# The Captivity Trail

*Group Captain
Ronny Arjun Das*

*(Retd.)*

The author was a career officer in the Indian Air force. An alumni of the National Defence Academy he also has a Masters in Military Sciences from the Defense Services Staff College in Coonoor, India. Both, highly prestigious institutions at par with West Point, USA and Bracknell, UK. His professional career as a fighter pilot spans across thirty years of training and service to defend India from which Pakistan was born after the Partition of India in 1947. He belongs to the post independence generation of thinking professional soldiers who understand Geo-Politics, Ethnic bias, the Multi polar world and International relations today as much as they do the Strategies of modern warfare. As a Combat pilot, Base commander, Flying instructor and also a Deputed tactical training instructor to the Indian Army he has vast experience in management and working at different levels and understanding the psyche of soldiers, their families and their fears and hopes. Prisoners of War and their surviving families, he says 'are not talked about as much as war heroes and some may still be languishing for no real reason.'

This is his first novel about prisoners, their families that struggle even today, their pains, uncertainties and simple joys that could all very well be true and is also about the meaning of Captivity– not just physical but also mental that many could be in for most of their lives.

# The Captivity Trail

*"Religious politics to divide Hindus and Muslims was given birth. Gandhi by default and the British in India became its legitimate parents. The rest is all history."*

*"Is there any authority that can say with conviction that both sides after a conflict have released every prisoner of war? Is there an assured method to declare a missing soldier as dead, alive or captured by the enemy?"*

*"Maybe it is really the women of nations that suffered the most and yet kept their sanity. The men probably have understood only sometimes through their women's grief; a fraction more about co-existence."*

*"Heal him from the nightmares of agonies that he must have faced as a prisoner of war. Let me be a good mother and nurture him the way I could when he was a child. You have brought him back to me. Grant me the energies that I need at my age. I thank you for giving me this opportunity again. Whatever it is, thy will be done."*

*"Women with active sensors know how and when to wait. They may suffer loneliness but come to terms with what men perceive as a kind of captivity while in waiting. For some women, waiting is a willing submission more like an offering to some cause. Their emotions in waiting are not diluted by feelings of captivity."*

*"Remaining captive to a loss can deny reception of so many positive changes that those so afflicted can sink into the ocean of self pity and reach the bottom where there is only hate, mistrust and depression going beyond the reach of any help. You can only rise up to the surface yourself. He would never realize that he could not free them of their captivity. He could only hand them a bunch of keys. They would have to open the doors themselves."*

*"Truth gets a price tag because of consequences. If there is nothing to lose, the abstracts of an attached price becomes trivial and converts into a synergy that could move mountains."*

This is a work of fiction. Names, characters, places and incidents either are the products of the author's imagination or are used fictitiously and any resemblance or similarities is not intended with reference to real people, places or incidents that may be or appear real.

© Copyright 2006 Ronny Arjun Das
All rights reserved. No part of this publication may be reproduced, stored in a retrieval system, or transmitted, in any form or by any means, electronic, mechanical, photocopying, recording, or otherwise, without the written prior permission of the author.

Note for Librarians: A cataloguing record for this book is available from Library and Archives Canada at www.collectionscanada.ca/amicus/index-e.html
ISBN 1-4120-8427-x

*Printed in Victoria, BC, Canada. Printed on paper with minimum 30% recycled fibre. Trafford's print shop runs on "green energy" from solar, wind and other environmentally-friendly power sources.*

*Offices in Canada, USA, Ireland and UK*
This book was published *on-demand* in cooperation with Trafford Publishing. On-demand publishing is a unique process and service of making a book available for retail sale to the public taking advantage of on-demand manufacturing and Internet marketing. On-demand publishing includes promotions, retail sales, manufacturing, order fulfilment, accounting and collecting royalties on behalf of the author.

**Book sales for North America and international:**
Trafford Publishing, 6E–2333 Government St.,
Victoria, BC V8T 4P4 CANADA
phone 250 383 6864 (toll-free 1 888 232 4444)
fax 250 383 6804; email to orders@trafford.com
**Book sales in Europe:**
Trafford Publishing (UK) Limited, 9 Park End Street, 2nd Floor
Oxford, UK OX1 1HH UNITED KINGDOM
phone 44 (0)1865 722 113 (local rate 0845 230 9601)
facsimile 44 (0)1865 722 868; info.uk@trafford.com
**Order online at:**
trafford.com/06-0182

10 9 8 7 6 5 4 3 2

Dedicated to the men and women who were or are still prisoners of war, conflict or just circumstances and their beloved who face the challenges of Captivity and wait for freedom.

*Author's note*

*Don't we all inherit? This is another summarized version of what we all have with some variations. Do we have the courage to shed it?*

# THE INHERITANCE

Families simply inherit from their ancestors. A country inherits from history. Factors like its geopolitics, ethnic evolution and importantly the influence of other nations vis a vis their own respective positions on the map of evolution plays a direct and indirect role in the accumulation of an Inheritance. Evolution of a nation includes its growth as we understand it and also its degeneration or stagnancy as it moves from now to the future.

Inheritance does not dictate future. It influences future sufficiently through needs that rely on this Inheritance. A need can be created. In the same manner the created need can be satisfied for it to become redundant or grow. For a created need to grow there is always a situation or conditions that demand fuelling. Manipulation can affect such conditions. This is where discretion succeeds or fails. Discretion to allow or disallow the growth of a need shows its eminence only in time. Future is what we want to enhance and so the need here to peep into India and the world's ethnic Inheritance.

In Ahmadabad the Army Cantonment enjoys being located adjacent to the airport. A common fencing with the airport exists even today. In pre-independent India, the British must have decidedly located the cantonment on purpose. They rarely did anything without some definite motive. Always for the benefit or at least in the name of the empire. The empire that had to ultimately withdraw. Great Britain, an island nation; it always gave the islanders pleasure to dominate larger countries that succumbed to their "shopkeeper's guile". And before reaching India they had developed adequate experience in trading. The sheer numbers that India had when the Brits schemed their way beyond just trading to ruling should have seen them routed and on the run. Our inheritance would have been different.

One can only presume that at Ahmadabad, the guile saw wisdom in the cantonment being closer to an airfield. Perhaps they could move at short notice and also the proximity ensured that those of the fairer race arriving or departing did not have to travel through the pre-independence dusty narrow roads of a volatile city that was home to the father of the nation, Mahatma Gandhi. Instead, they could hang out in their self-contained pristine cantonment. The Mahatma, Patel, freedom, democracy, secularism and Ahmadabad are synonymous. Ironically, Ahmadabad not so long ago was honored on the front pages of Indian and World media as a showcase of the failures of democracy and secularism with its communal riots. For similar displays, blaming the British or later Indian leaders that were in charge would be in bad taste but it is time that generation next stops the rot started by ancestors. The British will not accept their responsibility in the division of India but who cares; history books? Popular opinion worldwide has reached conclusions in its intelligentsia or at "polite conversations", in the leftover Victorian living rooms, swanky bars and at coffee houses that have made many street corners famous meeting points.

Indian leaders of yore especially from Ahmadabad adorn the walls of government offices even today for they were icons, born of the struggle for independence from the Empire. Successors of that legacy in the India of today surprisingly are more like inexperienced buccaneers on a ship without a captain. Of course they have selectively inherited some of the British guile as an essential pre-requisite to being in the business of politics now treated more like trading and even auctions. They have become masters in creating needs that they can rapidly satisfy by manipulating the conditions that can control needs.

The inheritance of divide and rule distributed to Hindus and Muslims of pre-independent India came from a need. The British were quick to realize that togetherness of the two ethnic followings was a double-headed poisonous snakehead for them. They played with the need to ethnically self determine. Tragically true is that we ourselves gave them their best option at that juncture; to light many little bonfires between the two communities. The fallouts of the British 'divide and rule' policy live on as the legal heir of many nations. Colonial Britain was known for thoroughness at implementing long-term strategic policies. Some nations have overcome the effects yet some continue to struggle against the deep-rooted malaise.

In the sub-continent, India and Pakistan appear to excel in the art of making this inheritance grow. The result of discretion exercised by our then leaders Nehru and Jinnah has become the poor inheritance of India and Pakistan today. It is helped on by "Powers that be" because of binocular vision. They cannot see India without a glance at Pakistan and vice versa. Weapons or technology to one must be distributed strategically to the other. The scope for divide and rule continues.

Speeches by politicians, gangsters, and film stars are generously littered with stirring words like secularism and of course long Kalashnikov bursts of terrorism and "the enemy". Blaming Pakistan, demonstrating anger on Muslims and advertising it has become a sure shot winning formula with the uneducated masses and fast food instant recipe generation that possibly is vaguely aware of only some religious differences for the "Partition". They follow the new flag in the sky. Its bearers are the modern day ethno-preneurs that seize every opportunity to implicate the minority community as violators of democracy and it gives legitimate reason for them to communalize issues that otherwise have solutions or justice well catered for in the Constitution. The manipulations to ethnically self determine has achieved a degree of finesse. If we grant the British that their discretion to satisfy an ethnic need existed in the 1940s; the same cannot be justified when we talk about global village and secularism all in the same breath today.

Tragically, the ethno-preneurs' flag has adopted a sacred saffron color. Ethno-preneurs, it appears, prefer to forget the fact that the first non-cooperation movement launched in India was for a reason that should have brought Hindus and Muslims closer in a bond that if nurtured could have changed the course of history in the sub-continent and quite easily the world. Destiny had other plans for the History of the World. The joint movement was against what was then termed as the "Khilafat wrong". The brotherhood of that non-cooperation movement is yet visible at times today through the dust but it is not in good taste for Hindus or Muslims to stand up for each other leave alone display it. It could be disastrous.

The necessity to quote The Khilafat wrong from history is purely to recapitulate for generation next that Mahatma Gandhi was in support of the Muslim agitation of undivided India in response to the Khilafat wrong. The Muslim community's fears were genuine that the British would desecrate their holiest places in Mecca and Medina including the Kaaba after the defeat of Turkey. And so it happened. These places were then under the charge of the Ottoman Khalifa. Many a congressman in India was not in support of an agitation as they considered it a religious and not a political issue. Is there a distinction between religion and politics, one may contemplate? Both have ideologies, faith and practices. Their application in daily life may have different realms but that is all. Ideologies and Faith in their interpretations and application also have a very wide spectrum of gray between black and white. What may have appeared, as a religious issue to some in the Khilafat wrong was politics to others from within the same single prominent political party; the Congress. Views can and must differ. One of the tenets of true democracy is that there will be diverse views. Against party opinion, Gandhi embraced a sympathetic opinion for the apprehensions of Muslims. As such it was indeed a justifiable issue that concerned not just Indians in their struggle for freedom, democracy and secularism but in hindsight, the whole world and Gandhi was crowned its first non-violent champion. Similarly Mohammed Ali Jinnah became the first citizen for his declared secular Pakistan. His apprehensions that Muslims would not get their rights after independence led him to galvanize the Muslim population easily through religion and it suited the British to bring down the curtain on their divide and rule opera with the final Partition. Gandhi was not wrong and Jinnah can also justify that he was right.

Religious politics to divide Hindus and Muslims was given birth. Gandhi by default and the British in India became its legitimate parents. The rest is all history. Today it has mushroomed into a vendetta between the Muslims and the rest of the world! Religious politics make no mistake, is here to stay but with newer colors. Let it stay but not sin by leaning on religion for justification. Can it quote from the Gita, Koran, Granthsahib or the Bible? Which one teaches communal politics leading to slaughter and disharmony?

Did not the Romans dabble with religious politics? The Pope continues to be a concern for political leaders, world over. The English mastered the art of religious politics: they continue to face the latent hate from the Scottish, Welsh and the Irish. Did not the Americans support Muslims in Afghanistan against the Soviets or the Iranians against Iraq? Ethnic upheavals in Europe and even the Middle East can be traced to religious politics. Have we overlooked Hitler? Or is he shortly going to be relegated to lower position as the brain behind the worst kind of religious politics; "racial executions". The world could soon see some who may better him. In the name of Hindutva we could well have our own Indian a.k.a Hindu candidates vying for that record. And so also, under the misinterpreted understanding of Jihad it is unfortunate that the Jehadi's blood continues to be the toast at august gatherings of politicians, businessmen a la weapons dealers and now film stars who find politics a good investment. Wasn't Vietnam something to do with religion or was it only political will? And many more died in Vietnam than during the war against Fascism. However "Vietnam" had the official nod of a "fight against evil". This is also something the world has inherited. State organized communal violence. Nine-eleven is just another thumbnail image of the artwork of religious politics. In its present avatar there cannot be one religion for the whole world. Multi-polar religious politics is another inheritance.

If the pain and fear of terrorism has come to be part of our environment, has it not been the legitimate child of religious politics. Why is the world today with a pitchfork against Islamic nations? What have those that follow Islam done per se? They are like any other people of different nations that have had to take their stand on internal or external issues that individually or collectively affect them. Islamic is black, white, yellow, democratic or socialist. So are Christians or Hindus for that matter. Yet terror has become linked mainly with Islamic nations like some default setting in the mindset of the much advertised, "brave new world".

As a natural response, Islamic retaliation is forced to continue. The need to retaliate is constantly being fuelled. It has only grown. Massive retaliation a left over of the nuclear deterrence policy of cold war between USA and the Soviet Union did not deter the proliferation or stockpiling of weapons of mass destruction and is unlikely to get to grips with terrorism. Rather, the terrorist may soon acquire nuclear status, certainly inline with the Inherited massive retaliation concept.

But who says we are not trying to reduce the divide between India and Pakistan? Don't we meet and confer. Is not the hate reducing with cricket matches hosted by both countries? Aren't we coming closer with students, culture groups and film stars visiting each other's heartland? Or is it another cloak and dagger façade of playing for time. Or are we witnessing real diplomacy, the skilful management of negotiations that can have far reaching improvements or unmanageable consequences. From 'Gunboat' to 'Cricket' diplomacies, newer methodologies or tools for religious politics are still evolving. The very concept of religious politics is fraught with dangers. Narrow mental streets between communities have sparked communal riots at the slightest brush. Communalization led to the Partition. It remains the basis for terrorist acts in the disputed status of Kashmir.

Is it possible for those that have suffered the gnawing pains of a Partition or lost everything in wars, to be healed with a cricket match or two? It is the people on both sides of the border that have lost. Diplomatic relations needs to grow beyond the signing of agreements. Visible adjustments and banning communalization as an anti-national act punishable by law followed by creation of an environment for genuine mixing of the two communities can lay the foundation for a route towards secularization needed by both nations. Today, does the soldier on the border on both sides of the fence stop patrolling; expecting a stray bullet anytime? Now they have a new net. A barbed electrified fence and some new orders to play shooting matches. Has it made any Muslim in Ahmadabad or anywhere in India feel more secure than before? The popular "Feel good factor" lewdly advertised failed to re-elect a ruling party that blatantly played the communal card into governing the country. That was "Paid with blood" realization by a mass of people that they were being manipulated into created needs that keeps the ethnic hate burning.

Unfortunately there is a whole new generation that has been softwared to not have the time to read, leave alone understand what is religion or one God, or democracy a garden where secularism could bloom. Should they be condemned to reap the punishment for ignorance or disinformation doled out by sensational reporting or inaccurate textbooks, both of which are manipulated by religious politicians? An optimist will yet contend that after all something good always comes out of everything albeit with time. Maybe a few more September Elevens and Akshardhams or controversial cricket matches? Surely we do not label these as very good happenings. The British were generous to leave good cricket in the sub-continent. Don't India and Pakistan excel in making that warring inheritance grow? Only the game and bookies truly benefit. Not anyone else.

No denial that Islamic nations have a history of turmoil generated from tussles between the clergy and the people. Also between the haves and the deprived. Islam does not recognize the institution of clerics. Nor does it accept the amassing of wealth. But clerics, wealth and power co-exist and those that have access are among the most powerful in their fiefdoms. Who can afford the risk of watching Islamic nations resolve their own issues? Will that not increase global insecurities? Consequently, "The Islamic nation" becomes a good business proposition as an investment to consolidate global security. Enter, the opportunist international ethno-preneur cum businessman weapons dealing politician. It will bring a smile to his eyes that could eventually qualify as the universally accepted worldwide smiley icon representing pure tilted to one side heady delight.

Do Islamic nations interfere between the Irish and the British in their conflicts? Is not apartheid a horrific experience in parts of the free world even today? Do we hear of interference by Islamic or other nations— to levels that escalate issues and marginalize whole ethnic groups? One may laugh and say that no Islamic nation has the capability to interfere. What is capability? Do the global police have courage or capability to confront Islamic North Korea or Saudi Arabia with their respective nuclear or oil designs? And is not terrorism also a capability? Why is there the current backlash of worldwide terrorism sponsored by various Islamic groups? They are compelled to join forces against those that identify themselves as the lawmakers. Here lies the danger, as history is dotted with evidence that suppressed minorities, be they with good or other ideologies: have in course of time, regrouped forces against their dominant suppressive powers. Capability can be achieved or is dormant and can be triggered to realization.

Let us not forget that we had the capability to oust the British but they were crafty to decimate the country in spirit. Did not Bhagat Singh and Khudiram resort to violence and they are our heroic freedom fighters. Mohamed Ali Jinnah a Muslim can be credited for the first successful anti Raj, Indian road blockade in Bombay. Did the British accept these as freedom fighters or were they not hated for their terrorist activities. Jihadis can also be heroes— given a cause. And they have been gifted a cause by the non Islamic: no doubt about that. Yet we neglect and continue to allow marginalization of communities on the sub-continent and the world at large. It is constantly fuelling the need to continue branding terrorism as Muslim.

However, can we recline and blame it on the British or Gandhi or Nehru, or Jinnah, or Bush or Bin Laden or Modi for that matter. We have a commitment or don't we? Haven't we learned that Ram, for example, took to banishment for fourteen years to honor his father's commitment or of Moses, who left the comforts of a princely lifestyle? Who is upholding any commitment of Gandhi or Patel that India will remain a secularist state that will encourage coexistence? Do we not have the sensitivity as a people to realize the fallacy of drawing energies from wrong analogies to whip up even more anti Islamic frenzy? Are we not able to feel and resist this infection? Has it not begun to creep in under our doors? Maybe we are locked out in some time warp: captive to inheritances, condemned to see more evil "interest" accumulate. Yet we remain proud bearers of the secularist flag at International forums. And the same world looked on as the Nobel peace award of 2003 went to an Islamic woman Shireen Ehbadi from a country like Iran that had been labeled as the focal point in the "Axix of evil" by the most powerful flag bearer of democracy – The USA. Was it a mistake, a miracle or a scheme? None, for it was a victory for the few committed voices that recognize the evils of religious politics and relentlessly champions the ideology to treat all humans equally. It reaffirms that it is not Islam that is evil. The religious politician and terrorist have to be contained without violence and any hidden personal agendas of such power peace brokers must be laid bare. They are active worldwide, in India and Pakistan as well and we are immune to the rising temperatures of stewing in the evil broth of communalism stirred on by such politicians and terrorists. Does Pakistan have any less internal sectarian problems or riots for that matter? Yet religious politics for them demands that a common enemy be identified and thus India becomes a branded religiously evil Hindu nation, its sworn enemy for decades.

A temple has to be built where there was a mosque. In the name of neo-secularism a mosque is demolished. Was there any dearth of leaders, forces or law that could not have prevented this rape of secularism? And also, Muslims were later asked to be tolerant and allow the construction of a temple in place of the mosque. Obviously the Muslim minority can presumably afford the adjustment. All under the saffron flag and neo-secularism. Next, it could be the demolishing of a Church or a Synagogue for the benefit of the Hindu masses as: there 'used to be a temple here, you know?' Which brand of secularism or democracy or religion stipulates that history should be rolled back to correct the record and what and who decides the cut off date. Can any country try the British for what many label as crimes or recover stolen treasures and straighten the records? Can we, or will the freethinking world digest this without a gut ache? We are allowing leanings on inheritance that can be discarded with a little courage. Much less courage than required for launching invasions on Islamic nations.

Yes, secularism could grow from temples, mosques, gurdwaras and churches. Is it not preached by every faith? But maybe it is time now to liberate secularism from its continued religious confinement denying those who misuse it for their own benefits. Secularism without the sanctum-sanctorum religious bond could make religious politics begin to look illegitimate. Independent from its neo colors; divestment from British legacies is overdue. Allowing our undesirable inheritance to manipulate the future is poor discretion.

One of the fallouts of such an inheritance and subsequent stoking of the need to ethnically determine is war or conflicts that have inflicted worldwide suffering and deprivation on a few who are condemned to bear it; not just in India and Pakistan but innocent people from nations that are still engaged in armed conflict with others. These few are the survivors of prisoners of war who remain missing in action. Not much talked about: illegally held PoWs from Indo-Pak wars or even civilians arrested for border violations and held indefinitely, significantly proves the smoldering suspicion and hate between two nations. It was mistrust that triggered the conflicts between Hindus and Muslims before partition. Thereafter, it has been wars and continuous low intensity conflict between the two countries that has only eroded the character of both culturally rich nations, precipitating more expressions of hate. The latent bitterness has now increased because the Islamic world also decidedly straddles the religiously political stallion and tent pegs India as one of the recognized hated few countries that supposedly threaten Islam. Religious politics and its manifestations have only led to more wars and wars legitimize death and the taking of prisoners of war. Have we not witnessed this in Korea, Vietnam, the Middle East, South America and Europe's ethnic violence, or Kuwait, Iran and now Iraq? Have we relegated the horrors of those that were exiled to Siberia as some fiction? Haven't we heard accounts of languishing lives behind prison bars and those that wait for their return? Mandela was obviously not a good enough example for the free world to realize the horrors of being a prisoner. And pray what was the reason for his unjust detention? His release is one of the biggest victories for secularism. We need more.

Freedom associated with secularism is not to be for these few that languish in enemy government or military cells for simply obeying military orders that are in effect the extension of a political will. Every warring country takes prisoners of war and there is never a guarantee of their release or whereabouts. If fishermen who have strayed in the Arabian Sea, where it is well nigh impossible for them to remain within territorial waters, have been held in Pakistani and Indian cells for over ten years; then what of captured men in uniform who were explicitly engaged in wiping out each others forces or territorial assets? How do we know if they all came back after the war? Do we lack a judiciary system that cannot put border violators to a fair trial, punish them and or release them? There is an accepted procedure and the Geneva Convention but apparently the release of prisoners of war has not been just a military, police or judiciary decision. Some prisoners who had even served out their sentences were not released in time. Some do not even know their crimes. Yet in contrast and shockingly true are the examples of politicians with proven criminal records that roam the world with impunity. Sad fact is that few can do little to liberate soldiers or civilians held as prisoners. Many express opinions and everyone shrinks from counting the many who weep silently due to the state approved practice of unreasonable imprisonment leading to separation that lingers on. Who really cares for these victims left behind to stumble around in a free world while their beloveds are kept pathetically alive behind bars?

Is there any authority that can say with conviction that both sides after a conflict have released every prisoner of war? Is there an assured method to declare a missing soldier as dead, alive or captured by the enemy? After the fog of war has cleared, can we be certain that there are not still those few that are being held. For them and those that wait for them, it is like imprisonment to some horrible prolonged nightmare. A veritable nightmare of hope diluted by doubts. A thought process full of uncertainties that increases in proportion with the continued hate generated by the followers of religious politics, both in India and Pakistan. Can any legitimate authority guarantee that countries like the USA or other nations in Europe or the Middle

East do not continue holding PoWs beyond conflicts and peace processes? One of the effects of latent hate and suspicion is that many PoWs on the sub-continent or other parts of the world for that matter will wait hopelessly for their release, in spite of the declared wars being over. And if they have been unlawfully held— can they be released now? What explanation will any captor have? One suspects that there is a trace of hostage-ism being followed here. Our emotions run high when we hear of an airline hijack or hostages. What of those prisoners of war that could still be held as hostages or worse, been done in. It applies universally to all nations. Unconditional secularism could promote trust and coexistence. Without it there is little hope of rapprochement and conditions that may precipitate among many issues, the return of prisoners, both civilian and military. We can take a cue from the Germanys or the Soviet block countries that had to break down the barriers and finally have even joined the European Union. Cannot India and Pakistan find a legitimate cause to re-unite? And release all prisoners. It is not impossible. Will the world allow it?

Ask, or look into the eyes of PoWs who were fortunately released. They continue to reengineer themselves from the disintegration effect in the enemy's cells. Are they not re-visited by nightmares of certain death at the hands of a religiously fanatical enemy? Or, ask them who wait with uncertainty for the return of the given up for dead, for it is a nightmare only they deal with. Theirs is a daily search to the limits of their mental horizons, relying that the pain and deprivation will vanish with the "return". Even a confirmation of death may be a preferred reconciliation for them. They are the most harangued victims of religious politics. A pathetic existence resulting from factors that include poor discretion in encouraging ethnic self-determination by the very "Proper" British on the sub-continent and others elsewhere in the world.

Their hopes slowly die as they struggle to keep it alive in the face of the divide between the two nations and communities. They have little choice than to wait. Such is the sometimes-undesirable endurance of a human mind that it can remain captive to a hopeless vigil. However, the horror if allowed to persist, awaits us in different forms in the near future. We could all become prisoners of our fears or uncertainties and remain in waiting for a day that allows us to breathe without having to worry about tomorrow's newer terrorisms. Secularism could help arresting such dreadful maladies to gradually move towards a dream many before us have dreamt. Yet secularism seems to be on the retreat. It is overdue that we consciously divest what the British and our ancestors left behind or even vehemently reject the marginalization being propagated by the self-styled law keepers of the world. Humanity needs to deliver justice to all those in captivity, be they prisoners of war or criminals all over the world so that they along with those that wait for their return or end can begin again. If we can ask Pakistan for the handing over of a list of twenty criminals declared by India; who supposedly roam free in Pakistan; can we not demand the freedom of every Prisoner of War? Or is it possible that we never knew how many were taken prisoner?

You may find some answers here or even better; generate some questions about the fate of those who remain prisoners long after the soldiers; tanks and airplanes have gone home. What lingers unnoticed is the pain of families who are trapped in uncertainties with dreams dying by the moment while their fathers; sons, brothers or husbands languish behind prison walls. They had never dreamt of such an Inheritance. It was thrust on them. Such suffering souls are real. Soldiers, world over often question; would it be preferable to die than to be taken prisoner? A surrender or capture continues to be an act of disgrace. Humiliation, suffering and wait are certain. Have we then surrendered to the divisive forces, condemned to wait. Are we allowing invisible chains to hold us captive to the fear of terrorism and violence? Or are we waiting for secularism? Maybe that is the question we need to address and self determine or stay on a Captivity trail that has no destination.

Haven't we heard this one before? 'They are those who gave their today for all our tomorrows.' It remains to be seen if secularism will find a nest in this world, for many have died fighting for its tomorrow; leaving behind the few, who must continue to strive for it and many obliviously wait for its fragrance. Some inheritances have to go.

## Ahmadabad, India

## 1987

'Are you sure this strapping bull is not going to make the grade in the selections? What a shame. We need exceptionally fit guys like him for the Para Commandos.'

'Yes sir I'm afraid that's true, his individual performance is exceptional but so far his marks don't seem to be making the grade. We have a detailed report on every candidate. Should I bring it for your perusal?' The Brigade major at the recruitment center stood his ground. 'And all the doubtfuls are standing in that separate group on your left sir.'

'I don't think it is my business to get involved in these selection reports but I am truly disappointed that this boy could not make the grade. I guess you have a tough process Major and I have no doubt about your quality control.'

The Brigade Commander a Para Commando himself and veteran of the 1965 and 71 war with Pakistan had an eye for good soldiers. He also knew his Brigade Major well and was a bit taken aback that one of the toughest and fittest candidates had failed to be selected for training as a soldier into the Indian Army. He turned and walked towards the staff car throwing one last look at a small group of ten young men who had been segregated as the "also ran". Some more tests, two more days and the results would be declared.

At the Army Divisional Headquarters recruitment center a group of young men were being tested for their physical fitness and stamina. Apart from testing physical abilities the tests were also designed to bring out the team spirit as well as leadership traits of a potential soldier. There is one candidate amongst them who has fire in his eyes yet always also has the beginning of a smile on his lips. He is fair, much better built than the others but his attitude does not visibly conform to his physical appearance. He appears rather withdrawn and almost bashful of his remarkable physique. He is Basheer Khan, the son of late Naik Azad Khan of the 9th Battalion of Para commandos. The Para Commandos are known for their courage in the face of the enemy and earned heroic battle honors from Alamein to the liberation of Bangladesh. The selection results are announced and Basheer Khan is rejected from recruitment because of his reclusive behavior. The physical test observations and the psychologist's report said;

"Although well built he is unable to tackle the team tasks and physical obstacles within the specified time with his teammates; Lacks ability to be part of a team".

So many of us have this trait but it is 1987 and the Army is recruiting soldiers from different communities provided they are able to work shoulder to shoulder like a team. Basheer did not show aptitude for team spirit exercises. He will never know the reason for his failure to be selected, as these details remain buried in the files. How can he know and would he ever accept.

*His conditioning from birth was that he was from the minority Muslim community. His psyche, 'will the team accept me,' had kept him out of many teams. And also, was the team conditioned enough to allow him in as a teammate, especially a Muslim under competitive conditions. We are sadly witnessing an environment inherited by the poorer sections of Muslims in India.*

Like his father, Basheer has very fine cut chiseled features but he is different from his father in that, although his looks are formidable; he is so soft spoken that one can barely hear him. He rarely speaks but his eyes are alive in a gentle manner and his lips always have the remnants of a smile. A spontaneous subdued expression simply incongruent with his predicament or joy. His mother and their clientele understood him. His pleasant manners blended with the decorum heard of only in Mughal courtrooms and it encouraged anyone to talk or listen to him. Gentility more than conversed with them through his eyes. It was as if he touched them. He was capable of silently setting an easy and creative mood with his attentive eyes and latent smile. He was more like a couture designer than a simple tailor. Basheer's presence encouraged the calm and expression. It obviously did not fit the bill for displayed team spirit desirable in a soldier.

Ruhaina is Basheer's widowed mother who managed to earn just enough to educate him through college. She ran the family tailoring business. Ruhaina inherited the fame of Rehmat Ali her father who was known for his exquisite embroidery. As a little girl she had seen the powdered charming wives of British officers and later, the boisterous, gesticulating and imposing wives of Punjabi Indian Army officers stationed in Ahmadabad. The latter came flocking in vociferous groups to her father's shop to get their gowns, saris, their tableware bed linen and even dupattas embroidered. Ruhaina's husband, Naik Azad Khan was the son of "Tailor master" Kasim Khan who was known for his expertise in cutting the perfect sheer party gown or elegant shalwar suit. Kasim's old world mannerisms fitted perfectly with the chivalry of the British that was later inherited by the Indian Army. His movements with a measuring tape, kneeling, bending and stretching were almost like he was romancing the subject.

Once in a while he would whisper, 'do you want the fitting a little closer or is what you are wearing all right?'

A bashful smile would convey but they always added. 'Whatever you think is better.' That was more often than not— every woman's reply. They had confidence in Kasim Khan.

The lady's measurements he was taking and the figures would all get recorded in his mind. He did not carry a pencil behind his ear lobe like many tailors who jotted measurements immediately. And it was not because the lady would find her vital statistics being noted, an embarrassment. He had his own code, categorizing his subject into a form. The sizes and shapes recorded themselves permanently in his mind as a perfect soft reflection. The fitting was always without an oversight and the women just felt very comfortable wearing garments tailored by him. Of course his cutting and tailoring of the three-piece dinner jacket suit and ceremonial gold embroidered uniforms of Indian Army officers had pride of place in the Indian Army's history. His brand tag on their battle dresses and the close hug fit instilled a sense of pride associated with fine grooming. It was as if the livery could fan the flame of bravery in a fight to finish bayonet charge or ignite chivalry on the battlefield as well as at poised courtroom decorum crystal glass mess functions. Have you got your "Kasim Khans"? 'Go and kit yourself,' were the favorite last words of commanding officers during introductory interviews of the young subalterns joining the paltan (Platoon).

Kasim Khan had lived, worked and died in the same place near the cantonment for most of his seventy years. His son, Azad Khan had joined the Indian army it seemed, as a natural consequence of wanting to wear the uniforms hanging in his father's glass cases to become a part of the dramas of bravery related by the officers as they chatted with his father. In short he wanted to emulate these impressive and powerful clients and strive to be definitely better than them. Kasim Khan had put up a frame of his son Azad's photograph in uniform on the wall facing the entrance to his shop. No one could miss it as you went up the wooden stairs.

*Yes, Azad was Basheer's father but father and son were so different in their image projection.*

Kasim Khan had shifted with Rehmat Ali, his tailor friend, from the slums on the banks of the Sabarmati River and bought a set of rooms adjacent to each other in the cantonment area. Kasim had three children and since few Muslim families lived in the cantonment area, he wanted Azad, Iqbal and Nusrat to grow up in a secure, large family like atmosphere. He had paid dearly for this small yet comfortable Muslim pocket place in the Cantonment area and shifted residence. It was in the heart of a door-to-door wigwam of a few Muslim families living close to each other so they even knew what was cooking for lunch, Biriyani or Dal Ghosht. These were warm-hearted generous Muslims. He was not communal but it was all about being in a comfortable environment. He had observed the early signs of neo-secularism seeping in soon after India's independence. Neo-Secularism was a Hindu choice in a Hindu nation. It was not blatant but Muslims preferred to stay close to each other.

Kasim Khan's friend, Rehmat Ali gave one of his four daughters, Ruhaina, in marriage to Azad shortly after he joined the army. They knew each other from childhood. The union had ingredients of friendship and romance but to the community their marriage was almost a business deal. Both had grown up watching their parents in the tailoring business. They understood the texture of materials; the joy of giving shape to a piece of cloth and the appreciative smiles of customers. It was like a natural cycle embedded in their psyche. Understanding each other would be easy and quite naturally take the business forward. However, Azad Khan disappointed everyone by joining the army. Yet Kasim would proudly tell the young officers visiting his shop, with a nod towards the frame on the wall.

'That is my son. He was the best wrestler in the whole Para regiment.'

After her betrothal, Ruhaina helped her father-in law Kasim Khan with the tailoring business. With her inherited talent in embroidery, the business and clientele grew. Kasim Khan was secure that his business would continue after him. Surely, Azad would leave the army after his compulsory service of fifteen years. Ruhaina and he could hold the fort for sometime. Would his fort survive the twist of fate that was set in motion with independence and the Partitioning of India with its unpredictable storms of neo-secularism?

His dreams though, died with the war of '71' with Pakistan. Kasim Khan never quite recovered from the shock of hearing that his son was missing in action. Ruhaina was pregnant. What would happen now? He would ask Allah every night and every officer who visited his shop.

'Can you find out from your sources, what really happened. He must be alive somewhere. Are some PoWs still being held by Pakistan?' He would ask, rarely getting a satisfactory reply.

Death could not touch his formidable wrestler son. They all promised to find out but after some time Kasim realized that these men seemed to forget his request even as they stepped out of his shop. Some even gave him hope that mistakes took place and Azad could still be alive or injured in some enemy hospital. Kasim dreaded the word "dushman" (enemy). It was being used in Ahmadabad, in his very street and they sometimes glanced at him as an alien. Where could Kasim begin his search? He had tried to enquire right up to the Army Headquarters in Delhi.

From behind the curtains separating the backyard tailoring workshop and Kasim Khan's gaddi (shop floor), Ruhaina would listen with the hope of hearing some information about her missing husband. It was futile but she stood there almost by habit every time she espied Kasim opening a dialog about her husband. Swallowing her tears was natural and almost had a quenching effect providing the energy to go on. Kasim finally died with the regret that he could not do enough for his friend Rehmat Ali's daughter who had to adopt widowhood. He had not been able to recover her husband and his son. Ruhaina had even silently refused his suggestion that she could marry Iqbal, the second son. This saddened yet left him with a sense of pride associated with a woman's chastity.

'Ruhaina my dear, today there was a very senior officer from Azad's regiment.' Very often during their meals Kasim would start a conversation to keep everyone's hopes alive.

'Does he know Azad.'? Ruhaina would ask.

'I have asked him and he has promised to find out. They have not declared him dead. So he is missing. Who knows where he is. The army is so huge.'

'I am sure they have the names of all their soldiers and officers; then why aren't they able to find him?' Ruhaina was not willing to accept any finality.

'He could be sick or injured somewhere in some military hospital. I am sure we will find him soon.'

Basheer grew up in this environment of the constant search for his father and a predominant feeling of uncertainty and gnawing insecurity. He became a survivor, yet those years had left their scars. He had watched his mother working on her embroidery and once in a while she would sigh and take of her spectacles to wipe the tears before they could be seen. Those eyes had worked silently wet. The uncertainties and insecurities grew with every incident of communal confrontation in the country. The fires of communal flare-ups spread fast. It was like being captive to this whole thought process of uncertainties. The rebel side of him decided that the day he was of age for recruitment, he would enroll in the army. That would be his liberation from the captivity of uncertainties. The Hindu community would not trouble them if he were to be in their army. After all he would be known as a fighter for the motherland against the "dushman", Pakistan. He would find his father or at least avenge his death. Simple ambition within seethed to rise from the ranks and become an officer someday and do whatever he could to bring unquestionable honor to the family. These were his dreams, as he grew up, a strapping physical replica of Azad Khan the wrestler. His mother was proud of him and had often chided that his father could drink three glasses of milk and was the wrestling champion whereas Basheer could only have one glass reluctantly. Basheer had attempted to join the Indian army and now he had failed. Of what use was the milk. His failure held him captive to the uncertainties. Only the chains got heavier now with the added weight of an unfulfilled dream and newer shackles of being frequently identified as a minority community.

*If we are truly secular, why is there so much hype about minorities and communities? Aren't Indians one community after all and specially in this* city of the Mahatma, Ahmadabad. Basheer thought he understood secularism but could never feel it. He was not being permitted to feel Indian. He wanted to change it all to an honorable fearless way of living. Oh! What a feeling to be young, free and Indian. Would he ever?

# Bombay, India
## 2001

'Isn't this the first time you are coming to my house?' It was seven in the evening.

'Is it too late Brother? Maybe I should visit your mother at a more appropriate time.' Sheila was apprehensive almost by habit.

'It is not late. You live far so I know you will spend little time here. I wanted you to stay for sometime but its okay. My mother will be happy to see you. She has tried to introduce me to some single women, every time we go to church. Maybe she wonders if I have any women friends at all.' Their stifled laughter was simultaneous and then there was silence that surrounded Brother James' last comment.

In Bombay there are many old winding streets and one such place in Bandra is Chapel Road. The belief is that this was one of the first roads in Bandra. And Bandra today is a major road maze by itself. Chapel Road is predominantly Christian. Truth is that there are many third generation Muslims living here too. There is always a sense of happy coexistence on both sides of the road and everyone lives quite "side-by-side". The road has lanes, by lanes and even narrow unpaved ravine like walk ways leading or winding between dilapidated three storied buildings, tiled roof cottages and new high rise apartment blocks that resemble a chest of drawers. A middle-aged couple is walking, their hands barely brushing each other. Every time their hands or arms brush there is a gentle knowing smile that begins but freezes before it can be noticed by passers by. There was discreet intimacy here. It was Christmas time. The man has a sling bag on his shoulder. He is slightly hunched but there is a firm erectness about his whole appearance. The lady is in formal wear. Her shalwar suit is simple yet very well carried. There is music in the narrow by lanes. Old English songs sung by Nat King Cole, Jim Reeves and Frank Sinatra. The cottages and apartment blocks have come closer to each other over the years. The distance minimized by even smaller shelters and mini dwellings and shops springing up in the gaps.

Somehow, the proximity of the dwellings does not affect clarity of the songs. Strange acoustics, the street has. It was as though the music followed the pathways in a very orderly manner till it reached the main artery of Chapel road itself. There was no mix up here. Songs from next door never disturbed neighbors, Parsees, Muslims or Hindus. Songs were to be shared by everyone here. Amazingly secular! As they walked slowly by, both of them were partially attentive to the words of these songs of days gone by. These were songs of their childhood. These words stuck, never to be forgotten and the Goans of Bombay absorbed every song into their heart and unsuspectingly pretty much into their lives too. It was a very congenial lot of Indians at Chapel road. The songs were a bit like having chilled old wine. Maybe this was the Goans' secret of being good musicians all.

The couple reached an old wicker gate and the man was distinct in his mannerism. He held the gate open with an old world charm bow for her to walk through and closed it behind him. The sound of a television set filtered through to the balcony of this old cottage.

A neighbor called out in greeting. 'How are you Brother?' and 'Brother James, have you collected your monthly quota of liquor from the canteen. Can you loan us a bottle of rum man. It is Christmas man,'

'Sure George, send your boy and take two.' Richard James was very aptly nicknamed "Brother" by his fellow fighter pilots in the Air force and it had stuck and come home to stay at Chapel road. Generosity was Brother James's trademark. It was almost careless generosity because he could never remember whom he had given what. He was just happy that he could give something to someone. Yet he had a sharp memory for certain things. Things he never forgot were old English songs and names of people.

Today he had spent the whole day with Sheila Rao and in the

evening she had agreed to visit Richard James's mother. After all it was Christmas week and she had taken time out from home and work to wish her. Brother let her in through the main door. Martha James was in a wheel chair watching television. She suffered from severe arthritis and it showed in her bent fingers that she always tried to keep away from view. Martha was leaning back with her dinner half finished in the tray in front. The television was her connection with the world. It had been her only companion after Tom had died. It never failed her.

' Mama, I want you to meet Sheila.' There was no response. The soap on the tube continued to run. It was a scene from a family drama serial that had gained almost secular popularity with the middle and fading generation. She was fast asleep.

Brother smiled almost apologetic, 'Maybe some other day, why don't you have lunch with us this weekend,' he whispered. Leading the way out so his mother would not wake up, they stopped in the small verandah that had a very neatly rigged swing. 'I can cook pretty well, it will be simple though.' Sheila was taken a bit by surprise. She liked to spend weekends with her only daughter Rani who was twenty-eight and into a mature relationship with Ravi who kept them laughing whenever they were all together. Sheila loved to laugh and was addicted to all that Rani shared with her. Like a wholesome meal these laughing and sharing sessions between two women kept her need for any other company away. The effect made the week go by without any longings. Could she give it up for a very painstakingly cooked meal by Brother only to preserve the link with her bygone past as the war widow of an air force pilot?

Richard had been meeting Sheila for almost two years and he had never asked her home. Why now? She remembered the date, 23 February 2000 when he rang the bell at their apartment in Borivili and introduced himself as Flight Lieutenant Richard James of the Indian Air force. Brother had promised himself that if he ever managed to escape from the prison camp, he would visit all the relatives of his fellow prisoners and friends; those who had died and those with whom he had fought the war of 1971. He had walked boldly into their drawing room, shook hands with her, picked up the framed photograph of her husband Kailash Rao from atop the refrigerator.

'Kailash and I were course mates at the NDA and we were shot down over Gujranwala on the same day in 1971. I am Flight Lieutenant Richard James and was a prisoner of war till January last year. I was lucky to be released due to health reasons. They had given up hopes of my survival. I am supposed to be under treatment for tuberculosis. Actually there is not much wrong with me now. This was the only way I could have been released by those Pakistanis. It is getting cured, so say the doctors. Don't worry.'

Sheila was stunned by this declaration; it sounded almost well rehearsed. The man had no worry about himself to be so casual about his own health, and then she was suddenly impatient about news of her missing husband. It showed in her eyes. She couldn't wait. Was Kailash also alive with him as a PoW? Prisoner of war was something she had only imagined and hoped for Kailash but could never have said it. It was not considered very honorable for any soldier to be a prisoner of war, she recalled. So she could not ask now. Rani their daughter, was always told, that the authorities in Pakistan were keeping Kailash and one-day he would come back. Now the grown up daughter did not ask anymore.

'Mr. James,' she had started, but the statement 'Was my husband Kailash also with you,' remained only writ on her face. Her eyes had welled up and Brother James understood without her having to ask. He was facing one of the most difficult situations in his life. Words had to be found and he needed time.

'Not Mr. James,' he joked to diffuse the rush of anguish he sensed, 'Flight Lieutenant James, now retired due to medical unfitness.' Laughing had bought him time. Sheila was amazed, that he could laugh with so much ease and there was truly no trace of regret or hate. She recalled faintly that almost all fighter pilots she had met could laugh without a care in the gravest situations. Strange creatures, she had thought. Secretly she had admired this trait as it always managed to make things look brighter at least for that moment. They all seemed to possess a never give up attitude that helped tide over the most trying situations.

Was he going to surprise her with the information that Kailash was alive, a prisoner, maybe sick with TB or something else but that he was alive and would also be soon coming home maybe in exchange for a Pakistani held captive in India. It all rushed through her brain. And this fellow Richard James was laughing, so the news had to be good. She waited. There was silence. In those few moments their eyes had met. She had not asked but got her answer. These answers were easily communicated through silence. With trembling fingers covering lips she indicated to him that it was okay if he wanted to be silent. Brother's eyes froze almost non-expressive, accustomed to the brutalization of captivity and here was a woman that had penetrated his thoughts with her simple expressive eyes. Her expression had changed from anticipated joy to that of being permanently lost and trapped.

Brother had seen this look on most of his fellow prisoner's eyes. His own— not an exception. It was now torture for him to see captivity visiting here again. It grew worse as she had released him without his having to say anything. She had made him feel that he was not under obligation to tell her anything. She was alive, communicative and responsive in comparison to him. Sheila had retained her sanity, in spite of all the tests and tribulations of being a single parent of a growing child in a big city full of its own brand of difficulties. The silent acknowledgement of his inability to say the unpleasant had touched Brother without warning to awaken emotions that had been exiled. He felt alive and not forgotten or dead, as here was someone who was more concerned about his feelings rather than her own. This simple realization was overwhelming. It was like the turning point for Richard to really want to live with a purpose; to put his captivity and lost time behind. It was no longer justified to put the blame on his captivity for so many issues that he was unable to cope with but wanted to. There is much more to do after all. The world was full of people who have been through trying times and they still have the energy and sensitivity to care for others. One tear escaped and then he found himself in her arms, being sheltered and consoled, for he was sobbing uncontrollably. Between his choking sobs, words spurted out in gushes like water from a garden tap that had remained unused for long. 'He got.... the bridge .... they got him. I was in the same formation...... we had met for the briefing...... at Halwara and had a beer.... the previous day..... Our code word...... was Sheila, to indicate....... that we had the target...... in sight. That.... was the last. We had both said...... Sheila together..... A little later,..... He was hit. I saw it happen. There was........ No parachute.'

'Its all right, I understand. Atleast I know the truth now. The others never told me the real truth. God is kind that Kailash did not suffer. I hope the air force acknowledges his effort. It would have cost them nothing to tell me the way you have.'

'They don't have the courage to even think about truths. They consider us just numbers on the wall. It is easy for them to wipe these numbers without caring about feelings.' Brother's words shocked.

'Come please sit down. Let me get you some water.'

Like a tide receding, the sobs reduced to a gentle quake of muted meaningless expressions. They had both finally accepted that Kailash was no more. He had not had the environment in all these years to mourn the loss of a dear friend. His dam had burst. Did she not know for so many years, he thought. *'Then why had she looked expectantly for good news? Had they not told her that Kailash's documents had been closed? She is not crying even now. And I, the fighter pilot, I weep like a boy. I think they should have just kept me in the camp. I would have died and wouldn't have to face cruel realities of this world again.'*

Richard was suddenly in control, almost jarringly composed as he withdrew from her sympathetic hold. He had learnt to be like that as a fighter pilot. He was here to meet Kailash's family to help them and not lean on them for emotional support. He was furious with himself and the Air force now. The Air force had not told Sheila that her husband was dead and also that he had destroyed the target on that mission? Why had she looked expectantly at him for news about her husband? It was a war fought thirty years ago and she was still waiting to hear about him. It had been the same with his parents.

They had been sent a telegram saying, "We regret to inform you that your son Richard James is missing in action, efforts are on to locate him."

Tom and Martha had waited and accepted the harsh and unreal. It had taken time. And then he had come back from the missing. *'Declaring a combatant dead is not easy when you have no evidence. How can there be evidence for every soldier dead other than his body or eyewitnesses.'*

Sheila had not allowed the tears to come. She had become collected and was already thinking fast. How was she to convince Rani and how painful it must be for Richard to talk about it to her after all these years? Holding Brother closely was like her last contact with Kailash. It was like finally sharing a loss. And she was thankful that someone had finally come and told her that Kailash was no more. She was liberated from the uncertainty. Now she had a choice to wear white like a widow or not and reconsider applying the sindhur that identified married Hindu women. Prayers could be said for his soul now and this itself was like a fresh breath of air for her.

'I am sorry to leave you like this after reminding you of all that you have been through. Kailash was a dear friend and I came to see if you were all right. Please forgive me for opening old wounds. If there is anything I can do; please don't hesitate.'

Brother had not expected Sheila's ignorance and the rationale of the air force in not telling her what he believed everyone knew. This was even more difficult to accept. It was shocking to him and he felt terribly disappointed with the Air force.

'That is very kind of you. You have not pained me. I had hoped that he was alive and somewhere, maybe a prisoner but the air force never told me the facts like you have. I will remember your kind gesture always.'

'It is so many years after that day in seventy-one but I have never truly been able to mourn Kailash. Today I am grateful that I have not forgotten to cry but I know it has upset you.' Brother stood regretfully leaving her doorstep.

'It is fate and I am grateful that you have released me from the waiting. Hopefully we will see you again.' She had withdrawn and gently closed her front door.

Brother left Sheila's apartment and returned home since he was at loss for words after the emotional upheaval.

Sheila had sobbed fitfully for most of that night after telling Rani and they had held each other close till fatigue had overtaken them. The uncertainty was over. In the morning she would be better prepared to face the world because she knew that Kailash was never going to come back. At least someone had the courage to tell her. Others had only given her hopes. She loathed them now. After what seemed like a lifetime here was a change from the usual lip service. Brother had comforted her unknowingly. She appreciated honesty and courage in a man.

In the following year Richard had been a source of encouragement as they had got to know each other. He was now asking her to have lunch with him on the coming weekend. She had fended off so many of these invitations from so many people and she was also suddenly aware that Brother had never invited her. She had expected an invite much earlier and had wondered that he had not. And now when he asked, she was undecided. He had never even asked her out till today but had kept coming to visit her every month almost like a routine. And once in a while he would call to find out if there was anything he could do for them.

In that moment as he waited for her answer, she had tapped on her defensive mechanism for a way to get out of this situation. It had become a reflex process. Only this time, she was taken unawares by the suddenness of his genuinity. It was Christmas time. He had wanted her to meet his mother and she was fast asleep. He was apologetic and sounded disappointed. He was inviting her to lunch on another day. There was no need for that. Sheila's mind galloped.

All she could say was 'I don't know about the lunch but I will try to come. I have to check if Rani has any plans for the weekend.'

'Of course, you must and if Rani is free, bring her along, it will be like the old times and I will tell her all about what Kailash and I used to do in NDA, in the Flying academy and the fun in the squadron,' Richard had said with mischief in his eyes.

Sheila suddenly wanted to share Richard and the Air force life that she had known with Rani who had no inkling of her past environment. Those had been the good times that she had known, just one year after their marriage. Brother's company was also reassuringly similar to the way she felt with Rani's Ravi. Almost instantly, she mentally admonished herself to be so presumptuous. Brother was not to her like Ravi was with mother and daughter. How could she compare. Anyway, it would be good for Rani to meet someone who knew her father so closely. In that moment Sheila realized that she liked Richard's spontaneity and decided to make the visit over the weekend and also have lunch.

However, she remained guarded, 'I will call you on Friday and confirm. Let me know if I can cook something and bring it.'

Richard warmed up to the offer and looking into her eyes said, 'this weekend, you don't cook, I will and I enjoy cooking for people who care for me. I appreciate the offer.' Sheila blushed secretly, turning away, as though Richard could feel her affection. She actually did want to come and share time with him. This ancient cottage was so quiet, yet warm. It gave her strength in an altogether different way from her own cozy nest in Borivili.

Brother had walked to the bus stop and seen her off. They shook hands as she thanked him for the outing. 'Wish your mother Merry Christmas, for me,' and Brother had nodded in smiling acknowledgement. She had promised to call him after reaching home safely. It would take her at least two hours.

And then he had put his mother to bed and retired to his own room. This had been where he grew up and the room had been his little world. There was an old brass four poster immaculate with a simple cover spread without a crease on it. Brother was very particular about his surroundings. It had been like that with him always. The walls in his room had photo frames and a few paintings. They were all of aircrafts in flight. There was a bookshelf near an old but well polished study table. The books were all about Flying, Tactics, Wars and campaigns in history, his training notes and journals before the war and he had a set of albums. The albums had photographs of all the places he had been to or served at after he had left home for training at the NDA at the impressionable age of sixteen. These had all been bundled and brought to his parents a few weeks after the war. The arrival of his belongings had truly declared him missing in action bringing the cold of death near but they had struggled to keep the house warm. Martha was strong.

Sitting at his study table, leaning back, recollecting the whole day that he had spent with Sheila, he thought, it felt nice to be with someone whom you can talk to, without any apprehensions. It had not been like that with anyone else. They were both fond of art and there was an exhibition at the Jehangir art gallery; the proceeds were to go to war widows. Brother attended all these functions in the hope that he would meet some known faces and share a few thoughts or information that could be exchanged with them. Taking Sheila along today was with the hope that it would make her feel that the country was after all doing something for those who had lost their husbands in the service of the nation. She would be with other women who had lost their men and it would have its own therapy. He was not sure if she felt about it that way. She had related her earlier experiences of the pain generated by the official system. There had been delays in sanctioning of the financial benefits to her as a nominee. It had been a traumatic experience for her to produce marriage certificates and a whole host of documents; sign them and it had still taken them over a year for her to start receiving the survivor benefits. With a small child and no other income it had been tearfully trying. Brother was just a bit agitated as he went over the day's happenings, to the extent that he had wanted this first outing with Sheila to be a cheerful one but it had turned out somewhat different.

At the gallery they had met a retired Air Marshal who had flown fighter missions during the war of 1971. Brother recognized him instantly with courtesy, 'You must be Nihalkar sir.'

'Yes son, I am retired Air Marshal Nihalkar, and you? Where have I seen you, let me see?' The Air Marshal had difficulty in recognizing him or recalling his name till he was told.

'I am known as Brother, otherwise I am Flight Lieutenant Richard James.'

'Oh, are you the same brother who belly landed a Gnat with bombs under your wings, I have heard about you.' Brother had flown a few missions in the same sector and in 1971 Wg. Cdr. Nihalkar was well known as he had been decorated for gallantry with a Vir Chakra for shooting down an enemy fighter. Brother was simply known for his daring.

'So when did you leave the Air force; must be long ago because you said Flight Lieutenant, didn't you?'

'Yes sir, I was shot down over Gujranwala in 1971 and was a PoW till January 2000.'

The Air Marshal tried to look away in disbelief— shock showed clearly. 'You were a PoW for twenty-nine years! Where were you, I thought the last batch of PoWs were returned in 1975 or 76.' Brother shuffled for an answer to the question and then the Air Marshal shifted his attention and concern to Sheila who stood one step behind. He had begun to say, 'I am so happy for you Mrs. James' and Brother, late to introduce her said, 'Oh! This is Mrs. Sheila Rao.'

'Her husband was also shot down during the strike on the Gujranwalla bridges; we were in the same formation.'

'Oh yes, Gujranwala, how can I forget, that was the day we lost quite a few boys but it had also been the day after which the tide had been turned.' Sheila managed a smile. How easy for him to say, *'We lost quite a few boys, and "tide had turned".'* A young lady in an escort's uniform had come to the Air Marshal, requesting him to give away one of the paintings sold to a well known Industrialist. The Air Marshall had left abruptly. Brother had looked at Sheila, apologetic for the Air Marshals' brusque manner and she had silently put him at ease with a never mind look. Brother felt cheated for Sheila. The Air Marshal could have offered to let Sheila hand over the painting.

Sheila had simply smiled and added, 'Isn't it good for you to meet someone who remembers your accomplishments even after so many years.'

'Sheila, you saw, I had to remind him, I am amazed, they thought all PoWs have been returned. He was a senior officer, he should know better.'

She said, 'You have tried to tell them, maybe you need to try harder.'

On the way home in a taxi, Brother had begun to discuss, 'It is shocking that even our senior officers believe that Pakistan has handed over all PoWs to India and that India has done the same and he never had a kind word to say to you about your personal loss.'

Sheila had just touched his arm and said, 'how does it matter, why let yourself get worked up, they are still not sure about Kailash, for them he is still missing in action. But I believe you.' In whispered tones, 'this is something we should not talk about here and she pointed at the taxi driver to indicate the confidentiality of their conversation. There are so many who die here in Bombay and do you think each one of them is identified and their families searched out and informed. Why should I be special? Just because my husband was a victim of the war none of us have truly understood. I am now like any other widow with my own memories. I don't need anyone to remind me of them.'

'But there are still many who are being held. They didn't believe me when I told them in my interrogation at Delhi, just because I could not remember the name or location of the camp. On the contrary they declared me mentally unsound with memory loss. Imagine— they took another month to let me go home because one interrogator thought I was not telling them the camp location for some motive or out of fear. Those soldiers still in captivity have got families here and there is no reason for them not to be released.'

Sheila had just looked out of the window and said, 'does what the Air force think still bother you, I don't think you are scared or hiding the location. You just don't know, because they ensured you didn't get to know and you were sick and it is also possible to loose portions of one's memory.' There was finality in her statement and it had comforted Brother to know that she believed him. It had also hurt that he could have lost some of his memory that could be the key to freedom for others. The rest of the journey home had been conversation about the general state of unemployment and Sheila's office where they were retrenching staff because of the financial cutbacks. Brother was looking for a job but there were none and it didn't bother him.

His health was improving and he was happy looking after his mother. He was even toying with the idea of writing an account about his PoW days but was unable to start because he wasn't sure if the experiences were worth going over again. The enemy had been very thorough. It must have been a big risk for them to release him. Or was it that they had decided to leave him because they believed he would not survive and even so they could dispose off the rest of the PoWs at any time to obliterate tracks if any account were ever written. The fear of being disposed off had always haunted him even while he was in the camp. It was vital that he had to remember the location of that camp. People would then believe him and more importantly, mobilize efforts to free his fellow prisoners still languishing there. His mother had not accepted that he could die. It did not seem fair that the families of his co- prisoners should live in the imprisonment of similar uncertainty.

Brother took out a folder from his study table drawer and from it took out the telegraphic message the authorities had sent to his parents. The paper was old and there were some stains on it. These must be my mother's tears, he thought, gently feeling the stains with his fingertips. He then reached determined for the bottom most drawer and pulled out an old map that was patched up with strips of tape. It was a map showing the western border of India with Pakistan. He tried to remember again. It was very important. He had to free them. Sheila had said he needed to try harder. Closing his eyes helped to recapitulate. *'We took off for the mission from Pathankot. Slipped over the Pir Panjal range north of Jammu to avoid radar detection, crossing the border north of Sialkot we flew west to hit the road and railway line at Wazirabad and then followed it to Gujranwala.'* He traced the route on the map and tried to recall more. With his eyes closed again, it started coming back to him in slow motion. There were four Hunter fighter-bomber aircraft in the formation in front of him. Abreast of him was Ashok in another Gnat fighter. They were the air defense escorts for the Hunters. Descending through a thin layer of morning haze, the twin bridges of Gujranwala had risen. Almost relieved he had smiled under his oxygen mask. He recalled Kailash whispering out 'Sheila' on the radio. Brother's own call was a fraction behind Kailash's as he watched the lead Hunters launching their rockets. A few seconds and the trail pair of Hunters fired theirs. He flew through the rocket smoke trails. Brother was in the dive when he saw a bright flash in the sky. The Hunter diagonally to his right in the trail pair had exploded. That was Kailash. Almost immediately he also saw the explosions of the lead rockets on the rail bridge through his gun sight and then had fired his own rockets. He had also seen Kailash's rockets finding their mark but the Hunter had disappeared. It had disintegrated completely. They had pulled out of the shallow dive and started turning when he felt a thud as his aircraft was hit and then the Hydraulic and fire-warning lights on his instrument panel had come on. He was on fire. He could see the smoke trailing behind in his rear view mirror. Brother had tried to turn around with the formation in an Easterly direction towards home but the controls were not responding and he was losing height. The remaining aircraft of the formation ahead were becoming dots in the sky as they pulled away and Ashok's Gnat flew across his path in a tight turn as if to circle him but then vanished from sight. Brother had felt deserted. He had to get out of this machine on fire. *'It is early morning so I'll have a chance of slipping across the border through the mist.'* He remembered pulling the ejection handle at a thousand feet and then it was quiet. He was coming down fast into a field and there were people there. They were waving at him. How strange. For a moment he thought he had ejected in friendly territory. And then fear had gripped him as he saw huge bamboo staves being angrily pointed at him. There were sickles and swords tied at the end of the bamboos. They would kill him. He thought about his mother. She would be devastated. He felt for his 9mm. It was there. He was close to the ground and it was time to brace up for the landing and then he would run. Going through the drill mentally he had observed a jungle to his left. It would give him cover.

He had touched down and rolled over with the impact. It had knocked out the breath from him but it suddenly felt good to be on the ground and alive. The Earth was just a little wet, soft, like lying on the riverside on a picnic he'd been to with the rest of the boys in the squadron just a month back. He had little time to dream. The villagers were crawling all over him. Feeling greeted he then realized, they were tearing at him like wolves as he tried to roll away. One of them had held on to his revolver and managed to pull it free from the holster. Brother had tried to prevent it. Their fingers had met, grappled and pulled free. The burly villager had shouted and the others had fallen back and then he felt the cold steel barrel being bored into his temple. He had seen the man's eyes narrow as he pulled the trigger but there had been no explosion as Brother winced. The ugly man had also recoiled. They had both expected a bang. It was not loaded. Instead there was a loud metallic sound. Their eyes met. The villager's eyes had hatred of generations there and then they were all beating him. Through it all he cursed himself for not loading the revolver and drawing it out as he parachuted down. He could have taken some of these wild animals before they got to him. Brother realized much later that his one carelessness had actually saved his life. He had broken a cardinal principle but it had helped him. As a PoW and even as he sat in his Chapel road room, the thought never failed to bring on a sarcastic smile. Especially when Brother had occasion to remember his colleagues, the hard core killer instinct variety who had sworn that if ever they had to bail out and escape was not possible, they would kill as many as possible and reserve one bullet for themselves. Brother had never argued as he had his own thinking on that one and had erred accordingly.

He recalled waking up on a cold floor and it was quiet. It was dark as he tried to focus his eyes. The throat felt dry and cold was reaching his very bones. He ached and shivered. There were footsteps approaching him. He tried to crawl away from the sound but a wall abruptly prevented any movement. Rage gripped him, that his hands were tied. Where am I, he wondered? It was pitch dark and for a moment he even thought that he was dreaming. Thoughts raced from his mother to his squadron mates and the mission he had flown. He had to get word to her that he was alive. Did he fly the mission today? It seemed so long ago. He felt hunted by the bright ray of a torch stabbing at him and tried even harder to crouch and crawl away. The sound of keys reached him to realize that there was another human being close by. This was confirmed with the sound of a heavy metal door being pushed open. The door was near but the sound seemed hollow and far. Suddenly there was light all around him. He had known this effect every time he had flown through the clouds into the bright blue above it all. Almost dazzling. He couldn't be flying now so how was this happening. The prison cell light hurt his swollen and bleeding eyes as he ducked away from the brightness. It was then that he realized that he had been captured and was in an empty cell. Eyes traveling along the floor he recognized the boots of the soldier who had come in, and then perceived the bars and dirty walls of the cell. With the light his swellings and pain took shape. He could not move his neck to look up at the face of the man and could only make out that he wore khaki trousers. Attempting to rise he was pushed down by something. It was the barrel of a rifle and the blow pierced his aching shoulder. It was natural for him to present himself in a dignified manner but his captor took it as an aggressive act. *'How can these goons be so scared? My hands are tied after all.'* Falling forwards he rolled to be face up. A blurred image came through his dazzled eyes. It looked like a policeman. How could a policeman dare to muzzle him? He was an officer. Policemen were not authorized to deal harshly with regular officers of the armed forces. They had to know, he was a fighter pilot. A bunch of keys and a torch in one hand he had the rifle in the other. It was a savage. The expression spelt hate. Those eyes had mastered the art of piercing a captor with apprehension and fear. The cold hatred almost grew every moment. His lips moved the way a butcher prayed before slaughtering a goat or a fowl. Back home in the market he'd seen lips move like that, like some prayer was being offered. Brother instantly realized what he was about to encounter. Blind aggression rose in retaliation. Hate was returned with scorn and the message had silently gone across. Brother saw the soldier's finger slide into the trigger guard as the rifle muzzle was lifted towards his chest. The barrel was now resting between his ribs digging for his heart and the duel of eyes locked in combat was rapidly moving against Brother. Instinctively, he realized the helplessness of the situation. He had to do something. The trigger had to be jammed from being pulled. Pain racked his body and he couldn't move. He had wanted to look at the finger on the trigger but he knew that it would be suicide to leave the assassin's eye. The irony of being tied up and shot in a jail finally overtook him and Brother couldn't stop a snigger from escaping. In response the barrel dug viciously into his ribs. Brother gasped and detected the beginning of a sadistic smile in the eyes he was dueling with. The animal wanted to enjoy this and that could give Brother time to recover. Brother had shrugged and laughed again. He could win. And then there was noisy interruption.

These were other voices. The duel was interrupted by a Pakistani major from the regular army storming into the cell barking something very curtly in Urdu. The policeman reluctantly straightened with the rifle leaving its point of contact and he and the major looked long enough arrogantly at each other for Brother to realize their occupational jealousies. He could sense that the army major had come to take charge of him. There was relief within him because the regular army would know how to treat him. He was a fighter pilot. He was elite. Izzat (honor) was high in the order of the value system of Pakistani officers. After all he was doing his duty and the enemy understood this well. There would be no personal animosity like there had been from the villagers and then the policeman. At least they would not kill him in cold blood. Or would they for he had heard crew room gossips.

Brother had heard the voice of this major somewhere. He was pulled up on his feet and more pushed than assisted down the corridor and up some steps into a small hall and then taken out to a waiting jeep.

'Where have I come across this major,' he thought. It was night and the street was dimly lit. Almost like black out conditions. Brother secretly yearned for a Canberra bombing strike at that moment and his ears almost heard the long drawn humming sound that preceded their arrival. The officer asked him his name in the same harsh tone that he had addressed the policeman. He knows how to command, thought Brother and appreciated this trait. It suddenly fell into place.

This was the major who had rescued him from being lynched by the mob of villagers after he had parachuted into the wet field. 'My name is Flight Lieutenant Richard James and I am grateful to you for saving my life sir.' Actually the major had saved him twice that day and that is what Brother had meant.

'Don't be too sure. Before the night is through, you will curse the day you were born.' It was a typical threat. On the contrary, Brother had expected him to say 'Oh its alright, we treat prisoners correctly.'

'What is this Brother on your name tag?'

'That is my pet name in the Air force sir.' He had smiled becoming more erect with chest out and proudly said, 'they call me Brother James.' The major had viciously ripped off the name tag, thrown it on the ground and stepped on it. The scorn was evident. Brother rushed towards him in a reflex but was restricted, his head pulled back by an ample hair growth by the policeman. The war had permitted them to grow hair beyond the regulation length to merge with the population for escape on occasions like this.

The major's face had a smirk and he leaned close to Brother's face, 'You had better cooperate tonight or I will send your jewels to your squadron by post.'

The knee hit his groin with the suddenness of a recoiled piston. Brother smelt the whisky on his breath. He was in pain, breathless from the unexpected assault, yet surprised. A good Muslim did not drink. The policeman then kick shoved him towards the jeep and held him back for a moment and in rapid fire, said to the major, 'Let me finish this dog, why waste time and food on these prisoners. We have barely enough for ourselves. You can always say he was trying to escape sir. I am good with the bayonet. We will not even waste a bullet.'

The major had just looked very hard at the policeman and then at him. Brother sensed the major contemplating, so he smiled at the major through the pain of his hair being pulled like he was some animal for slaughter. The smile had lit a fire in the major. Brother had heard to his relief,

'No, I want to see for myself how tough these pilots think they are. I have a batch mate who is a Mirage pilot who thinks fighter pilots are the toughest. Let me appreciate this for myself.'

'Oh yes, give him the full dose sir and if you ever need professional expertise, call me, I am Ata-ul-Hasan,' the policeman had said. With that Brother's journey had begun. His nametag lay on that street in Pakistan; he missed it even now.

Brother had just collapsed on the floor of the jeep. He realized that his sense of balance had gone. Both ears were swollen from the beating. 'What is wrong, why am I falling like this,' he thought. I must stand up erect and be strong. I must get my energies together and I will escape,' he thought. For him it was like a boxing match and this was just one more round. The coach at NDA had always said, 'reserve a bit of your strength in every round even if you are being bashed and you will always get the opportunity, look for it and then, go for the kill.'

'I have to get my strength together and go for it,' he thought, as he lay beaten on the jeep floor. He recalled the Geneva Convention that protects every PoW. You only need to give your rank, name and service number. He had resolved. It gave him some consolation and strength. He was fading. I must keep awake. Where are we going? He almost asked and shut up.

The major looked over the seat and said, almost kindly, ' Did you say something or do you need something.'

Brother was thirsty. 'No nothing,' he had nodded. There was an evil smile on the major's face that Brother could not see from his position on the floor.

The drive was on a good road. It was smooth with lampposts at frequent intervals. The major had snapped at the driver. 'Why are you turning left?'

'That is the way to Muridke, sir,' he replied in Urdu. Brother realized that he could follow the language without much difficulty. Who are these people we are fighting against? They speak like us. Strangely, it gave him some comfort that he was, if not home, not very far with people who definitely would be like those back home.

'Turn right and head towards Wazirabad Brigade Headquarters.'

'Yes sir.'

Brother was sweating, bent over his study table, the faded map in front, eyes closed, deep in his thoughts trying to remember every little detail like he had never done before and it was an exercise that was making him try to recall newer, very minor incidents and details so he could connect with his lost memory. At times it was fearful as he relived the memories that randomly flashed. He had never done this. Sheila had implored, 'You need to try harder.' He was trying, sometimes wanting to stop the agonizing madness. And the sound of children singing Christmas carols from the street outside his window took him back to the PoW camp where he used to sing carols during Christmas time and all his fellow prisoners had sat around and learnt to sing along with him. He had to somehow recall the name of the location because he owed it to them. They had suffered together, laughed at fate arm in arm, looked death in the face and they had been by his side when he was sick and left to die. He would never give up trying.

They took him to Wazirabad for initial interrogation. It was a comfortable cell for three or maybe four days. The interrogation was not so important. He had to remember the place or at least the route to the place that he was taken after that and held captive for so many years. Trying to refocus, the phone jarred him from continuing. The phone had rung so often during his interrogation and the mustachioed Brigadier had picked it up. Between questions, coaxing, threats and cups of tea the phone had on those occasions given Brother time to think. Even tonight he was thinking. The phone on his table rang a few times. He straightened a little nervously to come out of the trance. Looking around as if it were a strange place he then realized, it was his own room. Who could it be at this hour? It was close to eleven at night. Brother looked at the instrument apprehensively and then with a hesitant smile of relief, picked up the receiver. It must be Sheila. She had reached home safely. And had promised to call. Brother answered it, listening very carefully. He was still in a different world.

She had asked with concern if the call had woken him up. 'No, I am very much awake and trying harder.' It had not made sense to Sheila at first.

She had said, 'Trying what?' There was silence because Brother had expected her to know that he was trying to recall names of places in Pakistan. Their worlds were so different.

Brother had later wondered about the total surprise to his, 'Trying harder'. He had to explain, 'I am trying to recall every detail of my days as a PoW from the very first day. You said I will succeed in remembering the name of the location.'

She had laughed, 'don't waste time, go to sleep, how is your cough; you need to rest and just try and recall the names of places or the route to it Richard. Why go into so many other details.'

'But you'd said that I need to try harder, so I was doing that.'

'Come on Brother don't punish yourself. It will come. I am tired but thanks for a lovely day.'

Brother couldn't remember being addressed so affectionately by Sheila or anyone for that matter. He did not know how to respond. This was not part of his training but he sure wanted to learn. In two years he felt he was witnessing his own change. They were getting closer. Was it out of a kind of sympathy for his age and health or did he see a relationship being nurtured by her. She had said to try harder and now she says don't waste time. Egging him on, yet concerned about his comfort. Strange. 'We will talk about it tomorrow, okay.'

'Yep,' he had replied like he had always said to any task.

There was a moment's silence; hesitation and her receiver had been gently almost reluctantly been replaced. He had held on to hear her receiver click shut and then put his own down. It was quiet again. So many dreams end with just these kinds of clicks, he thought. He shrugged, smiled and folded the map that was spread in front of him. She sounded so good tonight. Brother looked at himself in the mirror as he brushed and couldn't help spluttering into a laugh. Was he being the vane fighter pilot? Who wants a relationship with me, I am old just out of an ailment and am a marked man. I was a prisoner of war. Relationships are for the balanced and normal and not for those put away for twenty plus years. The number of years gone by sent him into cold sweat. Had he become immune to affection in captivity?

His mother had called from her bed in the adjacent room and Brother heard only her third or fourth call. Coming out of his reverie, 'Coming mom.' He wiped his brow and went to her side.

'Whose call was that Ritchie?' Only she called him Ritchie. She searched his face through her failing eyesight. It looked like she was seeing him, her only son from the bottom of a pond. The water was still, yet his face was so wavy and distorted. It had bothered her. His loneliness. Who was he talking to, so late in the night? And then she tried to smile; he always liked her to smile. 'What happened, you were to bring your friend Sheila home for dinner.'

'I am sorry that the phone woke you up Mom. We got late so she went home.' Brother did not want her to know that he was disappointed. She had been asleep when Sheila had come. Mother and son had both smiled at each other. Brother in understanding and she just happy to know he was there. He had come back from something like a life sentence so he would always be ready to forgive anyone. And she had smiled because Brother was smiling and it was so good to see him smiling like that. A little like Tom…. she had often tried to reach him through his pain and all the lost time but he had always talked good about the friends he had made at the camp and the things he used to do to keep himself occupied and fit. He had made it look so plain but deep inside she knew, there was pain. He was beyond the age for her to take him into her arms and she was not agile anymore, like in the days when he would come back from a lost football game or a frustrating day with the teachers at school. Even as a young boy he used to gently push her away when she had tried to hug and console him. She had not imposed then so she did not pry too much now. They were very comfortable with each other.

She turned to one side and said, 'Ritchie, can you open the blinds son, I like the sunlight to wake me up.' He had opened the curtains facing east and remembered that all those years in the PoW camp he had always slept facing the east because that was home and he had always wanted to escape and run east. It had also been the last thing he had tried to do before he had ejected from his battle damaged aircraft. The East had meant life. So he pulled the blinds open. Let there be life. From his prison cell window he had observed birds flying away to the East before sunset and had envied them. Now at last they had flown him home with them to the east.

Coming back to his study table, he opened an old diary that had hardly been used. It was an unused diary of 1971 that had been sent with his few belongings after he was declared missing in action. He opened it to fourth December and quickly wrote just a few sentences and some points. He was trying harder to remember dates and places and must make notes. He must for he had to free the others left behind. There had to be a way of locating the PoW camp reserved for just a few special prisoners. With that he had lain down thinking about the days proceedings, the Air Marshal, the paintings, Sheila and then the other prisoners that were left behind, Naik Azad Khan, Colonel Sunderam, Major Ganguly and the young Indian Army doctor Pawri who had just one years service and a few others who were surely still there in the camp. These were the officers. The other prisoners were plain soldiers and even some civilians. Where? That was all he had to recollect. Sheila had seemed so close tonight on the phone, as if she knew more about his mind than himself. She was pointing him in some direction and his gut feeling was that he would succeed. She was so confident that he would recall the name of the camp. Why was it that he couldn't remember? Or was it better this way. Who likes to recall captivity when the whole world was breaking free day by day from the past and even the previous day?

Thoughts raced as he lay in bed. He was blindfolded before they had entered the town of Wazirabad. His blindfold removed only when he was indoors within the headquarters complex. How he had hated being blindfolded not even sure of his step and being led by a rope and often pulled from side to side. His lost status had retaliated and that had brought abuses and physical pain. He remembered how he would become dizzy due to the long hours of questioning and he was made to sit blindfold while they would have their lunch. He could almost recall the aroma of the spices. It had felt good but he never got to eat it. They would give him some lentil soup and hand made dry "chapattis". They had then moved him at night after the four days of interrogation, threats and insult at the Brigade headquarters. After a whole nights drive and late in the afternoon they had reached Campbellpore. They had removed his blindfold for him to relieve himself off the road and he had espied a milestone nearby. They were heading towards Campbellpore.

He was then taken to the sub area PoW camp and it was just survival there for four years. It had been torture because it was just the beginning. A total attempt to shatter self-esteem. He had been forced to clean the toilets of the camp officer in charge and even the sentries' washrooms. Sweeping the cookhouse or the camp roads was routine. There was then an escape attempt by three co-prisoners. Those three had suddenly gone missing. They had wanted to execute him so they tried to force a confession in writing that he was re-arrested after an escape and caught trying to blow up an ammunition dump. Brother remembered refusing to do so and the physical torture and the days without food and water in a small compartment where he could barely move and how it had become maddening due to the stench of excreta. He had prayed for deliverance and had begun to converse as if with his mother in a delirium. He would even hum the NDA march past tune that played like a record with its needle stuck but only in his mind. It provided the arrogant courage required for survival.

That they had let him off was a miracle. He was frequently questioned about the air force's training pattern and location of squadrons and Brother would laugh in a stupor. The interrogator would hold a pistol to his head and pull the trigger. There would be a loud metallic sound and he would fall off the chair in auto response every time. Through the haze a scornful interrogator would be laughing at him. And then there was the cold water thrown on him and it had felt like he had gone onto the next world. Reborn. There had been a sudden disappearance of a lot of PoWs. Those that were kept back had whispered and conjured that these disappearances could either mean freedom and return to India or death or transfer to some other camp. He had been moved to another make shift camp at Kalabagh to work at gunpoint on a construction site at Daud Khel.

He recalled the river Indus at Daud Khel. The working parties were allowed to take a dip in the rushing waters on a few occasions after the days work. The construction work of the so-called granary towers had taken three years and on completion he was again moved with three other prisoners. They had spoken in hushed tones, 'these are ammunition storages or construction for an atomic energy plant.' Six prisoners had been shot at the riverside in Daud Khel just one month before work completion; on the pretext that they were escaping. They were a group with one officer from the army and they had repeatedly fought the authorities about the illegal work PoWs' were being made to do and the food and poor conditions of living. And they had not tried to escape; he had seen them minutes before the gunshots. Brother wondered about the shape of those towers. Could they be something other than granary towers?

The physical work had made him weak and he had developed a severe cough. It was diagnosed as throat infection. Two fellow prisoners had died of high fever in the new camp within three years. Another move had again been in the middle of the night. He was given no warning and in less than thirty minutes, huddled into a military vehicle blindfolded and moved. This ride had been in a truck lying on the floor and he just could not remember anything other than a very bumpy ride over rough roads. The journey had been mostly through wooded and hilly terrain he guessed because of the slow speed and constant shift from side to side as the vehicle zigzagged in low gears that were changed often. He had been tired and slept rolling on the floor of the truck. There were three such moves at night by road and rail in the years to come and he used to be very unwell with a bad cough, so he would be tired and sometimes in high fever unable to follow or know where he was. The last move was in 1992. He was resigned to an end. Death would bring his freedom. Thereafter his world had not extended beyond the fencing of the unknown camp for the next eight years. The Pakistani army camp doctor had diagnosed Tuberculosis. Brother had not felt anything on being told that they could only give him some medicines that were authorized for his condition. He would have to continue with these substandard medicines. Lieutenant Pawri a doctor who was also a prisoner had assured him that he would recover if he ate and exercised. He had knelt and prayed, thought about his parents and looked east at every dawn and many times throughout the day especially in the evening at the birds that always flew home to the east. His condition had worsened and he would be indoors bedridden for days. Fellow prisoners had often helped him with food, taken him to the toilet and held him in his weakness and sometimes carried him outdoors to get some fresh air. Their constant encouragement and support prevented him from giving up.

There was only one prison guard who could not suppress his compassion and they had become friends. Brother could never forget Nazeer. Brother had taught him English and Nazeer would teach him a few words in Urdu but it was all very discreet. Brother had given Nazeer his address in Bombay with a request to write about his being alive to his parents but Brother had never received any letter from anyone so obviously Nazeer had not dared. They had both known the consequences and understood each other enough to accept the situation. Through their friendship Brother had begun to realize that it was just possible that all Pakistanis did not hate Indians after all. He recollected Mustafa the cook who used to tell them jokes and couplets. Many an evening after the prison officials had left for the night, the dormitory cell would witness Mustafa in his elements. And Brother had played the guitar for the prisoners to sing with him. All the Indian prisoners liked Mustafa but he could never give them the food that he cooked for his own camp staff. How could he, there had to be a difference. The cooking was very often from the prisoners' rations but there had to be a difference as required by the camp management. Secularism, leave alone basic human rights and equality, had not yet strayed into this corner of the earth.

Brother smiled as he drifted off to sleep his eyes half open. A change that had taken place in the years of horror. His half open eyes were always watching for an opportunity to escape or looking for the guards who may come any day to take him away. Where will they take me? Uncertainties had made the living look like dead. Their eyes always stared. The possibility of freedom was enough to dissolve the pains of captivity. The hope of freeing the others held him captive now. A lot of the pain had gone.

# The Year 2002

# Chapter I

From the hospital bed where he lay in bandages with his mother Ruhaina sitting by his side, Basheer Khan replayed his life from the day he was rejected by the Indian Army. He was now thirty-one years old and had not married. The tailoring business had grown. He had started a home school of embroidery classes and employed more than twenty-five Muslim girls, to learn and undertake embroidery work for him. Their creations were being supplied to major garment manufacturers all over India. His grandfather's old shop was redecorated and looked bright. Most of his clients were Hindus and he had no difficulties with them. In fact they became like family to him because he was accommodative, patient and never went back on his word. He never troubled them for his payments. His deliveries were always on schedule. He had seen Izzat O Iqbal engraved on the belt buckles of the gunner officers of the Artillery Corps and that had got embroidered in his mind. It was the Artillery Corps motto. It became his too. 'Izzat' (honor) was the only important thing.

Basheer Khan, the son of a martyr Naik Azad Khan lay in the municipal hospital a victim of the riots that were triggered off by the tragedy at Godhra. *'Why me, what have I ever done to deserve this,' I want to fight those terrorists and the Pakistanis but here my own countrymen are trying to kill me.'* He had been beaten badly and his fingers on one hand were all broken. This was the work of someone who knew him.

A malicious attempt to destroy those God gifted fingers. Tears escaped in a slow river from his once alive eyes. His mother wiped them off one by one. But the flow continued sometimes streaming and mostly just a trickle. A mother has to do that for her children. Absorb their pain; listen to their angst and even accusations. And gracefully keep the home fires burning and tuck the uncertainties away. She was softly reciting the holy Koran as she gave him her soothing touch. On that fateful day Basheer was dragged out from his ancestral tailoring shop not far from the Divisional headquarters of the army. Was the new color of secularism knocking shamefacedly even in the backyard of the armed forces? The services. One big family that did not differentiate between race or religion. Yet there was that "dushman" and how can men in uniform forget what they had heard in hushed tones about the Muslim 'mujahideen' and even Pakistani troops and their torture methods. This Hindu mob had rushed in and attacked him without any warning. Some of them entered the room behind the main shop and mercilessly dragged the young women busy in their embroidery onto the street and into a van. The shocked and screaming women had clutched the lace and embroidery as though it would protect them. Everyone respected the workmanship and knew Kasim Khan's reputation. Anything connected to Kasim Khan, even his embroidery will ensure our honor, they had hoped.

Through his bandaged pain and tears, the voices of the holocaust came at Basheer like tidal waves. ' Kill him, he is an ISI agent and he runs a brothel of these women who entice our Hindu soldiers for the secrets of the army, kill him, he is a Pakistani agent, he thinks he has deep connections with the High court judge and he has the guts to flirt with his daughter. How dare a Muslim traitor dally with a Hindu girl, kill him, burn him alive, so we can dispatch him straight to hell.' 'Hurry up; the police will arrive in fifteen minutes. We must finish him now and leave. Where are those unholy women, get the van moving. Muslim women have to be punished for their sins. Their men are allowed to marry four women. Let us now enjoy their women. They can also have four men. Come on; let us take them to the farm. We will hang them with their dupattas to liberate them.'

Basheer's mind kept returning to relive the horror of that morning. Major Dilip Bahadur of the 3rd Para Commandos was in his shop to collect his new battle dress for he was moving shortly to the front in Kashmir. Pakistan had increased terrorist activities and the Indian army was in full deployment to prevent mercenaries from Afghanistan and Kashmiri militants from infiltrating the valley.

Moments before the incident Basheer had asked Major Dilip entreatingly about his missing father and related the story of his failure to get recruited. There was a silence almost akin to the quiet on a beach in front of an approaching cyclone. 'Is there some way that I can join the army even now?' The Major had no words and then Basheer broke the silence with an apology, with both palms joined. Major Dilip had wanted to pay for the work done. Basheer said, 'I do not charge anyone from my father's Parachute regiment for their rank badges and the regiment insignia. This is our only contribution to keep his memory alive. Baba would have never charged his own regiment boys. We have heard a lot about PoWs kept in confinement by the Pakistanis, for bargaining, is it true?' This question remained unanswered as the shop came under siege. Major Dilip was pushed and he fell, hitting his head against the glass sliding doors of the display cupboard. It knocked him out. Basheer was stunned at the suddenness and severity of the attack. What was happening? These marauders had huge spears and swords and they were already bloodstained. He had never seen their faces. They were from some other area. Then how have they reached me? I will not be afraid he decided. They have hurt my officer Major Dilip. I will show them. The eyes that were always gentle became fireballs. He had fought them off with the solid steel measuring meter scale, but they over powered and dragged him out. He recalled the smell of petrol being poured on him. "Ya Allah!" 'I will not let them glorify in my pain. I will take them with me.' He struggled because he had never known what is giving up. And then there was a battle cry. It was the blood curdling battle cry of the 3rd Para Commandos.

Basheer recalled the horror of seeing the pool of blood around him. He had been stabbed and there was a smoldering rubber tyre around his neck. He was being held down as he resisted with all his might. Well built he had the courage of a wounded lion. Every muscle strained in spite of the wounds. Basheer's struggles were becoming weaker and the feel of petrol from his clothes was chilling, but the battle cry had relit his desire to live. They were the same words. A slogan that he had heard about from soldiers and officers belonging to his father's regiment. He turned instinctively towards the power of the sound and imagined that he was a soldier and this was war with the "dushman" and the Major was his officer in the lead of a charge. His struggles became more powerful. At last I am in the army with the 3rd Para Commandos and his vision blurred. Soon I will find my father and kill those who took him away from my mother.

Through the blur Major Dilip had come flying out of the destroyed remnants of Basheer's shop. His revolver out, a rage in his eyes and face distorted with the force of his battle cry, he was trying to reach Basheer screaming soundlessly at the mob that *'Basheer is a patriot who wants to fight for the country. Leave him alone.'* A mob only hears its own fury. And then there was gunfire. Basheer thought the major had been shot and he struggled, turning to look for him with his last bit of energy only to be struck down but then the mob suddenly moved away. Major Dilip was holding a sword to the throat of one of the mobsters and had his revolver in the other hand covering the mob. Like a possessed creature, he dared anyone to move, his hoarse rage forced the mob backwards. He screamed at them to leave or he would slit the throat of the man he held captive. 'Touch Basheer and I will cut this man's throat and you can kill me after that but you will have my whole Regiment hunting you for generations to come. They will liquidate your families; now get out of here or I will kill. Run while you have the time. My men are on their way.' The women from Basheer's workshop had already been huddled into a van and dispatched during the commotion. The mob leader quickly gave instructions, there was some argument and suddenly it was quiet. They had disappeared even faster than their attack. The last thing Basheer remembered is that the Major was picking him up in his arms like a child. He had asked him, 'Where are the working girls?' Major Dilip's eyes searched the street and his head drooped with fatigue and shame. He had wept. A major could cry; not possible; that too for me? Basheer felt the heat of emotions as Dilip hugged him to his breast. This Major is a Hindu and those murderers here were also Hindus? Dilip's tears were hopeless and Basheer recognized them. The major's face then turned into the face of his father Naik Azad Khan. Basheer had never known the cradle of a father's arms. He imagined he had died and reached heaven and was with his father. *'At last I am liberated, I am a good soldier and I have killed those "dushmans" and have found my father. Now I shall tell Ammi that I have found him. She will be happy at last.'* And then he blacked out to wake up in the hospital with his mother holding his broken bandaged fingers in her delicate hands. Would he ever be able to create anything with them? How beautiful the embroidery from his fingers had been. She had seen but never praised him. In fact she had always something to say about some little defect. Now those fingers were wrapped up; would she ever kiss them again or see his emotions come alive in the lacy work.

On coming to Basheer had asked about the women who were working behind the shop and his mother just shook her head and a tear fell from her eyes making a wet furrow on her weary face. Basheer just stared in disbelief. He had rarely seen his mother's tears really falling. These tears were like something his mother was revealing to him at last. That she also hurt and cried. She had always been strong. He turned his head away to hide his own shame, afraid of what else she would reveal. He realized that the fate of those women was sunk in the divide being widened by the evil forces of greed in the politician's belly. Some of them were in their teens. *'Allah is this your mercy? Why then was I spared?'*

A turbaned man with a moustache appeared at the door of the hospital ward. The fear of dying again rose and Basheer tried to move and protect his mother from this Hindu who must have come with a sword. He collapsed back on to the pillow, his mother holding him in her arms. In the doorway he could see what could not be real. From behind the turbaned attendant emerged, Smita Choudhury, the judge's daughter, his college days flame.

She wore pink but today the color evoked fear. They had discussed marriage in a casual way. The relationship was closed, as she couldn't go against her father's wishes. And then she had married and also joined the bar. Her husband was Nikhil Banerjee a civil engineer with the state government. She continued to get her clothes stitched only at Kasim Khan's and Basheer would not let anyone touch the material that would be left in his care. On many an occasion Smita had accidentally touched Basheer's hand as she handed over the cloth or advance payment for tailoring and said, 'Basheer bhai, will you call when it is ready. I will come.' He had never replied because she was telling him silently that she knew he wanted her to come. He would only smile and she would be gone. He would cut the cloth so gently and stitch them with even more care and always with that smile on his lips and so many dreams. He would weave those dreams into her clothes. So she could also dream. He stayed connected to her this way. The truth that he could not marry her was slowly accepted. They had both understood the impossibility of it and kept it away in the once lit now locked corridors of the heart. She had gone on to study law and he had taken up helping his mother with tailoring. His mother had known. She had found Basheer with Smita's half stitched clothes in his lap. He would fall asleep on the floor in a squat position. Ruhaina would just smile and carefully put the clothes away and cover him with her shawl, while he slept. Today, Smita was to collect some clothes given for Zardosi work. It must be all destroyed he thought and *'I could not protect them, or her, she is also covered in blood, why did they have to hurt her simply because I am a Muslim?'* He recalled the screaming accusations of the mob about his association with Smita. It numbed his mind. He fainted. The agony was too much. *'Allah, please liberate me from this pain and uncertainty. No wait, I have to find Baba and demand rights that go with a free state and not be condemned to the uncertainty or be branded as minority.'*

# Chapter II

Prisoner of war Naik Azad Khan was kneeling with his arms crossed at the wrists in his lap. In prayer just as Brother used to be on his knees praying in front of a cross painted on the wall of his cell next to his bed. Azad was deeply disturbed for he had heard the prison guards talking about some trouble between Hindus and Muslims in Ahmadabad at a place called Godhra. He thought of his wife Ruhaina and his brother and sister. He had gone to the war when Ruhaina was pregnant. He knew. She was embarrassed. He was exalted. His father and Ruhaina's faces drifted into his vision. Baba may not be alive. Would he be with them again? Allah had heard Brother's prayers so he will hear mine, he firmly believed. He prayed for his near ones. He had assured Brother that he would survive the illness and never to give up. Brother's deportation details were not known to anyone. He was just taken away one evening. Brother and Azad had become very good friends. They knew everything about each other's families and lives to the day they were captured and brought to this remote camp. It was early evening now. Azad was facing west with his folded arms reciting the namaz. He now suddenly felt alone. Finishing his prayers he sat and stared at the cross painted by Brother on the wall. It was still faintly visible on the stone. His cellmate, Brother, had been taken away to a hospital to die. Who knows, it was two years ago. At least he got out of this prison.

Azad Khan prayed regularly for Brother. In the army everyone celebrated and prayed together at every religious festival and on such occasions they all visited the temple, mosque, gurdwaras and church, as the occasion demanded because these places of worship were always built side by side. It was a special brand of secularism. Yet what were these guards saying about Muslims being butchered in numbers at Ahmadabad. About some train being set on fire by Muslim fanatics and a coach full of Hindu pilgrims being burnt alive. The guards rejoiced at the pilgrims' fate and also taunted Azad that his kith and kin were being butchered and raped so why didn't he join the mujahideen and go back and fight the real "Hindu enemy". They had assured him his freedom. All he had to do was to give his willingness to serve with the mujahideen. Azad had kept his rage under control. The years had taught him to curb his wrestling instincts. Instead he would just look at the guards mutely and go back to his prayers. They usually left him alone during prayers.

Azad closed his eyes and tried to pray. His mind drifted from prayer to the day Brother was taken away on a stretcher. Barely conscious, Brother had smiled weakly at him as they took him away. Their hands had clasped tightly and they had both realized that this could be the last time they would see each other. Brother had tried to memorize Azad's address in Ahmadabad. Azad then recalled the day Brother was brought to the camp and he had helped him to get used to the routine of this secluded high security camp. They had exchanged notes about their families, units, the war and what they planned to do after returning home. Azad would go and continue the family tailoring business and Brother had planned to teach music, as he knew how to play the guitar, flute and organ. Both had regretted being captured but they gave hope to each other of a life beyond the prison camp. If only he had not got separated from his platoon that dark night..... His thoughts drifted to that fateful night.

It had been on a night patrol that he got separated from the rest of the platoon. He was young with a lot of steam. Separated but courageous he headed east towards their own lines but in the darkness little did he know that he had silently been surrounded by a Pakistani section of about ten soldiers and one very young officer. He had seen them first but had been in a terrible dilemma to open fire on them because he couldn't differentiate them from his own troops. They could well be from his own platoon. What he hadn't realized is that he had also been seen by two Pakistani scouts of this troop he was shadowing and they had closed in on him rapidly from behind in the cover of darkness. He had suddenly felt the barrel of a semi automatic in his back, pushing him face forward into the sand and then pinning him to the ground. There had been a short struggle but he was overpowered. They had gagged and tied his hands and pushed and butted him like some animal being taken for the slaughter.

The enemy had been known to brutally murder and even leave amputated bodies of Indian soldiers behind on the sands as a warning and for its demoralizing potential. Such visible and gathered information of torture and death in enemy hands with gruesome details was adequate to shake the inner fibre of many a soldier to the extent that they preferred death to being captured and humiliated. These are not issues discussed at schools of tactics or combat training centers. Uniformed men who claim access to secret documents about the enemy sometimes share information in hushed tones. The gory narrations silently flow and find their way into the rage and fear centers of almost every soldier's heart. Especially so after the rum has reached the depths of a stomach that is conditioned to absorb messages of angst from the brain and send a bolt of anger induced adrenalin into the heart. Not in the military textbooks but it has helped during battle.

Ironically, it had the opposite effect of demoralization. The soldier's sense of belongingness and pride of the unit, the flag, bolstered by regimental discipline and tradition, turns him into a raging bull that will fight until death. He would prefer that. Some may qualify these as foolhardy, desperate or even glorious acts of suicide. However, this strange chemistry has shown results of dedication and motivation of an intangible order. It has been the underlining factor of many an impossible and unexplained victory, however at a cost. These are again rarely analyzed or discussed in august gatherings but mentioned or just celebrated with medals, wreaths and emotional speeches of re-dedication.

*Surprisingly sometimes such near impossible bravery is justified by tacticians as inadequacies and mistakes of the enemy that gifts a bonus victory where a few overcome many. Ask the few that were captured and became the prisoners of war expecting a gory end everyday of their lives. They have very little to analyze or argue. The living horror makes many into mental wrecks and others become so hardened that they almost seem disconnected with life after a period of time. Living under a life threat and humiliation without any contact with the rest of the world and the dwindling hope of being reunited with your own comrades in arms and family after the* war is like slow poisoning. History has many examples and no country, race or community can claim that it has not imposed these horrors on their prisoners of war: unfortunately also into the lives of others, directly and indirectly. The damage is permanent, sometimes perceivable and more often dormant. Something akin to radiation exposure. The internal or external scars are irreversible. War itself is an atrocity, sometimes unavoidable. Consequently, there is not much one can offer to the wounds and effects of this atrocity other than, nursing them to a degree of restoration. One of the silent yet horrific fall-outs of wars continues to be the plight of prisoners of war and their survivors. There are celebrations of D-Days, Martyr's day, Victory days and Independence days but there are no days commemorated to the memory of a missing soldier; the prisoner of war. How can there be and what will be celebrated or commemorated. Does anyone know for sure the date, time and place where and who was captured, left dead on the battlefield or is in some unmarked grave. Only a few are ill fated to become prisoners, therefore there is only a small associated population of families and friends that bears the brunt. Those that live in captivity as PoWs and their near and dear who remain imprisoned to the hope of reuniting, continue to suffer. They could also be classified as a minority since 'minority' has now become a household word. There can never be a prisoner of war day for this living dead minority community or for those that remain captive or escape or were released. Everyday continues to be a trial.

Azad Khan was captured in the semi arid area close to the border opposite Anupgarh in the territory that had been captured after a severe battle for two days and nights. His Battalion had been located off Suratgarh.

The first question he was asked by the young Baluch officer was 'Where is the rest of your unit.' Azad had pretended not to hear. A soldier in a Pathan suit had put a booted foot on his chest and sprung open the bayonet on his automatic rifle. In one motion he had inserted the sharp edge under his battle fatigue shirt and ripped it open from waist to throat. The tip had connected with his chin and Azad had felt the warmth of his own blood.

'Tell us where are the rest of the dogs or we will cut you open and leave you here for the vultures.' Azad was gagged to prevent him from crying out for assistance.

He made an attempt to speak and the officer said, 'Open his gag let him speak. If he makes a noise, kill him.' The bayonet was held with just sufficient pressure to hurt him and not much effort would be required to pierce through the throat. They removed his gag. The officer asked him with a questioning nod. Sound travels distances in the desert and he wasn't going to invite an ambush.

Azad had pointed with his eyes and said in Hindi, 'They're, all around you in the dunes.'

The dunes were all over and the captors realized that they were in imminent danger and their prisoner was not going to be of much help. No more questions were asked. The soldier with the bayonet had looked at his officer and asked permission to slit his throat. There had been a moment's hesitation, the officer's eyes blazed with anger at the suggestion of murder and then he had indicated to gag him and take him along. Azad had seen the expression and choked at the rise of emotions that Allah after all had been merciful and there were honorable Pakistani soldiers after all.

Azad's first thought went to his wife, Ruhaina. She was pregnant when he left home for the front. Will she have a daughter or a brave son to take care of her, now that his own survival was uncertain? They had pushed the enemy back in the two preceding nights after a pitched battle of heavy fire and had finally charged across the dunes to destroy the enemy bunkers and machine gun nests. There had been jubilation. This was their first night patrol to counter any infiltration and counter attack. He had survived the merciless shelling and the charge just the previous night and becoming a prisoner of war was quite far away from his imagination. How would the unit explain that he was alive or dead or taken prisoner? Families had to be told. It would give Ruhaina hope that he would return soon after the war. It would let her know that he was alive. She was carrying his first yet to be born. He also felt a sense of shame. I should have died in the battle last night than be taken prisoner. Allah knows what will be my fate. I am a musalman. They will treat me like a Muslim traitor and surely torture me. I must escape. And there could be some of his own colleagues who may even suspect that being a Muslim he had deserted. He prayed hard that someone from his patrol would sense his predicament and activate a search patrol or an artillery barrage. It would give him the opportunity to run. He may get injured or even die from friendly fire but it did not bother him now. Why can't they open up with the artillery. Why is everything so silent tonight? There had been a fire plan to commence shelling just after midnight but that was a couple of hours away. He was missing so they would conclude his capture and suspect the presence of the enemy to start a search for him, or start firing and shelling any minute now. This fatalistic thought process gave him hope. The shelling never started and his journey across the sands continued. His spirit did not die. He just kept waiting in anticipation for the shelling to start. After an hour of stumbling through the sands he could make out some prepared defenses in the near distance. Enemy pickets and bunkers, he guessed. Good, this was well within the artillery range. The scout patrols would have spotted it and he would make a run for it at the first opportunity. A suicidal thought but it was his best option.

Approaching the enemy picket they had stopped. The young officer had given brief instructions and the troop had split into two small groups. Azad Khan guessed that the area ahead was mined and therefore they were to follow two predetermined routes free of mines, known only to the enemy, to reach the picket safely. He had been blind folded. It had taken them more than fifteen minutes for the detour. On the detour he was in the group that did not have the Baluchi officer with them. In his absence the soldiers had all taken their turn in hitting him and one had even spat on him, laughing. Azad was surprised that the officer had left him at their mercy. He had resisted and struggled. That was his training. Resist and fight the enemy's interest in trying to break you. It could keep you alive. Through his bruised eyes he saw the face of the soldier in the Pathan suit. He had detached the bayonet fixed to his rifle. Holding it like a dagger, he ran it across Azad's throat.

'I should slaughter you. Your soldiers shot one of my men last night in cold blood. He had surrendered after the picket was over run. They dragged him on the dunes behind a jeep and used him for target practice. Tell me why should you live then?'

Azad was dumbfounded. All he could do was offer an arrogant stare and in his heart call upon Allah to be merciful.

*It took little time for Azad, now a prisoner of war to appreciate that once captured he was at the mercy of not just a few people. Azad thought to himself. This is probably the hatred of generations. The propaganda of politicians. It could be personal vendetta. Or just whims and even sadistic pleasure. Although the Geneva Convention protects all military prisoners, the enforcement of it is something that cannot be monitored and controlled by any independent agency. This is something all soldiers know and it is only the very honorable, principled and determined men in soldiering that are able to demand or implement the convention in the heat of battle or inside the dungeons for PoWs. The captured soldier therefore can only keep hoping. In desperation he can only evoke the honor code of the enemy to uphold the Geneva Convention. Any kind of brash behavior can only reduce the possibilities of the enemy respecting the convention and turn into impulsive violations. For a life and death issue, on the battlefield, respect for the*

*Convention was very situational, almost left to personal choice. Soldiers can be unpredictable in the battlefield with prisoners.*

Azad was resistant to being moved and his physical capabilities dominated his actions preventing him from comprehending that his resistance would have to be more focused and reserved for critical situations. Although he was bound, he was in fact retaliating every time he was struck. The soldier with the bayonet at his throat ordered him to get on his knees. Azad had refused and when he was being forced, he had swung at the two soldiers holding him. The bayonet was no longer at his throat but the soldier was raising his rifle to fire at him lying on the sand. The scuffle had resulted in sounds and there was a shout from the enemy picket.

'Who is there? Identify or we will fire.' A shot had been fired over their heads.

The scuffle ended and the man in the Pathan suit announced himself, 'Najib.'

An authoritative officer's voice rang out over the dunes. 'Bring the prisoner here at once. We need some information immediately. He must talk.' Najib lowered his rifle very disgruntled and hit Azad on his chin with the butt.

Blood with broken teeth spewed out. ' By tomorrow morning you will regret becoming an Indian soldier. Now move you kafir.'

They had entered the picket area. It was a semi circular cluster of six trenches, well camouflaged, dug into the sand with heavy machine guns in each. Azad was led towards the officer's bunker. He could hear the officer talking on the radio to someone superior from the tones and marks of respect.

'Huzoor (Sir), we have got him here with us. I will make him tell us about the enemy's plans sir. Don't worry I have a seasoned fellow in Najib. He can make a dead man talk. I assure you sir. We will take back the positions that we had to give up last night.'

Azad had followed every bit of the Major's dialog. There was no way he would tell them anything about the artillery barrage planned for that night or for that matter about the actual offensive action planned further north in the Fazilka area. He knew that the artillery barrage in this area was to draw away the attention and reserves of the enemy. His Battalion with two other Battalions and a Squadron of Armour was to create a diversion. The actual penetration with the Armored Strike corps to cut off the Multan to Lahore road link was to take place somewhere north; the exact location of which, he was not privy to. He could not part with any information on his life. Taking this decision he accepted with it that he might not live through this night. He was at the mercy of a beaten back enemy determined to gather any piece of information that may help survival or retaliatory operations. 'Let me die honorably. I am of little use to my comrades unless I can keep the plans secret. I will bear the pain. Allah, please be merciful. Let it be over quickly.'

Azad was made to kneel on the sand with his hands and feet bound. The sand felt soft and cold. His gag had been removed and he was given a glass of water that he held between his bound hands and brought to his lips. The Pathan, Najib had different ideas. In one swift motion Azad's hair was pulled back to an impossible angle and he was asked about his name and unit. He had no fear but there was doubt about what they would do with him after discovering that he was a Musalman.

'My service number is 3487653, Naik Azad Khan sir.' The grip on his hair was loosened and there was an eerie silence. The truth that he was a Musalman soldier in the Indian Army had them dumbfounded. Though just for a moment. It was the Pathan who was quick to realize.

'Let me deal with this traitor Huzoor, he is a kafir and a traitor to Islam, fighting against his brothers.'

'No Najib make him talk, we need information, you can deal with him later,' the officer intervened. Azad understood that he had to play for time and every moment was like a bonus. The artillery barrage had to start very soon and he would get his chance. Or they would kill him. Both were acceptable.

The water was taken away from his hands and his shirt was ripped off. He was now bare from the waist up. 'What unit do you belong to and what forces are we facing, tell us you pig.'

'I told you I am Naik', he was cut off with a sharp blow to his back that sent stars shooting into his brain. Falling forward on his face Azad felt the boot of the Pathan digging into his spine and the rifle muzzle poked him viciously in the back of his neck. The barrel was deathly cold. There is pure hate in this Pathan he thought and the only way I will survive is to resist. Ya Allah give me the strength; I cannot let down my comrades. What will happen to Ruhaina if they kill me now? Let them. I will not betray. With that he struggled to raise his head from the sand and another soldier pushed his face nose down into the sand. I am a champion wrestler and cannot give in so easily. He was choking and heard the laughter at his struggles. Azad stopped fighting the force pushing his face into the sand and held his breath. With a little movement he created a gap sufficient to breathe and let his body go limp. He expected a bullet at any moment.

'Don't kill him; we need the information Najib,' came the urgency from the officer in charge.

'Oh yes we will get more than information, we need some entertainment desperately and lets get that first. What do you say major sahib. Shall we slowly roast him and hear him squeal?' The major was silent and Azad concluded that it was approval.

Najib growled at one of the soldiers ' go and get a can of petrol, we will see how he keeps his silence.'

'Ya Allah,' thought Azad, 'they are going to burn me alive.' He turned towards Najib with hate in his eyes. 'I will see you in hell you kafir he hissed.'

'Oh he wants to say something, give me the can.' With that he poured petrol on the sand all around Azad and struck a match. ' Naik Azad, tell us where and what troops are opposite us in this sector.'

'Never you animal.' Najib lit the petrol in the sand. Azad found himself trapped inside a circle of fire on the sand. The heat and the fumes of ignited petrol cut into his nostrils and he could barely breathe. Neither could he roll out of this cage of fire, as it was all around him. The hair on his arms felt the heat as he dug his face in horror into the sand as if burrowing to safety. 'For the sake of my brothers in arms l will not disclose anything,' he kept whispering to himself and braced himself as the heat came closer.

And then there was an explosion with sand raining down on him. Azad thought he was dead. Must be a mine or someone had fired at them. He saw the enemy soldiers running for cover. Another… and then another explosion. It seemed as if the desert had suddenly woken up with the heat of the fire around him. It suddenly dawned on Azad that this must be the artillery barrage from his own side. They must have spotted the glow from the ring of fire around him in the desert. He had prayed for it to begin. But why were they firing at him, he shouted at them ' not here! They are a hundred yards further, take proper aim and let them have it.' The fire around him had reduced as the flying sand from the explosions settled and extinguished it. Azad found his opportunity to escape. He rolled towards a gap and got up to run when he was hit on the back by a blow that sent him sprawling into the sand.

When he awoke, it was silent and he was lying on something cold. He could not see or move as his hands and feet were bound and he felt a rope around his neck too. Azad remembered the days of his childhood in the lane where all the boys used to play "robbers and cops"; he always enjoyed being the thief who could not be caught or the one who always escaped from the make shift jail; over powering his captors with sheer strength. Rubbing his cheek on the floor Azad realized, he was lying on the metal floor of a truck and there was very little room for movement as he was wedged between heavy boxes. They are taking me somewhere. The events immediately after the artillery barrage from the Indian side remained a blank in his memory thereafter.

' Azad bhai, it is time for lunch,' Mustafa was announcing to the prisoners. It was very similar to a farmer calling his cattle "come and get it". Azad was shaken because he was on the cold floor of the truck and how could someone be calling him for a meal. He opened his eyes and could not totally disconnect from the chain of thoughts of the day he was captured. And now his mind again raced to his family and home, hinged to the bits of gory news of riots in Ahmadabad. The guards had taunted him about his misplaced loyalty to India and aggravated his 'wrestler's psyche' only to mentally grapple with the unknown fate of his wife and family in a country that he had served with his lifeblood. Why were prisoners here not allowed to write or receive letters? Through the Red Cross this was permissible. Why had they never seen the Red Cross after being dumped in this camp? *'We are being held against all conventions. Why?'*

He was sure if released Brother would have contacted his family in Ahmadabad and soon the government of India would do something to free them all. Had Brother been released? Or was he dead. It remained unanswered. Positive presumption gave him the required strength to overcome a sense of helplessness and he got up to move towards the common table for all prisoners. The others were already there waiting for him. They never began meals till the three officers and everyone else was there. Colonel Sunderam the senior most would join and ask them to be seated and they would eat. "Jai Hind" always preceded their collective activities.

*Meals were such a binding force. How sincerely secular. It was just a matter of order, functional discipline and empathy for each other. Almost a culture. Azad felt at home in spite of being the only Muslim prisoner. The other prisoners had silently accepted him as a role model for his continued resistance to succumb to favors and concessions by the captors. If freed, these would be the fittest men to uphold true secularism and possibly abolish the usage of the word "minority community". Azad ate very little for his mind was in Ahmadabad.*

# Chapter III

Smita had moved Basheer to a private nursing home from the municipal hospital. It had not been easy.
She had to overcome her father's firm opposition, to get personally involved in such matters. He had relented to her request that Basheer and the family should be provided with police guards. Smita knew enough about the police organization and its history in the communal incidents of Ahmadabad to visualize how the Judge must have expressed his concern in very civil tones and how equally gracious the Police Commissioner would have been in agreement with the volatile situation and agreed to detail "lip service" guards. With her father, Smita had pursued her basic argument like a good lawyer that Basheer needed better medical care and a secure environment. Her astute understanding of a Judge's concern for his own public image and also concern for a daughter's sensitivities had won her the day. There had been debate but Smita had presented her case to appeal to his basic humaneness. How could he let her childhood friend suffer in an unhygienic municipal hospital where he would be given second-rate treatment if at all, under the prevailing communal emotional upheaval? And to aggravate the situation it was unlikely that even basic security would be extended to injured Muslim victims. The mob could very well reach Azad in the municipal hospital.

Her father Judge Sudhin Choudhury had personally called the Police Commissioner to permit the discharge of a riot victim from the municipal hospital. However he cringed at what the commissioner had said, ' Will you take the responsibility of this Basheer Khan in a nursing home or would it not be wiser than not to have the media and the minority community at your door step should anything untoward happen to this man.' A Judge helping the minority community in distress he thought, is after all not bad publicity, in fact he was showing the way for other Hindus to protect their Muslim brothers. It could also backlash on him. Yet it was all-important that his daughter continues to see him as a good human being.

The Judge listened, thought and gently weighed down on the police boss, ' the family of this victim are known to me for years and I want you to accord the patient and his family, appropriate security.'

It had its effect on the Policeman, 'Yes Sir.' And then Smita had personally supervised the shifting of Basheer Khan to their family doctor's nursing home. She had insisted that Ruhaina and the ladies of the family move into their outhouse within the compounds of the official quarters of "Judge Choudhury".

Ruhaina had resisted and said that, 'we have lived here with Allah's mercy and if He so desires, we shall become one with Him.'

Smita had called her 'Ammi' (mother) like she had heard Basheer during their college years, ' I will not be at peace if you refuse me and would you have refused your own daughter?' Through her grief Ruhaina had blocked tears and weakly smiled at the recollection of Basheer's college days. She had finally agreed. Smita had a way with convincing. More compassion than a lawyer's staunch arguments worked well in these situations. Ruhaina had quickly gathered some essentials and with her came sister-in law, Dilawar. The other neighboring families looked on and when Ruhaina had asked them to send their women folk with her, had refused. Time had stood still for those few moments. The shattered glass of the shop and the debris of the attack remained where they had fallen. It was traumatic for Ruhaina to leave the place where she had grown up, married, had extremely happy memories of and now held the fort for her husband Azad to return. Leaving it was like an amputation or desertion. This was her only bridge with the past, across which Azad would hopefully return someday. Smita understood and could feel the turmoil.

'Ammi, I will bring you back once things settle down, you are not leaving this place forever.' And so Ruhaina stumbled out not forgetting to take with her the photo frame of Basheer's father Azad Khan. Smita with a couple of her trusted servants and two armed police guards to accompany them packed a few things and helped them shift. She transferred Basheer to a private nursing home close to their house and it had not exactly been very pleasant to deal with the municipal hospital authorities.

The commoner in India was still so vulnerable. Her experience at the hospital was not very different from what she had read about in the history of India under the British. The system was so full of bureaucracy, preferential treatment bordering on feudalism and total apathy. Secretly she recoiled at herself for using her father's offices to move the machinery that should have in the first place not allowed such a disaster as Godhra. Her guilt was mitigated since there was little time to waste and things were getting out of hand in the city. She would move heaven and earth to bring help to a family that she knew, for were they not on the verge of being annihilated? Smita was acutely aware of her feelings for Basheer but those were adolescent tides. She had later grown to appreciate him as an adult who had shouldered the responsibility of a missing father from an early age. And he was truly a gentleman compared to all the colleagues she had in the high court. Smita surprised herself that she could recapitulate her adolescent feelings for Basheer so clearly. In spite of the prevailing tense situation it did not fail to bring a faint glow to her eyes. Her thoughts, she realized could travel quite easily into the past and it felt good because those youthful days had been so full of feelings. Some of those feelings and values would be directing her energies to help in healing the pain Ruhaina and Basheer would carry for the rest of their lives. She however, decided to stay just a little detached in their grief. Caring yet unwilling for involvement and healing beyond the tide line so that everyone stayed comfortably anchored. She liked to be in control of her emotions especially those that included Basheer.

*How do some feelings survive and others slowly die or change without any definite reference to time? Is the mind an abstract independent control center with a reservoir of feelings? Feelings that surface triggered by an environment that stirs the reservoir. So there is a possibility that true independence and secularism are also feelings that reside in all minds. Who will be the Mahatma to make this intangible into a tangible environment and conscious reality so there can be genuine intent for coexistence? Collective thinking minds can attempt to do so. After all neo-religion, the brand building exercise for adulterated secularism and destruction 'a la Godhra'* were also collective deviant mental mechanization that had its own visible and tangible messiahs who also must surely have had their individual devil's workshop reservoirs. What lies at the bottom of such black reservoirs? Is the human 'mind' really the control center that can command the brain, its physical agent to perform such uncontrolled acts as those at Godhra? When the masses rub shoulders for revenge, is there some chemistry that obliterates the mind from its natural reluctance of inflicting pain and grief, or does it become hyper sensitive to drive the super ego into a maniacal state. Or were there still minds like the Mahatma's or lesser mortals of the likes of Smita Choudhury that could maintain a balance and be worthy of being called human beings. Hopefully there are and although secularism has retreated into the distant horizon, these few minds can always weigh heavily to maintain just adequate balance to prevent the volcano of communal frenzy from frequent eruptions or in the least, work at damage control by freezing the hot lava.

Can reality ever-that Godhra, the Mumbai bomb blasts with communal carnage; Kashmir, the rape of Bangladesh, the twin towers in New York or the smell of death in Palestine or the stench of Vietnam, be buried to fade even like a reluctant sunset through clouds? Only to rise again? So many minds would have to relate and erase, accept and come to terms with large portions of their consciousness. Perhaps collective consciousness will have to undergo a major re-engineering on a spiritual plane. Or it may well nigh be impossible to escape from the imprisonment of these horrors created by devilish minds. Jewish survivors still hunt Nazi killers like bloodhounds. India and Pakistan will need a therapy in their consciousness for generations and then there may come about a change or something like secularism or some new state of co-existence could take birth in our mingling. After all it was a major decision for so many Muslims to reject the promises of a Muslim state in Pakistan and continue to live in India as a minority community with some dignity at least for some periods of their lifetime.

Unknowingly, Smita was working towards a change and so were Basheer and his imprisoned father Azad and so many nameless faces worldwide but mostly without knowing or having links to harness their collective capability to strengthen the always-existing camouflaged bridge across communal divides.

Across the courtyard of Judge Sudhin Choudhury's villa was the outhouse in which Smita had given shelter to Ruhaina and her sister-in law Dilawar. Dilawar suffered from chronic chest congestion and had a cough that could be jarring even from a distance. After dinner with her parents and husband, Smita came down the old wooden staircase with a torch in her hand. As she walked down the narrow path her mind was in a state of flux. At dinner her father had only asked if the family in the outhouse was comfortable and had something to eat. Smita had not replied because it sounded like a statement made in the courtroom. She had in return enquired, 'has the Police Commissioner assured you that the nursing home will be guarded all the time.' It was the judge's turn to respond and his eyes looked up from the plate and nodded in the affirmative. Their eyes had met and he had understood instantly that Smita had doubts written over her face so his eyes remained locked without any visible expression. He had spent too many years with many tough cases to remain cool under penetrating eyes.

After what seemed like a deep breath he tried to put her at ease, ' I have told him. I think he will listen to my request and I ought not pressurize him since the police force is already stretched and he is well aware of his commitment to me. Were the constables not there when you brought them out of their place in…..,? ' The cantonment,' Smita had to fill in, in almost a languishing whisper.

Rani Choudhury, Smita's mother had come to the rescue of this duel, 'have you seen to them that they have eaten and have all the necessities. The outhouse has not been in a very good condition for long.' Smita had got it vacated of the family furniture and other luggage that was to be disposed in any case. She was glad that someone was at last living, where her maid and companion of childhood had lived for sometime and due to age had gone back to the village. Smita had an attachment with people and places and she felt disappointed that her father had become so disconnected and insensitive with the ways of his profession. Would she also evolve in the same manner? No, she would consciously keep her self in touch with herself and it was easier by being in touch with those who cared and had shared something with you.

Smita approached the outhouse and observed that it was not lit very brightly. Maybe Ruhaina does not want too much light. The thought made her wince that people had to hide in the darkness because of not wanting to be seen by others. There was something very pathetic about such a fugitive psyche. She wanted to do everything to make them comfortable and tomorrow she had decided to even go into the areas that had been ravaged by the riots. She would join hands with the agencies and non-governmental organizations in the relief work. Or better still; fight cases for those Muslims that suffered at the hands of the masses or even the police. She wondered what her father would have to say to that. She had to shed the halo of her father's position in the high court. He was always very politically correct.

As she came into the ragged grassy patch in front of the out house Smita could see the silhouette of Ruhaina, sitting alone on the concrete platform joining the pillars of the outhouse verandah. She stopped just for a moment suddenly feeling like an intruder to the silence, without even knowing what to say. There was only one light kept on inside the outhouse. It threw a diffused glow into the porch. The glow moved ever so gently with the light breeze caught by the hanging bulb that the whole verandah seemed to be in a rocking motion. Even Ruhaina and the few plants that were there appeared in rhythm with this movement. It was as though the storm had passed and now the sea was undulating in its calm. The gloom was there yet there was strength in the immediate vicinity that Ruhaina occupied like a statue standing guard. Smita felt this and gravitated to the source. Her footsteps light as they were, was enough to just startle Ruhaina back to her present for she had escaped far back into the happy past.

Smita heard the light gasp and apologized, ' Ammi it is me, I am sorry if I have disturbed you, are you not cold.' With that Smita took off the light shawl from her shoulder and laid it across Ammi's back.

'There is enough warmth here in your shelter my dear and with you nearby there can never be any cold.' Only a woman could truly sense the genuine inner warmth of another. It reminded Smita of her days in college when there had been a few occasions to meet Basheer's mother at their tailoring shop. Ruhaina had then seemed to her like a Mughal princess in her simple yet flowing traditional attire and she would say very little but it was always with so much compassion. Smita blushed in the darkness now at Ammi's affection as she used to in the past when Ammi would compliment her poise and the fit of her clothes. Smita had presence and an innate grace that came from serene surroundings and controlled upbringing. Of course Ammi had tailored her clothes those days, as Basheer was still learning to cut and sew.

Ammi took both Smita's hands and gently kissed her fingers saying, 'what you have done for Basheer and us will be rewarded by Allah.' Smita could only cling to Ruhaina's fingers and accept the blessing. With that she sat beside Ammi with one arm around her waist as they both came to terms with each other's situation. And then Ammi broke the silence ' I wonder if bringing us here is the best thing, after all there are others who are still at the mohalla.'

Smita interpreted this differently as a question that was it all right for Judge Choudhury to give refuge to a Muslim family.

'Ammi, I have brought you here so that you are safe and my parents have no objection.'

'Maybe you should listen to your father. We can go back tomorrow.'

'Not at all, you can stay here for as long as you wish, at least till Basheer is fully all right.'

'Smita, you are like my daughter but will you understand if I tell you that people from my community at the mohalla who are still there will consider my coming away as an act of desertion. Our lives have been spent together and we have always shared and helped each other in times of joy and grief. Basheer's father would have wanted us to stay together.'

'I appreciate your feelings Ammi and am genuinely concerned that Basheer should get good medical attention and the nursing home is close by, so it will be easier for you to be with him.' These were sensible words but was sensible always the best or right path to follow.

Ammi turned towards Smita and searched her face. 'I will have to go in a few days and will always remember your kindness and affection. I hope my Basheer will survive for his wounds are deep, he has bled a lot and his heart is broken for many reasons.'

'I understand Ammi and tomorrow we will get a specialist to attend to him; he will be alright, have faith and I will also spend sometime with him if that can heal his heart.'

Ammi held her face in her hands and her lips quivered with emotional currents, 'I am fatigued with so many years of uncertainty after Basheer's father went missing but you bring some hope in my heart that these communal fires will die down someday. Basheer adores your courage and kindness in this man's world. It is people like you in the younger generation that can make it happen. I cannot believe that such a fate would befall us in spite of the sacrifice of my husband for this country. He disappointed my father-in law by not taking up the business as he felt his true destiny was to serve shoulder to shoulder with people from different religions or cultures like he saw with the army men. He used to talk about 'qurbani' for the country and see maybe his dreams were realized. Poor Basheer, he has not known the affection of his father and he still believes that he will find him. He also dreamed of joining the army and I did not stop him but Allah wanted a different fate for him, I guess. He was very depressed after being rejected by the army and I suffered it with him. It is a mother's fate to laugh and cry with her children's success or failures. What you and others are doing for us now Smita, will hopefully teach future generations never to allow such disasters to repeat. You are a great one, I always knew from your college days. I am sure you will be a very loving mother.' She smiled in adoration and Smita could sense much more than was being said. The sensitivity of the moment was overwhelming and she hugged Ammi and wept freely.

'Ammi, we are unable to have children as it could be fatal for me.' They were both treading on fresh grounds of sharing. Only women have the courage to emote with the intensity of a tornado that can destroy yet reaches up to kiss the sky and subsides back to the depths of the ocean floor.

'I am not unhappy for you Smita because maybe Allah has greater plans for you. As a great judge you will have the opportunity to uphold the rights of so many and that could make so many needy children happy. You could be a mother to thousands Smita, unlike me, I have only one, Basheer. And he was not easy to raise.' She laughed, 'You will be a great mother to many without having to put up with all their quirks.' They broke from the embrace reluctantly and were both smiling through a few tears now.

'You have such high aspirations for me Ammi; I hope I can live up to that image because I am not like my father. He is strong and I am weak at heart.'

'Smita, that is because we as women are designed to build and have inbuilt resilience. Our strength is different from that of men. They are more conquerors than builders. It makes them look stronger yet they also have a soft core and struggle with themselves to build. Sometimes they succeed.'

'You speak truly like the Mughal queen I used to imagine you as when I was in college. Such simple yet powerful logic.'

Ammi broke into laughter at the irony of her statement and Smita could not but join into the bubbling dance of two women laughing at themselves. Even the single light from the room within the outhouse picked up the tempo as a fresh breeze arose as if in appreciation of the simple yet dynamic bonding-taking place. The shadows swaying in the light strengthened the rhythm of this dance. The mutual admiration was spontaneous and cut across all boundaries of the frail social fabric that often does not take kindly to mingling between people of different social status, color, culture and religions especially between Hindus and Muslims. More so during communal upheavals.

*Was this mingling and coexistence synonymous with secularism? Maybe the women of the future can make secularism a reality. Secularism after so many ravaging incidents and the splitting of two nations will need a lot of nurturing, building and only women possess the determined resilience to withstand and re-construct through such traumas. Maybe it is really the women of both nations that have suffered the most and yet have kept their sanity and the men have probably understood, only sometimes through the woman's grief; a fraction more about co-existence. Unfortunately a lot of these women have or will pass silently into history before the dawning of tangible secular thinking and then, after all, had anyone forecast the re-unification of Germany nor have those women that may have silently bled for and created the stage for it, been ever mentioned in History books.*

'It is getting late, I think you had better be with your family Smita. Convey my gratitude to your parents.'

'You are also my family Ammi and it will always remain so. And you are cold so keep my shawl. Tomorrow I will take you to the nursing home. I have already spoken to a specialist orthopedic surgeon for him to treat Basheer for the finger injuries. Soon he will be able to work with his hands as before.'

'Inshallah,' was all Ruhaina could sigh.

# Chapter IV

**M**artha James was at the piano while Brother led a couple of young boys and girls of a small group of children and teenagers learning music and songs. It was an old Hindi hit film song they were practicing. Even as he strummed the guitar and led the chorus, Brother's mind drifted to the PoW camp because this was one of the favorite songs in the prison camp. Even the prison guards would join in as they sang. In spite of the animosities between the two countries, they loved Indian film songs. What neo-religion funda could explain or prevent this. His voice choked, emotions falling over each other, preventing the words to flow smoothly with the tune but he continued strumming and hummed loud enough, sometimes injecting words that would urge the group to continue singing. The cottage was small so Brother and his singers were in the verandah and Martha played on from the living room. It became coffee break time for nearby Chapel Road residents whenever Brother conducted his music classes. He had started this class because music was really the best thing he could do next to flying and sadly his fighter plane had been shot down thirty years ago. This was now giving him the joy of doing what he loved to do. Sing and he was getting paid for it too! What could be better? And Chapel Road loved music and songs. It was the culture here. If you played the guitar and sang, you had to be a good soul. And if you were teaching children to do the same you were in high esteem since you were keeping them off booze and drugs. Even in February 2002 this was a time and tested Chapel Road analogy. Somehow this locality had the stoic conditioning to resist being touched by neo-religious orators or the vagaries of secularist political rock shows. It was like the innards of a fortress. Everybody in this fortress no matter what color or caste seemed to happily co-exist. Even Hindus with Muslims.

The children were from different communities but they would sing hymns, carols, nursery rhymes and even film songs. And for Brother, unconsciously, it was working as a silent therapy to cope with the changes in society and value systems that had left him behind. Just the interaction with young minds was better than any psychotherapy that a lot of released PoWs had resorted to after their return from Pakistani prison camps. His music had a way with the children and they all looked like a group of friends rather than master and pupils. It had been Sheila's suggestion. His age and lack of any professional training for a world rapidly moving towards professional specialization would not get him a job to make a living. He was good in playing musical instruments and singing so he could try starting a music class at home. Brother had mooted the idea impulsively purely because it had the flavor of praise for his skill as a musician. It was his natural response to reject the sounds of self-esteem. He had forgotten to receive or even understand what praise meant to others. In his captivity the mind had become more programmed to receive insult and taunting as a routine. Yet he had taken out his old guitar during Christmas and bought a new set of strings and tuned it. It was one of those evenings that a group of street children were out singing carols for donations that spurred him to call them into his cramped porch. He had asked one of the girls who looked like she was leading the group to sing for him. They needed no further encouragement. So Brother had taken out his guitar and played with their songs and it developed into an impromptu audition and celebration. In about fifteen minutes there was a small group of old ladies returning from church that just stood outside and listened. And then the windows of the neighboring cottages had swung open with curious faces framed against the bars and his one time football partner now addicted to alcohol had started an impromptu jig. The hero had come home finally and he was entertaining the neighborhood like the Brother, a fighter pilot, used to at air force parties. Brother was synonymous with his guitar amongst squadron mates and even those who knew or even had just heard about his exploits in the air force. He had left his heroics far behind.

Brother realized that there was not going to be a red carpet welcome home for him. The interrogation at Air Headquarters had set the mood. It had not been the most pleasant experience for him, more so as he had expected to be given at least a welcome back and hopes for his mission to free the others left behind. He had not shot down enemy planes to be in the headlines, so how could they give him a hero's reception. Of course it was also partly because not too many politicians had wound their way through Chapel Road nor had the shark like marketing executives been permitted to lead road shows down the street for anyone to realize that they could have put up banners, 'Welcome home Brother'. The street was too narrow. Marketing was not required here. Chapel Road bought whatever they wanted. So, Brother was saved the rush of being carried on willing shoulders like a product being displayed for advertisement and sale. There was a whole new generation in the pigeonhole cottages that had only read in history books that India had gone to war with Pakistan in 1971. Some high school children not so good at remembering dates would even get this answer wrong when they had to fill in the blanks in their tests at school. Most would just leave it blank. It is so easy to forget. Maybe this was best forgotten. It was so long ago that Chapel Road had no particular reason to remember one of its sons who had fought that war. The few who knew had sympathized with Tom and Martha at their loss. In fact the intrusion by a dilapidated Air force jeep that brought Brother home on the last leg of his journey from the railway station to his home was viewed as a museum relic and the street children had crowded around more to touch the jeep than even look at Richard James.

The same street children of Chapel Road had finally cheer led his first liberated Christmas and ironically that to at his behest that he would give them some donation if they sang while he played the guitar for them. They had been his first pupils and it had grown from there to almost a full class of twenty children. He was on his way up almost like he used to zoom up into the air in that littlest fighter, the Gnat. This time only in spirits.

Brother continued to hum and play the guitar. Sheila had parked her car at the gate enjoying the song before she entered the cottage porch. She was amazed at the chemistry here and wanted to absorb some of the youthful energy. Rani and Ravi had also come along as the three of them often frequented the popular shopping arcades at Hill Road in Bandra. Shopping was supposed to be cheaper here.

These were times of recession. Sheila did not have endless resources yet she wanted good things for her Rani. Brother saw them, smiled and waved her in without a break in the song. Their presence at his gate took away his attention diversion to the PoW camp and mates singing this same song. Getting his voice back Brother lent his full baritone to complete the chorus. Sheila had heard about these classes from Brother. He would tell her everything nowadays. They were coming closer as companions and there was no rushing pace here. Both had experienced harrowing uncertainties and waiting had been thrust on them by fate. While mastering the art of waiting they also suffered the yearnings that can easily encroach on middle-aged single hearts. Men and women are both subjected to its tugs. Sheila was at an advantage because she knew how to balance her thoughts. Brother was like a gurgling brook in the valley of emotions. His response was that of a bird suddenly released from the cage where it was forced to flit around the bars of imprisonment. Yet he was discreetly hungry for more. Sheila had survived in this big city and brought up her daughter. It was not that she had never felt the need to be loved. She had all the opportunities but the fear of another heartbreak had conditioned her mind and with it dampened the fluttering heart from any romantic liaisons. She did not have any such feelings for Brother but from his behavior, she had begun to suspect that he was floating down the river of mature attachment trying to carry her along surprisingly without the usually associated persisting towing affect. Just letting her feel the ripples as they washed her feet while he was wading into waist deep. It had a refreshing affect on her. And although Brother was often her breath of fresh air, she was adept at inhaling with control. Between them there was really no commitment. Sheila was grateful for the release from the uncertainty surrounding her missing husband and the definite presence of Brother. Content that she was just a comfortable link between each other's past and now.

 He had been uncertain about finding Kailash's wife. During his interlude with the authorities, he had gathered her address from Air HQ. Brother had yet to find the families of the other prison mates. It continued to be an element of nagging uncertainty in his life. He had been uncertain of his fate when they carried him away from the camp on a stretcher but he had promised Azad and the others that if there was any chance of his release; he would find their families and move the bolts to open their barred doors. It was a huge commitment willingly given by him without even knowing about his tomorrow.

The income from his music classes had gradually unhooked him from one more small yet fearful rehabilitation uncertainty that worries the unemployed middle-aged. He was gradually moving away from captivities; exploring newer possibilities; becoming more certain everyday.

Sheila had been living in uncertainty because Kailash had only been declared 'missing feared dead'. It had been a relief for Brother when he traced her and for her it had been the final confirmation that her husband had died in the war. The expectation that your loved one was still alive had its own binds that could waver with time but stands on feet that slowly grow numb. Brother had untied those bonds for her with his arrival and she was grateful that someone had finally told her the truth.

Uncertainty between them could only creep in if expectations took root. Sheila was careful not to create any expectation between them but she had recognized a slippage gently taking place. There was no real solution to deal with it than to draw the curtains and she was not willing to do that on Brother. The man had after all freed her thoughts from an anchor dragging on the ocean floor. And she had also felt his need for a foothold on the wall of self-resurrection. In the beginning she had looked at Brother as a relic that had lain beneath the rubbles of a destroyed kingdom and had suddenly been found. Twenty-nine years of imprisonment in an enemy prison camp followed by a return to civilization was not the same as was for criminals locked up at Arthur Road jail. It was more like coming back from a lost planet. She was trying to help him recall and develop methods of coping with the ways of life in the city of his birth as well as assisting him to remember the location of his captivity. He had told her that he had to free the others and also reach out to their dear ones to bring them the joy that their men had not died. They were alive and he was going to get them freed. This mission required a steady boat and Sheila was determined to stay with him at the helm. Any other thoughts of a possible relationship with Brother had to be kept on hold till mission accomplishment. She was not yet sure about her own feelings.

The song over, Brother left his pupils and came out into the porch to welcome Sheila.

'Nice surprise, I wasn't expecting you here at all today or I would have freed myself earlier.' This was Brother. He was simple and could do anything for those he cared for.

'We hadn't planned to come to your place but were here for some shopping for Rani so we thought of having some tea with Aunty and you, here, these are for you, pastries we picked up at the bakery. I am sure your mother will also love them. How much more time will your class take?'

'Oh! It is almost over. These children are going to participate in the talent contest being held at St Andrew's school next month.'

'Then I think you should finish your session while we take a walk to Bandra bazaar. Rani has never seen this place before.'

'Why don't you stay. This will take maybe another ten minutes and then we could all have tea and walk down to the market together?' 'Mom, he called loudly, Sheila, her daughter and friend are here with some lovely pastries for you. Can we sing some songs to earn these?'

'Sure son, ask them to sit down. I am afraid there are not many chairs there.'

The three of them sat on a bench against the railing of the verandah and Brother took his position at the head of his class. From the living room Martha James struck the keys of "My Favorite things" from the soundtrack of the famous film, "Sound of Music". Brother, with one leg on a stool gave it the rhythm on his guitar slung round his neck and the children picked up the song. Sheila was struck by the spontaneity of the whole group. Like one cohesive team they all looked up at Brother and followed their own cues. The man had a presence. She watched Brother as he smiled at each one of the children who was to sing a specific line of the song and there was such harmony. The music touched her enough to make her hum along. Even Rani and Ravi had unconsciously joined into singing along. Martha could not see this happening. She was happy to play the piano after so many years and specially because Brother had coaxed her into it in spite of her arthritis and bent fingers. He used to massage her fingers everyday to keep them active and ease her pain. She was amazed at herself to have re-started playing the piano. It was more to make him happy that she had begun and after all those lonely years it was nice to have so many people in the house.

She had not known that it was Sheila who had sown the seed in Brother's mind. Did it matter? Maybe this was the greatness of women to nurture that had given Sheila's natural instinct the impulse to suggest music classes to Brother. She had unintentionally nurtured Brother's inherent capability and also given him the resilience to make a place for himself in Chapel Road and life again. And it had led to an invisible bonding between so many, young and old and what Sheila did not know was that the entire street was timing themselves to Brother's music classes to reduce the volume of their sound systems; switching off their televisions or putting down their chores to quickly brew a cup of rich black coffee taking a break or pushing their grandchildren in perambulators down the street or just humming along in their balconies. Rich play ground of feelings and belongingness. Sometimes one could even hear someone call out for a request song and Brother's group would oblige. Everyone had time for each other and time would stand still during practice sessions. The bonding was strong here and no one probably was aware of the big word of secularism here because it was just natural to be like this. They had been like this since Chapel Road came into being. Neither the British rule nor after that had any "ism" force find refuge here. Chapel Road was the epitome of its own secularism.

*Was it the proximity of the dwellings? Or was it the people who inhabited Chapel Road? Could it be that people from different religious communities living together learn to accept each other's ways? There had to be some bonding force that Gandhi, Patel and Jinnah had missed out on or did they know but knew not how to deal with the British in preventing the Partition between two communities that led to "two nations". The flavors of music on Chapel Road had changed with time from Jim Reeves and Nat King Cole to Brian Adams and Britney but the people had managed to stay untouched by religious politics that destroy a mosque to build a temple. It was from this secular home that Brother joined the air force to be swallowed into a war between two nations that had fallen apart as victims of divisive forces. Was it the nurturing of this street that had given him strength and dignity that kept him sane through those years of captivity to come back with an impossible mission? He was once again thriving in the warmth and bonding of Chapel Road secularism where "Lucky" and "Jeff" caterers doled out Biriyani and all the "Aunties" also baked Christmas cakes and Easter eggs for sale. And it was all happening side-by-side. Biriyani and Easter eggs were the products of two different races but like trees - bloomed side by side.*

The song ended and everyone clapped. There were claps from the street too and Brother took a bow. Sheila was truly happy for him. The children broke into their own chatter as Brother tried to tell them what to practice at home and when they could all come for another session. No one in particular was being addressed, yet Brother was confident they would all be there on time. Confidence born out of trust on them and in himself. The children flew out of the porch into Chapel Road and disappeared into the narrow lanes. The small audience outside the wicker gate also reluctantly departed. Brother and even Sheila and Rani helped rearranged the porch with the few chairs and benches. In a few moments the music classroom was neatly set up for the unplanned tea party.

Martha had wheeled herself to her kitchen to make some tea. Sheila's presence had taken away Brother's attention just sufficiently to give Martha the opportunity to get into the kitchen. This was her haven and Tom and she had shared many sweet moments here and also wept together on the old mahogany dining table when they received the telegram about Richard going missing during the war of 1971. She knew her way in this kitchen blindfolded but off late Richard had started encroaching into her domain and keeping things in new places. Today she just couldn't find the copper kettle. 'Richaaaaaaard, where have you put that kettle my dear.' Brother heard her call and excused himself and almost tripped as he hurried into the house. Sheila, Rani and Ravi followed him into the living room. Sheila was tempted to offer in making the coffee but held back for reasons of her own. Every woman likes the preserve of her own kitchen. Lots of chemistry originates from here and Sheila recalled some very intimate moments with Kailash in their kitchen just after their return from a honeymoon at Goa. She was not about to barge into the whispering between mother and son trying to make coffee together. Secretly smiling that Brother was taking care of Martha she was even happier than watching him with the children singing. He was at last coming back to his own world. There was hope then that he would be able to move on in his mission.

Sheila was carrying the day's newspaper and the news was not good. The paper had been brought on purpose for Brother to read a small clipping among the other shocking full-page accounts about the communal riots at Godhra in Ahmadabad. She remembered hearing him talk about a fellow Muslim PoW who was still held in the same camp at the time when he was taken away sick on the stretcher. He had mentioned the name as some Khan who happened to be a tailor's son. And he had promised that he would find his family at Ahmadabad and tell them that he was alive. Brother had also told the interrogators at Air Headquarters about all the names of PoWs who continued to be held by Pakistan. It was futile because he could not give full information on the location of the camp. She was quite certain that the clipping she had read in the paper was referring to the Khan's family. The name was not mentioned yet the descriptions and the tragedy triggered feelings that drew visions of a tailor family that was mentioned often by Brother. Brother had referred to the tailoring shop as Khan Clothiers & Embroideries. There was no mention of this in the clipping yet the account of the mishap seemed to fit. Reading it in the morning had set her heart racing. She had wanted to call him on the phone and then decided not to as it could create unnecessary turmoil in Brother's mind and she never wanted that for him. It would be better by far to call him at the end of the day or maybe drop in at his cottage after they had finished shopping at Hill Road.

Martha sat next to Sheila as they had coffee and the pastries were passed around. Brother was trying to show Rani the basics of playing a guitar and Ravi laughed as she tried to strum. It was a happy get together where middle class manners did not put too many demands of etiquette. It was very acceptable to talk and eat at the same time. The British had left behind table manners that scorned on such behavior but Chapel Road had not much room on that narrow street for such values. Brother had been through the etiquette routine in the Air force and he could put on that act almost automatically. He would, whenever he visited Sheila's house; get up if seated whenever Sheila got up and finish chewing whatever he was given to eat, put his cutlery on the plate neatly ensuring his elbows were always off the table and then with his hands under the table, straighten up and make conversation. Sheila had noticed this and it had become a joke between mother and daughter till one day she had told Brother, 'If you are going to stop eating while talking we are going to have to eat so silently that it will feel like the last supper.' They had all laughed and Brother had implemented the required concessions.

Sheila motioned for Brother to come near her and she gave him the newspaper saying, 'I want you to read the clipping that has been highlighted on page three.'

'Sure, what is it about?' Taking the paper, Brother moved into the well-lit porch and found an article with "Read carefully" scribbled by Sheila with a color marker.

Ahmadabad riots: Indian Army Major injured: saves Muslim Family. He read further, Major Dilip of the 9 Para Regiment in Ahmadabad was badly injured, trying to save a muslim tailor from being lynched by a mob of Hindu reactionaries in the aftermath of the Godhra train burning incident. The tailor suffered stab wounds and burns and was taken to the Municipal hospital by the Major's troops. Witnesses said that tragically the tailor was the son of an Army soldier who died during the 1971 conflict with Pakistan. Also it was reliably learnt that the tailor himself had been rejected from recruitment in the Army a few years back. The mob paid little heed to the fact that the shop was located in the heavily guarded Cantonment area of the city. The tailoring shop was patronized by the Army personnel and was almost completely destroyed. The tailor would have certainly been killed, had the Major not intervened in time. The family does not want to make any official complaint to the police.

Brother read the article a few times as though he was searching for something. A name, an address? Had he missed it? Was it somewhere between the lines? His eyes settled on the Army cantonment as his first thought stop. Folding the paper, he went inside and Sheila's eyes locked with his. They knew each other's thoughts. He needed a starting point. Sheila had so far succeeded in holding him back from undertaking the strains of a journey in a blind search for the relatives of his fellow PoWs. Brother had frequently wanted to start out without any address with just the vague descriptions by his mates. His health had not been up to the levels required. It was now, after two years that he was looking and feeling better without any recurring bouts of fever and cough. It was time to move now. He would have to break the news of his plan to Martha. She would not be happy at letting Richard go away for long durations. He had been away for twenty-nine years. Brother felt, he would have to go soon and his mind raced from the evening's warm gathering in his mother's cottage to the dark and damp prison cells and then onto unknown addresses of families who had waited and probably given up. He had to let them know that their loved one was alive and then mobilize enough forces to get them their freedom. He was sure that he had hit on one clue about Azad Khan's family. His belief that he would find the others became more tangible. The belief now had a beginning.

Sheila sensed the anxiety of Brother wanting to discuss his future course of action. She had learnt to wait and felt that a discussion should also wait for sometime. She understood him sufficiently to know that in time he would make a plan and then discuss it with her. He needed time to accept the enormity and weight of the challenging mission he had so far only talked about and for this he was best left alone. She had learnt that his strength lay in the depths of his solitude. The coffee party at Martha's seemed over. Sheila got up to leave and so did Rani and Ravi. Martha had hoped, they would stay a little longer and she held Sheila's hand gently for just a moment before allowing it to be withdrawn. They smiled at each other. Both had waited a long time with uncertainties, which throw up questions giving the mind endless roads to travel. There was thus a similarity here in their smiles. They seemed grateful for what was there today.

Brother saw them off closing the door after Sheila settled into her car, with an understanding that she would call after reaching home. Verbal assurance between them had gradually changed from words to a nod and today just a smile seemed appropriate communication. They understood each other a lot better after two years. The car drove away and Bother watched it go round the corner before returning to his thoughts and Martha. The picture of Rani driving her mother home stayed for a while with him. He felt happy that Sheila did not have to travel in busses anymore. Rani and she had saved enough to buy a car. He preferred to travel by bus and train as it kept him in touch with people. He had been disconnected for a long time.

# Chapter V

On the way home Sheila's mind traveled randomly from the time Brother had first found her apartment to the subsequent visits that gradually gave vent to emotions surrounding his PoW days. To the war of 1971 that sent them both into exile. To television clips of the Kargil war of 1999, shown vividly by the media and of course in comparison the distorted Pakistani version that was fed to Brother and other PoWs. The devastating accounts of the behavior of Pakistani prison camp officials related by Brother. To the simple understanding of secularism in Bother's words and how he detested the current overdose of religion in politics.

The frequent communal disturbances that had occurred after 1971 and the current flare up at Ahmadabad seemed to touch her more closely now. She worried about the constant guilt that Brother suffered from. His guilt at the impossibility of the commitment to free his fellow mates that often ended in, 'It is unjust that I was released instead of those with families and children.' She saw his guilt but could not fully comprehend. Her thoughts today seemed to churn the very soul in an attempt to decide whether it had been wise to draw Brother's attention to the news clipping. Did he not want to work towards locating the families of his prison mates? There should have been no dichotomy in her mind. The random thoughts spun even faster, leaving her without any definite conclusions about questions that arose. She was not even able to stop long enough with each thought to understand her real concerns and doubts. There was a current that was drawing her into undefined territory.

Reaching home she had called Brother and excused herself from any further discussion. Brother had tried to persist and she had to tell him that she was just too tired after the whole day. It felt harsh at not allowing a discussion. *'Let him think about it and let me also understand the direction of my thoughts,'* she had reluctantly, yet without conveying, put the receiver down.

After dinner it was routine for Sheila to walk in her balcony. It had been so ever since she had moved into this apartment. The balcony was not long enough to qualify for a walkway. The walking portrayed her like a caged animal. Yet, the patrolling relaxed her and the pace reflected her thoughts. Accelerating when there were unresolved questions and slowing as the solutions took shape. This apartment was all she felt attached to. She had been the only child of parents who had lands and property between Bareilly and Delhi. She had sold some of it after they had expired to afford a comfortable two-bedroom hall apartment in Bombay. Rani now had her own room but spent a lot of time in Sheila's bedroom watching television. They could never forget the years that were spent in a much smaller apartment with her parents; soon after Kailash was declared missing. She was only a commerce graduate, just twenty-three, carrying a baby when her world had caved in. Kailash came from a very large family living in Hyderabad. His parents had wanted Sheila to settle close by. However, she had managed to convince them with the help of her parents that it would be easier for her to be close to her own mother during child birth. The sheer size of Kailash's family and its business atmosphere choked her. She came from a family of teachers. Both her parents had been professors in the University of Bombay. She had kept up with Kailash's parents for a long time with her routine yearly visits during Rani's summer breaks. Those had not been her best memories but it had helped strengthen her conviction that she was happier living in a different city on her own. There had hardly been any savings when tragedy had struck and it was a natural consequence that she moved in with her parents in their one-bedroom apartment at Chembur, a middle class suburb of Bombay. After both had passed away, Sheila had sold the apartment and some land, to gather enough resources and afford this larger apartment in Borivili. It faced the sea and her balcony overlooked the road along the sea front. The view had grown on her for fifteen years and she had furnished the apartment the way Kailash would have liked. Simple and very functional with a lot of books that belonged to her parents and some of them included her own collection. Books had become her closest companions. She was now fifty-four with a thirty-year-old daughter who was climbing up the ladders in a multi-national bank. Sheila was determined to continue her professional life for as long as she could. She was the Chief accountant with a successful Information Technology company.

What was the bottom line of her thoughts? Pacing along her potted plants in the balcony she gently brushed the leaves to steady her thoughts. Was it the news clipping given to Brother that nagged at her? She had felt that it would give him a possible starting point for his mission. In the last two years, he had tried in vain to adequately convince the local military authorities or his few old colleagues. They did not disbelieve him and even that had been encouraging for him. There had been a woman's organization that was willing to take up his cause for the sake of the unknown PoWs' families left in the lurch but efforts at getting the government machinery moving always reached a dead-end. Brother's pleas drew sympathy followed by questions; he just could not remember the location of the camp. Now there seemed to be this strange clue, of a Muslim tailor rescued in riot strewn Ahmadabad. So, why am I perturbed, thought Sheila? Was it some latent insecurity gnawing at her? She had lost her husband and now she was leading Brother into a search that had undefined frontiers. Was there a possibility of loss here? Had she become so attached to him? He was just a very good friend. She had waited for information about Kailash. He had brought her that release. There were others who were probably still waiting like she had. Kailash was gone but other loved ones could still be alive in captivity. It had been sorrowful relief to finally be told that she could be a widow now. Imagine the emotions of those that Brother could possibly trace and the sudden bright lights in their minds, ' *Your husband, father or brother is still alive.*' She imagined so and it took her to newer heights of joy laced with the unforgettable pain associated with the disappointment of her own loss.

Then what was it that worried her? Sheila had grown accustomed in a conscious way to the mind search that she was involved in. She could search and simultaneously detach from her within to watch herself in this hunt. Leading an independent life and having to make all the decisions had trained her mind to delve to the bottom of many dark alleys. And she had watched herself negotiating the bends to straighten and move on. Watching herself and also searching for solutions or discerning between needs and wants did not make her infallible but it did provide the signals to cross or hold at the junctions. There had been the odd occasion when she had skidded.

Her walk was more of a prowl now. The pace was steady. She had gone into a rewind, using past experience as a datum to match her present feelings. It was 1981 and Rani was then, ten years old. She was growing up watching her mother routinely dressing up for work. Coming back exhausted. And helping with the household chores. There was very little in their regimen in terms of a social life with friends or relatives. Any company was a welcome change in both their lives. The emptiness of those years stayed fresh even as Sheila measured her pace in the dimly lit balcony. There had been a cousin brother of Kailash and he was a commercial pilot. Indrajeet had been very helpful over the years. He had come into her life at the time of her father's hospitalization and death. Stationed at Delhi he flew to Bombay frequently. The visits to Bombay had increased after he had got to know her. They shared a passion for reading books about self-improvement. He would call her every time that he flew into the city and made it a routine to visit their house at Chembur. They could sit for hours discussing a book or he would tell her the experiences of flying an airliner. Flying connected her with Kailash and she would compare previously heard experiences with those of Indrajeet. These became the comfortable emotional playgrounds. They had known each other for about two years when he surprised her by inviting her out to a theatre. It was the comedy, *'Adrak ke Panje'*. They had laughed at the peculiarities of the Hindi dialogues spoken with a twisted rustic accent. Laughter had provided a release for deeper emotional expressions. It had allowed much more than eye-to-eye contact.

She had flinched, the first time that he leaned into her during the show laughing almost uncontrollably and laid his hand on hers in a moment of innocent intimacy. They had dined out and he had dropped her home before returning to the hotel that he stayed in. It was then that she realized that she was getting drawn to him. He had held her around the shoulders as they walked up the stairs of her parental home. And then he had pulled her close to him just outside the door. Sheila had not resisted. She recalled even smiling up at him. She had enjoyed his company and the evening immensely. It was the first intimate closeness with another man for her after Kailash. Ten years had gone by and she had not yearned for a man's company or touch but Indrajeet holding her had felt good all the same. Their comfort levels made it so. She had been married for just two years before tragedy had struck. The bonding within a marriage that grows with time and sharing had been denied to her. She could only imagine as a witness of her parents' life. There was never any craving. She had accepted her situation and more so, there had been no information or ceremony that could change her mindset to that of a widow. In the two years that she had known Indrajeet, they had come close. There had been just comfort in the beginning that someone cared to call whenever he was in town. Then there was the mutual admiration while they shared their impressions through a common book. The relationship had inched forward. Recommending books to each other, buying and gifting them with underlined portions that appealed to their common understandings of life. Through it she had not forgotten Kailash and it never failed to cross her mind but she was getting to know Indrajeet more closely. *'Where is Kailash or what had really happened to him in that war'* never failed to intervene.

The freedom of expression congruent with an environment of learning and teaching was familiar in Sheila's life. It also helped her to easily distinguish her own distinctly different emotions for Kailash and for Indrajeet. The planes were different and could not be compared. It was not as though Indrajeet was replacing Kailash's absence in her physical or mental consciousness. She was sensitive to her own positive emotions that originated from either of them. Both men were also at such spaced out stages in her life. It took her a little time to realize that the inputs were different although leading to a similar result of emotional gratification.

Closeness with Indrajeet was pleasant. He had grown fond of without too much encouragement from her. Marriage had been mentioned in passing.

It had led to a discussion about Kailash and she found it strange that he could say with ease, that, 'If he is alive the air force would have definitely known and told you.'

Sheila absorbed it as an attempt to help release her from the realm of unknown and consider the possibility of a fresh start. He had respected her feelings and never brought up the subject again. She had gradually implemented control mechanisms in the relationship with Indrajeet. At that stage Sheila was not ready to accept that Kailash was no more. And knew that Indrajeet was not really expecting her to do that. He had tried to be helpful. Their bonding had grown naturally without any overtly conscious tending. And she was not willing to lose in a relationship again. She was thus unwilling to invest. That had been her silent decisive logic in controlling the relationship. Controls meant setting up of invisible barriers. And relationships without commitment do not grow when controls are applied. They had remained in touch and then Indrajeet had married in Delhi. She had been happy for him and happier that she had controlled the relationship, so when he did get married, it was not like a loss. There had been some pain and she could only understand it as a tidal emotion resulting from her own deprivation.

Tonight, Sheila was pacing the balcony to understand the reason for her unknown apprehensions. It was a bit like a sense of foreboding. The apprehensions had begun after she had read the news clipping. She had waited all day before giving the news to Brother since the fears had taken newer shapes. And then, after giving them to Brother, the uncertainties had assumed proportions that seemed to envelop her into them. She was trying to pinpoint those apprehensions and in the process doing a very rapid comparison of her feelings and relationships with Brother and other men. Brother's presence in her life seemed different from what Indrajeet was to her. Those days, Kailash occupied her memories and intimacies and it was not that Indrajeet had transgressed. His closeness had always made her secure. Yet it also had the effect of nudging her conscience awake. She was young then and deprivations had not seasoned her terminally to erase all desires for the company of a man. Clearly, she had liked Indrajeet.

Brother had come to her from the unknown. Kailash was still there in his seat within her mind. He remained her silent Buddha giving her the courage or motivation and even the enthusiasm to indulge in the comforts and entertainment that were being made available in the age of consumerism. Brother had been the messenger that she had searched for many years and given up. There had been no one who could tell her with clarity that her husband would return or had gone into history. They had all played for time and been polite and sympathetic. That is not what a woman wants when her husband's whereabouts is suddenly unknown. This man had told her without any apprehension and had been surprised that she had not been told. He had gone into a rage that there had been others in the formation that would have seen Kailash's fighter being hit and surely they would have known that no one could survive a direct hit. Brother had hoped for a parachute; it hadn't been there and he had told her so. He had related the happenings to her and she had not stopped him. She had heard him out in a daze but registered every detail. The narration had its own thereauptic effect. She had not wanted or waited to hear the end. It had the effect of releasing her from a logjam to flow gently towards the sea. The waiting was ended.

Sheila had grown to like Brother for his simple honesties. He had narrated all that had happened from the time he had been shot down to the time of his returning home. There were times when they had shared their fears, weaknesses, achievements and shortcomings and it had always been Brother that would begin these natters. It had taken time for Sheila to open up to him. She would get drawn into these "on the coffee table for two" discussions more as a listener and later she had become an equal participant. Sometimes even leading the way. It always left her feeling fresh and hopeful. There was an element of willing submissions in their interaction. Brother could laugh at himself more easily than he could at her quirks. There was no conscious effort between them to change or improve each other. Sheila had never even felt the threat of being on assessment. On the contrary at times she had to remind Brother to stop being harsh on himself and also learn how to accept compliments. Brother had given vent to his feelings and had cried without any shame at times and there had been occasions when Sheila too had allowed a few tears to roll. Holding hands or even a hug was never far and such intimacies had increased with the passage of time. They even understood that each one liked simple intimacies. It was spontaneous without any dilution stemming from controlled discreetness. They would encourage each other and Brother's mission had occupied her mind in a large measure. She had wanted him to be successful in that for she knew what it meant to wait. Let him find them and bring joy to them. Maybe he will even be able to get them released. For that he would have to get moving and she had inadvertently shown him the way.

The way was leading him to Ahmadabad. Sheila stopped pacing. Leaning on the balcony railing she was looking down at a street cat in the lamppost light. There were mice in the drain near the lamppost. The cat was waiting to pounce. Was Brother's mission like the cat? Would it pounce on Brother and take him away? She had faced deprivations for the better part of her life. Why did she feel a sense of loss here? Brother was on a well-defined platform in her life. Or was there a doubt here? Did she want more of him in her life in some other way and was there a chance of losing him? There was no definite answer to this last question. Her attention stayed focused on the cat in the street. A mouse had scrambled up the drain and scurried across the road before the cat could pounce. Sheila smiled almost in relief. *'Brother if you have survived that PoW camp, I think it will be reasonable to presume that you will survive the difficulties of this search and the mental confrontations that await you. I will wait for you – though I know not if you feel what I feel for you, even at age fifty-four. I suppose I have to wait for some more time.'*

Sheila had known about Brother's feelings of guilt that he had not been able to progress in the commitment to his prison mates. It used to gnaw at him and had the unhealthy effect of an emotional drain out. Would he be able to cope with the varied responses he gets from the families he finds? They would have moved on in their lives and he would be intruding. Would he cope with a failure to find any or all of them? These then were the probable reasons for her apprehensions, she thought. She realized that her assessment of Brother was, "Not yet Ready". And also surprised herself at the depth of fondness for him. She was ageing but not yet old. Her post supper walk over, Sheila could now distinctly identify the issues that had put her into gentle turbulence. She could not resolve them, as that was the prerogative of time. She could only trace the possible course of events in the near future: centering on Brother. His mission successes or failures would not alter her conclusive attachment to him but it had the capability to fulfill them both. There was no decision to be taken or solution to adopt, nothing to confront except one's self and she was never shy of that. There would also be time for that. The pacing had brought in a calm. Sheila preferred the certainties associated with being in rhythm with her consciousness. She could wait; she had enough experience on that.

## Chapter VI

    The Ahmadabad sky flickered from the glow and smoke of many a destroyed Muslim future. In February the nights turn pleasant but the days are sufficiently warm to yearn for sunset. That year it was no different. The city had known communal disturbances since independence yet in 2002 there was a difference. The media and technology in tandem provided momentum in vectoring the fetid air into every home irrespective of the air-conditioning, décor or immunity provided by being upwind: only the poor and weak no matter where they are, are condemned to be downwind of such storms. This storm enveloped the whole state of Gujarat and its peripheral effects had not spared the entire nation. The gargoyle of communalism seemed to draw energy from every killing and the innocent blood spilt so wantonly had sent bloody spray into the air that no one could escape inhaling its effects. Mixed with the smoke of burnt homes the very soul of every living being seemed to want an escape into cleaner air. The British were not to blame for this. This flaming sky was now only an effect of a revenge cause revived into motion. The British horizons had long ago retreated for everyone to know that the sun after all did set in the empire.

    The early morning cool never disappoints trembling bodies after a restless night. Ahmadabad needed its healing coolness. It swept in gently from under closed doors and through half open windows. The nights were pleasant but the early morning chill brings with it, reason to huddle together. This was nature reminding that we still have the capacity to generate and spread warmth that nurtures life. Everyone in Ahmadabad needed cool mornings but those weeks in February; for some, even daylight meant death. They were hurriedly searching for darker corners to hide in.

As the night cooled, Smita and Nikhil had kept awake and talked till late. They were disturbed. The law and order system was almost non-existent and the Army had not yet being called out. Why was there this delay? It had not taken so long in the past. Both had agreed that Ruhaina could stay with them indefinitely. Smita admired his patience and understanding. It had not bothered him that they were sheltering a Muslim family. They had enough space in the sprawling judge's estate. On the contrary Nikhil had even suggested setting up a small camp in tents for Muslim families threatened by the wave of terror. The thought had opened a new window for Smita to look into his mind. It had touched her to realize the depth of his kindness and also chastised her for overlooking this all-embracing side of him.

They had made love in the cool of dawn and she lay sensitive to her thin skin in his arms as he clung to a receding slumber associated with a disturbed mind trying its best to gather some more calm. For it did not know what the next day would bring. Their half asleep unobtrusive search for each others body and the passion of being entwined together was like a drowning body floating upward to the surface for that breath of life giving air. Death and destruction had come so close that it was triggering some primeval desire to procreate and be reassured that you belong. Smita lay still not wanting to break his link with the calm. Her mind was however discreetly detached, away from the warmth of his body. She stayed there for the touch yet the resilient woman in her was climbing out of the surf of emotional fulfillment. It searched for solutions and she was faintly aware that the room was illuminating from shadows to shapes as the sun brought in another day through heavy curtains.

*'Could this be happening really? In 2002, in India? Is it possible that a train with passengers gets halted in the middle of nowhere and a whole compartment is torched? Is there no fear of the law or repercussions? No concern for human life. Could they totally disregard the backlash of communal disaster unleashed after an act such as this? Organized violence could escalate and swallow entire communities. Who is right or wrong in the mosque and temple tug of war, anyway? As a practicing lawyer how can I*

suppress my conscience to the court corridor whispers that the bloody incidents possibly taking place even at this moment have powerful support and worse still, the police could be deliberately looking away as the mobs burn, kill, rape and loot. Can we rule out the possibility that Muslim fanatics had actually set fire to the train carrying Hindu devotees? Or did miscreants for blood money orchestrate this death dance. There are too many ghosts here. Father and I will soon be dealing with cases that will surely have well tutored witnesses swearing by the 'Gita', 'Koran' and 'Bible'. It could leave permanent stains on those holy books.'

The sun came into her privacy without permission today.

'What will I do if Basheer's case has to be fought? Will I fight for him? Without a doubt, I will. So what if he is a Muslim. His father was swallowed in a war for this nation. He was an Indian Muslim in a war against Pakistan, an Islamic nation. How tragic! And the Hindus are blind to such sacrifices. When will we all think as Indians? This has destroyed Basheer's only means of earning a livelihood almost crippling him for life. I wonder if he will ever be able to use his hands and fingers. There must be many Muslims in the armed forces. How are they feeling? Poor Basheer; he had also wanted to join the Army, but they rejected him. Was that because he is Muslim? It is a wonder that Muslims yet have the desire to serve the nation through the armed forces in spite of being victimized. I am glad Basheer could not join the army to fight some war against Pakistan and then come back to find his whole family destroyed. No, I don't think Muslims are visibly subjugated but yes, they are always treated with suspicion. Is it ' Hindu' to treat other communities with such contempt?'

The reality about terrorism can be so biased.

'Why is there a very real worldwide antagonism towards Muslims. It is not just in our India. The Jewish athletes at the Olympics, the New York World Trade Center; the war in Afghanistan against the Taliban. It is Muslim groups that claimed responsibility for these ghastly events. The bomb blasts in Bombay in 1993. That was also the handiwork of Muslim fanatics. Is it Islam or the Moslem people of the world? Why is the world blaming Islam as the only 'terrorist' culture and taking severe punitive action? Why is similar anti-terrorist action not taken against the IRA, or the Israeli gunmen or the Liberation Tigers of Tamil Elam? Are they not terrorists? It is unethical that a political identity is given to the IRA, LTTE or the Zionist variety of violent activists that gives them immunity from being termed as hardcore "terrorists". Why is it now more Islamic terrorists and militants? Why isn't there a war or concentrated International action taken against the other icons of terrorism? Why only against the Islamic brand. Am I biased because of Basheer? Violence leading to loss of civilian lives is terrorism. In that case American weapons and soldiers killing civilians also amounts to terrorism. Civilians do not fight wars. Any State sponsored killing of civilians is therefore terrorism by definition. In which case the killing of civilians in Ahmadabad without the protection from the law and order machinery makes them accomplices in terrorist activities.'

Muslims of the world are all being looked at with revulsion. There seems to be an association between Islamic upheavals and global insecurity. Is it because of these violent incidents? The worldwide action against Islam is becoming endemic. Muslim Arabs in the US, Muslims in non-Islamic South Asia, Muslim Turks in Germany, Muslim Algerians in France. They are always the first ones to be arrested.

The morning has never been so disillusioning. Something has to be done and soon.

'But here in Ahmadabad, it is the Hindus that are enmasse involved in uncontrolled butchery of Muslims. And it is Hindus that demolished the Babri Masjid. Did the Hindutva brigade not understand that it is very possible that Hindus will also soon be associated with violence, insecurity and terrorism? Or is this title reserved exclusively for violence originated by the Muslims. Maybe we will soon have some new 'ism' for the Hindu variety of violence. Organized American violence is labeled as "Liberation". Is it truly so in Afghanistan or in Iraq? Media and technology will not take much to start a worldwide propaganda of this Hindutva brand of terrorism. Maybe Hindus and India is already considered a semi-terrorist state.'

Smita shuddered at the vacillations in her mind. Maybe it was her lawyer's logic and very often it did not align with real life. She sighed. Nikhil stirred in his sleep in response to her emotional tremor. His senses could detect her signals of turmoil through the post dawn misty bliss.

Her mind withdrew home to Ahmadabad and her home. It hovered and resettled around Basheer and the tragic course of events in his life.

'The violence has engulfed him. Had he been in the Army, things may have been different. It has been a big blow for him resulting in total rejection. He has often told me that he never felt this weird Hindu and Muslim phenomena and that he could not understand the loathing that Hindus have for the Muslims. Basheer comes from a family striving hard to meet all ends. Their value system considers all human beings as equal. We were such close friends and it grew from admiration to fondness and there were pleasant humane intimacies. He was an exceptional athlete at college and had single handed, turned the scoreboard around for our house to win. I was the house captain and proud of him. I will stand by him through everything always.'

Her mind raced back to the romantic playground of her youth. Was it right to have these reminiscences now? She was happily married and Nikhil was holding her close in a very possessive embrace. Yet she dared to travel into the past. A smile escaped unseen. Women were better at concealing thoughts.

'Basheer used to read Ghalib for me and I would read Tagore's 'Hungry Stones'. Both of us were fond of literature, art and music. Basheer's physique and good looks did not reveal the fertile pasture of his core. I had got to know from the books he would take away from the library almost secretively. I remember needing 'The Golden Treasury'; a compilation of poems and the book was overdue in the name Basheer Khan. Basheer's English was not very fluent. He wanted to reach levels where he could express himself the way I could at all the college debates. He used to cycle down to college while I traveled in a chauffer driven car. Yet in the college campus there were many occasions that Basheer gave me a ride from the main block to the library on his shining cycle. I enjoyed those rides. We were college mates on a cycle in the campus, at the theater, in the botanical garden or simply frozen in an intimate embrace. Basheer was always reserved. It was as though such intimacies were not his right. It had been such an issue of debate amongst my friends that Basheer had never wanted to even hold hands with me. Imagine they wouldn't believe me. The others had all those titillating tales about their boyfriends, dates and kissing!'

Smita had brought Basheer home once. It was to show him her collection of books. Her father was then a renowned lawyer at the High Court and they had a nice bungalow near the cantonment. The now judge; Sudhin Choudhury had been quite a liberal then. It had only been later that he had begun to play golf and associate with the political who's who of Ahmadabad. It was in that bungalow that she had presented Basheer with a copy of Shakespeare's complete works. Basheer had been so touched by the gesture that he had spontaneously held her in an embrace. That remained the high mark of her youthful romantic dalliance with him. She had not struggled but had just been a trifle fidgety. Yes she had felt very effervescent but it been so quick that very often she had wondered if it did happen at all. And it was only when her mother had cautioned her not to be seen with Basheer in public but was alright to hold hands at home did she realize, that they had been seen in the library. It had come as a shock and her intent to debate the issue about "being seen by the world" fizzled out. The argument died in her adolescent embarrassment. 'It was good that mother did not think it was wrong to hold hands at home.'

The unspoken secret shared with her mother always made her feel more intimate with Basheer. A bee seen to settle on a flower was a proud moment for the gardener. Gardeners usually do not carry tales. Ma had seen and not made an issue. Smita then disregarded the caution and they had been seen publicly even going to Basheer's mother's shop. Smita had gravitated to Ruhaina from her first meeting. Ruhaina in her simple yet very intricately tailored salwar suit had fascinated her. There was some regality in her presence and Basheer had some of that charm. Her youthful senses liked the flavor and sounds at Ruhaina's.

The relationship grew through her law college days. Basheer had given up study after graduation. He had the natural talent of his grandfather and began assisting Ruhaina in all the departments of a tailoring outfit. They would meet less frequently but kept in regular touch on the phone. Basheer had spoken about marriage to her in the manner of a discussion. He had not expected any answer; just wanted her to know that it was a dream. The impossibility had not lessened their affections but it had tempered the relationship to its new avatar. Smita remained bound to the enormity of their understandings and lack of any visible regret displayed by Basheer. Their visual exchanges grew more astute without losing its warmth. This was a totally new realm of love that could exist between two people that understood and shared affection on a plane of mutual respect. It had not been easy for Smita to understand till Basheer had told her that he was not disappointed. 'Muslims cannot marry Hindus, without being ostracized,' he had laughed. And they had allowed these words to cement in their minds and it had not caused any pain. Only some youthful rebellion.

Smita stirred gently in Nikhil's embrace and wondered whether she was still in some kind of emotional captivity. Surely her emotional and other needs were fulfilled. She wasn't about to dive into fantasizing.

*'With Basheer, have I not given enough; reciprocated affection? Then today, why am I feeling as though I have never got across to him the way he has with me? He will never know that I had truly wanted to marry him and that there had been a huge debate in the house? It was Ma who had gently comforted my shattered emotions and left me to understand. I had not felt it appropriate to include Basheer in these happenings. I knew it would distress him. Is he still waiting for me and did I put on hold something that I should have shared with him long ago? There is no doubt about my deep attachment and bonds with Nikhil. Yet after our marriage, I have kept my association*

with Ruhaina and Basheer. They do all my tailoring. Basheer did not attend my wedding reception and it has remained unexplained over the years. I never thought it correct to ask and he was so courteous the first time that I had gone to their shop to get some clothes tailored before our vacation in America. Tailoring my clothes has continued to be the basis of our association for the last ten years. What is it that I feel now? Sympathy? Why?'

Smita gently lifted Nikhils arm from around her waist. She knew that he was now snoring in deep sleep. Her mind was made up. She would visit Basheer in the nursing home and share something with him that she may have saved for an appropriate moment. This had waited for long enough. She did not know how but she knew that she had to get across and maybe let Basheer know that she still cared and that there was still hope for all his other dreams in a world without the fears of being from a minority community. She was a lawyer and would try to do justice to this relationship. She looked down at Nikhil's relaxed face as he slept. *'This is something I will be keeping from you my love but it is not because I love you any less— I am like an ocean and can absorb the water that flows down every mountain. Basheer's tears need to find a resting place. I have learnt the meaning of devotion from him and it is you Nikhil that has always received that from me. Let me only show him my gratitude. He has waited long. I think you will understand this.'*

It was as though Nikhil had received the message, 'Why do you have to get up so early Smita,' he mumbled. Smita leaned over him for a moment. She smiled without any trace of the turbulent, just concluded mental exercise.

'I have a lot to do today Nikhil.'

'Don't let all that is happening, bother you Smita, is there something I can share and do?'

'You know I will manage Nikhil; just be home early today evening.'

With that she got up to leave and Nikhil clutched at the sheets that covered her. Smita looked at him, suppressed a laugh and let the sheets drop and walked bare towards meeting her day head on. She stopped as her reflection in the mirror arrested attention and thought. *'There will never be anything I have to hide from you Nikhil. The truth is that I have to make Basheer feel wanted. He must rise from the debris in his life. The reassurance that I truly loved him will be enough for his heart. He needs to move on. I have. Or am I still captive to some emotional trail?'*

## Chapter VII

    Mission day had arrived for Brother. He was pushing a suitcase on casters. He could do with well-greased wheels, as this was one mission that could take him miles in many directions. He was beginning a search. Sheila carried what was going to be just 'a snack' for him. She had insisted, to his refusals. It was carefully wrapped in brown paper and she also had a talisman tucked away inside her handbag. She had checked for it about half a dozen times to make sure that it was there. It was to protect him and maybe give him the success that he needed and there were so many waiting for his fulfillment. She would give it to him at an appropriate moment.

    Bombay Central station had been a take off point for Brother in the past. It occupied a special place on the tracks of his life. He had caught a train from here that had taken him to Delhi for his medical exams prior to joining the National Defense Academy. All his vacations while in the air force had ended here. He was familiar with the feelings that a fighter pilot has when he leaves home and boards a train to go back on duty to fly. Often to some far out location in Kashmir, Punjab or Rajasthan. Trains to the North of India mostly departed from Bombay Central. It was also the station where Brother had finally set foot after he had completed the formalities of a deported PoW and also declared unsound of mind by the authorities at Air Headquarters in Delhi. A start or destination for trains. Just another milestone in most people's lives; Bombay Central. For Brother today it was more. It was the beginning of many things.

For Sheila it had been the station that had received her during the war of 1971. She had stepped off the Frontier Mail and the dams had burst. Her parents had waited on this platform. They had come to receive their only daughter. She was six months into her pregnancy. Kailash had been declared missing in action but they were sure to hear about him soon. That had been the hopeful mood. It had helped to wait for every sunrise. Sheila also associated Bombay Central as the station that used to make her board a train during Rani's summer breaks for their ritual visit to Kailash's parents. She was not particularly fond of this station.

The Gujarat Mail stood in its place on platform number four. For Brother it was just another train. He had been on trains before and it did not bring any journey related excitement to his psyche. He was looking much ahead in the distance. At what, he was not sure. Every now and then as he crossed other passengers he would feel urgency and a goading commitment to his friends back there in the Pakistani camp. It was two years after his release and he had not been able to even start the search. He had no address or telephone number. In thirty years a lot could have changed with their families. He had thought about them everyday maybe more than once and his inability to make a start would leave him ashamed and wondering with guilt. This very guilt held him prisoner to a sense of remorse. And he had longed for freedom. The news clipping was just a straw in the wind but he was willing to hold on to it and begin navigating wherever it dictated.

He had navigated his way back to base in worse situations. Those had been the few occasions that he had to fly his fighter above clouds without any visual references of the ground. Sometimes not even in radio contact with ground control. He would skim above the wooly carpet; something he truly enjoyed doing; a bit like skiing that he had only wanted to do and then dive through a gap when he could see the earth. There was always either a railway line, a river bend, a village with a temple, a canal bend or even a quaint looking tree. These had been clues; frozen snapshots in the brain, seen just once as he flew past them at eight hundred kilometers an hour and he had fortunately not gone wrong. Those clues had brought him back to the safety and haven of a dark gray runway and he had landed the bird at times with the fuel gauge reading zero. For Brother, the newspaper brought to him by Sheila was more like an arrow pointing towards mission commencement and not like breathless moments looking for a hole in the clouds just to spot a clue. It was time to dive through the clouds. The train or Bombay Central and the other memories that tried to crowd his mind were rapidly rejected to back seat. He was already flying down the track to Ahmadabad. The injured Major had saved a Muslim tailor located near the cantonment and most tailors knew others in the same locality. Fellow prisoner Azad Khan had described the cantonment area very often. He could not remember those descriptions too well but he would find Major Dilip of the news clip as he could get access into the camp being an ex-serviceman. He would then find other clues to continue his search. Azad Khan was from Ahmadabad. Someone would know him.

The noise level on the platform was without its usual cacophony of hawkers, porters and passengers. The Gujarat Mail was a favorite with businessmen as it left Bombay late in the evening and got into Ahmadabad in the early hours. It gave traders and businessmen a whole working day in Ahmadabad for noisy negotiations. Brother knew that Gujaratis were a talkative lot. If not the stock market, they could be discussing politics, films, cricket or even their own family problems. And they were vociferous. Perhaps it had something to do with the trading in the stock market that demanded loud voices. That was Brother's understanding of Gujaratis. Tonight the platform was devoid of any gregariousness. The riots must have discouraged travel to Ahmadabad. Or had the terror seeped in like slow poison into everyone's psyche. It was evident from the few silent passengers. There were more than a handful of armed guards from the Railway Police force. He disliked the presence of guards. They took him back in time. He had noticed that the number of retail stalls on the platform had increased. His attention had been caught by the display of wares in the stalls. They had become more colorful with brighter packaging. He had wondered at the products being sold here. A journey by train reminded him of eating snacks. He used to buy a lot of those packaged food products and munch and share with other passengers while reading Leon Uris or a Max Brand. Those were hot selling paperbacks in those days and readily available at almost every railway platform bookstall. Thirty years back you could get beverages, biscuits and cigarettes from the same stall. Now it was all segregated. Categorized. The cigarette stalls were missing as smoking was now banned on railway platforms. Tea had maintained its best selling product status. He had crossed a trolley being pushed by two men and it carried what looked definitely like ammunition boxes. It had startled him but he concluded that this was probably meant for the police and the riots in Ahmadabad. Why should we have to fire on our own citizens? Could these bullets calm the fury? His sense of urgency was rekindled and he wanted this journey to get over so that he could find the Muslim tailor in Ahmadabad. It was now or never. He had to start.

Brother and Sheila found their paces increasing. It was as though the train would leave before they would find his berth number and seat. They stopped on the platform looking at the list of names on a sheet of paper stuck inside a glass-covered board. The print was small to read.

The shape of the train extending ahead of them on the platform accelerated their pace. They were now searching the names on sheets of paper with passengers' names stuck on each compartment entrance. The compartments appeared to stretch forever and there was not much time left for departure. They had decided on the phone that Brother would make this trip to Ahmadabad. And then Brother had stood in a long queue to book his ticket and it brought back memories of standing in medical check up queues at the prison camp. He did not want Sheila to see him off but she had picked him up from Chapel road and driven into town to drop him. It was well past eight in the evening and would take her at least two hours to reach back her apartment in Borivili.

'Brother, there's your name I think,' she had shouted since he had already gone past the compartment onto the next one. Brother looked back at her shout and she was smiling.

'How did I miss that?'

'Never mind, the typing is not very clear but I think it is your name.' She pointed it out for him and he gave her his most sheepish smile. The name on the list was in fact Richard James.

'The last time that I was really anxious while looking at a list was when the merit list for my selection into the National Defense Academy was printed in the papers. I had not missed it then; maybe my eyesight is growing weaker?' There was relief in both their smiles and Brother put his arm around her shoulder in a gesture of gratefulness and she just patted him on the back.

'You get in and get your bag in place, I will wait here.' She had this finality in her voice that Brother willingly accepted and almost responded. 'Yes sir.'

It was an air-conditioned coach with six berths in an open cubicle.

Brother found his lower berth and pushed the suitcase under the seat. An elderly couple sat in the opposite lower berth and Brother smiled at them. It did not have much effect. They looked worried. These were troubled times. The communal riots at their destination did not warrant smiles from fellow passengers. The frozen stare had left Brother feeling very brazen.

'I am just going outside to say bye to a friend.' He had said it loudly like an announcement, not addressing anyone in particular but just so that the couple accepts that he would be back traveling with them. They certainly did not look very comfortable. Chapel road had taught him differently— to get along with everyone. Nobody was a stranger if you extended your hand.

There was still sometime for the train to leave. Brother stepped out of the train a little relieved after finding his berth and Sheila handed him the brown paper package. 'Smells good!' He smiled.

'There are some sandwiches made by Rani for you. We know you like chicken sandwiches.'

'Of course I do but where was the need. I could have managed a meal from the train catering or from some wayside platform stall.'

'I have something I want you to have.' Sheila dug into her handbag and found the talisman. It was a faded locket with Sai Baba's image on it with a black string passed through its ring that made it possible to wear around the neck. She handed it to Brother and he accepted it with a quizzical look.

'Is this supposed to bring me luck?'

'It was Kailash's and I want you to have it. It should keep you safe.' Brother thought looking at it; *'had this been with Kailash, things may have been different,'* and then slipped it over his head and under his collar and shirt. It felt different because he was also wearing a gold chain that used to be his father's, given to him by Martha. He smiled; now he had Jesus and Saibaba to take care of him.

He never had any fixations about praying or asking for blessings from Gods. India had so many religions and Gods. For him it had all been one. The air force way of life had been very secular. They had prayed at Hindu temples, Gurdwaras for Sikhs and even the tomb of a Muslim saint located next to a runway at one of the airfields in Punjab. Nobody had any qualms about these issues in the armed forces. It was not so much about praying as much as it was "we respect your place of worship and your sentiments that go with it". All religious festivals were recognized and colleagues made it a point to visit and exchange greetings. Regional belongingness and favoritism was there but there was never any visible discrimination based on religion. The rules, regulations, opportunities and privileges were applicable to all.

In Bombay, Brother had been provoked by some advertisements in the media. Some apartments were not for sale to Muslims. Of course there were also some blocks of apartments and localities that were reserved only for Christians, Sindhis or Pharsees. Communal preference was also evident at admissions to schools and colleges. Schedule (lower) castes and tribals were being uplifted into mainstream life with job reservations and even admissions to higher educational institutions. Such privileges violated regard for aptitude or entrance examination merits. Brother had not come to understand these burning issues. They did not affect him. The visible application of these had however made him wonder. To him, Secularism had looked fractured at times and at other times coexistence was very visible. He knew that secularism demanded that no differentiation or preference was to be made based on religion or any form of worship. Policies of governance, education, civic rights and social customs should not consider religion as a factor to differentiate. For him, Partition of India into two parts based on religious factors was a non-secular policy and act. It was however given a democratic hue under the rationale that Muslims had the right to have their own nation and governance and if that required a nation to be split: so be it. *Is there a conflict between democracy and secularism?*

Brother had come to these conclusions during his captivity. There had been many hushed discussions between fellow prisoners and sometimes the more liberal prison guards would also express their own views. Their declarations, for or against were always regarded with suspicion. These conclusions were not the result of any research or systematic debate but there was always consensus that the Partition had been a wrong precedence and there were vested interests in it. The British were always the villains but that was a decision set into motion by Hindu Indian leaders. Therefore it could be suicidal, blaming Pakistan while you were in their unlawful custody. The participants at such forums in the camp were all soldiers. Their approach to democracy, secularism and freedom was more like looking up the meanings in a dictionary and interpreting them according to the law of the land. Politicians and ethno-preneurs on the contrary had a business like approach. Whatever kept them in power was spin doctored to be correct. They all agreed on this.

Time stood watch at Bombay Central. Sheila had spotted his name on the reservation chart and that had taken some wind out of the earlier rapid movement of the clock hands. Brother seemed quite motivated and certain that he had found a useful lead that was taking him to Ahmadabad. His mission now had the ingredient of resolution. After all Sheila had found the clue and he was going to give it his best shot. There were just five minutes for the departure of the train.

'Sheila asked him, 'Brother, what will you say to this tailor who you presume to be Azad Khan's son. Have you considered that he may not believe your past? It is so many years and you have no documentary or other proof to convince them of the reality.' There was a moment's silence and they could both hear the squeaking of wheels as a porter pushed his overloaded cart with mailbags. The squeaking mocked at him. Did he have an answer to that? This was also one of the reasons that he had not begun his search.

Brother replied with resignation, 'no one will believe my account of the PoW camp. The authorities at Delhi did not look very convinced. Though, I am certain that if I find the families, it will not be very difficult to make them believe. I am thankful to you for giving me the first clue. Hopefully now, I will find the rest and maybe even free my mates. This is not something I can achieve alone.'

'I will help you Brother. You do not know how much relief you gave me by telling me all the details about Kailash. We will try and help the others. They will not have to wait in uncertainty like me.'

The two tone broken voice electric horn of the train sounded, "Am coming soooooon." Brother touched her on the shoulder, the train jerked into motion and stopped. Brother laughed, 'It waits for me Sheila,' and she pushed him gently towards the train to board. These fighter pilots could laugh anywhere at anything.

'You get on board and don't worry about your mother, I will visit her.'

'Drive home carefully, it is a long way to Borivili.'

'You have a much longer journey; you will be successful I know. Do not lose hope.'

How will he deal with the disbelief and reactions of relatives who may have moved on in life, was her apprehension more than the likely frustrations he may have to deal with at not finding the relatives. He looked happy about keeping his commitment to his mates. She admired the energy and courage. He just needed a start. The carnage at Godhra was the least desirable trigger.

Brother waved from the doorway as the Gujarat mail slowly

pulled away from a lonely platform. Sheila stood waving a handkerchief till the curve on the tracks took him out of sight. Brother felt the tug in his belly It was poignant like the old times. He was leaving home and going back on duty. He would find a way to convince the families. Many approaches had been thought of without any convincing solution. Yet he always felt assured that the situation would take care of the issue. When you spend twenty-nine years in confinement with someone; you get to know his likes and even the quirks. Poor Sheila; fate had allowed her only two years with Kailash. Brother and Azad were confined for years together, also by dictates of fate. He would know how to deal with relatives. Brother leaned out of the door to look ahead down the tracks as home was again left behind. The breeze narrowed his eyes. He was finally on the trail.

Walking like a seaman as the train tested his balance, Brother moved between the bunks to his berth. He would have some sandwiches and read Exodus. Leon Uris had dealt well with minority community psyche. He would get a glimpse into the minds of people that were cornered and their survival threatened. Jews had got their promised land but were having to struggle and kill to keep it. Could traces of their psyche be found amongst the Muslims in their mohallas and mosques in Bombay, Ahmadabad, Lucknow or Calcutta and across the spread-eagled map of India? He opened the brown paper package to set his plan moving. The book was easily reached by opening the zip of his suitcase. He did not like locks and keys. That was related to captivity.

'Are you getting down at Ahmadabad or somewhere in between?'

Brother was bent over looking into his suitcase for an air pillow. His mind raced. He had smiled at them when he first came in to locate his berth. They had just looked through him. Why were they curious now? Let me pretend to be a bit deaf. The question was repeated after a moment.

Brother looked up and smiled at them again. Maybe we can make a new start, he thought, a smile would break the ice. The lady shifted as if the smile had touched her body. Brother smiled again.

'Do you know him?' The man asked her.

Brother smiled and said, 'I am sorry, my hearing is not too good.'

'I said, are you going to get off at Ahmadabad or in between and why do you smile at her eh?'

'Oh! I know you are Mr. and Mrs. Shah and are traveling to Ahmadabad. It says so on the reservation chart at the entrance. My name was just next to yours,' he added with another knowing smile again. The man was visibly flustered with his smiles.

The years of hedging around questions shot by prison camp interrogators and guards had taught Brother the technique to avoid giving obvious answers. He was doing well because the question remained unanswered for the man opposite him.

He said to his wife, 'he cannot hear too well.' Brother took out his sandwiches and offered it to them.

The lady smiled reluctantly, almost coyly and asked, 'is it vegetarian?' Brother kept his hands extended with a gesture that she should help herself. The man reached forward and opened one of the handiworks of Rani. His eyebrows went up forming perfect half moons. 'That is chicken isn't it?'

'You are right, do you like chicken.'

The lady twisted her nose in disgust covering her mouth with a handkerchief pulled out from inside her blouse and realized her visible impoliteness and apologized, 'we are vegetarians but only he eats chicken outside the house. We do not cook chicken at home.'

'So then have one please.' The man reluctantly took one. Keeping it in his hand he watched Brother biting into one.

'Don't worry these are home made and fresh.'

Mr. Shah hesitated and said, 'these days a lot of passengers are duped from eating food with sleep inducing drugs in them.'

Brother laughed, 'Do I look like a trickster?'

'Sorry, sorry sir, I did not mean that.' He came sniffing at Brother again, 'Are you getting down at Ahmadabad?'

'I may get down at some station in between.' The man turned to his wife immediately, his hand halting the journey of the sandwich to his mouth and they both looked very uncomfortable. 'I like to drink coffee at night, so I may get down a couple of times in between.' A smile of relief escaped from the lady. Brother had understood their concerns for security because he had also heard that theft on trains was not uncommon. Thieves in the guise of passengers would get off at wayside stations and walk away with luggage belonging to other passengers.

While munching on his sandwich, 'Is Ahmadabad a nice city, I have never been there before.' The couple now leaned back on their lower berth, relaxed. Brother had relented and answered Shah's previous query and added his own question. Mr. Shah bit into the sandwich at last.

'It is the best city in India.' Brother smiled encouraging Mr. Shah to go on. 'It is a very modern city. Good roads, lots of shops, movie complexes, good business and economic growth, good hospitals, schools, colleges. Cost of living is lower than your Bombay. Brother observed the stress on "your Bombay".

'And how are the people?'

'Oh! They are very friendly, helpful, peaceful and sober like us, not like the younger generation dresses in your Bombay.'

'Then why is their so much unrest and communal riots in Ahmadabad.'

'Those Muslim hooligans, they burnt the train so they deserved the punishment.' He almost allowed a laugh but it stalled as Brother's eyes became narrow. Mr. Shah quickly added, 'You see Ahmadabad is a very secular and democratic city, so something like Muslims burning a train and killing Hindu devotees is a serious undemocratic behavior and they should not go scot free. It is always the Muslims and their disturbing acts that leads to communal trouble.'

The battle lines were quite clearly drawn. Brother had not wanted to engage in any more conversation. He had expected some trace of regret in Mr. Shah's description of the people of Ahmadabad or criticism for the failure of the law to prevent the revenge killings. Maybe some remorse at the whole issue of Hindu and Muslim riots; a backhanded tribute to Mahatma Gandhi's non-violent and secular beliefs in the very city that was close to Sewagram. On the contrary he had devoured the sandwich with a little more gusto while speaking about the Muslims.

'The Muslims cannot kill Hindu devotees returning from the Ram temple in Ayodhya and get away without any retaliation.'

That snared Brother into a soft duel. 'Mr. Shah I think it was criminal to destroy a Muslim place of worship in the first place. The democratic government of India guarantees its citizens freedom to practice their own religion. It is absolutely un-secular to allow the demolishing of a Muslim place of worship with the law and order watching as mute witness. Secularism does not base its policies or decisions based on religion or prejudices. The government should have protected the Babri Masjid. Why has the government decided to excavate and research only into the past of this particular mosque? And now the issue of temple or mosque is left to the decision of a court? Two wrongs do not make a right. The mosque may have been a temple and it fell prey to warring forces. To demolish the mosque and reinstate it as a temple is not secular. How far in history are we to go to correct or demolish and rebuild temples and mosques. Babur, Akbar, Chengiz Khan and even the Dutch and British are a part of our history of demolitions. Why are we not demolishing all the buildings and the architecture created by the British? Would you want Lutyens' Rashtrapati Bhavan, (the President's residence) to be pulled down and perhaps rebuild whatever existed there before? To my thinking the whole issue of the temple and mosque was originated by un-secular forces and given wide publicity to the Hindu poorer sections of society to whip up emotions and gain favor in the electorate.'

'Are you a Muslim?'

'No, I am an Indian. A Christian. A retired air force pilot, Flight Lieutenant Richard James.' He extended a hand as formal introduction.

'Politics is not like the armed forces Mr. James,' they shook hands. 'It is a business, you see. If your product is a need, it sells and you get profits.'

'You mean Hindutva and demolishing the mosque was a need?'

'I don't know because I am not a politician.'

'Then you must be a businessman for sure.' For a moment there was silence. Brother took the opportunity to pick up his book and Mr. Shah was left without audience for any further glib sales talk. Brother wondered if sharing a sandwich was a mistake.

It was past ten at night and the train had settled into a steady rhythm. Brother had put on his reading light and struggled to get past the Prologue. His eyes seemed to droop for every eight beats from the wheels. And then it sagged for every four. Sleep intervened as he tried to focus from his argument with the businessman to the lines in the book. His concentration was divided. Sleep won the battle. And he was subconsciously glad for the respite. His residual energy drifted to the mission ahead: finding the family of Azad Khan and the others.

He tried to recollect Azad Khan's features. A description of features may help in convincing his wife and son. *'What were the names of the father and wife? Was it Ali or Kasim? It had to be Kasim Khan and of course it is good that I can remember some names. I may not know the relationships but that is acceptable. The wife was either Ruhaina or Nusrat or was it Fatima? Oh! It is not Fatima. How can I forget her; she was the deaf and dumb sweeperess at the camp. She had almost been raped by one of the Pakistani guards. Lieutenant Pawri had intervened and fought of the armed fellow and saved her as he was in the dispensary at that time. Poor Pawri, he had been bullied a lot for complaining about the soldier. Pawri was the youngest prisoner. He was strong. What a pity; to be captured, just into the Army as a doctor. Fortunately, the rapist had been punished and moved* out of the camp. That Pakistani camp Commandant was a good man.'

The train had picked up speed and was moving at a steady clip. His bunk was comfortable and almost the same size as the bed in the camp. The camp beds were hard. He smiled even as he was being lulled into a semi- state of reasoning. *'If I can get a detailed map of that area, I may be able to reach some conclusions from the mountains I remember so clearly and there must be a village nearby with a name. Who will give me a map of Pakistan? In Air Head Quarters they had shown me a map and I had said that I was able to see the Nanga Parbat; that bare rocky peak in a North Easterly direction on clear days and there were other smaller mountains all around. It was like being in a bowl. They had doubted me. I can't blame them. Yet I am certain it was Nanga Parbat and not some other peak and the journey by train from Daud Khel had taken more than twelve hours. The Air force intelligence officer had mentioned some names like Nowshera, Charsadda, Tang and Malakand. According to information available to them, there was no prison camp or even a terrorist training camp in that area. I know there was some kind of training being conducted there because outside the walls they would fire together for sometime and then it would be quiet. The gaps must be time for the trainees to reload for their next session of firing. I think they just didn't want to believe me, as it would fuel so many complications between governments. As it is, the Pakistani's had been clever in faking my handing over papers. Imagine the story. I had stayed in Pakistan illegally after the war and then worked as missionary converting people from Islam to Christianity. And then I was detected and jailed for two years. Our authorities believed their story and not mine. How else could the Pakistanis explain my custody for almost thirty years? It is just fortunate that even the Air force doctors did not give me a chance of recovering from Tuberculosis or they would have put me behind the bars for desertion. It had taken a lot to convince them about our plight. And finally they had accepted my version after I had told them the names of officers and men who were falsely implicated in an escape bid and shot at Daud Khel. How could I remember some names and not the prison camp? That a blindfolded train journey and confinement without any contact with the world could do this was beyond their comprehension. It had taken the Army three weeks to confirm the names of those executed soldiers. It is fortunate that those names were still on record and that I could remember them. I am lucky to be free but this mission may land me in trouble again. No, I will not give up. I had promised them that I would do my best to reach their relatives and also free them. What a chase I have got into.'*

The Gujarat mail ploughed through the night and was he hearing the sound of a familiar horn. At the camp they would hear the long drawn horn with two short blasts of a diesel locomotive. It used to be twice a week.

'Is this the sound of my train to Ahmadabad or am I seeing Azad Khan in his bed smiling at me. He always smiled when we heard that horn. It was the sound of freedom and it had never failed to bring that infectious smile on his face. He had made so many plans to escape but they had remained dreams. That camp was just the bottom of some inescapable pit. There was just one entrance and walls all around. It looked like an old fort.'

'I don't know what fighters are based in Pathankot. I am Flight Lieutenant James and my service number is G-5794 and I am an Indian.' The nameless eyes of this fair Pathan officer are boring into me but I will not give any information.'

'Give him a bath, he smells.' Brother rolled in his bunk as though the jets of steaming hot water were tearing into him and then he shivered from the air conditioning as though cold water had been sprayed on him. He was suddenly in a cage barely a four feet cubicle with just one small six-inch square window.

'It feels like an oven in the open sun. I cannot look outside but the light and darkness comes and goes. 'Oh! This is hell. They cannot make me sign on that paper that I was part of the escape plan. That National Defence Academy march past tune is so good. Let me whistle that tune for company. I still remember graduation day. Mom and Dad were there. The view here in Daud Khel is so beautiful. Some of the places in Kashmir are so similar. The memory of Lidder River at Pahalgam will always be with me. That was one good vacation Mom, Dad and I had gone for. Why the gunshots? Oh! They have shot those three prisoners as they washed themselves in the river. Why did they do that? They were not escaping. Why this sudden pain in my back. You have no right to hit me. I am lying at the bottom of a beautiful grassy slope on the riverside, hit in the back by a rifle butt, I am shouting back at the Pakistani guard.'

'The guard is coming towards me and saying, 'you saw them trying to escape? The same fate awaits you dog. Come with me.'

'They were not escaping; they were bathing after the days work. How dare you shoot them in cold blood?'

'You want to see how well I shoot?' Silence.

'Major Pillay is dragged out of sleep at night. They blindfold and gag and take him away. There is no other sound in the night. After an hour there is a shot and now they have come for me.'

'Give us the answers to a few questions or else you will be shot like Pillay. Can MiG-21s take off and land at Awantipur? How much time does it take to refuel and re-arm a MiG-21. Tell us all the combat tactics in a four aircraft mission?' They are trying to brainwash me about the Indian authorities not caring about us prisoners. We are not being released because the Indians are not willing to exchange for us; we are junior officers after all. They are only concerned about Indian senior officers being exchanged for Pakistani PoWs.'

'I have no knowledge of MiG-21s as I have never flown them and it is five years now since I flew in the war. How can I remember the combat tactics? It must have changed by now.' They hit me on the head with a blunt object and the next thing is that I am in this dark cell lying next to someone. Are we dead? I am touching someone and he finally wakes up. In this darkness -who can it be.'

'Who are you?'
'I am Flight Lieutenant James and you?'
'Major Pillay.'
'Oh! So you are alive.'
'Do you have some doubts', he is sniggering.
'They told me that you had been shot for not cooperating.'
'That is an old tactic. Don't they teach you such things in the air force?' Silence.

'Mustafa, the cook in the camp is standing at the table while we eat his cooking. He is joking with us as usual and asking if the food was tasty.' 'You will never get such Biriyani in India. We Pakistanis are the best cooks in the world.' ' We are all laughing. It is a Sunday and we have to eat Biriyani on every Sunday. The Biriyani over we are washing our plates and glasses and walk back to the cell dormitory. I am suddenly jabbed in the back by a stick. It is that Subedar Abdul Kareem, the senior most Non-com Pakistani officer at the camp, with his polished baton. We are at the morning exercise routine.'

'Can't you keep in step with the others, you air force flyer boy? Do you want to fly to heaven? I can send you there? Come on keep running and don't look at me like that or I will put you in the cooler for a week.' 'I am not scared and he hates my looks. They have again thrown me into that dark cell with rats and spiders.'

Brother woke up in a fit. He had fallen out of the bunk and was lying on the floor of the Gujarat Mail. It was so good to be free. Even the floor was quite acceptable. The sound of the wheels sounded friendly and not like that Pakistani train. There were no rats here. The blue night lamp threw an eerie glow around and everyone was sleeping in the compartment. Brother rolled over to get up and back into his bunk. He could see the businessman or was it a camp guard, looking down wide-eyed at him from the upper berth. He didn't offer to help him get up or have a kind word to say. Maybe he was keeping a watch on his luggage so no one could make off with it. 'All your luggage in tact?' Brother whispered. There was no reply. The face just turned over and went into a snore almost immediately. Brother got up and sat in his berth and drew open the curtain at his window. It was a beautiful moonlit night. It had been a long time since he had last traveled in such comfort and beauty. There was hope in the moonlight that he would find Azad Khan's family and the intense joy it would bring to them brought tears to his eyes. He hadn't given up positive thinking. And he was used to sleeping in sitting position and this was not some uncomfortable dark prison floor.

*'The Gujarat mail is removed from riots and bloodshed. It is very comfortable. Let me watch this moonlight and forget about that nightmare. I wonder why does this happen every time I think about Azad Khan. Maybe it will leave me after I find his family. I cannot deny, that at least these nightmares bring back their faces to me. How else will I remember their features and mannerisms to describe to their relatives and keep the fire burning to get them their freedom?'*

Brother had fallen asleep at the window with moonlight for company. The coach attendant woke him up. 'Sahib, we will reach Ahmadabad in thirty minutes, would you like some tea?'

'Of course, I would love that, here take the money for it.'

The man in his khaki open jacket looked a bit surprised, he said jovially, 'You can pay me later.' The lighthearted start to this day seemed auspicious to Brother. He tipped the attendant well and was saluted for it a couple of times. Did I pay too much? Why was he so grateful? *Not all were businessmen or politicians expecting freebies.* Three cups of tea and thirty minutes later Brother stepped onto the streets of Ahmadabad in search of Azad Khan's tailoring shop. It was another beginning.

# Chapter VIII

It was another cold wintry day at the prison camp. The peaks in the distance had their snowcaps firmly in place and it would be another few weeks before some of the lower ridges began to show their rocky façade or barren slopes. Seasons would make the hillsides don new colors. These images had become picture frames for the inmates of the camp. They had all known that this was somewhere near the North West Frontier province but the name of the adjacent town or village remained a mystery. Brother had been good with maps as a pilot to point out the Nanga Parbat peak on the Indian side to them. They had no reason to disbelieve him.

The prison guards had been briefed well not to disclose the location and they were all very loyal. Guard duty was just another soldiering job for them with clear instructions that names of places were not to be part of any talk with prisoners. Not much interaction took place between the few prison cell guards and them. Newspapers had never been given to them during Colonel Akhtar Hussain's tenure as the Camp Commandant. The new Commandant Colonel Arif Sami had recently introduced the luxury of a one per week video film screening of an Indian film. Sepoy Nazir, a Baluchi soldier had become friendly with Azad.

'This Colonel is a very simple yet strict man. He even tastes the food that is served to you fellows and unfortunately this looks like his last assignment. He is not very popular among the senior Generals at Islamabad so they have placed him here as a punishment posting.'

Azad would get such information from Nazir whenever he was on duty. Nazir had lost an elder cousin brother, a Pakistani army cavalry officer, in the 1971 conflict with India. He had related many a tank battle to Nazir and in turn these were whispered to Azad. They had very often exchanged their personal impressions about India and Pakistan; the futility of all the wars and now, the mujahideen strikes in Kashmir. Nazir would smile and claimed that he had some relatives in India. They had not moved to Pakistan during the Partition. They were permitted to visit Karachi once in three years.

Azad had tried to appeal to Nazir. 'Just give our names and Indian addresses to your relatives from India. It is the only way for us to reach our near ones.' Nazir had never said no but loyalty or fear had kept him from doing it. There would be no mercy for him if the leak were traced out. His eyes would lower in a silent confirmation to Azad, that he had failed him. His presence as a friendly guard was a confidence factor yet he was kept out of many of the hushed discussions between the prisoners. Was he planted there on purpose?

Azad had seen the two-day-old edition of The Dawn, a Pakistani daily. It had given vivid details of the communal riots in Ahmadabad. There were a few photographs that were not very clear. Names of localities were familiar. It had made him feel like a lion in a cage. He had gone into silent prowling. Some of the other guards had even called him aside and taunted him about the treatment meted out to Muslims in India.

'Why don't you to join the mujahideen and fight against the kafirs? Look what they are doing to your sister, wife and children. How can you be loyal to a Hindu nation when they are raping, burning your homes and treating you like some hunted animals? You are a coward, not fit to be a Muslim. They have forgotten about you Azad. Your officers and men abandoned you in the battlefield on purpose. They did not want you in their ranks. They suspected you. Be thankful that we took you as prisoner and have given you shelter for so many years and are still willing to set you free. We are not going to allow kafirs to rule this world. Did you see what our brothers did in New York? They are a nation of cowards who fight battles only in foreign lands. Have they ever had a war on their own soil? They are two faced like the Indians. First they gave arms to our brothers against the Russians and now they are trying to take over Afghanistan. And the Hindus; they supported the Mukti Bahini to split us as a nation but look how they are killing Bangla Deshis as infiltrators. Indian soldiers are looting and raping Moslems in Kashmir. We will liberate Kashmir soon. Do you want to be part of that liberation force and get pardoned by Allah for being a traitor?'

Azad battled with lunch while the others ate and then he retired to his corner in the dormitory cell. They were watching his torment. The insults and humiliations were not so painful as the knowledge that this time the communal fires looked like it would swallow his family or whatever remained of it.

'Ya Allah! What is happening in your kingdom? Why have you kept me alive to see this day? Am I cursed to remain alive and watch my family consumed in this hell fire?'

He withdrew with his Koran and began reciting in the lilting way that Moslems do at prayer meetings and mosques. Colonel Sunderam had observed Azad and the guards and he wanted to know but held restraint. Sunderam had a hunch, as he had been a confidant for everyone. Azad had been taken aside by the prison authorities periodically and such occasions were gradually increasing. There was some pressure building up there.

He was like their father. Sunderam had long ago understood that the mind is best soothed after finishing a battle within. The darkness and illumination were all in the minds and true feelings could surface only after the storms of rage or regret blew itself out. Any interruption to that process would only confuse and delay the process. Some distraction may provide a relief but the debate must come to its logical conclusion from within. Azad was in that muted debate with himself.

His mind went back to his youth at the cantonment in Ahmadabad. He had been through this before but today he stood erect with his arguments and the Lord would have to convince him that the Pakistani guards were misleading him. He needed a powerful lighthouse to remain homed in.

'Did my friends at school and college taunt me about being a Muslim? In fact my best friends were Hindu boys. My wrestling coach was a fine Hindu. He would take special care of me and show me grips and throws that he did not share with all. The crowds would cheer me at the matches. They never treated me as an outcast. My father used to tailor uniforms and clothes for all those Hindu officers and their families. They were always in praise and behaved more like friends than customers. Did we feel insecure during communal riots in the past? Our neighbors were Hindus and always had a kind word or assured us that they would not let any miscreants enter our* *premises. Was I treated differently from the other soldiers in the Battalion? The colonel and other officers and men were proud of me. I was the champion of the Regiment. They would carry me from the ring on their shoulders. The cheers are still loud in my head. And in fact the Major sahib had not wanted me to go on patrol on that ill-fated night. The area was mined and he did not want to lose me. There had been an argument and I had managed to convince the Major that I would be fine. Poor fellow, the Colonel will never forgive him for losing me like that at night but it was my fault. I had suspected the presence of the enemy and wanted to get at them. It was not their fault that I got lost in the dunes. We had been cautioned to stay close. I had wanted to get my sights on the enemy patrol but it is unfortunate that they got me first. My officers did not abandon me or ever gave me the feeling that I could be sacrificed. There was no one who could be sacrificed. Just the previous night we had fought off the enemy and over ran their bunkers together. We had been brothers side by side in the blood soaked sand and anyone of us could have taken a bullet.'*

*'Then why are they killing and looting Moslems in Ahmadabad? Who are these people? Don't they know that even Muslim soldiers have given their life for India? Did not my father decide to stay back in India in spite of all those promises that Jinnah made to the Moslems? We were never involved in any communal hate campaigns or action. Diwali and Holi are Hindu festivals that we truly enjoyed with all our friends. Will those friends protect my family now? Have they ever considered that I never got the opportunity to even see or hold my child? I wonder if it was a boy or a girl. I am not sure Ruhaina and the others will be safe this time. And am I going to remain a memory for you my wife while I am actually breathing here in captivity? I feel as though I am hiding away from you all. Ruhaina please forgive me for shattering all your dreams. Baba, you had not wanted me to join the phauj (armed forces). How could I not? From childhood we had heard about all the glorious victories that the Para Commandos had won. You always looked into my eyes in those powerful moments of gallantry. My greatest gift to you was to become a part of that dream. I had already joined the Para Commandos when I was in school. I used to be in those battles in all my dreams. Your stories always had happy endings. And I had carried the Regimental flag in every dream. Then why am I here? Oh Brother! You had promised to reach my people if they released you. I cannot believe that you didn't make it and are now no more; then take me away too or do something to protect my people. There has to be some way that we can all be free. I have to reach Ahmadabad soon. Brother, you had said that there was a road in the mountains into India and if you keep the Nanga Parbat to your left and head east, the border couldn't be more than a two day march. It is so many years*

and we had planned so many escapes but somehow it was always discovered and how can I forget the punishments thereafter. Maybe it is time for such punishment again. This time I may not come out alive from that underground hell. Let them drown me in that torture cell or maybe it is better to get shot escaping than stay in stagnant water for a week. Ruhaina, I will keep your face in my mind till my last breath. But I do not wish to die. I have to reach you and I think we had a son. He must be a young man of thirty, maybe married with children. I could be their grandfather? At fifty-one I am young for that but will have many stories to tell my grandchildren.'

'Why do they keep offering to release me? Does Subedar Abdul Kareem really believe that I will join the mujahideen and fight for the liberation of Kashmir? He hates me like a traitor. Nazir is not in favor but he says there were a lot of Sikh army deserters trained in the border towns who had fought as the Khalistani force for the liberation of Punjab. I have already refused to train or join the mujahideen. Could it be that now they may really allow me out of this camp to train these animals and also become part of that force? I am a Para Commando and can teach them many tactics. That makes me a traitor. I cannot do that and leave behind this disgrace for Ruhaina and Baba. What if they make me train them and then kill me? I could escape before they do that. But they may not accept my services now. It has been very long since they last made me that offer. How will I explain all this to Colonel Sunderam and what will the others think of me? We have all suffered together for all these years and even they have families in India. If they can suffer, why am I making plans to escape by becoming a traitor? Can I sit here while Moslems and my family are being murdered in daylight? Will I ever forgive myself if something happens to Ruhaina and my child? I will escape and also fight tooth and nail to liberate Colonel Sunderam and the others. I will come back here and free them if the government cannot. Allah, give me the strength to overcome my doubts and let me take the first step. I do not wish to take revenge against Hindus. Just help me to get out of here and reach my family so that I can protect or perish with them. The root cause of all that has happened in our lives is this Hindu, Muslim divide and India and Pakistan. How can I change that? I am sure there are many Pakistanis like Nazir that realize the futility of all these wars between the two nations. Their habits and thoughts are so much like ours.'

'Then why can't we become one nation again? Colonel Sunderam feels that this is possible but will require a very strong yet considerate leader on both sides to carry their own people along. To become strong he may have to be harsh and in that process guard against becoming hard, forgetting the basic element of concern and kindness. And he also says that if the people are allowed to interact; the momentum of their understanding, realizations of *bygone follies and longing for a revival of suppressed common culture can strengthen the hands of leaders to take a bold stand to overcome any kind of opposition to a reunification. I have to live to see this and want to be with you Ruhaina when it happens.*

His lighthouse and dock was always Ruhaina.

Evenings were the time for any discussion between Colonel Sunderam and the few that were left. The guards were more relaxed and would not be listening. Azad had not approached him throughout the afternoon. He sat on the floor in prayer and thoughts. He would do this often and it did not look very unusual to the others. They were just four of them left after Brother had been taken away. Only the Colonel had noticed that Azad had been summoned aside by the guards, before lunch. He would wait for Azad to come. The sun dipped behind the rugged western hills. The twilight always gave a sense of secrecy to the inmates and they became bolder to talk about subjects that could easily excite a negative response from the guards.

Azad glanced at Major Ganguly. He was a good painter and was working on a canvas with snowcapped mountains and a herd of mountain goats grazing on the lower slopes. The goats had the freedom that he had lost. Ganguly was a cavalry officer and he had painted the battle scene of his capture. It was now in a makeshift frame and hung on his wall. It was a miracle that he had survived a direct hit and crawled out of his burning tank only to find himself facing a Pakistani officer's pistol. He was tied to the enemy tank man's turret and taken home as some prize of war. He had prayed for an air strike but it never came. His paintings and sketches were his survival. The Camp Commandant and some guards had even bought his sketches and paintings. Ganguly would always buy some sweets or biscuits for the others with such earnings, that he called prize money. He had also given a loan to Fatima the camp sweeperess.

Lieutenant Pawri, across the cell from Azad, sat by his window side table, looking for any discoloration in the medicine bottles that had been allowed to him for the common ailments of fellow prisoners. His convoy had been ambushed in the Uri sector and he had stayed with the wounded. Recovery troops had not reached by sunset. The Pakistanis had encircled them at night and that had been the end of Pawri's short career as a doctor in the Army. The only son of Dr Sohrab Pawri, he had joined on a short service commission and after the war would have gone back to his hometown at Nasik. They had decided to take him prisoner to treat Pakistani casualties. The Indian wounded had been left behind on the roadside in the bitter cold. He had overheard the argument between Pakistani officers that it would be a big risk to release him. He would get back and give away their position and supply routes. So Pawri remained a prisoner; yet in the true traditions of a military doctor— never hesitated to treat enemy soldiers. There was always a short supply of good doctors so he had been shifted from camp to camp treating Indian PoWs or the enemy casualties alike. The earlier Commandant and Subedar Abdul Kareem hated him. He had seen too much and could not be released. He was not permitted any further treatment facilities in this camp. Like many of the camps there was no prison doctor here so Pawri had waited and won over the new Commandant to allow him to treat everyone. He had helped save at least two guards from bad attacks of dysentery. The last three years had seen him set up a small dispensary in the camp. The new Commandant had even managed to get him a sterilizing unit and instruments to undertake minor operations. Pawri had however become a marked man. He had intervened and saved Fatima from being molested by one of the guards in the dispensary. It had been late in the evening and Pawri had suspected something amiss because Fatima would always come to their dormitory cell before leaving for the day and ask him to inspect the dispensary for cleanliness. Today she had not come till much after sunset, so Pawri had gone to inspect. She was deaf and dumb. Pawri had physically intervened and struck the rapist soldier from behind, just as he was about to ravish her. At the trial the Commandant had believed Pawri's version and it had resulted in severe punishment for the Pakistani guard. Subedar Kareem had protested but the Commandant had been firm. Abdul Kareem had promised Pawri that his days were numbered after the departure of Colonel Rahim. It had not bothered Pawri. Fatima had then gravitated towards him. He had developed a special sympathy for her. Feelings travel and he was amazed that they needed only eye contact to communicate emotions. He always had some humor going in the camp. Soldiers everywhere always regarded a doctor as special. He could save them a lot of pain and this camp was in a far removed remote place. He was only forty-eight years old but they called him Pawri Baba. Even Subedar Kareem may need his help someday. Pawri had no doubts that he would do his best even for the vile Subedar.

Azad wondered as he looked at all of them in turn. Pawri and he were about the same age. Ganguly, a few years ahead and Colonel Sunderam was touching sixty-five. Were they all destined to die here? Not he. Brother had been a good friend. Was he is still alive and where could he be? He was very sick when they took him away. He must have died in some hospital. Azad's insides churned as he remembered Brother's songs and the descriptions he had given of life in his mother's home and the narrow street they lived on. His parents would never know that he had talked so highly of them. I will find out his house and tell them. I have to escape.

'How do I approach Colonel Sunderam and tell him that I am going to offer my services to the enemy for training the mujahideen? How do I explain to him that it is my subsequent plan to make a bid to escape from their training camp? He will be livid. How do I have this discussion without Ganguly and Pawri knowing? If Sunderam agrees, my going away must look as though they were shifting me to some other prison. No one must get to know my escape plan or I could be dead. And after my escape, I will have to convince the Indian Army that I have escaped from an enemy prison after so many years and that there are still three of my comrades left behind and who knows – more in other camps? If the Indian Army gets to know that I trained the mujahideen – I could be punished with further imprisonment. Would they shoot me in a firing squad? There is no war on now so I cannot be declared a traitor or deserter in active service during operations. What will happen – will they have a trial? I can handle that as long as no one knows about my involvement with the mujahideen. It will be such a disgrace. If I do get free – Sunderam will know about my involvement with the mujahideen. He is a good man. I have to tell him all the truth. He will understand. Trusting him could be the final word to exonerate me and then there will be nothing between us Ruhaina. There is no assurance that the guards will not talk about me becoming a traitor. Ganguly and Pawri will never believe them but it will be strange for them. Ya Allah, it is a long route and there are risks but that is better than rotting here. I wonder how things are in Ahmadabad after these riots. Am I too late? Will they be all right when I reach Ahmadabad. Allah, please protect Ruhaina and forgive me for the wrongs that I am compelled into. The intention is not to help the enemy or anyone. I am not a traitor and only want to be back with my family and return to India.'

Azad waited for what seemed like eternity after the lights were put out. There was only one light permitted in the adjacent toilet for the prisoners. Sitting in his bed he could hear Major Ganguly's steady snore and Pawri also seemed to be asleep. Colonel Sunderam was a light sleeper and he had shifted sides a few times. This was Azad's only opportunity.

'It may all become impossible if Col. Sunderam thinks it too risky or dangerous for the others. I will still go ahead. I cannot continue being a spectator to the butchery at home. I will tell him but still do what I think I have to. Allah, you are my guide, help me please. I have to get out.'

'Sir, it is me, Azad.' He had touched the Colonel lightly on the shoulder and realized from the response that he was awake.

'Yes son, what is it.'

'Can we talk?'

'Is it about today, with the guards; did they brainwash you?'

'Can we go to the toilet and talk. I have a plan to discuss sir.'

'Can we not talk in the morning?'

'No sir, I cannot let the others know about this. What I will tell you is only for you sir.' There was silent urgency in what he said. For a few moments they could hear each other's breathing. The Colonel sensed that this was not going to be easy. In all his years in service and as a prisoner, he had been loyal to his subordinates and to the traditions of what he had learnt as a cadet in training. Here was another subordinate that probably needed a hearing and support. He would help as it applied to the situation. Azad on his part assumed a calm. He had set the wheels rolling and knew there was no looking back now. It was like all the ammunition was over and the "fix bayonets" order had been passed. He was ready to charge forward. Azad moved towards the toilet and waited for the Colonel to follow. The Colonel was very proper. He had his toothbrush and paste in hand as he came into the dimly lit toilet. It was the first thing he would do getting out of bed. The time never mattered. They smiled at each other and Azad knew he would have to wait for the Colonel to finish his brushing. It gave him some more time to backtrack along the dusty route that had blinded him the whole day.

Colonel Sunderam had looked Azad in the eye and heard out the whispered plan. He had seen the same look in many a soldier's eye. These were simple sons of the soil and once they had made up their mind to be absent without leave; nothing short of physical confinement could prevent them from taking off. Locking them up would only strengthen their resolve. He secretly admired Azad's determination to face the dangers that were imminent. There were no detailed explanations. Azad had requested his silence from telling anyone.

Azad would break a prison rule to be taken away and there would be no explanation.

' If you do manage to get us freed, are you aware that we will all face a court martial as a standard procedure.'

'Yes, I know about it Colonel sir.'

'Azad what will you expect me to say if I am asked about your escape from here and your association with the mujahideen?'

'I do not expect you to tell any untruths for me sir. I am only requesting that you should not tell Major Ganguly and Pawri or the Pakistanis that you know my plan, till you are all free. You can tell the court-martial that I conspired with you? Or don't if it endangers you sir. I leave it to your judgment sir.'

'You can be sure that I will speak fearlessly, Azad. Frankly I don't think the Pakistanis will even consider your offer. The security measures here to prevent an escape will increase. There is also just a chance that they may make you some other stupid offers. Be prepared and careful.'

'The communal situation in India is enough reason for them to accept my offer to join the mujahideen for revenge against the Hindus sir.'

'I wish you luck. And there is every possibility that they will kill you at the slightest excuse.'

'That will not be easy for them but I am prepared for that too sir.' Blood rushed into his eyes.

'You are brave but don't be stupid. You have my best wishes. And I have some suggestions.'

'Yes sir.'

'It will be better for you to tell the Indian authorities the entire truth, including your involvement with the mujahideen. They will understand. You know that I will speak the truth if ever I am freed: so it will all get known. And if we are not freed for any reason, I will take it that you did not make it alive to India. So you still retain the choice to decide whether you wish to get us freed or want your secret to die with us here. Lastly, there will be many opportunities to escape. Most of them will be traps. Your best bet is to do the unexpected. It may appear impossible and stupid. That will be your best opportunity. But it may not be the safest.'

A Hindu and Muslim soldier shook hands and embraced in the dim light of a Pakistani prison. Dawn was not far away. Colonel Sunderam prayed that Azad would not succumb to the pain he would experience with Pakistanis outside these prison walls or retaliate foolishly due to the self-consuming guilt of training the mujahideen. He had known Azad for over seven years in this prison and the Naik had come through well after the humiliating punishments for attempting to escape.

The Para commandos were a tough arrogant breed.

Azad fell into a peaceful sleep. He had crossed the biggest hurdle. Colonel Sunderam was like a father and he had never had to conspire with him. It needed blind trust. Sunderam generated lots of it. Hindus were not all 'Muslim haters and killers'. Even Pakistanis were not all enemies. It had taken almost a lifetime to experience Pakistanis. He would find friends out there, he was sure. They would assist him to reach India. And he would tell the whole truth. Someday. His grandchildren would build a truly secular sub-continent.

# Chapter IX

Two trolleys serviced Judge Sudhin Choudhury's breakfast table. One had consumables placed in bone china plates, shapely wide mouthed jars and bowls of different sizes. Fruits were a very essential diet content in this manor. Watching the judge cutting into an apple to make evenly sized slices or peeling a golden mango and then carving it into comfortable cubes was an exposure to concentration in slow motion. He would automatically reach for a specific knife for the fruit before engaging into a discussion that demanded deliberate thoughts to be worded. Thoughts became precise expressions almost in tune with the pieces of fruit as they were shaped. The other smaller trolley had newspapers, magazines, printed papers in clips and his dominating briefcase. He could alternate his attention from the fruit to read a well-folded newspaper article or the foolscap brief for the day's cases without much loss in the quality of fruit carving. Smita had been his bouncing board for a long time and these were the occasions that made the mother glow with visible pride. The judge would always be out voted whenever a consensus was required. Nikhil would join father and daughter for breakfast a little later. This gap provided the few morning minutes required explicitly for cryptic professional exchanges and also familial bonding.

'The police chief had called; they have got the van that had brought the attacking mob to Basheer Khan's shop. It was abandoned in a hurry not very far from the shop and fortunately there was no harm to any of the girls working for Basheer.' The judge looked for a favorable response.

Smita was visibly overjoyed. 'Have they apprehended the attackers? How are we so sure that the women were not harmed?'

'The van was a stolen one, so there were no arrests.'

It was Smita's turn to scorn. 'I had expected that and also am quite sure there are no eye witnesses.'

'Your conclusions in riot cases is remarkable.'

'So this is one more dead end case where the criminals have got away in broad daylight.'

'It is not over; they will look for clues and maybe make arrests at a later date.'

Smita looked determined. 'I will visit the police station and find out whatever I can. They have to take some action on the complaint that I have lodged on behalf of Basheer. I will be visiting the nursing home after the police station and then be in the court. My assistant has got two cases from Muslim victims of the riots.'

'Do they have any witnesses?'

She looked at him and said, 'Unlike your days lawyers now have to work to get some real witnesses and protect them also.'

'You have my best wishes and blessings.' The judge had the last word.

Nikhil had learnt to stay at the edge of these discussions. His attention would be more occupied and amused by the gentle sparring between father and daughter. His only visible involvement would be to offer subdued smiles to both of them. He had mastered the art of not getting baited into offering support or criticism. He would be more concerned that Smita left for work in a balanced state of mind. And he also knew the art of diverting the attention of both father and daughter without making it too obvious. Today he could sense a calm. Smita had not retaliated about the police not making any arrests of Basheer's attackers. The morning had been refreshing for both and the day begun gently with his mind still lingering on in the fragrance of total bonding. He remembered that he was to return home early.

Smita did not have an easy day ahead. It was four days after Basheer had been admitted to the nursing home. He had not wanted any plastic surgery for the wounds on his face and was also reluctant for surgery required to set his fingers correctly. He had stab wounds and there were multiple fractures on both hands but he had only said, 'Let these remain as they are, Allah will set them right and it will help remind me to struggle against the social discrimination. If He does not wish them to work again, I will know.' Ruhaina had not known how to cope with it other than pleading with him to take the doctor's advice. Smita had tried in her own persuasive way that used to bring positive responses from him in the past. Basheer was not one who accepted any favors. He was more concerned about the women that worked for him. He would ask about them everyday. Today Smita had a lot of things to tell him and she could hardly wait.

*How does one emote or comfort a person recovering from wounds, almost beaten to death during communal violence? Violence generated by your own community. You are a Hindu and your childhood friend; a Muslim is lying in a nursing home with his body and soul battered. He was also your first brush with romance. Both of you have no communal qualms. You love the presence of flowers in your surroundings and want them for him. The hospital attracts flowers. Those are for the sick to get well. But they also bring in a fresh breath of life to heal. And then they wither. Fresh flowers replace dying ones. More freshness is brought in. Flowers are also placed as a mark of respect for the dead. And flowers celebrate the arrival of a newborn. They speak a language using colors; universally accepted for so many messages. Can it heal the wounds of a physically damaged and mentally humiliated friend? Flowers wouldn't make a very pleasant apology here. Through the pains, it may bring in hope but it does not soothe the innermost that has been permanently scarred. Smita had decided on taking some roses for Basheer. His spirit needed a silent reminder that people cared and understood his anguish. He would never be alone. She would be his flower today and leave some of herself behind in the bunch of roses for his spirit to rediscover the colors. Flowers from her could do that? Yes. And she had something to say that may pain or soothe him or both but she felt it would have the effect of extricating him from the withdrawal that was setting in.*

Smita watched the streets for signs. It was devastating. A tornado like force had ripped through the city and left behind debris without any pattern. It was just strewn around as though the wind had changed directions rapidly and finally escaped upwards into the clouds. The police station in charge had shown her the progress on the First Information Report complaint that she had lodged. It had the blasé remark: 'Under Investigation'. They had shown her the signatures of about eleven women who had been rescued from an abandoned van. The names were of Muslim women. The policeman gave her a look that was meant to convey; *'we have taken adequate action on your complaint; please be reconciled.'* She had wanted a copy of the document with their signatures but that could not be given under the pretext of requirement of a court order. There had been some argument when she took out her diary and made note of the names. Fortunately, one of the senior policemen had recognized her as the 'Judges' daughter. She was allowed to make the list. The bile had arisen but Smita kept her calm; secretly satisfied that the women had been rescued and at least the signatures and thumb impressions had the appearance of genuineness. It would bring some respite to Basheer. He had frequently asked her and Ruhaina about them and had looked away to avoid their silence and his guilt.

Clutching her multicolored bunch of roses she walked up the stairs of the nursing home. She looked supple in white. White softened some of the sharpness of her poise and glowing eyes. It was Basheer's favorite color. The salwar suit was perfectly tailored and had the light green collar tag with "Kasims" embroidered on it in gold. Her trousseau had a lot of clothes with that tag. It never failed to divert her thoughts into the past. There were two policemen with communication sets at the entrance of the nursing home. Protection was provided on request by the "Judge". She saw a man in Army uniform at the reception counter. He was in conversation with the nurse on duty who showed immediate relief on seeing Smita.

'This soldier has come from the army cantonment with a message for the patient, Basheer.' It was in a brown envelope.

Smita took the envelope and opened it to read.

Dear Basheer Khan it read. Is it possible to meet you or any of your relatives, as I have some important information for you? A Major Dilip had signed it.

Smita in her typical lawyer's mask looked at the soldier and asked him about Major Dilip, listening, while scribbling her own telephone number on a piece of paper.

She said, 'Please ask Major Dilip to call me on this telephone number after three in the afternoon? And also kindly give me his number so that I can call him when I am free.'

The soldier gave her a number, took her telephone number and saluted leaving the way he had come. Smita read the note again. It was just one line but when she looked up to see the soldier, he had gone. What information could it be? She had heard about Major Dilip from Basheer and wanted to meet him and express her deep gratitude that he had saved his life. He was also an eyewitness to all the happenings. She would need him soon. The message had broken her chain of thought linked to Basheer. She was here today on a personal mission but information about Basheer's team of women workers being rescued and Major Dilip were distracting her.

Looking around for help she found a nurse. 'Sister is he awake. Can you arrange for a flower vase in his room.'

'Of course madam.'

Smita entered Basheer's room. The windows had plain off white curtains that filtered away real light. It gave the room a bit of an ethereal feeling. Not dim but not too bright either. In the filtered light one could miss the faint lines or expressions on a face that leathers in sudden self-control. For someone from the dazzling harsh world it had the effect of calm. But for someone who was cocooned in this abstract lullaby; the entrance of someone from outside was like being jarred into realities. Basheer was facing the window curtains in a half reclined propped up position.

Smita entered and called to him. 'I hope I am not disturbing you.'

Basheer turned slowly and as always had a smile for her. His face was bandaged but his eyes conveyed the joy at seeing her and then the surprise at the flowers. Surprise waned to resignation. His eyes always did more of the talking.

Smita arranged the flowers on a table in the corner of the room. 'Can you see them here?'

He could see it all the time but they were out of his reach. To touch them he would have to step out of bed and walk. He had not shown much enthusiasm in his treatment. It would take effort to walk.

'So Basheer, I am told that your operation is fixed for the day after. How are you feeling?'

He mumbled slowly through the bandages. ' There is no need for the surgery. I am feeling better and my fingers will get reset on their own.'

'That could happen but it will take very long and then there is a possibility that you may have to forget doing embroidery work that Kasim's Clothiers are famous for.'

Basheer drifted further away. 'My work must have made someone jealous. Why else would they break my fingers? They could have killed me anyway but they did not. The shop is destroyed Smita. The girls who worked for me have also been destroyed. Their lives are over now. What use are my fingers now? Embroidery will only keep reminding me of their ill luck to be working with me.'

Smita pulled her chair close to his bedside. Leaning forward with urgency she said, 'the girls have been found! All eleven are safe. The police found the van abandoned. They could not make any arrests but here, I have noted the names of the girls.' She took out her diary to show him. Basheer just stared at her and something from deep inside arose, choking his very breath. It was pain mixed with disbelief and gratitude. Allah had been merciful.

'*Is she giving me false hopes?*' He saw every name and recalled their faces through cloudy eyes as they cried for mercy and then his tears trickled slowly. They looked at each other and she nodded that it was true. The girls were safe.

'The girls have signed on the paper in the police station saying that they have not been harmed. Some are just thumb impressions but I have seen it with my own eyes. The police are investigating and will make arrests soon. I will fight your case and they will be punished and fined. We will get your shop completely repaired with the compensation Basheer; I don't wish to tailor my clothes at any other place than Kasim's. What I am wearing today was made by you, do you remember?'

He shifted his hand and placed it in hers and then gently withdrew. The touch had flashed its message; he would relent for the surgery and his wonderful fingers would weave even more beautiful patterns. 'You can withdraw your complaint. I do not wish to fight any case in the courts. Allah had wanted this punishment for me. My shop was to be destroyed so that I could build it again. This is my life's mission, to keep my father and grandfather's memory. By punishing them, nothing can be built. It will only transfer my pain onto them. Let the pain end here with me.'

'And Smita, do you remember those lines from Tagore? Remember, it went,

'Where the mind is led forward by Thee,
Into ever-widening thought and action...'

Basheer turned away abruptly silent and sighed in the painfully true irony of the verse. Touched deeply, she recalled, hesitated and recited it for him .........

'Into that heaven of freedom,
My Father let my country awake.'

And wiped a tear before Basheer could see it. Past memories and hopes collided to become a logjam in her throat.

*Basheer was humiliated for no offence than being a Muslim. The fear of*

*those moments and the helplessness along with thoughts that erupted into pain and regret would haunt forever. Was it a sin to be a Muslim in India?*

Basheer's eyes were saying, 'I have to be magnanimous and forgive my unknown assailants. I accept this act as the will of God. I have to be resilient and climb out of the ruins. I will pick up my flag and fly it for the day that it may also be honored.'

*Perhaps it would give him strength to be fearless in the future. There are few like him but their minimal numbers is adequate. The warmth of these few could incubate the seeds of secularism for another day. It is the others that will rage in silence and wait for opportunities of revenge that will finally turn around and fatally sting them; they will remain captive to hate.*

*A train compartment of Hindu devotees converted into an unbelievable flaming trap. What devilry could plan such action? What offence had the devotees committed? And then the frenzied revenge against innocent Muslims. Such negative energies only spawn Godhras, New Yorks, Munichs and worse. Fearless of the state law systems, some are arrested and many escape. They have raped the very system of democracy that has nurtured them. Latent rapists have always lurked on the face of the earth. Cannot all of technology, science, literature, art, education, humane feelings and love cure these violators? It can, but first there has to be forgiveness and unconditional understandings followed by other process. Not futilely impossible, it needs time and Godly leadership. Hard to come by.*

"We have no time to stand and stare.
In this life so full of care, with leaders in a constant scare".

*Everyone will not be forgiving like Basheer. Some Muslims would. Some criminals will escape the reach of the law. They will get back to their daily life. Systematically convincing their conscience that what they did was honorable for their religion, for their political party, for the country. And they will visit temples or mosques to offer prayers and seek blessings. Death will come to them also. Their punishment is their own slow cancer of a nagging conscience. Ceasing to breathe will be their deliverance. Perhaps the universal and secular God will have forgiven them for they knew not. It is not too late for them. Did not the great Emperor Ashoka give up war and violence after the battle of Kalinga?*

'Basheer, you may forgive those that have caused you this grief. But if the law catches up, let it deal with them. Allow me to fight your case if the situation arises and you may then withdraw your case by forgiving them in court. I will not pressurize you to change your stance then.'

Basheer could see the difference in their approach to this situation. She had always been very righteous. He nodded and lowered his eyes in agreement. They looked at each other for a few moments before Smita broke the silence. Those few moments were like the watering of souls. It had been over ten years since they had met on emotionally irrigated fields.

' Basheer, I have to tell you. Your Ammi worries for you. Are you not going to marry? Will you not give her the pleasure of grandchildren?' Basheer turned his head slowly towards her and their eyes met. He was asking a silent question in reply.

And she replied. 'Look at me; with all the comforts and love in my life, I still don't and cannot have children. Maybe this is the pain I have to carry.' Basheer listened but closed his eyes to make it easier for her to speak. It was like this even when they were in college. His eyes always spoke. In pain they would remain closed.

'I always feel that I have let you down because you had wanted to marry me. I have never told you about the pain that even I went through by giving in to my parent's wishes.'

Basheer opened his eyes and looked at her and then slowly turned his head away towards the refuge of the windows. His one glance conveyed that he had known her traumas.

'I am happily married and Nikhil is a very nice man. I still think of you often because those were very happy days and they will always stay with me. I want you to understand that I still care for you and want to see you happy. You never came to my wedding reception and I understand your feelings. You are very present in my life Basheer so forgive me if I have hurt you because I could not do otherwise then.'

Basheer lifted his hand and she took it. Through the bandages fingertips met and held. He turned towards her and his eyes smiled and he spoke, ' you have not hurt me ever. It is my fate that I am born a Muslim and am proud of it Smita. I have not married because I am happy this way. My best companion is my work. I share my affections with you whenever you give me your tailoring work. Your work makes me strive for better quality and it has uplifted me in many ways. My only concern is that Ammi keeps waiting for Baba. I wish to wait with her.'

'I can understand that. I have lots of tailoring work for you. You will undergo the surgery and get well?' He nodded and agreed with his eyes.

They had knowing smiles in their eyes now. It was reminiscent of their youthful gambols. She had remained captive to some of her unexpressed feelings and had taken the opportunity to release it today. A load suddenly lifted off her. He had heard and shared his genuine thoughts with her. A new bonding was welded. What was amazing is that they could respond instinctively to each other even after all those years. It was love on a different plane. And they had not shared it for ten years. Both had traveled on separate roads only passing each other at the crossings.

*Hindus and Muslims will continue their travels on roads towards destiny. If they remember to be humane or secular: they could also meet at the junctions or roadblocks. A wall or fence that can dam the power of human love, understanding and truths is yet to be built. What we face now is a maze of barbed wire fences that keeps us from reaching home. We are still captive to throwing the dice of our inheritance for the jackpot of our future. It will wear out and some simple events and words may renew old bonding. There is hope. After all it takes planets and some rare eclipses so many years for a return to be viewed again. India and Pakistan or Hindus and Muslims are much closer and have many more opportunities than planetary movements can afford, light years away, to come together at least in spirit. Even Pakistan has an inheritance that surely has its ulcers and craters. It is futile to blame the clergy, the opportunist politician, the Hindus or the western world for their continued apprehension and aggression on the Islamic. Forgiveness and acceptance by everyone will have a price. Are we willing to foot that bill?*

There was sudden lightheaded freshness in the nursing home room. The flowers suddenly came alive. It was just opportunity and simple expressions of the heart that gave them both wings to soar higher and fly on. ' Should I tell the doctors that you will be ready for the surgery in two days?'

'Provided I get some fresh tailoring orders from you Smita.' He smiled.

'Oh! You have a lifetime contract Basheer,' she laughed.

He nodded with a weak gesture.

'I will leave you now Basheer bhai and maybe bring Ammi in the evening. I have to be in the court in fifteen minutes. Oh! There is a message from Major Dilip to you. He has some important information to give you. Should I speak to him? Maybe it is something to do with the attack on your shop. I will call him up and let you know.'

He agreed with his eyes. She was always in command. It felt familiar. He liked to drift into their youthful cavorting in a make believe. It had helped him to keep moving on but then the frequency of those dreams had reduced. For many years now he had stopped going into those memory lanes as it sometimes left him chastised for self-indulgence. Today's bonding was a new sunrise. He had all along known that Smita had cared. Yet her plain submission had quenched his thirst for what had stayed out of his reach. He had only wanted to hear a few words from Smita. It made him feel very light again. He could fly freely and she was already airborne. He was released from his own shackles. They were both free.

# Chapter X

The Ahmadabad cantonment houses an Army Divisional Head quarters. Brother sat under a tree, outside the room given to him by the Indian army unit for his stay in the city. He had shown them his retired officer's identity card and it had been his passport to some privileges. Permission was granted to stay in the Officers' Mess. The room given to him was in a little more dilapidated state than the new main block. The main block was an epitome of cleanliness. Retired officers sometimes get second preference. The mess comprised of an anteroom, the dining hall and a plush bar. He had seen traces of British tradition in the bar. A newspaper on his lap, he recalled the Air force officers' mess at Halwara during the war. Somehow all messes had peculiar warmth. It was after all the home of bachelor officers.

He now recollected the events of the last two days, waiting for a message from the Adjutant's office. It could be a memorable day.

He had traveled all over India in his air force days. Ahmadabad, he knew was like any other big city in India. It was a textile manufacturing and trading hub. In the last one week it had hit the headlines for unprecedented ethnic violence. He was traveling light. Just one suitcase carrying some clothes and a book was adequate he thought. Coming out of the railway station had not been easy. The platforms were overcrowded with people trying to catch trains out of the burning city. From their garb most of the people looked like Moslems. It had surprised him to see refugees in peacetime huddled together or rushing to somewhere with fear on their faces. It was full of policemen and some army soldiers as well. Women constables were supervising a long queue. It was one for free food being provided by some charitable organization. That had been a welcome sight but the people in the queue seemed to be scuffling among themselves. Like a pecking order; there was some shuffling going on. The elderly and ladies with small children were being given preference and moved up the queue while those that got relegated; expressed discontent. There was one man with his head heavily bandaged and Brother could not take his eyes away from the red stains. In the process of moving on slowly Brother was jostled around and it suddenly felt as though the crowds would swallow him in their motion. It became a jarring entry to the city. Brother had worked his way through it all and finally hailed a motor cab to take him to the army cantonment. Bombay Central had been so different.

He was beginning his search at last. The crowds at the station and the whole atmosphere had left him wondering if he would ever find his way around at all. The newspaper clipping was safely folded in his shirt pocket. It was like a reference map for his search but was quite abrupt. There were no meaningful names of anyone in it. Would it be better if he went to the newspaper office or the local army authorities? There were moments when he wanted to go back from the station itself but just the one possibility that he may find Azad's family drew him deeper into the mire. On the way he had observed that some shops were completely gutted by fire and surprisingly the very next shop was left untouched. The driver had explained that the destroyed shops belonged to Muslims. He had never experienced something like this. The discrimination however brought memories of Azad Khan being singled out in prison for insult and rebuke by the Pakistani guards. Pakistani Muslims discriminating with an Indian Muslim? And now here again Muslims singled out for destruction. In the armed forces one was quite protected from upheavals and discriminations like this but then you were also exposed to a few things that only soldiers were meant to face.

The driver was a good conversationist. 'Where do you come from and why? What do you do for a living? Where will you get off at the cantonment? It is quite a spread out area. Why do you look so worried? This city has seen so many communal upheavals. This one will also pass. Such events don't allow us to make a decent earning.'

'I am shocked at your casual attitude about these communal misgivings and am visiting a friend and once we get there I think I will recognize the place. It is after a long time that I come here. Now that I am free I have lots of time to go visiting.'

'Wrong time to come here sir. You should always come before Diwali. Do you know the festival of Navratri?'

'Yes but I am Christian.'

'Oh I know Christians here too and in Ahmadabad everyone enjoys during Navratri. Are you married with children?' Brother had laughed at the irony of the last question. He hoped the questions would end but the driver must not have had any customers the last few days so he chatted along incessantly.

'Married? I never felt the need to marry.'

That had taken the driver by surprise but he had laughed and said, 'Muslims can marry four times,' and then there was silence. Thereafter he kept looking at Brother through the rear view mirror. Brother did not miss the frequent looks. Playing a silent game with strangers had got embedded in his character. It was fun, like baiting the prison guards in Pakistan.

He recognized the cantonment area (they were alike all over India) and on impulse had asked the driver to drive him around to show him the market area. The driver had stopped and asked him if he had some address to visit. Brother had replied that he was looking for a tailor's shop.

'Do you have some clothes to stitch or collect?'

'Yes, I have to collect some clothes for a friend,' Brother played on.

'What is the name of this tailoring shop. Do you have some bill or telephone number?'

'No, but I will recognize the place if I see it.'

They had driven around for half an hour and the driver suddenly reminded him that he would have to charge him extra for this tour. Brother had replied, 'please charge me by the meter,' and the driver had pulled up.

'By the meter was up to the cantonment but if you are going to take up my time and not pay me extra then you better let me go.'

'I will pay you extra but how much.'

'Hundred rupees for an hour.'

'Right, here is your hundred now drive slowly without speaking.'

Brother had surprised himself at this mute submission to the unreasonable demand of the driver. The driver had also felt strange that there had been no haggling or argument. He had then gone on to apologize that these were curfew days and he had to earn enough by sunset and it was always better for him to get as many fresh passengers than drive around slowly the way they were. Brother had allowed him to ramble. His eyes were searching for tailoring shops. The name of the shop was Kasim something. Azad had mentioned it at some point and he would know the moment he saw it but there were so many things he had said. Disappointment was already nagging at him. Maybe the name had been changed.

They had reached a street that was cordoned off by the police. He was asked the address of his destination and Brother reluctantly had no explanation other than, 'I am looking for a tailor's shop. I think it is a Muslim tailor's shop.'

The police inspector had brusquely replied. 'Don't you know this area does not have too many Muslims? Are you a Muslim? No one is allowed to enter this area unless you live here. There have been some nasty incidents here so if you are visiting then better wait for a few days and then come back. Are you a Muslim?'

'No I am not.'

The policeman laughed sarcastically, 'then why do you search for a Muslim?'

Brother had felt close to his objective but things were getting more difficult. His mind worked rapidly. Should he show the newspaper clipping to the policeman? Hesitatingly, 'I have a Muslim friend who is a tailor and lives here, I remember.'

'What is his name?'

'It is Azad Khan.'

The policeman shouted the name to his colleague who came out from a van and took a long look at Brother. He then looked at some papers that had names in it. 'There is no Azad Khan here. We have all the names of people here. He may have run away. Many have.'

'No he is not the kind to runaway, I can assure you but anyway do you know if there is a tailoring shop in this street? Azad Khan owns the shop.' Brother could sense the impatience grow in the policeman's attitude. He persisted. 'Please tell me if there is a tailor's shop that has been destroyed recently.'

It was met with, 'have you come to repair the shop?' There was laughter and Brother joined them. It had the effect of diffusing the situation.

The cab driver now grew impatient and said, 'I think you better let me go for in any case I will not enter that street.'

'Are you scared? I am with you.'

'Just who are you pray?'

'Okay I think you better take me to the army authorities and I will let you go.'

The driver immediately became apprehensive. 'Are you threatening to take me to task with the army? I am not scared. I have not done anything. Why are you threatening me?'

Brother reluctantly took out his retired armed forces officer's identity card and showed it to the driver and the policeman also had a look.

'So you are a retired officer.'

'Yes. Now can we go to the Army camp?'

The cab had slowly moved forward and doing a turn away from the market headed back the way it had come. *'Was the army feared or respected? How come this chatter box has suddenly piped down.'*

'You wish to be dropped at the army gate number one or two sir.'

'Any gate will do.' With that Brother had mentally resigned and waited to reach the army divisional head quarters.

'You must be getting pension sir.' Brother was in no mood to converse so he just gave yes or no answers to the fresh utterly respectful questions of the driver. Fortunately the distance was covered in less than five minutes. His mind was again reaching frustration levels. How would he find the officer who had saved the tailor's life? Was the newspaper clipping genuine or was this propaganda and a wild chase. *'No one seems to like questions and specially about some vague tailoring shop belonging to a Muslim. And I have to ask many, just to locate the shop or even the chivalrous army officer. Let me first get into the army camp. I have to work on this slowly. Let me get to the Officers' mess and I think the barman will help.'* Barmen in the armed forces usually had all the news.

Entry into the military camp was not quite difficult. He had to explain the purpose of his visit on the telephone and the officer at the other end had been very courteous. Brother was visiting some friends in Ahmadabad and needed a place to stay for a week. He had decided that the newspaper-clipping story would be too jarring for starters and specially on the phone. So the fabrication of "visiting friends" was a ploy to get in. The driver had waited for Brother while he showed his identity card and entered his name in a register with the gate guards. They recognized his rank and saluted him as he left. Brother was quick to return it. He suddenly felt at home. Even the driver had suddenly got out of the cab to hold the door open for him. They smiled at each other. Brother appreciated courteous behavior.

At the mess, the Subedar was respectful but had no intimation of his arrival. He had to call his officer to confirm before allotting a room to Brother. During the wait Brother had taken in the well-manicured garden and the polished furniture. There were wall photo-frames of generals, sporting events and a tabloid with the names of war heroes on the wall. The Mess Subedar had beckoned him to the phone and the same officer was online. Brother had just spoken to him from the entrance gate. He was the unit adjutant.

'I am extremely sorry that you have had to wait but we are having a busy time so I could not inform the mess in time.'

'That is perfectly all right. Is it possible to come and meet you?'

'What is it about?'

'Something personal sir,' Brother added with respectful appeal.

'I am Captain Jamwal and am busy the whole day today but maybe we can meet at the mess bar in the evening?'

'Oh! That will be a privilege Captain.'

'Then, is eight o'clock fine?'

'Sure sir, anytime is okay with me.' Brother felt a lot of hope compared to the dead end at the police blockade in the market. The opportunity to meet in a casual atmosphere was unexpected and certainly welcome.

The day had been uneventful till the meeting at the bar. Brother had just stayed in and caught up with reading Leon Uris' Exodus. There were not many officers in the mess during the lunch hour. The waiter had said, ' they are all at some exercise and will be back in the evening.' Most of the noon had been spent pacing in the room and then he would go outside and walk impatiently in the area outside. It was pleasant and far removed from the chaos he had experienced in the morning. (All military camps had this tucked away ambience. And the surroundings were always so clean and orderly. You could identify the start and finishing line of a camp because the area just after it became noticeably dull and shabby with strange odors). The officers' mess quarters seemed so distant from reality that at times he felt cut off. It did help in his recapitulation of conversations with Azad. He would have to repeat all about the PoW camp to the family. He had explained so many things to the army authorities at the sub area head quarters in Bombay. They had found it hard to believe and offered help but nothing had happened in the last two years. He now even wondered about Azad and his well being. Anything was possible at the prison camp. Urgency had suddenly grown with emptiness in his stomach and he couldn't wait for the evening in the bar. Thoughts were the wild horses pulling him in all directions. He needed to collect himself.

Dressed in a shirt and tie Brother had walked into the bar well before time. He had ordered a glass of orange juice and asked the bar man to introduce him to Captain Jamwal as he was new here. It was Brother's turn to shoot questions. Amused at his own behavior now he recalled the cab driver's curiosity. The barman was a much better listener with a smile compared to his recent acquaintance— the cab driver. *(Barmen all over the armed forces are the ones who are witness to officers coming and going from a station. They get the opportunity to talk with all visitors. And they know a lot more than they often should simply because they stand like deaf mutes but monitor every bit of conversation between visitors. Yes you could say it is something of a concern. But they generally do not carry tales. Something akin to a professional code.).*

'Is there a market nearby to this camp?'

'Yes sir, it is called civil lines.'

'I believe it is closed these days.'

'It is not closed because I live there sir.'

'Are there good tailoring shops there?'

'Yes there are many tailoring shops around this area. What do you wish to tailor sir?'

'Nothing, I am just looking for a tailoring shop that was destroyed during the recent riots.'

'Many shops have been destroyed and most of these are owned by Muslims. So much hate has never happened in the past. The cantonment market has never been affected by communal problems but this time it has also been hit. There used to be a Military police post in the market but it has been removed for the last two years. The recent attacks could be a result of that.'

'Has anyone from this station been involved in any disturbance?'

'They will never touch anyone from the military sir.' Looking over Brother's head the barman stiffened, Captain Jamwal is here. 'Good evening sir, this officer is looking for you.'

' I am Captain Jamwal. You must be Flight Lieutenant James.'

'Yes and I am pleased to meet you and thank you for your help in accommodating me. Can we sit at a quiet place and talk? It is of a personal nature.'

'Sure, let us sit at the other end of the room. Normally all officers sit near the bar counter.'

'Oh! That is a fine place.'

'I am the adjutant of the station so maybe you are with the right person if your matter is a personal one.'

They had laughed like only men in uniform could after meeting for less than five minutes. Adjutants are like the chief administrators of discipline and orderliness of the unit and they have all the current information and records of all happenings. Brother had reached inside his pocket and handed Jamwal the newspaper clipping. It was read carefully and then the adjutant had looked at Brother.

'Interesting that there is an article like this. We have not seen it.'

'Let me explain. I have arrived from Bombay. The article is from a Bombay daily. I was a prisoner of war for a long time and there was an army Naik called Azad Khan from the Para commandos with me there and he is from Ahmadabad.'

'Oh! You are searching for him?'

'No I am not searching for him but his father had a tailoring shop in the cantonment market in 1971 and it is likely that this destroyed shop is now run by one of his relatives or family. ' Azad Khan is alive, still a prisoner in Pakistan and I have to convey this to his family, that he is alive. They probably don't know and have given him up for dead.'

There was silence. In that silence their eyes remained locked and Brother thought he could again see disbelief and suspicion.

'Please don't ask me to repeat my entire story because you may not believe me like everyone else. All I am requesting is that, let me meet this army officer who saved the tailor and let him take me to that shop. It may not be Azad Khan's shop. I am only searching. I will not ask for any other help from you.'

The pleading tone had made the adjutant wonder even more.

'You can tell me your entire story if you want to and yes we have an officer here who was involved in an episode.'

'Is it possible to meet this officer?'

'Yes, he is a trained Para commando and belongs to the Jat Regiment but I have never heard about any Para commando Naik Azad Khan or his tailoring shop. All that Major Dilip told us was that the poor Muslim tailor was almost beaten to death and he was in the shop during the attack and had taken action to save him because the attackers had assaulted him too. Umer Singh please get me the cordless phone.'

Brother waited while the barman brought the cordless phone on a silver tray for Captain Jamwal. He couldn't curtail a smile of appreciation for the silver tray and the barman. (British Cavalry tradition has it that even a cavalry officer's spurs were brought or taken from them on a silver tray). The adjutant had dialed Major Dilip's number and in the silence of the bar they could both hear the bell ringing at the other end. Brother was praying that the call be attended.

It was. 'Sir there is a retired officer who has arrived here from Bombay today and he wants to meet you in connection with the attack on you a few days back. He is a retired air force pilot and has a long story and he also has a newspaper clipping about you that we haven't seen here but it seems you have been made out as quite a hero.'

There was laughter and then the call was over. 'You are lucky; he is on his way to the bar.'

'Get me a drink Umer Singh, the standard please. Will you have something other than what you are having? And I am interested in your story as a PoW. It must be amazing because I have not met a PoW and if there still are Indian prisoners as you say, then we should do something to get them released.'

Brother considered for a moment and then said, ' I don't mind a whiskey with lots of ice.'

The Captain echoed, 'you heard that Umer Singh, please get it.'

The barman sensed an interesting evening and scurried away to get them their glasses. And Brother was in a dilemma as to where to begin his narrative. This was the starting point of his search for all the families of those that he had left behind. His earlier narrations had not had any fruitful effect but this time there was a glimmer of hope. He thought rapidly.

*'The tailoring shop has to somehow be Azad's. I have to find the shop. There is hope because I have found this Major the 'savior'. With him I will at least reach the area where this injured young man grew up and maybe trace the family from thereon. Why have I not done this before? The negative responses, officialdom and suspicious behavior of the authorities suppressed me. I just need one person from the armed forces who will believe my story. Major Dilip could be my man.'*

The fear of not being able to remember the name of the camp location came back to him like a wave and recollection of the official report from the Pakistani authorities that he had deserted and stayed back as a missionary almost overwhelmed him. The faces of his interrogators in the Air force headquarters came back to him like ghosts. They had looked at him with suspicion and believed the

Pakistani story. *'Will this attempt to locate Azad's relatives lead me into their questioning cubicles again?'* This newspaper clipping was like a dandelion in the wind. Sheila was the only one who had believed him from the first day. But that was because she was herself waiting for some news about Kailash. *'If only this shop belongs to Azad and I can meet someone who waits for him. It will all be complete. Is it only the ones that live in some captive memories that believe in the impossible truth? I am still captive to my commitment of trying to find emotionally captive families of people who are alive yet captive in Pakistan. I will not give up. Let me take a slightly different approach.'*

Their drinks had been served and the adjutant had been polite to ask him if he was comfortable in the room allotted for his stay. Brother had just smiled and said, ' those are nice, very old rooms, maybe from the British days, right?'

'You are right. We are thinking of maintaining them as heritage buildings. The legend is that a very famous British polo player lived in the room you are occupying. I cannot recall his name but the unit records have the history of this whole camp.'

'Your unit history may also have Azad Khan's name. He was a famous wrestling champion.'

'Yes, we could check it up tomorrow morning for sure.'

Brother's hopes rose like a surfing swell. 'There will be a way of finding out I am sure,' he thought. Meeting in the bar had been a good decision. He was spared the official and closed-door cross-examination environment. A gentleman with an arm in a sling walked in and the adjutant stood up to greet him.

'Sir this is retired Flight Lieutenant James. You will need sometime with him and a drink of course?'

'Yes Jamwal thank you and I am pleased to meet you Flight Lieutenant James; I am Major Dilip Singh. What can I do for you.'

'Call me Brother, I am glad to find you because I just need to find the shop of this Muslim tailor you saved.' He took the newspaper clipping and handed it over. 'I think this article is about you.'

The Major read the clipping and was without any comment. 'Why is it that you are interested in this destroyed shop?'

'That is because there is a possibility that the shop belongs to a Para commando Naik Azad Khan.'

'Why should that be important to you?' The Major's drink arrived on a tray and it gave Brother time to respond to the question. This was an interesting beginning. *'Instead of me narrating, let them ask me questions.'* All his earlier debacles with the authorities reminded him of his monologues and a few people staring at him in silent disbelief turning to suspicion followed by disinterest.

'It is not important for me but maybe it is for the current owner, the army and also the nation. I mean the injured tailor of that shop maybe related to this Para Commando Naik.'

'Why would it be important to him Brother?' ' Because the PoW Naik could well be his father and is still alive and it is possible that the relatives do not know about him.'

'Where is this Naik?'

Brother looked hard at him and asked, 'You are a Para commando?'

'Yes I am and how does that matter sir?'

'It matters Major because the Naik was also a Para commando.'

'I don't understand.'

'If you are a Para commando; you could have access to the names and addresses of the next of kin of any of your regiment soldiers Major Dilip.'

'That makes sense but this fellow Azad Khan could be from any of the many battalions. We are not just one battalion. Anyway I think you have reason to believe, because Basheer Khan, the owner of that shop has told me time and again about his father who was in the army and went missing, but that happened long ago and I was in school those days. So I may not know about this Naik that you talk about at all.'

Brother's excitement was visible. ' Can we meet this Basheer Khan? I am beginning to feel that he maybe Azad's son. His wife had been pregnant when Azad was sent to the border.'

The major's face grew grim, 'Basheer was badly injured and if alive, must be in the municipal hospital where my troops had taken him.'

'Major sir, can we go to this hospital also?'

'Yes we can do that tomorrow but where is this Azad Khan, who you say is alive?'

Brother was encouraged by Major Dilip's confirmation that the shop was linked to a missing soldier and so he narrated his story and that had accounted for a few more drinks and a strange kind of respect came over the army officers listening raptly to him. This was a total change from his past experience. He had suddenly become like a father figure and they looked at him with visible amazement. There were questions that he took time to answer and explain and the patience coupled with eagerness of the officers to hear his story gave him the enthusiasm and energy to recapitulate the horrific incidents in detail. Brother assessed his performance as "Most Convincing".

'Have you made an official report about all these happenings?' Brother smiled in response silently.

'Do I presume that you would like to believe in all that I have said?'

'I do not disbelieve but find it a little difficult to understand that you have no idea of the location of this camp.'

'Yes, I was court-martialled as a normal procedure and gave my reports and wonder how would knowledge of the location help without a system to verify it? Will any independent agency or the government take it up or be permitted to verify my facts and do you think our friends across the border will wait for an embarrassing situation like this to develop. It was only in the official prison camps that you got to see the Red Cross and there was no real head count and thereafter we never saw Red Cross or United Nations' observers for the next twenty-nine years. What would you do Major, if someone came searching for PoWs after all these years? Shift the prisoners to some other place or would it be easier to just do away with them and avoid the embarrassment? I consider it just providence and their kindness that we were allowed to live. And if the issue is taken up officially, I do not know what will happen to those remaining prisoners. There may be even more in other camps, who knows.'

'What was the benefit in keeping you and the others there?'

'Well Major, they always told us that India has also kept some of their very important officers as PoWs and we would be released only in exchange.'

'I have not heard of any left over Pakistani PoWs. Just suppose your story is true and you find this Azad Khan's relatives and also the others; what is your aim?'

Brother responded instantly, 'would you not feel grateful if someone told you that your father or husband or brother is still alive and yearns for you and will it not help to release you from the feeling that he is not missing or dead and that he is alive?'

'Brother sir, do you think they will believe you, I mean the families?'

'I have no proof other than living with their own kin for twenty-nine years and I think I will be able to tell them all about how my co-prisoners talked about home and them. They will feel it and I think it will be convincing? I have already told you about my colleague Flight Lieutenant Kailash. I saw his fighter explode but his wife waited to hear about his death for all these years. His status was missing in action for so long. Who would you believe? I was an eyewitness. In her case she was released from being captive to the thought that he was still alive. My mission is to reach these relatives and free them from their captivity of the mystery of their dear ones. Here again I am an eyewitness— luckily sent back. On my own I am not capable of convincing people to get my co-prisoners their release but maybe if there are more people who ask some questions; the authorities may react.'

'So, are you trying to get support to start a movement?'

'That is not my primary aim Major and if that happens it will convince more people and maybe get them their release or like I said it does bother me that the enemy may shift them or simply terminate their existence. However, I will keep my commitment to my brothers there. I cannot breathe freely with the knowledge that no one knows about them. At least their nearest ones can be given some good news after all these years.'

'It may not be good news Brother sir. They may have moved on in life and resettled?'

'Yes, that is very possible and if they have moved on; the news I bring will probably reattach them and make them captive to some new pains and yearning. It may also bring joy. But that is up to them. It is my promise that I will carry this information to them. I am sure none of them will be disappointed to hear about their near ones being alive. It is another issue that they may never get to see or meet them. That will be for them to pursue or come to terms with. We are all soldiers and joined the armed forces of our own free will and these are the challenges that cannot be avoided. The destiny of our families is quite linked to our own fate, isn't it?'

Major Dilip leaned back in contemplation, 'I guess you have made your point but you have not told us about the treatment they gave you and did they torture you or what were their methods of questioning. Would it be difficult or unpleasant to recount for us?'

'I can appreciate your professional interest Major. Does that give me the confidence that you do believe in all that I have said so far and should tell you more in answer to your questions,' Brother smiled at last. There was silence— he had taken them by surprise but they were smiling too.

Brother pre-empted, 'I will make a deal with you. Take me to Basheer Khan and I will tell you whatever you wish to know but it will all be unofficial. I am not here to rake up issues or stir up an

International broil. If it does develop into an International issue and my friends get their freedom; I shall remember that you helped me find the first window for their freedom. You can learn a few things from my experiences as well; you are soldiers and will have to fight someday. Shall we call it a day now?' He waited for their response. 'And Major, I thank you for your patient hearing.'

'Yes this is all very amazing,' was the Major's reply. 'Brother sir, if I show you a map of that region, will you be able to give an approximate location.'

'I could but of what use will it be.'

'There are ways and means of finding out. You must be aware that Pakistan is presently gripped by unrest and there are these terrorists and our troops confronting each other regularly. Maybe we could get some information from captured terrorists.'

Brother became more eager. 'I wish I could tell you in some official capacity. You could then initiate actions for someone to locate or collect information about this secret prison camp?' Brother's statement hung threateningly in the bar room smoke.

'I will show you the map tomorrow morning. I understand the maps that pilots use. We were taught at the Para trooping School by air force instructors.'

Brother smiled,' I would love to see a map, it has been so long.'

Brother slept little that night. He was battling with the realization that there was a very big possibility that the families would not believe him and if so they could create an uproar and that would take him back into the clutches of officialdom that he hated. He was aware that Sheila was also concerned about these possibilities. She had mentioned it at Bombay Central, he recollected. He prayed, *'Basheer Khan has to be Azad's son. There has to be some way of letting Azad know that he has a son. He will be fulfilled.'*

The next day was busy. Major Dilip had taken him to the adjutant's office and shown him a map. Brother had looked for Nanga Parbat, the peak that was clearly visible from the prison camp. From it, he had drawn a line southwest and reached the bowl between the hills. There was Katlang, Malakand and Tangi that had a railhead.

'That could be the rail head from where we heard the sounds of trains twice a week.'

Dilip and Jamwal had both made a note and said they would try to find out from their intelligence resources and also colleagues in the Jammu and Kashmir areas. *'Oh well, this assurance maybe like so many earlier ones. What can I lose? If they find out, we could all gain.'*

In the morning Major Dilip had taken Brother to the municipal hospital but to their disappointment they were told that the injured tailor had been discharged the same day. There was no further information of his whereabouts. The discharge of a seriously injured patient surprised them because the doctor on duty had checked up the patient's case sheets and told them that he had severe stab wounds, fractures and burn injuries. Why then was he discharged? Where could he be? They had then driven in the Major's jeep to the market area and stopped in front of what remained of the tailoring shop. Brother wondered if he had reached his destination. Looking for clues in the backyard of the shop cum residential building he had come across a metal board lying face down. On picking it up he saw what he wanted. He was at the correct place. The board read. "Kasim Khan's Clothiers and Embroiderers". The words lit up his face and Brother felt a shout rising in is throat. Azad had told him proudly about his father Kasim Khan the tailor. They had then gone into the mohallas and he had asked for Ruhaina and this had drawn worried and scared looks. Strangely no one volunteered any information. The Major then requested some elderly residents and very reluctantly they had told him that Ruhaina had gone with the High court judge's daughter. Brother had been dropped back at the officers' mess as the Major had some urgent work in connection with deployment of troops for aid to the civil administration. It had been disappointing that he had not been able to meet with Azad Khan's family. That he would have to wait for another day made the anxiety acidic.

It was as though it had taken him two years of waiting to reach this far. And if the communal riots in Ahmadabad had not taken place he may have had to wait for even longer. The irony of it all just seemed to exasperate him. The next evening they had once again got together at the mess bar and he was once again the center of hushed discussion. The Major and Jamwal had wanted to also keep his presence and mission at low key. The private meeting had the shades of a conspiracy. These two officers were not in a hurry to be identified as the ones who had helped instigate an outcry for the freedom of some PoWs that they were not very certain of. Brother had somehow captured their imagination.

The Major had meanwhile enquired from the local Air force Command headquarters that one Flight Lieutenant Richard James had indeed been commissioned into the air force in 1967 and had been declared missing in the 1971 conflict. The air force list of officers confirmed it. So, Brother was not a fake. They had talked about their individual training days at the NDA and how it helped in making men out of boys and that these days there was more stress on academics than making mentally strong real officers out of them that could lead men into the face of death. It was all very debatable and it was good to have an old boy from the NDA who had fought a war and been a PoW. Brother felt like an ornament being praised.

Azad Khan's name had been traced out from the station sports archives. He was indeed the champion wrestler that Brother had described to them. There was adequate credibility here but the subject of PoWs still in Pakistan was very delicate. Two junior officers of the Indian army couldn't do much when the top brass at the service headquarters had pointed out the inaccuracies of Brother's version and had in fact declared him of disturbed mind due to prolonged illness. He had been let off due to his terminal condition. But he recovered slowly and not many keep track of retired officers in any case. Not someone who may die soon and claimed to have been a PoW for twenty-nine years. People like Brother were best forgotten. Brother had the devil's luck as his squadron mates always said. You needed that to belly land a fighter with its undercarriage stuck in the up position with two bombs under the wings that luckily do not go off as the aircraft slithers to a halt in sparks and smoke and a smiling Brother jumps out of the cockpit.

Reminiscing under the tree outside his room in the officers' mess for news from Major Dilip, Brother wondered what today had in store. The injured tailor had been traced the previous day to a private nursing home and a message had been sent to him that the Major had wanted to meet him. Brother waited for the Major to confirm that they could finally meet.

A jeep drew up. He could see the Major's smile behind the windscreen. 'I have some news for you Brother sir.'

'Did you get a time to meet Basheer at the nursing home, he asked in eagerness.'

'No, said Dilip, but we will meet a lady. She is the daughter of a Judge and her name is Smita Choudhury. She is the one looking after Basheer and his mother. She took him to a private nursing home for better treatment. The mother and sister have been given shelter at the Judge's house, as it is closer to the nursing home. I spoke to this advocate Smita because she had received my message meant for Basheer Khan and she called back at my number. I have not told her the purpose of our meeting Basheer because it is best that you explain everything. Basheer is recovering but has severe injuries and is due for surgery. Are you ready to go for this meeting?' The major wondered if he had done things the right way.

'Yes of course, this is what I have come for.'

The major didn't want to get too involved as he doubted the ethics of what he was about to get involved in as a serving officer.

He hesitated, 'is there a requirement for me to come with you Brother sir?'

'It will be better because I need your presence to provide credibility about my credentials. I am sure you have done your homework to find out that I am actually a retired ex-air force officer and was a PoW. Haven't you? Nobody will believe me without someone like you vouching for my background. I will need support in many places Dilip.'

The major smiled through dark shades like he would, at any of his buddies. Brother was almost a buddy now. Brother knew the fears and danger confronting a serving officer getting involved with a retired officer on a mission to free some PoWs and worse still that too with an ex PoW. The Major laughed, 'Brother you are a survivor,' and then with almost an apologetic smile; 'you don't need my help but I will come with you. Let us go.'

'I like your attitude, Dilip. You could have been a good fighter pilot.' Brother thumped him on the back.

They headed off towards the high court for the meeting with Smita Choudhury. He was getting closer. And his fears began to bubble again but he kept them behind a pair of shades and a tight-lipped smile. Thoughts went back to the camp. *'Azad please forgive me for taking so much time. I hope you are alive and well. You will be surprised. Soon I will be meeting your son and also Ruhaina. Will you ever understand my apprehensions for taking so much time? My own colleagues in the air force here did not believe about us in that camp and I was also scared like I have never been before. I was scared of being dragged into situations where I would not be able to prove anything. I was probably more courageous as a PoW. I hope your family will understand and believe that we spent twenty-nine years side by side in a prison. Will they believe me? What should I tell them? How do I start? Please be with me. Azad, my dear friend I will tell them that you are alive and that we will get you out. I hope I am not too late and you are all in good shape. We will try to get you guys home soon.'*

It was becoming similar to the upheaval he had before narrating the story of Kailash to Sheila. He was however becoming surer of himself.

The court façade loomed ahead with its grim stone architecture. It brought him back to realization that he was meeting some lady advocate and not Azad's family as yet. That in itself was welcome relief. Although eager to meet them it was buying him some more preparatory time.

# Chapter XI

The prisoners and prison staff were out in the backyard at their routine morning exercise that involved some jogging and then a game of volleyball with the guards. Azad Khan showed no interest in the game.

Major Ganguly tried encouragement, ' Azadbhai you are our best player. We have to win the volleyball match prize again this year. How can you allow these guards to score so easily? Come on I will set up a volley for you.'

Azad only glared defiantly,' I am not interested in playing this stupid game while my people are dying.'

With that he just threw the ball at the Major's face and stomped off the court. Colonel Sunderam asked him to come back. Azad kept walking defiantly towards the dormitory cell. The Colonel had never raised his voice but now firmly, 'I am ordering you to come back.'

'Keep those orders for yourself Colonel, you and your Hindus,' he shouted. 'And don't you try to order me around anymore. You heard me?'

The colonel was not to be shouted down so easily. Turning towards the Pakistani armed guards he said, 'arrest Naik Azad, for breaking parade without permission. You are inviting punishment for disobedience Azad, come back, this is your last chance.'

'What can you do, let me see who arrests me, these are my Muslim brothers.' The guards playing with them got together and moved towards him keeping a bit of safe distance. Azad scoffed at the Pakistanis, 'aren't you ashamed of taking orders from an Indian Army Colonel?'

A shot rang out. It was from the revolver of Subedar Abdul Karim. Leaning over the window overlooking the playfield, he said, 'bring that kafir to my office.'

Azad resisted, there was some grappling and the guards overpowered him. The morning exercise was curtailed and the Colonel, Ganguly and Pawri followed a guard into their dormitory silently. They were stunned at Azad's sudden erratic behavior. Misbehavior from any prisoner generally brought retributions for all.

Subedar Abdul Karim knew his job well and it always gave him extra pleasure in punishing Azad. He was after all an Indian Muslim traitor. Azad was escorted in chains between four guards to the Subedar's office.

'For breaking the exercise parade you are liable to be punished and this is the fifth time you will be punished in the last three years. Your limit is one punishable offence in a year. You have already crossed all limits. So this time let us see what is your tolerance? You will not live through this one, you kafir and traitor to Islam.'

Azad was defiant, 'you may punish me sir, but I wish to say something in privacy.'

'What is it?' 'I can only speak to you in private or you can take me to the Commandant sir.'

'Guards! Leave us alone and close the door.' He rose from his chair swaggering, pistol cocked in one hand. It had its intimidating effect. Leaning on the table with his face thrust at Azad, 'tell me what last wish do you have.'

Azad reached inside his pocket and brought out the newspaper clipping, cut from the daily that carried reports of communal riots in India and handed it over to the Subedar. 'Who gave you permission to keep paper cuttings? This is another offence. You've had it this time.'

'Yes sir, but,'

'But what?'

Azad looked at him in the eye, 'Muslims must take revenge on Hindus.'

'That is very easy. I can arrange for you to get a knife and you can slit the throats of the other Hindu prisoners at night. We will not punish you for that. I will also see that after this you are even granted the opportunity to join the mujahideen.'

'That is of no use sir, these are my comrades. It is the politicians and Hindutva people in India.'

'What do you take me for Naik Azad; some greenhorn?'

'No sir, you are the only one that has the correct indoctrination against Indians.'

'You are right in that for once. I have sent four Indian prisoners to their Hindu Gods. The problem here is that we have a Commandant who also seems to be a traitor like you. The day he goes I will ensure that your doctor Pawri joins his friends with their Gods made of clay statues. He is having an affair with that sweeperess. Shame on him for being an officer.'

'But he is a Parsee and not a Hindu sir.'

'Don't talk out of turn you traitor. So, tell me,' he whispered, 'are you going to redeem yourself from being a traitor? Finish those three kafirs in the cells tonight? If you chicken out, we will try you for possession of dangerous weapons and if you fail to kill them and are caught, we will try you for assault on your own officers. Hah! I am sure you know the sentence for these offences. Choose how you wish to start your revenge Azad.'

'I will not kill my own officers. You can punish me the way you want and do you remember, I was offered to train your mujahideen boys in making booby traps and setting up ambushes and taking them into Kashmir and creating havoc among the Hindu population there? I am a commando and am willing to do that now; I am ready. I have to take revenge for what they are doing to Muslims in India.'

'You are not only stupid but have the audacity to make deals with me? Guards! Take him away and put him in the underground tank till his body rots and disintegrates. We will feed you to the rats. They are hungry for a traitor's flesh.'

Azad had resisted, there was a scuffle and he was hit on the head, knocked unconscious and dragged by the guards across the yard for all to see. They threw him into the underground water tank and it had brought his senses back only to suffer the stagnant water and acrid odors. There were rats already scurrying along the stony walls. The day had dragged on and he knew that night would take away whatever little light penetrated the cell through a barred skylight in the roof. He had suffered this before. Food was lowered to him through the bars in a tin can at the end of a rope. The Subedar had come at sunset to see him through those bars and wish him luck.

'Start reciting whatever you remember from the Koran you kafir. This time I will have my way with you.'

Azad had retreated to a far corner of the water tank, as there was not much here as foothold for the rats. He would have to fight them off from whatever little sound he could catch as they approached him in curiosity. He could stand on his toes with chin above the water in this corner. They had adjusted the water level well. He alternated between sleep and alarmed wakefulness leaning his head against the corner of the surrounding wall.

Three days had made him into a total mess. The skin all over his body had become wrinkled and there were sores in the places where the rats had been able to bite him. This was the worst punishment. There were two other punishment cells but those were not like this. One was a small cubicle made of steel kept in the open and a man could barely sit on his haunches with his head between the knees. At the end of three days the legs would be cramped and the back bent over stiff that it would take a day to just straighten out leave alone getting sufficient balance to stand or walk. The third was a cell where the prisoner would be tied in such a manner that the ropes or chains would be adjusted to prevent from allowing him to sit or lie down. You just had to suffer standing till the weakness would make you lean to one side in a semi conscious state where the body remained in a suspended stupor. The food in all three-punishment cells was a watery soup with some rice.

Azad was brought out on the third day and given a wash with hosepipes. He had just lain there on the ground while the water beat into his face and body sores. The Subedar appeared in his vision, eyes squinting from the sudden bright daylight. He was then taken into a proper cell with a cot and a toilet. Fainting from cumulative lack of sleep he found himself fighting off imaginary rats on the cot at night. A guard slept just outside his cell on a comfortable well-made bed. The logic was to humiliate and break the will. They had all been through each of these punishment cells and had been strong enough to withstand and survive it without parting with any information. Azad recalled Brother coming out laughing in a delirium from the underground water tank. You were never sent back to your dormitory cell immediately. Solitary confinement and no conversation even with the guards was the second stage before being returned to normal camp routine. Azad used the time to gather himself for the next round. It was another two days before the Subedar summoned him and he was taken in chains to his office.

'Have you made up your mind Azad?' There was a commando's knife on the table. 'The knife is for you to use on your comrades or do you prefer the underground for a few more days?'

Azad glared at the evil eyes. 'I have told you that I will not harm my own officers. You can do whatever you wish with me sir but you forget that I am an Indian soldier who will not raise his hands on his own officers. And you also know that I am a Muslim and I cannot see my brothers and sisters being harmed by the Hindus in India. Give me the opportunity to take revenge. You are not able to accept my services now because I have refused you many a time over the years. You fear that I will escape if I am allowed the freedom to train your mujahideen.' He smiled contemptuously.

The Subedar shook his head in agreement, 'you are amazingly intelligent.'

Azad stood his ground and lowered his voice in desperation, 'why don't you try me out for sometime and let your mujahideen shoot me if I attempt to escape? Take me for a raid on the Indians to prove my loyalty.'

After a pause the Subedar relented. 'The Commandant will see you tomorrow and decide your fate. I have recommended that you be handed over to the mercenaries as a prisoner and not as a trainer. They do not have any mercy like us. And they do not waste bullets on prisoners or traitors. The jobs they give; you will not last for even a week. They are my friends. I will brief them. You would have been welcomed like a hero if you slit a couple of Hindu throats here. Now you are a dead man. Be damned now.'

The Commandant Colonel Sami had been very firm. Two guards escorted Azad to his office. Subedar Abdul Karim was strangely kept away from this interview. It surprised Azad that Colonel Sunderam was seated in the Commandant's office before his arrival. He felt betrayed and scared that his conspiracy with the Colonel was out.

'You have been the worst troublemaker in the last five years. That is what your prison record says.'

Azad was respectful; 'it is the duty of every prisoner of war to resist the enemy sir.'

'I am aware of that Naik Azad Khan and am glad that you remember it. It is also the duty of the captor to try and break the will of a prisoner and extract maximum information from him. What is it that I hear? The Subedar says that you wish to join the mujahideen? Can you explain to me?'

Azad pretended to hesitate in the presence of his comrade, the

Colonel. The Commandant egged him on. 'Go on tell me and don't worry about the Colonel. His life will be over here anyway.'

Azad mumbled, 'it is unbearable to watch my own brethren being humiliated and butchered in communal violence sir.'

'I can appreciate that Azad.' Azad looked at Colonel Sunderam who looked away.

'Your Colonel has recommended that you be shot as a traitor if you join the mujahideen but we cannot do that. That is for the Indians to do. You will be betraying your own country. That is if we decide to hand you over to the mujahideen commander. He is from Kashmir. What do you wish to say?'

'I have already said what I have to say and you have got your report from the Subedar sir. I have nothing to add.'

'Colonel Sunderam do you wish to speak with Naik Azad.'

'Yes sir I wish to apprise him that the mujahideen are an anti Indian force and he will become a deserter and traitor by joining them and that is a serious offence. Collaborating with the enemy is the most serious crime for a soldier. It is worse than desertion of duty.' Colonel Sunderam looked Azad sternly in the eye and played on. There wasn't even the faintest trace of their midnight conference in the toilet. In fact Colonel Sunderam was seriously condemning him.

'I am not anti India sir,' Azad tried to justify politely. 'I am only against the Hindutva, Colonel sir. Would you sit back and watch Hindus and your family being massacred in a similar manner. Will you sir?' The Commandant listened to the duel. No one could guess the inner thoughts of three seasoned soldiers. Three sets of values. Each on a different platform. They were not in conflict. They just had their own three sets of reasons.

'Very well Colonel Sunderam, I will hand over Azad to the mujahideen and his well being ceases to be my responsibility.'

The Colonel in his best military voice said, ' Commandant sir, I am sure you are familiar that handing over your prisoner to another enemy of India makes you an ally of that force. Which implies that the Pakistani army is supporting the mujahideen.'

The commandant laughed aloud, 'Colonel Sunderam, you are well trained. There will be no proof of that and have you forgotten that you Indians helped the Mukti Bahini to create Bangladesh. Azad is dead for us. We will make his papers for you to sign.' There was a hush. The Colonel looked for a longtime at the Commandant and then at Azad.

Azad requested him, 'please sign my death certificate sir. How does it matter now that you also think of me as a traitor.'

'The mujahideen is badly in need of porters to carry their rations, ammunition and they also need human shields to penetrate Indian mine fields. Will you sign his death certificate as a witness, Colonel?'

'I will never do that.'

'Then we will make his papers ourselves, the commandant said with finality in his voice. I can sense his desire to escape and he is of no use to us anyway. He is only a soldier but the other three of you are officers. You have worked in the construction of critical Pakistani military installations. I will have to keep you here. At least he has the spirit of a true jehadi. Let him escape and get his revenge if he survives. No one will believe him in India. We know the Indians well. They have given you all up for dead long ago. The mujahideen need Jehadis and will in any case make him cross the first minefield they suspect and there will be no need for any death certificates after that. I am against torture and ill treatment to prisoners. But don't take my fairness for a weakness. I am sufficiently patriotic to understand the importance of the liberation of Kashmir. You created Bangla Desh. We will have our turn to celebrate the liberation of Kashmir and can use every dedicated volunteer like Azad.'

There was hate in this room. Azad felt like a loser but he was determined to try.

'Transfer him to the mujahideen commander by tomorrow. Let Azad be "azad" (free),' he ordered sarcastically into the intercom. The meeting had not taken long. It had left no doubts in anyone's minds.

Azad wondered about Colonel Sunderam being called into the meeting. *'Hearing him declare me a traitor to be shot for wanting to join the mujahideen is shocking. Does he not know the real plan?'*

Colonel Sunderam appeared surprised that Azad wanted to go to his death for sure. *'What could make a man do such a thing?'* He also suspected that the Commandant knew that Azad would escape. *'Was the Commandant helping Azad?'* Azad could be their last hope if he reached India: or would it hasten their end by a bullet shortly?

The Commandant knew about a PoWs desire to escape and had his own logic to utilize Azad as a gladiator. He was willing to take the one chance that a truly vicious jehadi could be born. They needed motivated fighters and not greedy mercenaries and debauch Muslims in the mujahideen. Azad had motivation and courage of a Jehadi.

Sami had left his audience baffled. Even the Subedar was taken aback with the Commandant's decision. But he was certain that the mujahideen would get rid of Azad within a week. There was no chance of him escaping for the Indians to know that Pakistan still had PoWs, or were actively involved with the mujahideen. Who would believe him? And even if they did or came searching: there would be no way of proving it. *'We can eliminate the other three and others to wipe off any tracks. Who will ever find out?'*

Prisoners like anyone after all, are captive to their fate. Some destined to be released but captive to the horror, forever. Death would finally only unshackle another spirit that has struggled to get free.

Naik Azad Khan began his journey to the mujahideen camp not far away. He was not even allowed to go back to the dormitory cell. The few belongings that he had were put into one sack and thrown at him. He was refused permission to even bid goodbye to the others. That would not be the right spirit. He was now a Hindu hater. On his way out the Subedar had shown Azad his death certificate. 'You are dead for us. The mujahideen will give you a new name. And they don't wait to bury traitors.' With those parting words Azad had been huddled into the prison van and driven out of the gates forever. The deaf and dumb sweeperess Fatima saw him leaving. Their eyes met in a silent goodbye.

Spring was not far away. End February is a beautiful transition as the winter withdraws gradually and the hillsides burst into splashes of color. Azad looked back at the prison gates close and swore silently that he would get back soon and liberate the others. *'I cannot leave them to die. An Indian commando raid is not difficult at all. I will lead them. My reports have to be convincing. And I have to survive.'* He was not afraid of dying and definitely had the desire to reach Ruhaina and also take home the Colonel, Ganguly and Pawri with him. *'It will be such a joyous reunion for all of us? Where is Brother? He was a jolly fellow. I miss him. Inshallah (God willing), he is still alive and the sickness has left him so we shall meet again.'*

The mujahideen camp was about five kilometers away. A group of huts with one large tiled roof cottage in the midst of tall Chinar trees and an unattended apple orchard. It appeared like a deserted farm. The van stopped at a wooden gate and they were met by a fair young lad of about fourteen years. Face covered he had a semi-automatic slung across his back under a shawl. Only the dark muzzle peeped out. The boy's eyes had not lost its innocence but had developed the shiftiness of a hunted animal. They were constantly moving and scanning.

'Halt, what is it that you want here, don't you know that all vehicles stop five hundred meters away,' he yelled at the van driver from behind the gate.

The soldier driver sniggered, 'open the gates you greenhorn, we have an Indian recruit for your entertainment.'

The boy took a long look at the van and its markings. He recognized the Pakistan army insignia and opened the gate. Unslinging the carbine and cocking it, he looked at Azad through the small rear window. They looked at each other hard. Azad was stunned with the boy's good looks. *'These young boys were ready to die for the liberation of Kashmir? There had to be something terribly wrong in all this.'*

An adolescent voice trying hard to sound grown up said, 'why have you brought this dirt here?'

'He will be part of your force, now open the gate and let us in. I have to hand him over to your commander Majidbhai.'

The lad stayed firm, 'leave him here. I have orders not to let anyone in for the next two hours. I will take him to the boss. You can go back.'

'Here is a letter from Subedar Abdul Karim for your boss,' the driver growled offended whilst cringing at the carbine covering him, ashamed to accept that he lacked the guts to push a trigger-happy mujahideen.

The locked van door was opened from outside by the driver. The boy stood two steps away covering them both with his carbine. It was the fresh chill in the air on his face that took Azad by surprise. The breeze felt good and full of freedom. With bound hands Azad stumbled out with his sack of belongings. *'This will be transit camp till I escape or it maybe my final resting place,'* he thought. He tried a smile with the boy to be met by the muzzle of the carbine sharply poked into his ribs. It had hurt but his inborn resistance prevented any visible display of pain. The boy was quick to observe it and gave him another jab. Azad just looked at him without any expression.

'You think you are very tough? Come we will see.'

With that he stepped back and told Azad to march into the compound. Azad did not know what to expect. He turned resigned to his fate and started walking slowly. The carbine bolt was again withdrawn and released in the action of loading the chamber. At the sound, he stopped walking only to be violently jabbed in the small of the back. *'It is best to do what I am told,'* thought Azad and picked up his fallen sack to start walking towards the main cottage. The van drove away and now it was just the two of them that walked slowly up the shallow climbing path leading into the grove. Azad's soul was singed at the sheer violence emanating from this young boy. Tempted though he was to make some conversation, he kept walking silently expecting a shot in his back. Maybe that is what the Subedar from the prison wants.

'Halt here.' He was pushed against a straight Chinar tree and his feet and knees were securely bound with a rope. 'If you try to escape Sher Khan will tear you and he is always hungry.' He whistled. A white and liver sheep dog the size of a small donkey trotted across from behind the huts, the intensity of snarling increasing as he drew near with eyes that turned bloody and a nose that sniffed the air surrounding Azad. The boy barked a string of abuses to make the dog sit a few paces away and it kept growling all the while till he marched off towards the main cottage. The growls rising and falling threateningly and now directed only at Azad. The slightest movement seemed to enrage it further.

Standing tied to a tree Azad wondered what kind of fate awaited him. *'I think it is written all over my face that I want to escape. How do I change that look and make them believe me? I have to display the violence that they associate bravery, loyalty and courage with. Oh! At last I am out of that prison and it is good to see the mountains and trees and flowers as they are and not from behind a wall or fence.'* He tried to shift attention away from the growls. *'I maybe dead by sunset but it certainly feels good in the open. There are four huts and one main cottage. That must be the headquarters and the huts must be the living quarters of the men.'* A thin wisp of smoke drifted up and away in a slant from one of the huts and he guessed it to be their kitchen. *'That must be where the well fed Sher Khan came from.'* He tried to shift and look over his shoulders. Sher Khan growled, got up and came dangerously close to him with a throaty frothing snarl. Azad froze immediately and started a polite dialog with him. It will keep him distracted from attacking. It worked. The beast sniffed looking at him up and down and growled backing off a few steps to sit on its haunches; ready to spring. *'The mountains are about three kilometers away. It will not take more than thirty minutes through the woods. I will have to avoid following the trail and go cross-country. From thereon I wonder how many hours it will take to reach the border. It is so many years since I have done this cross-country march. Will my legs manage it? I have to. Before that I will have to convince this Majidbhai that I could be of help to them and my looks have to become harsh like one of them. That is something I have very little time to acquire. What makes them like that? Are they trained to show hate or do the living conditions and habits get laminated into their souls? Maybe it is their years of hopeless struggle that breeds contempt to levels where face muscles adopt a permanent frown. Even I have struggled for years in that prison and there was very little to hope for. But my face muscles have only aged and the lines have become more prominent. My wrestling was aggressive but can I develop this cold-blooded merciless facial expression? Are these really freedom fighters or are they just thieves and opportunists. What can I ever teach them?'*

Sher Khan suddenly jerked his head towards the cottage. It was a fraction before the cottage door opened and the sharpness of the movement and keen anticipation brought a gasp from Azad. The dog sensed his alarm and snarled looking at him sideways. Azad stared him back and realized that he had to change into a "Sher Khan". *'I have to be also growling from within, all the time. Actions and expressions are the easiest way to convince these killers. They will not understand words. They need to see hate spilling out in every breath. Even walking will have to appear malicious as though you hate even the ground that you tread. That's it. Thank you Sher Khan for teaching me.'*

Two men accompanied the boy as they approached the tree. Azad could feel their eyes sizing him. The men were dressed in light gray Shalwars and dark loose fitting kurtas that came to below their knees. They had belts of ammunition around their waist and one of them had a revolver in a dull weather beaten leather holster. He was obviously the senior in whatever hierarchy existed amongst them.

Poking Azad's ribs with the barrel of his AK-47, 'what do we have here? A kafir and traitor? Of what use are you?' Azad maintained a sullen silence. 'Come on speak up or shall we make you sing,' he coughed a cruel short laugh. The boy and the other one sniggered as if on cue but in a rather subdued manner. 'So you were a Para-commando? Look at you now. You look more like a goat tied to a tree. What can you do for us?' Azad kept looking at him in the eye. 'Do you know how to recognize a minefield?'

'I am not like you. I can diffuse mines,' was Azad's cold reply. 'Recognizing is for beginners.'

'You have a sharp tongue for a traitor.'

Azad interrupted further comments, 'you asked me a stupid question.'

The hawk eyed one reached for his revolver, drew it and moved closer to make the cold barrel just touch the center of Azad's head. He drew back the hammer and Azad stared him in the eye with contempt. This is the first message. *'They have to understand that I am* not scared of death. I have to be convincing.'

'We are not like your Subedar Abdul Karim. He has become soft. The mujahideen don't take any insults you kafir. I will reserve you for the minefield. Take him to Majidbhai.'

Azad thought he detected a sense of relief from the other two. The mujahideen for Azad appeared to live in a dramatic world full of glorious dreams splashed with blood that made them appear so fearfully charismatic. As a Para-commando he had learnt that honor was very important among the Kashmiri tribes that hailed from the Northwest frontier and life could be sacrificed for izzat (honor). They were earlier called razzakars and naturally lived in a state of bravado never knowing fear or even caring about death. The mujahideen came later. The few words that the hawk eye had said were all very highly charged dramatic expressions and aggression was the instinctive response to almost any input. Everything was somehow linked to honor. If that was what they understood, it was best to deal with them in the same language.

The march to the main cottage was a relief for Azad as his legs had been bound without any room for movement. The hands remained tied. He was pushed into a small room to wait for the summons. The young boy stood guard outside. Loud voices in argument filtered through closed doors and gaps in the roofing and then he was called. Led by the boy Azad entered what was the central hall of the cottage. On a raised platform with rugs and cushions was a man reclining with a hookah and watching television. It was an Indian film. Azad recognized the Hindi language and it took him closer to India. Majid Khan had the letter from the Subedar in his hand and seemed to be re-reading it.

'So you are Naik Azad Khan and you wish to take revenge on Hindus. You also claim that you can deal with mines?'

'Given the opportunity I could do many things but as good musalmans we have forgotten how to greet our friends. My hands are still bound,' he bellowed, raising his bound arms in front. 'The mujahideen are known for their courage,' he added with sufficient contempt in the tone. 'Are you scared of one Indian soldier much older than all of you and you have the advantage of young blood and weapons?'

'Release his bonds,' he hissed, 'so how do we trust and know what you say is true?'

'Time and opportunity will prove, Azad shot back and I have been told that I will die here soon, so why do you ask me so many questions.' His hands were set free. Azad smiled and acknowledged the gesture.

Majidbhai drawled, 'you will get your opportunity shortly but if you so much as dream of betraying us; we will feed you to the vultures alive. Show him the photographs of that Indian soldier we had captured and how he was fed to the birds.'

It was a series of photographs of an Indian soldier spread-eagled and tied to a rock. He was alive struggling in a few photographs and then there were vultures flying above that came and perched around him. They attacked him while he was bound and the birds had been quick. Majidbhai watched him closely as he glanced at the photographs. Azad looked up and said, 'I will prefer a bullet.'

Majidbhai grinned, 'that is what I want you to understand; we show no mercy to traitors and bullets are too precious. You are free to walk around within this camp but we are watching you. The cleaning of the huts and kitchen will be your task. Let us see your dedication. Salman, keep him in your room and if he as much as tries to spread his wings; you know what to do? You will be on trial till you bring back the head of an Indian soldier. And the area around this camp is mined by us so keep to the roads and pathways or you will make a good meal for the dogs here soon.'

Azad displayed immediate rebellion, 'I am a Para-commando and can teach your men the art of unarmed combat, laying an ambush, read signs and teach tactics followed by the Indians. Why do you give me the lowly job of cleaning your filth.'

'You will do both the jobs,' barked Majid, 'before I change my mind and from this moment onwards you are Abdul Aziz. Azad Khan is dead. He died in the prison camp long ago. Have you understood?'

Azad growled, 'you can give me whatever name, I don't care.'

'Good, you are wise,' Majidbhai smiled wickedly.

Salman was the young boy who had tied him to the tree. Abdul's hands were untied now and he was told to follow. The new man, Abdul Aziz felt the first rush of freedom and massaging his wrists, looked around. These were not very complex people. Simply ruthless and brutally hateful of Indians. Abdul Aziz would have to wait for an impossible least expected situation to become Azad Khan again.

Stepping out of the cottage he picked up his life's belongings and smiled, 'Salman bhai, where do I keep these?' The smile went waste.

'Come with me. You were a real Para-commando, were you?'

'You don't believe me. I can teach you how to make an explosive from a few rounds of your AK-47. It is easy.'

'Yes I would like to learn that sometime but you better start cleaning the place first. Majidbhai has a very short temper.' There was a faint trace of awe in the boy's expressions.

Realization that Abdul Aziz could be of use to the mujahideen was the only reason for Majidbhai to accept him into their fold. *'I will have to work on Salman for a while before I can take him into confidence. I need all the help I can get to find my way out of this trap. I have to find out more about him first.'*

*'I am Abdul Aziz. Why have they made me Abdul Aziz? Was there really some other Abdul Aziz, now dead? How does it help them to recreate another one? Where is the real Abdul Aziz? How does it matter really? When I return to India I will be Azad Khan. Nothing can change that. Or is there some grisly scheme that they require a dreaded and wanted criminal mujahideen Abdul Aziz to be handed over to the Indians in return for prize money. I have to find out more about Abdul Aziz. Who can I ask? Let me wait for sometime. These things have a way of floating up with time. At least I am free here and have a chance of making my dream come true. Ruhaina, I will soon be on my way. Will you recognize me after all these years? I have to be patient. Please help me Allah. The Colonel was right. They will give me ample chances to escape but I must watch and do the unexpected.'*

The next few weeks were without much happening. Abdul was accommodated with Salman and two others. One was Rasheid and the other Hamid. The huts were small and had space enough for five in each. The insides were sparse and quite unkempt. Walls were made of brick and wood. It had a tin roof. There was just one window and the gaps in the walls allowed the cold wind to moan through as if to lull them to sleep at night. One cot was used as a general dump for weapons, ammunition, their copies of the Koran and some personal belongings. The walls had rusty nails bent into hooks from which hung their few clothes. The mujahideen slept on the floor. It was part of the hardening process. And they would pray five times a day; with their semi-automatics always near. The AK-47s were an extension of the body. It even went to the toilet with them. Praying was a welcome pass time for Abdul. He used to wonder what they prayed for. Abdul prayed for these sub-humans to give up their killing ways and his own deliverance. How could you kill and destroy in the name of Allah. But even the Hindus did that at Ahmadabad. Or was that just very highly politicized as usual. How would he know? He was cut off for thirty years but definitely suspected Indian politicians.

It took some time for Abdul to figure out that the huts were inhabited on a regional basis. Sectarian feelings ran high even among the militants here. Abdul's hut was for the Kashmiri (Indian origin) fighters. There was one for Pakistani inductees and the third one was for the mercenaries from Afghanistan and neighboring provinces of China adjacent to the border and also from what was once the USSR. The fourth hut was a common kitchen for their vastly differing palates. Food was cooked in rotation by one of their own team. Everyone had to eat according to the cook's whims. It was part of building a cohesively hateful team. Hawk eye was known as Ozero and hailed from somewhere in the hills south of Tashkent. He was the number two to Majid Khan but looked meaner than all of them. He was there for all the meals. They had to eat together. His eyes would dart from his plate to each one's face without any movement of the head. Abdul was frequently under scrutiny. Abdul's characteristic smiling eyes drew an even fiercer look from Ozero but that did not deter him. Abdul had the same expression for everyone. Salman was the only one that still smiled back in a fading kind of illusion that ended abruptly. It always left Abdul in doubt; *'did I see that smile, or does his smile suddenly end because he knows that he too is being watched and my days are numbered. Smiling at condemned men brings doom was the belief. Well whatever, atleast he is not devoid of emotions through his battles to develop the hard bred look like everyone else. Why does everyone want to get the same look like Ozero? Oh! I remember now, this is the same thing we did in the army. Emulate the "Company Havildar major" looks and expressions ET all. This sure is disciplined grooming in process ah?'*

The teams had gone out on two raids. The snows were melting. They would go for over two weeks at a time. Abdul was left behind with Salman. He had discovered the deep-rooted hate of a young Kashmiri wanting independence from India. Salman's village had been surrounded and fired at by Indian soldiers. They had come at night to capture the four mujahideen that had taken shelter in their village. There were always some traitors who would inform the Indian army and they would come and open fire at random. Their mud and brick houses would be left in ruins. Some of them even looted and carried away their women. There was no one to listen to complaints. The four mujahideen had come to recruit young men and boys. Salman had helped and escaped with them. He would go back to his village after the liberation of Kashmir and meanwhile he would kill as many Indian soldiers and Hindu Brahmin traitors in the villages. Kashmir was the valley for musalmans and India was the oppressor. Pakistan will help to achieve independence. Salman's mother was still alive and he hadn't seen her for over six months and Indian soldiers had abducted his sister. They had not seen her for a year now. He would find her and take revenge against her captors.

'You see the jacket I am wearing, Abdulbhai? I took it off the soldier that I had killed about six months ago. And I have four grenades also that were on his belt.' He matter of factly added, 'what you find becomes yours. I have some watches and gold rings too. At the Khyber Pass you can buy any weapon with gold, poppy seeds or watches. One of these grenades will be saved to liberate me. I will never become a prisoner and will take at least a couple with me if they try to capture me. No mujahideen allows himself to be captured.'

'Why is that?'

Almost spitting venom Salman raised his boyish voice and said, 'you are lucky the Pakistanis never tortured you. The Indian soldiers parade us naked in front of the women and then cut of our testicles and leave us to bleed to death. They have often burnt our supporters alive in locked huts. They can never stop us from getting our independence. Majid Khan's strict instructions are never to take prisoners. We never torture them. We just slit their throats.'

'Have you done that?'

'No I have not got that close but soon I may get the chance. I hope my sister had the courage to commit suicide. She will never be accepted back in the village.'

Abdul was stunned, 'what will you do if you find her?'

Salman had looked deep into Abdul's eyes. 'I will have to kill her. She would have been polluted by the kafirs.'

It was Salman's turn to ask questions. 'Why have you joined our group?'

Abdul thought for a moment and decided to take the opportunity of creating a religious bonding. 'I am a musalman and the Hindus are killing my people all over India. I could not bear that the country I served is turning against us so openly. If they think we are traitors, then why should I remain loyal? It has taken me time to realize this and I want revenge before I die. We were kept prisoners of war in exchange for the release of Pakistanis kept in captivity. The Indians forgot about us. They praise and value soldiers only during a war. After some time they conveniently forget.'

Salman sneered, 'You are lucky to be alive?'

With open arms towards the sky Abdul accepted, 'that is Allah's mercy. Maybe he kept me alive to take revenge.'

Salman looked around to ensure that noone was listening and

then in lowered tones said, 'you may get a chance soon. I think there is a plan to attack some convoys very soon. And there are some villages there that have many spies. They have formed village defense committees. We will attack shortly. You will get your opportunity but if you try to escape, I will have to shoot you. Those are my orders.'

Abdul couldn't prevent a resigned smile, 'I know Salman but I have no desire to escape. Why should I escape? Who will accept me back in India? I am like you now. I do not wish to be captured and declared a traitor by the army and neither can I escape and hope that they will believe my story. I have no proof. You have your village to go back to. What do I have? Let me help you in the search for your sister and don't kill her; she is your own blood.' Abdul got up and put a hand on the boy's shoulder, 'Allah will cleanse her. Let her live.' The touch was to convey sympathy.

'You are too kind. As a mujahideen, you cannot show kindness even to yourself. Kindness is a weakness and will overtake you and be the cause of your death. Do you want to die?'

Abdul had to be convincing, 'I have no fear of death, especially now that I have chosen the path of revenge. Like you, I will also keep one grenade for myself.'

Salman was throwing a challenge, 'you have to get an Indian soldier's head before Majidbhai allows you to carry weapons and even the weapon has to be a captured one. Will you be able to kill an Indian soldier, get the weapon of one of your own brothers?'

'I have little choice in that matter and if I fail I know Majid or Ozero or maybe even you will kill me. There is no other way I can remain alive to get my revenge on the Hindus.'

Abdul was amazed at the ease with which Salman had talked about revenge killing. There was no hesitation in the young boy's mind. No controversies and conflicts like his own. Was life in the valley so harsh that all the ties and affection surrounding family values, religion and conscience get bleached to fade like the bare mountain rock face washed by razor sharp cold winds? Salman had a cause. The liberation of Kashmir as vengeance. He had no qualms about killing his own sister to keep the family honor in tact. *'I have a cause too. I will reach you Ruhaina even if I have to kill. Let me die knowing that you are alive and well and not harmed in anyway. I wish to see you smile for it was upon my honor that I took your hand from your father. But how will I kill Indian soldiers?'* Abdul was disturbed by the dichotomy in his mind. He had to make up his mind and act accordingly or live in constant conflict and fear of being discovered.

*'Everything else be damned. I have managed to survive and get out of that prison camp alive. I will reach my goal. And I will get the others out of that place too. Brother, you had promised to get us released but maybe the sickness got you. So forgive me but this is the only way I was left with to redeem myself. To escape by whatever means was our dream. And Colonel Sunderam knows about my plan. He will stand by me if required. If only I did not have to kill Indian soldiers.'*

Abdul had been asked about how the Indian army laid an ambush and what was the best way to get out of it. And he had recalled his training days to explain to them that in an ambush it was suicidal to turn back. The retreat in a well-set ambush always resulted in more casualties. It was by far better to take cover in the terrain and return the fire and charge into the enemy and break through the sidelines for an escape. He emphasized the importance of a scout who should reconnaissance the area ahead before the main advance. The mujahideen always moved in small groups, merging with the local population and Abdul's tactics were for larger numbers but they began to understand the importance of having scouts. Abdul was a wrestler and was still adept in unarmed combat and the use of just a strong wooden staff. He taught them a few blocks and throws and how to use the staff as a weapon. Majid would watch these training sessions with Ozero showing open scorn. The mercenaries had their own way but the Kashmiri and Pakistani recruits appreciated his skills and began to regard him as a good fighter. Soon they all began to carry a staff in addition to their "best mate" comrade Kalashnikov. The staff helped them climb steep slopes and was now also a potent weapon for them. After three months Abdul was taken on his first raid.

It was an early misty morning when he first saw the closest railway station with a damaged and fallen signboard that said 'Tangi'. *'So this is where the train blew its whistle twice a week. So this is where we are. The prison camp will be within three kilometers for us to hear the train whistle but where is Tangi in relation to the border?'*

They boarded a goods train with open wagons. Ozero knew the railway staff and he commanded almost feudal respect. He traveled in style in the engine cab while the others were in the open goods wagons. From Tangi the train would take them to Nowshera. He looked back at Tangi as the train pulled out of the remote station. My journey home has begun he thought. It was exhilarating for Abdul to feel the breeze on his face. The countryside was still quite green with scattered wild flower bushes. It was the month of May and summer was setting in fast. There were undulating hills in the near distance and he had not known so much beauty at close quarters for a long time. It had the effect of increased energy in his limbs and he chatted with Salman till he found him dosing. The mercenaries were two wagons ahead and had lit up their country made cheroots. He could see the puffs of blue smoke escaping as they exhaled carrying the acrid raw green tobacco leaf smoke smell to him in the wake. It smelt strong and rich exciting a wild kind of freedom. Behind him two wagons away were the four Pakistani recruits. *'They like to keep me in the center, Abdul thought and smiled. I am not going to run till I know that you wouldn't dream of it and you can be sure I will get my opportunity.'*

At Nowshera the weapons were wrapped into rough blankets and concealed within gunny bags. They were to board a passenger train going to Islamabad. Abdul became their baggage carrier. He was strong enough for the load and they were going away for three months. This was the time the tracks in the hills would be free of snow and they could cover distances hopping from village to village. The baggage consisted mainly of ammunition and crude sleeping bags made from blankets stitched together. Personal clothing was only what they wore as they already had some clothes at their advance camp destination in a village. The passenger train moved faster than the goods train and it did not stop at wayside stations enroute. Abdul found this quite similar to what he remembered of train journeys from Ahmadabad to Delhi in a passenger train with Abba. The mujahideen had occupied seats together so that Abdul was kept away from other passengers. He was at the window seat and was warned not to talk to anyone. In fact none of them spoke to anyone, not even among themselves. This was very unlike Abdul's travels in India.

In India on train journeys everybody made friends and got chatting to the extent of asking very personal questions. Ozero bought some fruits and they shared it. That had been their lunch. Abdul had climbed up into the upper berth and slept fitfully till it was time to disembark. This was his first train journey in thirty years and his body had forgotten the swaying motion, so he slept fitfully than being lulled by the usual rocking motion. He studied the faces through half closed eyes in between naps. It was evening when the train drew into Wah. They climbed out of the train with Abdul carrying the baggage. Ozero had some kind of a pass in his wallet that got them through the gates everywhere. No questions or tickets were asked for and the ticket collectors had a respectful look for Ozero as he passed. The pass he later learnt was an endorsed certificate from the army that the holder could travel with his helpers anywhere in the country. Salman had proudly claimed, 'we don't have to buy tickets. The army has given us a pass and Ozero has it. Isn't that great, free travel?'

At Wah there was a trailer wagon that could take the nine of them in it with the baggage and one man in the trailer. Salman was made to ride in the trailer while Abdul was between two of the mercenaries. Ozero and the others knew the driver. He was jokingly told, 'Rafiq bhai lets go for the wedding. This is the season and they had all laughed. We have a new groom to offer; this is Abdul Aziz.'

Rafiq had responded with the customary, "Salaam", and Abdul had returned his greetings. They drove out of the small township of Wah taking the back roads and Abdul was appalled at the poverty all around. Ozero had bought a sack of dry fruits but didn't have to pay for it. He just made an entry into a register and the Pathan grocer was very polite and happy at the sale. Abdul thought, *'there must be some understanding everywhere. How does it matter; but these are indications that such operations by the mujahideen is very organized and sponsored by someone powerful or an organization.'* The drive into the countryside was over narrow and broken roads. They were soon in the hills and passed through Haripur without stopping. Abdul made a note of all the places he was passing. It was important information he would be carrying back for the Indian authorities. From Wah they reached Abbottabad in four hours and Ozero called for a dinner halt outside the city. The driver new where to go and they were soon seated in a make do wayside restaurant called "Dilkhush". Rafiqbhai placed the order for food while Ozero and the two mercenaries settled to drink from a bottle they had carried with themselves. The two Pakistanis and Salman with Abdul stretched tired and cramped limbs on small separate wooden cots literally thrown at them by the owner of Dilkhush. Frontier ways and mannerisms were sure brusque. The Dilkhush husband and wife got together to quickly make a meal from rice and lamb. The smell of herbs and the frying of lamb meat in its own lard was enough to increase their appetite after a whole days journey that had kicked off on the back of a goods train. Abdul lay on a cot and looked at the stars. The way of life here was not very different from what he had experienced in rural India. The trains, the roads, the poverty, the countryside, the warm hospitality, even the language was similar. What then was the real problem? Why was there so much hate between two nations that shared even language and customs? Could it only be the religion or were there some deep-rooted deprivations and jealousy? If the Kashmiris truly wanted their freedom, then why not? His mind and body was in a trance after the whole day. Lying there he took in the smell of the cooking. *'Who cares, Kashmir or not anymore, I have to eat well get strong and run free soon. This cooking smells good.'*

Ozero presided over the meal as usual. The food was typically spicy and the steaming rice helped carry the aroma that had tremendous revival capabilities. Abdul was not used to the spices and needed to wash his mouth a couple of times. It provided the humor for the evening. Every morsel made him feel stronger. Ozero gave his approval, 'Muzaffar bhai, the meal was fantastic. Is there anything you want from India?'

'Get me some good Hindi music cassettes Ozero, I like the ones composed by Rehman.'

'Here is money for the meal. I don't know when we'll be back but I will try to get your music.'

Abdul realized that the Pakistanis loved Indian music from the films of Bollywood. *'Strange people, they hate India but love its music and there is no ban on it. How do they tolerate the black marketed films with scenes that have temples and idols?'*

They moved into the night and after two hours of driving through hills where the road was non-existent in patches they arrived at Nathia Galli. A small settlement of one large cottage and a few huts made of rocks and wood. It was going to be home for the next few months. Fazalbhai was expecting them and came out to greet them with a lantern. 'There is no electricity for the last two days. There was a storm and some poles carrying the overhead electricity lines have fallen. I have some hot Chai, if you care.'

'Yes and we need an extra cot for Abdul, said Ozero. He was an Indian Para commando and prisoner of war in Pakistan. Wants to take revenge, Hah! And is with us on his first trip. We will soon see his capabilities. If you have any reason to doubt him Fazalbhai, free his soul for good.'

'I will look at him in the daylight,' was Fazalbhai's response. Meanwhile have your Chai and rest. We can update tomorrow.' Abdul wondered at the scheme of things and the constant reminder given by Ozero that he was dispensable. He was constantly on the periphery between life and sudden death. The mujahideen have a strong bonding among themselves and you can never get accepted unless you prove it. Till then you were always a suspect under scrutiny.

Fazal had a small farm on the hill overlooking the Jhelum River. It was not full moon but the starlight was enough for Abdul to see the river frothing far down in the valley. It blossomed a plan. Ozero read his mind. As if he could intrude into your very being without notice. Even his conversation was in short abrupt bursts like the firing of a carbine. 'You getting ideas? That's the Jhelum. We could send your body down it.'

'I know Ozero but you won't have to, I have given my word to Majidbhai.'

'That's the river where we will wash and bathe everyday; you know how to swim?'

'Yes I was a good commando. I was a decent swimmer but am now totally out of practice.'

'Then better be careful or it can wash you away. It is fast.'

'Thank you for the advice; maybe you will feel happier if you tie me up to a tree before letting me into the water.' Abdul heard Ozero laugh for the first time in so many months.

'I will not tie you but if you try to escape; there are many groups like ours operating here and they will not spare you. And we know all the villagers here; so they will be looking and let us know. And as for the Indians— they will never believe your story. Tomorrow we will take you with us to our observation point. I want you to carry our stuff and also remember the route. Soon you will be making trips back and forth from here with food and ammunition.'

'Sure sir, I never forget cross country routes.'

Abdul followed the others into the farmhouse. It was built on two floors with a narrow staircase leading to the upper floor that was more like a platform with a roof. It had walls on three sides with the front stretching onto an open balcony without any railing and precariously overlooked the valley. Each man took his weapon and checked it before finally spreading a rug on the make shift cots that were laid out dormitory fashion. Abdul found one free and made his bed. Like the others he said his prayers and sat for a while. *'Tomorrow will take me closer to my India. Protect me from any hasty decisions Allah. These mujahideen will have no mercy if I fail them in anyway. You have brought me so far. Whatever is your wish, thy will be done. The view of the river from here is so wonderful. India and Pakistan have such natural beauty. But they are enemies. And I am just a log drifting in all this rugged beauty. Oh! When will I be with you again Ruhaina?'* His mind flowed with the rush of the rapids and he continued thinking in the same praying posture.

'There have been three wars between India and Pakistan. The last one was at Kargil. I wonder what were the reasons for Kargil and what really happened in it. According to the guards at the prison Indian soldiers were massacred enmasse and Leh was cut off from Srinagar. That means Pakistan has liberated or taken over some more areas from India. Their general then became the President. And he was a Muhajir (A Pakistani whose origins were in India). Does he never feel like an Indian? He wants to liberate Kashmir someday. What is it that makes a man believe that he can justify all his actions as the ones that Allah truly dictates? Does it never occur to such men that so many lives are disrupted with wars? The environment remains disturbed much after the battles are over. These killings in Ahmadabad, what in Allah's name is that for? Or is it true that we Muslims are really hated by all Hindus and will always remain at the receiving end. It may have been better then that even Abba had come away to Pakistan when he had the choice. I would have never been in this situation. But Oh! Ahmadabad is such a beautiful city and so is the rest of India. At least I did get to see a lot of India by being in the army. We fought Pakistan together, Hindus, Muslims, Christians, Sikhs and others side by side, in all those wars. How long will I now be captive in this mujahideen role? Will I be able to kill an Indian soldier to prove my loyalty and then be allowed to carry weapons? If I have a weapon I will feel more confident of attempting an escape. But what has the weapon got to do with my escape? At the most these fellows will worry that I can fire back at them. I wonder, because they don't seem to care for their own lives. Nothing deters them. Will I have to kill them to escape or will they get me. The prison camp environment was not so dangerous. I wonder what Colonel Sunderam, Ganguly and Pawri think of me. If only I am able to get them freed someday. They will then support my action in joining the mujahideen. That was the only way I could ever hope of getting out. It was such a big chance and it seems to be working so far. Tomorrow maybe a different story. I am sure that I will be able to convince people on the Indian side. I must head for the nearest army unit and surrender and what should I tell them? It is better that I tell them the whole truth. Why should I expect the Colonel to protect me by saying untrue things? If the Indian army puts me into a prison, so be it. At least Ruhaina will understand it all. And she will know that I am alive and always thought of her and had to do what I am doing to reach her. Allah, I know you will be merciful. So, I will escape but have to first cover some more distance, both in building trust between these fellows and me and also get closer to India before I plan to run. I have no idea how far am I from the border. Maybe I will be taken across soon for a raid. Nanga Parbat you look close. You are my beacon of freedom.'

The anticipation of crossing over the border back into India, the country of his birth brought a deep longing sigh. Prayers over, sleep came in whimsical waves to Azad Khan as he tried to keep awake comprehending the situation. There was no looking back now. Captivity was not restricted to prison walls. He was captive to so many factors and feelings even now. But he was at the base, climbing the rock face to freedom. At least that was what he hoped and prayed for.

# Chapter XII

'I could be in a lot of trouble for being here with you on this visit to this advocate and then to this nursing home. Do you really need my presence?' Major Dilip was appealing to Brother.

Brother put an arm on the Major's powerful shoulders. 'You are brave and I will be grateful always. I am fortunate to find you. Your presence gives my being here a lot of credibility. Thank you.'

Brother waited with Major Dilip outside Advocate Smita Choudhury's chamber at the Ahmadabad court. The Major was just lending support. Brother was full of apprehensions. Looking down the long corridor that took a turn and vanished he wondered. 'Am I getting closer or is this going to turn out to be a useless exercise. It will be almost impossible to get people to understand the last twenty-nine years. It will be difficult to accept that someone close to them is still alive and a prisoner in an enemy country and that the government has no information about it all these years.' His thoughts always became warning screams.

'And here I am; someone they don't even know leave alone trust and I bring them news about their father and husband. Will this news be a happy one for them or will it increase their pain. They are already in a traumatic situation due to these riots. Whatever it is, I have a commitment to my *friends still held behind those walls. It was not easy to tell Sheila that Kailash was no more. That was an ending to expectations. Here I will be rekindling expectations that may already be partly dead in their minds. There will be disbelief, frustration, anger and pain but I have been there before. Let me try to help them transit into the new hope that I bring. Oh Lord! This may reopen my battles with the air force and government but who cares. The truth is that some of my best friends are there left behind and not dead. Their wives and children must know. Maybe this lawyer is the best thing to happen. She can help us all but I have to be convincing.'*

The swing doors opened and a peon ushered them into the office. Behind a desk full of thick volumes and papers Smita got up to welcome them in. The Major was recognized from his uniform but Brother was in his favorite jeans and cheque shirt. She motioned for them to be seated and introduced herself. The major introduced himself and then Brother as retired Flight Lieutenant James. The steel cupboards and classic wooden shelves from a bygone era towered around creating a cocooning effect. And in the middle of this collapsing environment of thick files, folders with rusted clips and a glass top table was a vivacious lady advocate scrutinizing them. It did not help Brother's confidence but he stayed resolved. He had seen similar decor in the air force of the past. Most government offices had an aura and smell of old paper that made one wonder, how did it all work.

Smita broke the silence. 'I have the note that you sent to Mr. Basheer Khan in the nursing home. He is seriously wounded and had told me earlier, that you have saved his life. We are grateful to you major.'

'It is just fortunate that I happened to be there and am glad I could help. But there were many women workers in the shop and it is sad that I could not stop those hooligans from getting away with them.'

The advocate in her typical matter of fact tones said, 'Oh! You need not worry about those women. The van in which they were escaping was a stolen one and they abandoned it and the women managed to escape. All the girls are safe.'

'That is providence and how is Basheer because he was unconscious when we took him to the Municipal hospital.'

There was a tone of urgency in her voice but out of sheer gratefulness to the man who had saved Basheer, Smita continued, 'thanks to you, he is better now but very disturbed. The surgeons will operate on his fingers tomorrow. They are badly damaged but we are hopeful that he will recover and be able to do his tailoring work soon.

He speaks very highly of you. You must visit him in the nursing home sometime.'

The major sensed that time was on a premium here so he filled in the next short gap in conversation. 'This gentleman has some important information so it is better he tells you himself. Brother, Is that okay?'

Smita settled and was suddenly keen to continue hearing them, 'is it something to do with the riots Mr. James, are you a witness and were you there?'

'I am not a mister, but am retired Flight lieutenant James. You can just call me Brother. I am comfortable that way.' Brother with his eyebrows raised, indicated over his shoulder and whispered, 'is it proper to discuss confidential issues or matters that are secrets, here in your office. Your door is open.'

'It is fine, don't worry Flight Lieut...Brother,' and she smiled to give him confidence, the smile extending not because she was the informal kind but appreciated the way he had broken the formal barriers that was the dull spirit of courtrooms. This man had an easy presence so she felt the need to reciprocate the informality.

'Mrs. Choudhury,' Brother began. 'You can call me Smita,' she interrupted eyebrows raised, head tilted to one side in friendly encouragement and it triggered spontaneous laughter from her visitors. It was an unusual start for an advocate's office. Her fingers joined forming a praying tent; Smita leaned forward on her table to encourage the discussion. Brother and the major were a bit slower than her to regain composure from the brief diversion. Her eyes focused on Brother to prompt him to continue. Brother smiled and looked around deciding where to begin. He was still a bit "fighter pilot" and was at his best whenever challenge was in the air. *So far so good, he thought, atleast she is a cheerful person. Let me then give her the whole story. I wonder what she is, to this Basheer Khan.*

'Basheer Khan's father was in the army and was given up as missing in the war of 1971 with Pakistan. The Indian army records show him as missing given up for dead in their records.'

Smita narrowed her eyes to understand the relevance of this statement with the present circumstances in Ahmadabad. There seemed to be none. ' I can't figure out the relevance,' she said.

Brother looked away into the distance and continued, 'I also fought in that war and met Basheer's father. His name is Azad Khan.'

Smita's eyes opened up wide with surprise. ' How did you meet him because I thought you said you are Flight.... Isn't that air force?'

Brother smiled and helped her out with his rank. His smile embarrassed her but he was quick to raise both his palms in a gesture to show that he forgave and understood the problem of civilians not being able to remember military ranks in the first meeting.

'Do I take it that you do believe that I did meet him?'

Smita was quick to realize that she had implied it by asking him how they had met. The lawyer's defense came up. 'I have no reason to disbelieve you but if your story is true, then where and when was this meeting?'

Brother continued with his most serious face, 'Have you heard of prisoners of war?'

'Yes, I know about wars and prisoners, you may continue.'

'I was a PoW and so was Azad Khan.'

'You mean he was released like you and you have come to find him, but I am afraid, no one knows his whereabouts here.'

Brother smiled and shook his head to convey that she had presumed wrongly. 'No no, he is not here I know but I do know his whereabouts and have come to inform his family. I came to Ahmadabad after reading an article in the news papers and this Major is the one that is mentioned in that article.' With that he handed the well-preserved piece of clipping that was almost omnipresent in his shirt pocket. Smita looked at the clipping and back at him before she began to read the contents.

Brother leaned back patiently. It was becoming complex but questions would always be there. This was just the beginning.

Smita's forehead wrinkled and she handed him back the clipping. 'The reporters must have found out about Basheer Khan's father and mentioned it to make it a bit sensational. And you claim to know his whereabouts? So then, where is he?'

'He was in the prison camp with me and I was released due to failing health but he is still stuck in there.'

'How do you know that he is still there?'

'I was released two years ago in the year 2000, and Azad was with me in the prison for twenty-nine years. If he is still alive, he should be there in the prison unless they have moved him or otherwise.'

Smita looked at the major for an explanation. The major in turn just shrugged his shoulders maintaining neutral stance but added in support, 'Brother was a prisoner all right. We have checked that out with the air force but beyond that we don't know.' Smita's hand went to her cheek as she tried to lean forward and get to the reason of their visit. With a resigned tight-lipped smile she showed her helplessness.

'How can I help you then, Brother? If Azad is still there as you claim; only the government can help in getting him back, so you need to report this to them.'

'I told the authorities when I was sent back to the country but they wouldn't believe me as I could not remember the location of the camp and also a fake story about my presence in their country implicated me.'

Brother had to repeat his story as he'd done for the Major and his colleague two nights ago.

Smita listened with awe; eight fingers entwined thumbs supporting her chin, eyes changing from narrow scrutiny, to surprise turning into helpless sympathy. 'Even if all this is true, it is something that will be stunningly unbelievable for Basheer and his mother. Though his mother believes that her husband is still alive so maybe she will be overjoyed.'

'Yes Smita,' Brother looked down at his feet and added, 'my purpose is to bring them the news that he is alive, remembers them and is proud of them. It will give them hope but also increase their helplessness, I know. It was a promise to Azad, to find his family and these riots have made that possible because I had no address to start with and the last two years have been difficult for me to settle down and also, I did not want to get caught in controversies with the air force and government. If I had known the location of the camp, it would have probably made all the difference to everyone but could be fatal for my friends in that prison. Wiping out tracks is very easy for the military regime in Pakistan.'

The impossibility of the situation made Smita grit her teeth and wonder if she was getting into uncharted waters. The woman in her responded with deep joy for Ammi, sympathy for Brother and angst followed by determination to find a way. 'I would like to believe all that you say Brother and am taking you seriously. Shall we first meet Azad's wife as she is staying with me? Would you like me to brief her a bit? It can be shocking so let me prepare her?'

'Yes, it will be a big help.' Both men shook their heads together in agreement and that brought a smile to Smita's face. *'These brave military men still needed help and suggestions from women.'*

'Then why waste time. You can come with me in my car.'

'We have our own jeep.'

'You come in my car and tell your jeep driver to follow us,' she hurried with closing some of her open files.

Brother sensed that Smita was taking control. It gave him confidence that his support was increasing. Maybe finding the families and support from them could lead to freedom for all.

Smita made a call to her mother and told her that she was coming home with some important people who were to meet Ruhaina and Basheer. There seemed to be an added spring in her actions now. The peon was summoned and rushed to put her folders and files into the cupboards and lock up the chamber for the day. It was only eleven in the morning.

Minutes later they were headed home in her Toyota Corolla. She was seated in front with the driver and the major with Brother relaxed in the air-conditioned backseat. 'Is your residence far from here.'

'It takes about fifteen minutes. Do you wish to go somewhere else, Brother.'

'No, it is just that you have very little time to prepare your explanation for Ruhaina.'

'She is like my own mother and has seen me from college days.' She was then all praise for Basheer helping the mother's business and making it one of the best tailoring shops in Ahmadabad.

'So you seem to know the family for very long, is it?'

'Yes Basheer was in college with me.' Smita made mention of Basheer failing to get recruited into the army and that made Brother look at the major and say, 'couldn't the army have helped him in that?'

The major was caught unawares and became almost apologetic. 'I was not here at the time of recruitment or could have definitely helped. It is strange that in spite of his father being in the army, he was turned down.'

Smita added, 'just as well, I think his mother was glad that he wasn't selected.'

The Toyota followed by the army jeep turned off the road towards a dominating iron gate. There was a uniformed watchman who recognized the car and opened the gate. Brother looked in awe at the well-kept garden and the double storied bungalow ahead. It was painted in keeping with its British ancestry. Cream colored walls with the doors, windows and wooden supporting columns in bright green. It all looked very fresh and official.

'You have a fabulous house,' Brother complimented.

'It is my father's. He is a judge in the court here. We live upstairs and my parents have the whole ground floor. The house is more than a hundred years old. Ruhaina with Azad's sister are staying temporarily in our outhouse.' The car maneuvered under a tiled roof wooden porch that had wooden latticework from the roof downwards making it an enclosure. Creepers and potted plants filled up the eternity between the columns supporting the porch. Everything was quite huge here.

Smita led them up the shallow steps to a spacious verandah. There was a coffee and a card table with intricately embroidered cushion backs and seats in the cane chairs. At one end was a cushioned swing, the size of a bed. It was suspended with smoothened woven coir ropes from secure iron loops in the horizontal teak wood beam. The atmosphere was relaxed but Brother could sense the urgency in Smita's footsteps. He wondered if she would be able to explain it all. *'I will have to repeat my story to Ruhaina and there will be so many questions. Many more and newer than Smita or anyone else had asked him so far. I owe it to you Azad and will go through this test. I am sure they will believe that you are alive.'* The major had wanted to leave. Now that Brother was going to meet Ruhaina and Basheer, he felt that he would have no role. Smita had almost ordered him to stay on. 'Don't you think Ruhaina will want to thank you for saving her son's life? And I think Brother will also be more comfortable with you around.' The woman's eyebrows were very expressive language, observed Brother. 'Both of you wait here while I speak to her and it may take a little time so would you like some coffee or tea.'

The two men looked at each other and Brother opted for black coffee and the major just agreed to whatever his senior said. He was trained to do that. With that Smita disappeared into the mansion and a liveried waiter soon brought them the coffee and the major silently added some milk into his coffee since there happened to be a milk jug in the tray. Brother preferred it black. He needed the strength.

Smita explained to her mother hurriedly and requested her to join up at the outhouse after a while. Mother listened to daughter's plan suppressing her own astonishment and mused at Smita's bubbling excitement. Anything to do with Basheer or Ruhaina always made "Mother" sit up and listen. She could now feel the eagerness and empathy in her daughter's rapid fire. Smita would do the initial explaining and then may need the support of someone the age of Ruhaina to be around. It would be the right mix of emotional ages. Her mother agreed.

Ruhaina was packing a few things for Basheer. She was to visit and be with him from midday onwards. Seeing Smita approach warmed her heart. 'Truly, you are over concerned about me Smita. I can go to the nursing home myself. It is not a very long walk.'

Smita, with all her experience and lengthy orations in the court suddenly found herself without the right words. How does one tell a woman that your husband is not dead and also that he is still a prisoner of war? The enormity of it was overwhelming. And you cannot make polite conversation and abruptly break news like this or drift from the mundane daily conversation to thirty years back in a flash. Neither can you not show from your body language that there is something that has to be said and is blocked for a beginning. Sometimes body language reaches out and touches and even speaks.

'Is something wrong Smita?'

'All is well Ammi and Basheer is fine, I met him in the morning but there is someone here today who says that he has met your husband and that he may be alive.'

Ruhaina sat down in a heap, 'Ya Allah! You are merciful; I am grateful that he is alive. Tell me more.' Ruhaina hugged her as though clinging for life.

Smita explained everything that she could remember and Ruhaina listened shocked but without visible expression. Smita was dazed at the lack of any emotional upheaval. She had expected and almost wanted it, so that they could share the fire and ice together but Ruhaina had stolidly heard her out with a calm that almost invalidated her own anticipation. It was purely to express her own heartfelt joy that she said, 'Ammi I am so happy for you and Basheer.'

And that had burst the dam. Silent tears flowed and Ruhaina went limp without energy or desire to wipe them as they formed and overflowed. It was melt down for Smita too. The reality of the possibility that this was all true was finally finding a resting place in their hearts. Ruhaina had often imagined that Azad was very much with them and part of their simple lives. And not snatched away by fate the way it was. He would have been proud of Basheer. And Ruhaina had also known Basheer's affection for Smita. Smita had visited her shop during their college days and there used to be a common glow on their faces. That his dreams had died had been confirmed when he did not go for her wedding. She had seen the invitation card. And that she still mattered in his life was visible from his attention to whatever Smita gave for tailoring. He had almost refused to marry. That it was Smita bringing her the news about Azad, her long lost husband, made her tears warmer. Ruhaina could have well, been a grandmother if Azad's dream with Smita had become reality but she was not. A life spent in deprivation flowed through her tears in a controlled stream. This was truly a confluence of joys for her. This girl that must have given her son Basheer joy, was today bringing her own husband back from the dead to her. At least it felt that way, through the mist of tears.

Malabika Choudhury watched them from the house and tried to feel the winds of emotions in her backyard. Covering her head with her sari, she headed towards them. Seeing her come Ruhaina wiped her tears and greeted her with swollen eyes. They fell into each other's arms and stayed silent, letting the moment pass.

Ruhaina released her first and looked down and joined her hands and said, 'how can I ever do whatever your family has done for us. And now, Smita says that my husband is alive but as a prisoner. Do you think it can be true?'

Smita's mother was visibly embarrassed at the gratefulness and she could just manage saying, 'Smita is like your own daughter and we consider you as a part of our family, so this is a very good news for us to share with you. Let us see what we can all do and find out more from the person who has come here to meet you.'

Ruhaina went into the outhouse to wash her face but the anguish remained stamped to her face. She covered her head and shoulders with a white shoulder cloth and put her hands on Smita's shoulders. 'I wish Basheer were here. And Dilawar hasn't slept all night. Her cough worries me. Let her sleep now, I will tell her about her brother when she wakes up.'

'Ammi we will all go to the nursing home together after meeting this man who was with your husband. Come let us go, I can hardly wait to give Basheer this news.' Her eagerness brought a smile to Ruhaina's distressed face.

Brother and the major stood up to receive the three women. Ruhaina was a bit puzzled at seeing the major in his army uniform but it gave the atmosphere the sanctity required. Brother recognized Ruhaina from her distinctly different attire from that of Smita and her mother. To his "namaste", Ruhaina replied with a "salaam". Smita did a quick introduction and they remained seated looking at each other for what seemed ages.

Ruhaina looked at Brother softly saying, 'have you any thing that will make us believe that Azad is alive.' Brother just looked at his own feet.

Smita understood the silence and said, 'I have told her all that you have said and she is grateful that you have taken the trouble to bring her the news. You can tell her whatever you feel like and I think she needs more information about her husband that will make her more sure and convinced that you were actually there with him.'

This had been Brother's rock face to climb. All his descriptions about the prison camp and his mates always ended with unanswered questions about the authenticity of it all, especially because the location was want for a name. He tried a different approach.

Taking a deep breath he began. 'Azad bhai was very fond of his sister and always felt that he had let down his father by joining the army instead of continuing the tailoring business.' There was no expression from his audience. 'He was the regimental wrestling champion and had kept himself fit even in the camp.' Ruhaina's steady gaze made him uncomfortable. Brother quickly added, 'our beds were close to each other and he said his prayers five times a day everyday. He told me once that he hardly prayed when he was here in Ahmadabad but after becoming a prisoner he found courage in prayer. He admired you for being the one who prayed regularly everyday.' There was recognition of this fact in the form of a thin smile from Ruhaina. 'Azad bhai used to say that you made excellent roasted duck and that your father was a very keen shot and would insist that whatever game he hunted was to be cooked by you. He also told me that you gave him the gold to get his tooth capped. He still wears it.'

Ruhaina's face filled up with pain from this remembrance and she trembled breaking her silence and sobbed, 'then where is he now? They cannot keep him prisoner for so many years. What wrong has he done? He was a soldier obeying orders. Can you not get him released?' She looked around helplessly.

The atmosphere was charged but Brother felt relieved that he could recall some of their conversations in the camp and this had led her to accept that after all he had spent years with her husband and that he was not faking. He had no reply to the 'where is he now'. But he added that 'maybe we could go to the government and ask for help in getting prisoners held in Pakistan released. There may be other camps too, so there is no assurance that they have released everyone. I have tried my best to describe the location to the authorities but they need definite names and facts. They had declared us all, missing feared killed in action. So when I was sent home, the Pakistanis had made up a story to cover themselves and I could not prove it wrong for lack of evidence. They had almost decided to try me as a deserter and punishment could have been imprisonment again.' Brother was surprised at his own appealing voice as emotions enveloped him too.

'No no, I don't wish that you get imprisoned again. What can we do Smita,' was Ruhaina's genuine plea.

'Ammi what Brother says is possible because the government cannot take a stand unless it has all the facts. This could become an international issue.'

Ammi looked at each one's face in desperation and then said, 'but don't the governments of both countries keep accusing each other of terrorists and other violations so often? How does one more accusation matter and will it not make a difference if the government of India provides the names of the prisoners that Brother confirms and then they could demand their release? I am willing to go to Pakistan to get his release. There are some relatives of my father in Karachi. We have not kept in touch but I can find out from my relatives here. I am sure the Karachi relatives will help me. I only want him to be released and don't want any compensation or anything. Let him live like a free man is all I am asking for. Can you describe the place to me Brother so even if I reach within hundred miles of it, I will search out the camp. I have no fight with any government but I want that my husband who did his duty be allowed to live like a free man. Can you help me Brother and you Smita, you know so many important people.'

'Ammi, we will do whatever we can.' Smita looked at Brother for approval and he nodded in agreement.

This was something Brother had feared. To make someone believe that death had not taken away their father or husband in a war may not be very difficult but to have explanations as to why the government could not get them released from a Pakistani prison camp was never going to be explainable. This was 2002 and things were not at their best between the two nations. The Indian government would have no starting point to demand the release and Ruhaina's going to Pakistan was suicidal, at least for him and he thought it would be the same for Ruhaina. They may not allow her to enter Pakistan, leave alone a search for a prison camp. The imponderables were too many. And a stir like this could threaten the further survival of the prisoners that were at the mercy of rabid soldiers like Subedar Abdul Karim. He was grateful to have survived the camp and then the Indian officialdom.

' Ruhaina bhabi, I had promised Azad bhai, that if I am released and reach India, I would find your house, to bring you this news and I beg your forgiveness that it has taken so long and has happened only after I read about this major and your son in the papers. Azad bhai was very close to me and I am grateful that all of you believe in what I say. Azad does not even know that I was released because they never told me anything when they took me out of that camp into a military hospital in Karachi. I have to find the families of the others now. Your faith in me has given me enormous courage. My journeys have just begun and you have given me the push to go on. I am sorry to have taken so long in coming here.'

Ruhaina's words from her heart were simple. 'On the contrary I am grateful that Allah has been merciful to you and to my husband and that you could find us is the greatest thing that has happened for me in all my life.' Ruhaina now conveyed a more sure and determined look. Her resilience was coming through. From behind her tearful face was emerging a tigress willing to stake her all to reach her husband. It was a bit of a threat for Brother but now there was no looking back.

Smita looked relieved that Ruhaina had responded positively and asked Brother if they could all visit Basheer and share the good news with him also. Brother could not help saying, 'Azadbhai does not even know that he has a son. It will be a privilege for me to meet my brave friend's son, Basheer. There is a lot I can tell him about his father and how courageous he is. Let us go then. What do you say major? You are the one that is the savior of this family and have also helped me find them.'

The major looked embarrassed at these words and Brother once again pulled out the clipping and gave it to Ruhaina who clutched it as though it were her passport to reach Azad. 'You may keep it bhabi. Without all of you I would never have made this beginning. It is a long journey ahead, let us meet Basheer so that I can go back to Bombay and renew my search for the others.' Ruhaina was disappointed that Brother could not meet Dilawar and they moved on to visit Basheer.

The nursing home was barely a ten-minute drive. Brother and the major in their jeep followed Ruhaina and Smita.

The major hadn't spoken much but he could not hold anymore. 'Brother sir, you are a retired officer but for me to get involved in this business of taking the issue up with the government will definitely get the air force and army involved. It could become an embarrassment for everyone and I will be in serious trouble. They will link you and Azad Khan's family to me. It will appear as though I have assisted in instigating the matter.'

'My dear major, I will be in a trickier situation because I have already been through the official cross-examination and was let off in spite of the Pakistani story of my being a deserter. I may be behind bars again. And you are not getting involved. You have just helped me locate the man you have saved. You may wind up with a medal for saving Basheer's life. Have faith and remember; now we have women and surviving relatives on our side. The government cannot afford not to be sympathetic to Ruhaina. We want those men in prison freed. Don't we?'

'Yes sir.'

Brother withdrew to his memories with Azad and felt emphatic for Ruhaina and Basheer. These were innocent human beings forced into becoming prisoners of a deprivation that could only end with the return of their man Azad. For the remaining drive there was silence but his mind whirled. *'I am surprised with myself that I never felt sorry for my mother that she did not know about my whereabouts or whether I was alive or not. We were just overjoyed to be reunited again. She must be a very happy and grateful mother today. But she does not know anything about the problems that I had to face with the air force after coming back and now that I am on this trail it may help to share with her. Why should the name and location of the camp be so important as prisoners can always be shifted? We have to act quickly and get either an International agency that can bring its powers to bear involved or it will have to be an undercover operation. This is turning out to be like an exercise in exposure of truth. Here, Ruhaina and the others all believe my story but that may not happen with everyone. All what is happening may just lead to the wiping out of Colonel Sunderam and others. Captors are ruthless but there were some that were nice. Smita is a judge's daughter. She could become the driving force in this mission impossible. I must call Sheila tonight. It looks like a successful day. She has been my supporter all along and I wonder what I would have been or done without her help and suggestions. Women are making all the difference in my situations. The Colonel is from Banglore and Ganguly from Calcutta. I wonder what will be the response of their folks. And Pawri a bachelor is from Deolali. His parents will be overjoyed. I must find these people quickly now. But where do I pick up further leads? Will I be lucky again?'*

Smita led the group into the room where Basheer lay propped up with his bandaged arms resting on supports. Basheer was glad to see her again today. Smita noticed that the flower vase with the roses she had brought, had been shifted closer to his bed, within touching distance. It warmed and also amused her. Basheer was getting re-connected with life.

Ammi went to his side and held his hand lightly and Basheer enquired about her and his aunt. And then he saw traces of her tears. He knew the signs so well. He had watched her so often silently staring at the road from their shop and home. And sometimes her eyes used to stay swollen for days. It used to pain him but he was a man after all. Emotional displays were acceptable from women. He would sometimes try and amuse her to distract her away from the brooding.

He tried, 'Ammi, why are you unhappy today. Tomorrow they will operate on me and soon we will go back home and restart the business. And did you know that Smita has found out that all the girls are safe.'

His cheerful words brought her immense relief, 'Allah is merciful, I am glad to hear that.'

'Oh! Ammi I have been busy and forgot to mention it to you yesterday.'

'You are doing so much for us Smita, it is alright,' was Ruhaina's ever-grateful reply.

Basheer could see the major standing at the door so he beckoned to him, 'Major Dilip sahib it is so nice of you to visit me, please come inside and take a chair. I can see that you have already met my mother and Smita.'

'Yes I have and there is someone I want you to meet, Basheer bhai.'

Brother was introduced as a retired air force pilot. The rest was up to him to do. Repetition of his past had become almost theatrical and he was adding finesse to it. He would need to do many more self-introductions and story telling in the near future. Brother went close to Basheer and took his extended hand gently. 'I am a retired pilot who fought the 1971 war and was shot down.'

'My father also fought in that war. It was before I was born.'

Brother smiled and said, 'your father would be very proud of you for the way you have looked after your mother and the ancestral business.' He turned towards Ruhaina, 'bhabi, why don't you tell him?' She was seated on the other side of the bed from Brother. It took her by surprise and she was speechless. There was a hush in the room. Suddenly the hum of the air-conditioner became audible and so did some faint horns of cars from the road outside. All eyes were on Ruhaina.

Smita moved closer to her and put one hand on her shoulder and said, 'Ammi, it is your privilege as his mother to tell him.'

'What is it that you all want to tell me Ammi? What is about? Please don't remind me of the riots or about going to courts to fight cases. I am grateful to you major for saving my life. Ammi tell me what has made you look as though you have been crying?'

'Basheer, this man standing by your side has been with your father after the war. He knows him well.' Basheer's face lost some color and he stared at Ammi and then slowly moved his head with some effort to look at Brother. He exhaled as though tired from exertion. Ammi placed a hand on Basheer's shoulder and added, 'they were both prisoners of war, her tears started trickling and he says that Abba is still alive but a prisoner in Pakistan.' She collapsed hugging Basheer. Basheer's eyes took on a questioning look and Brother could feel them searching for an answer from him. Brother was spell bound listening to Ruhaina trying to explain to her son. He hadn't heard many people talk about him like this.

Basheer propped up his mother and avoiding her eyes he said, 'Abba would never let himself be captured. I have spoken to so many officers and soldiers. They all say that, it is a disgrace to become a prisoner. It is better to die for the regiment than allow yourself to be captured. My father was a champion and brave man isn't that so major?'

The major's nod was more to give courage to Basheer than agree with him that his father would never surrender.

Basheer's eyes went towards Smita. She sensed his desolation. His own belief about his father stayed resolute in his eyes. A man, who never saw his father, only heard about him in a way that brought pains of deprivation and memories of the grief of his mother, was not going to condescend easily. Smita felt defeated. Brother wished he had some evidence to prove the existence of Azad; something to show that belonged to Azad. He was on the edge of being disbelieved. Ruhaina knew her son's determination and arrogance. She had anticipated his response. She believed Brother and wanted Basheer to know that she was grateful to Allah for his mercies. Her mind had already galloped towards getting Azad's release. She needed Basheer to travel with her thoughts.

'Basheer my son, Brother has told me so much and it would not be possible for him to know all that unless he was with your father. I believe him and we will get your father out of that prison soon. I have faith in Brother.'

Basheer's eyes never left Smita. She returned his stare with a look of plea and nodded almost invisibly in agreement with what Ruhaina had just said. 'Ammi, do you really think Abba is alive and a prisoner and for so many years? Can I believe that? Is he telling us the truth or is it just another hope. '

'Yes, unfortunately and mercifully, he is a released PoW and knows your father for sure.'

Basheer collapsed back into his pillows and stared at the ceiling.

Brother moved closer and touched his injured hand. 'There are others with your father in Pakistan. We will try to get all of them freed Basheer. I am so happy that now you know that he is alive and we will try to have him back with us. He was my best friend and a brave man.'

Basheer's bandaged hand moved towards his mother's face, his eyes leaving Smita just long enough to compare the looks of belief in Ruhaina's and their eyes. Could they be trusted with this joy or were they trying to cheer him up? Suddenly they were all three in an embrace with heads bowed and Basheer sobbed silently.

'Ammi, one day our sorrows will end. We will get Abba back. Hopefully that will be our new beginning.' Their collective sobbing tapered to gentle moans of joy.

The Major and Brother stood still. Military men do not usually display too many emotions publicly. Brother's thoughts stayed immersed in his gratefulness at finding Ruhaina and Basheer. His resolve to find the others grew stronger. Was it the Major who had been the key or was it the riots and what if Sheila had not seen the newspaper. He wondered and also felt a new kind of courage to overcome the fears and ridicule that had haunted him and almost succeeded in burying his quest.

# Chapter XIII

'Can I get your baggage sir?'

It was a young boy in disheveled rags, working as a porter on the Borivili local train platform. This was Bombay, the dreams of so many. From the few mainline trains; these porters could make a few bucks, enough to buy them two meals for the day.

'I don't have much other than this one bag. I prefer carrying it myself but here take this anyway.' Brother turned to the boy and slipped him a coin. 'Go get yourself a cup of tea. I am happy to be back here in Bombay.'

The Gujarat mail from Ahmadabad to Bombay stops at Borivili for five minutes early in the morning at six before heading towards the terminus at Bombay Central. Brother had slept soundly on the journey home. He stepped off the train at Borivili to switch platforms and catch a local train to Bandra. Sheila had been overjoyed at his call after he had been through with the reunion at the nursing home. The partings at Ahmadabad stayed like a perfume on him. Every now and then he would catch himself smiling at the fragrant happenings. Ruhaina made him feel like a family member. Basheer had not spoken much but had conveyed his gratefulness by joining in his mother's relief and joy. Smita had offered help and assured Brother that he would be protected from those that disbelieved him. She had also noted the names of the other prisoners with the promise to try and locate the relatives through whatever channels and contacts. Major Dilip had been dragged into the search team with the tacit understanding that he would be kept out of any media or government attention. His direct association with Brother and the relatives of PoWs could precipitate an embarrassing situation for the government and put his career on the block. But he would discreetly try to help through his military contacts in locating the relatives of the other prisoners.

On the way from Bandra station to Chapel road, Brother stopped the cab at Bandra bakery on bazaar road and bought some freshly baked bread. He loved the aroma of fresh bread dipped in hot tea and so did Martha. Reaching home he was greeted by his mother. Brother had called her briefly before boarding the train at Borivili to announce his return. She had prepared tea and some sandwiches for Brother. It was like the old times when Brother would come home on vacation from the air force. They sat in the balcony and watched Chapel road wake up from its late night reveling. At Chapel road there was always a 'do' everyday somewhere. Martha listened to him attentively as he recounted his experiences at Ahmadabad. She just said, ' Richard you really look happy as though you just met some long lost friends.' 'Well they are like that for me mom. Ruhaina's husband Azad was my best friend out there.' 'Oh! There is a letter for you Richard, I have kept it safely in my cupboard on the top shelf.' 'I will get it mom.' Brother felt good to be back home and was waiting for it to be eight o'clock. That's the time Sheila would be ready and at breakfast before going to her office. He would call her.

Brother found the envelope and looked at the postage stamp. Who would write to me he thought. It looked like it was posted in Bombay from Byculla. He didn't know anyone there. Going into his room Brother sat at his study table and carefully opened the envelope. There were two notes neatly folded and inserted separately. He opened one. It was hand written. It read.

Dear Mr. James,

I am a cousin of Elizabeth Fernandez. You can contact me on phone number 23724862. I have just returned from Karachi.

Yours sincerely
Victor Gomes.

Brother's mind spun as he started opening the second note. Who was Elizabeth Fernandez? And Victor Gomes, just returned from Karachi? Is someone trailing me after my visit to Ahmadabad? Is this something to do with Azad? Have the Pakistanis got wind of my attempts to find these relatives? Are they worried about being discovered? Is this a threat for me to stop? Fingers fumbling, mind racing and eyes trying hard to focus, Brother opened the second note. It answered a million questions in less than a second. It was typed and not even signed.

Dear James sir,
You left your address with me at the Karachi hospital before they sent you to India. Victor is my cousin brother who visits us once in two years. I could not write directly to you for it is risky. I gave this note to Victor to post at Bombay. Have you been able to find any clues about my brother? I saw your documents in the hospital record office and finally know the camp from where they brought you here. Cannot tell you but you can send me any important message for the others that you mentioned are still there. I can try reaching them. It is dangerous. Don't promise. Ask Victor for my e-mail address and please be discreet. Please look for my brother. My mother and I believe he is alive like they kept you.
Regards
Liz

It was like the cold barrel of a gun touching him. There was danger here and also many possibilities. Brother sank into his lean back directors chair and re-read both the notes. *'Did I actually give my address to that nurse in Karachi? I must have. She had come to me one night when she was on duty and told me that her brother in the army was also missing since the war of 1971 and that I was being sent back to India soon. What was her brother's name? I could ask Victor. Can I use this note to convince our authorities that there are prisoners still in Pakistan? I can but I must not. It will put Liz into a dangerous situation. She is smart, as she has not even signed the note. That rules out any further usage of it as evidence. He looked at the note from Victor and reached for the phone. Wait, should I call him or let me think about it, especially after this visit to Ahmadabad. Let me talk to Sheila first.'*

He looked at the old cuckoo clock and it was five minutes to eight. Brother dialed Sheila's number. It rang for a while and then he heard her voice.
'Who is this?'
'Its me, I got in this morning.'
'Can you give me sometime as I am dressing. I will call you back.'
Brother waited and re-read the notes. He had to think this out

clearly and keep his apprehensions under check and be rational. He wouldn't tell anyone. Not even Sheila. *'She will get alarmed by my fears. No, she is cool; she will have some better ideas than me.'* He debated. *'Why am I all the time worried about people trying to lock me up again? I have not overcome the fears of twenty-nine years behind walls. And am doing things that are still linked to that prison.'* He waited for her call.

Brother shot out of his chair as the phone bell rang. He was shaken out of his doubts and fears. The voice at the other end was welcomingly warm and calm.

'Hello Brother, its great to hear that you are back, I'm sure you are happy about the trip?'

'Yes the trip was great encouragement and at least one family knows that they have someone given up for dead very much alive. It made them happy and wouldn't have been so without you.'

'Oh! Brother you give me too much credit. Anyway I am dying to hear all the details and your further plans but have to rush to work after a breakfast.'

Brother realized that this was not the time to invade her mind with his fears about Elizabeth. So he asked, 'can we meet at some point today?'

'Sure, why don't you come into town and we can drive back together and talk on the way.' This was typical of Sheila. Making use of traveling time to catch up on news. Brother would have preferred her living room comfort for a discussion but he agreed to meet her at the office at closing time.

Throughout the day Brother looked at the phone and debated calling up Victor. Something told him to keep it on hold. He simultaneously, replayed the events at Ahmadabad in his mind so that nothing would be missed out with Sheila. Before leaving home he called up Sheila and that increased his pace into town. She was going to be free earlier than usual. He hadn't even unpacked his suitcase after arriving home as though it would take away Ahmadabad from his memory. In the cab from Churchgate station to Nariman point he made up his mind to tell Sheila about the note from Elizabeth in Karachi. But he would tell her that last of all. He reached her office building and called her from a telephone booth and she came down in minutes.

In the car Sheila drove and Brother talked. Somewhat like a schoolboy traveling home with 'mama'. Every now and then Sheila shared his excitement with her exclamations and praise for his achievements at Ahmadabad. It had been her worry; that he wouldn't know how to handle the dead end situations of his story and get dejected by any adverse response with consequent dilution of spirit. But he had been a winner. She sensed his anxieties about Ruhaina and Smita moving the authorities to make an official attempt to free the others.

Digging into his fear zones she asked, 'does it worry you that the authorities could get nasty with you for reopening this issue of prisoners in Pakistan?' The question instead of drawing his fears out had the opposite effect.

He was firm, ' it doesn't matter anymore Sheila because it is only the government or the United Nations that can help in freeing them and the process has to begin and any response that affects me adversely is also a part of the same process. I have been in a process for twenty-nine years so another few don't really matter because the gains for everyone is immeasurable.'

She smiled at him and he understood that she knew it had taken him time to reach this bolder attitude. She had not coaxed or encouraged him in spite of his even wanting her to do so. His own thought process had strengthened him and he was getting stronger by the day. He had a better chance of winning now, she thought.

It was time to tell her about Elizabeth's letter. And her response was, 'at last, you have someone helping you in Pakistan Brother. What could be better than being able to communicate with your friends in that camp? It could lead to more options than you have now so pursue it but with a little discretion. I know you don't want anyone to be dragged into a mess. Do you have any plans of how to locate Elizabeth's brother?'

Brother admired her grasp and positive attitude. She never allowed fear to touch her doorstep. He would call Victor tonight and Sheila had promised to help him send the emails to Elizabeth. Suddenly help was rushing in from all sides. 'I really don't know where to start looking for her brother who was taken prisoner by our army but I guess I will try to find out through some Army and Air force friends. I wonder if they will know and it is such a sensitive issue that they will just back off even if they knew.'

Brother admired the way in which Sheila wound her way through the traffic. They were approaching Bandra and he would be getting of and going home to Chapel Road and his mother. He wanted to be with Sheila for some more time and realized that he had missed her for the few days that he had gone away. He didn't know how to tell her. His emotions were like deep-sea air bubbles rising and growing as they wobbled towards the surface

'Where should I drop you Brother,' Sheila began to edge towards the left lane so that he could get down at the kerb.

'I think I will get off at your place and catch a cab back home,' he said, smiling but not looking towards her. She glanced towards him. He looked at her and their eyes met briefly as she couldn't afford to get distracted in the evening rush hour traffic. She had caught his thoughts.

'Your mother will be waiting for you. You have just returned today from your trip. She missed you and told me when I visited her.'

'Yes, my mother told me that you brought her a lovely plum cake in my absence.'

Sheila laughed, 'Rani loves cakes, I was buying one for home so I picked up one for her too.' She maneuvered the car back into the main traffic lane in silent approval of Brother's need to be with her.

Borivili had a mixed community but Christians predominantly inhabited Sheila's locality. It was different from Chapel Road. In contrast there were tall buildings but every now and then was a small cottage reminiscent of the days when there was only a convent and a fishing village populated by converted Christian fishing folk. The faces on the street close to her apartment block were similar to those at Chapel Road. But their attitude was different. They had become distanced and closeted in their apartments. The few that had retained their cottages were trapped between two worlds. Somehow, the developers had spared some trees and it compensated for the spirit of Chapel Road. The road to Sheila's block was a shaded avenue. Brother had noticed the similarities and differences every time that he had visited her but happily the atmosphere was easy for him to blend because the people bonded in a comfortable way very much like Chapel Road. Christians of Bombay were a friendly bunch.

They were all smiles taking the elevator to her fifth floor apartment and she offered, ' maybe I can show you how to log into the Internet and send e mails to Elizabeth.'

'Yes that would be nice Sheila because computers and e mails is all new for me.'

'Oh! You will pick it up fast. I used to be scared of computers but Rani taught me in no time and now I work on it and find it good company.' Brother couldn't figure out a machine being good company. They entered the apartment with her key. Tension and apprehension showed easily on his face. He had never been with her alone at her apartment and felt he was trespassing or breaking some rules. But he also felt closer because she trusted him. It wouldn't have been very difficult for her to convince him that he needed to go home instead of traveling home with her to Borivili.

She put him at ease. 'Rani will be coming home late. She has an important project and is preparing a presentation at the office with another colleague.' It was as though she was saying he was allowed to be with her for some time. He hesitated just for a moment and Sheila looked surprised at having to beckon him into the apartment. She could sense his every move and Brother understood her eyes asking, *'Aren't you coming in?'*

Dropping her handbag on the sofa she went into the house calling, 'do you want some hot tea or something cold?'

'Oh, anything will do. I am a bit thirsty all right.' Brother always just stood around taking in the atmosphere. He was not uncomfortable but just a bit unsure.

She came back quickly in her casual clothes. In a pair of snug jeans and a loose shirt with her hair tied high up she was a relaxed picture. Brother had never before seen her in western casuals. She would dress formally in Indian attires for work or even while visiting. Sheila appeared like a very different image to him today. Brother caught himself staring and was quick to divert.

'I can make good tea, he said. I used to do that in the squadron and even sometimes at the prison. You remember that cook Mustafa I told you about?'

'Yes I do but I can make it, Brother. You can watch TV while I do that.' Brother insisted that he make it so she permitted him into her kitchen. It was functional but not very organized. Martha's kitchen was much more systematic, he realized. Yet it always reminded him of a museum. Sheila's was simple but tasteful and modern compared to Martha's.

The tea was brewed with cardamom. The aroma building an anticipation of its taste associated with sweetness and relaxed company. Brother poured it into two cups that Sheila had left for him and called out to her. She had left him to switch on the computer in Rani's bedroom.

'Brother you can bring the tea in here. I am on the computer and want you to see how to send an e mail.' She did not find it awkward to let him come into the bedroom but Brother was not ready for the intimacy of a woman's room nor was he geared to handle a computer. Standing in the hallway he called out again.

'Can we have the tea first and talk about the letter sent by

Elizabeth?' Sheila failed to sense his uneasiness and called him into the room again. Brother entered hesitatingly.

Rani's room was typical for her age. There was a low couch overflowing with cushions of different sizes and shapes. The unoccupied couch came alive with stuffed animals. A bead curtain with bells and a wind chime on the window ensured a tingling like suspended giggles in the air. There was freshness emanating and the dull finish furniture in the room enveloped you in its intimate embrace. Brother stood at the doorway with the two cups of tea in his hands. Sheila invited him in with a smile and rolled herself away from the computer on a stool with castors. There was a cushioned cane stool that Brother pulled away from the computer table and sat down handing her the cup of tea.

'This is a very beautiful room.'

'Yes, Rani keeps it very tidy but there are too many things here. Mine is comparatively bare. I like space.'

He made a note of it and said, 'I guess she has inherited this from her father. He liked a lot of things around him all the time.' Brother's mind raced back to their NDA days. 'Kailash was always buying small decorative things for his room and used to get punished for it. We were banned from displaying any other things than those permitted by the regulations. He was always a bit of a rebel.'

Brother had no clear course of action about dealing with the letter from the nurse at Karachi. *'Was this the best time to discuss with Sheila?'* He had missed her and wanted to communicate but didn't know how and where to begin. He was just very happy to be with her alone for the first time in two years. The intimacy of being within walls with someone you have a lot of admiration for feels good but if you didn't know how to express; it could be like a traffic jam of emotions. Sudden overwhelm like a speedy overtake was dangerously possible. For a moment as they sat it was on his lips but then she put her cup on the table and said, 'let me show you how to operate this for e mails.'

Brother turned towards the computer and followed her instructions with his eyes. He realized that there was a procedure being demonstrated and it felt at home for him, as he was familiar with procedures that were so necessary in piloting. But his eyes drifted every now and again to the back of her neck from where her neatly tied up hair began its upward weave. Sheila faced the screen and he couldn't help admire her presence. Some of what she was saying stayed and some of it got lost while his attention drifted. He would have been happier writing down the instructions. It would be easier to follow instructions in a step-by-step manner. The way she rapidly operated the mouse or the keys; the screen staying alive with changing images or message boxes just amazed him. He was left behind but had been even quicker than this in the cockpit. It auto-generated a "you are fantastic" smile through his eyes.

She had said something that needed no response but he had mechanically said a yes. Her hand froze on the mouse and she straightened and swiveled round slowly. Brother was looking at her neck all the while and in a flash he found her curiously wide eyes suddenly very close and looking steadily at his rapidly fading embarrassed smile that left only traces in the eyes. He was stuck for any explanation. His gaze touching her skin had been discovered.

'Are you alright Brother?' Looking away he could only manage a nod in the affirmative.

Her fingers moved to his cheek and her whole image grew soft in his focus.

'Why are these tears Brother?' He looked down at his feet and found hers close to his. Toes almost touching.

She was getting up from her swivel stool but had both her hands cupping his face gently lifting.

'Come baby, let me hold you. I know your trip and the future is rough.'

He arose from the chair her hands controlling the ascent. He regained control and allowed just one more big tear to roll and fall away. And they stood eyes locked in speechless dialogue. Her touch on his cheeks grew warm and enclosing but ever so lightly. Reluctantly they slid down to his collar like a sheet being gently withdrawn from a sleeping body. He caught their descent, her eyes lowered and she leaned on his chest, her breathing controlled but discernibly heavy while he kissed her knuckles, as they grew white from gripping his shirt and more. Letting go of her wrists Brother let his arms come to rest by her side.

Sheila sensed his reluctance while battling with her own emotions but she had already climbed sure footed onto a plateau, now beckoning him to follow. Brother looked down at her hair neatly tied up and dared a brushing kiss hesitatingly. She couldn't have seen it but felt his fingers slowly undoing the clip that held up her tresses. Her arms went around his waist and she looked up at him. He found the courage and longing in her eyes to release all controls.

Sheila had experienced passion but Brother had never been there.

They had moved to her bedroom and discovered that time could be made to stand still in their busy lives. She guided him and he grew stronger by the moment quite preferring to be led till he was sure of riding together onto a whole new landscape that spelt fulfillment. After the dams had burst and desires quenched, Brother hid his face and confessed, 'Sheila I have wanted you as a woman for sometime now. I hope you understand this?' She snuggled closer in reply. Now he found the words more easily to express that he had missed her even more on the trip to Ahmadabad. He felt suddenly released to tell her all with all his senses in harmony.

'Had it not been for your sharp eyes I would have never found the newspaper clipping and possibly yet be wondering at how to go about finding these families. You lit up the way and gave me the push.'

'Oh Brother! You would have always found a way. I have seen the urge in your every breath. You would have found them just the way you cared to find out about me. You are the one that finally gave me my freedom. I would have continued my life wanting to know the truth about Kailash. In some ways I was also a captive like you. I, to my beliefs and you in a prison.'

Brother could not resist teasing, 'Is it good for you to be free now?'

Enveloping him she mumbled, 'well, aren't you happy to be here,' a gleam in her eyes and a gurgle in her throat that was like a mountain stream bursting over rocks splashed shamelessly on him.

He moved to her again and they couldn't get closer. Words would have found it difficult to fit in. There was no space. Between frozen moments and quenching of a thirst that had been put on hold by circumstances and the barriers of conscience their eyes spoke of a distant language. Both had existed far away from passion for a long time. Their cocoon unfurled only to the distant ringing of a phone; their own sounds ebbing to a conversation that moved to Ahmadabad and his experiences; the letter from the nurse in Karachi and what he thought about the communal riots and how amazing was the co-existence of Azad's family; Muslims at Smita Choudhury's Hindu villa. Their inner feelings had just met.

The telephone bell came from far away. It was from Rani. She would be late and Sheila was not to worry or stay up. Ravi would escort her home. Their newly shared intimacy was permitted to linger like a fragrance and both knew that he could not stay for too long.

Sheila mumbled, 'I have never kept anything away from Rani.'

Brother took a deep breath and said, ' I understand it and never want to become the reason for any change in your understandings.'

As he left her apartment Sheila whispered holding him close.

'Please don't harbor expectations from me. Let me just be myself and you be yourself and maybe there is still time for us to be fulfilled in some ways.'

Brother was never good at reading between lines. So he just kissed her and said, 'Behind prison walls, one learns to wait with expectations dwindling. At some stage you learn to accept so there is not much I will not be able to endure or accept between us. Does that make sense?'

'I do not know about the future and do not want to disappoint you Brother and your mission has just begun. I can only assure you that I will be there.'

'That is more than I expect and they both laughed.'

Brother jumped into a cab and headed home to Bandra. Wavering between feeling at rest and latent guilt he grew impatient at the traffic jams. *'Where are people rushing all the time in Bombay? Where am I going in my life? Did we succumb to impulsive desire or was there a longing that we have been denied. I hope Sheila didn't allow me into her heart in a wave of sympathy. Her need for me was strong. I felt it. Why do I feel regret? Have I let her down?'*

He did not have the words in his heart but felt liberated and loved more than he had ever been. Was this the ultimate expression of love and trust of a woman then? *'Is this what has bypassed me in this life? Well, whatever; didn't she say, maybe there is still time for fulfillment but what was the bit about, have no expectations? And it can wait.'*

He had to establish contact with Victor Gomes and Elizabeth Fernandez. Sitting at his table after a sumptuous homecoming supper made by his mother, Brother was being eaten up by a churning urgency. It had been two years since he was deported from Pakistan. Would Azad still be at the same camp? Away from it but closer than ever in a different way, he realized how easily the Pakistanis could move the prisoners or do away with them and no one would ever know. He would call Victor the first thing in the morning and then depending on their conversation he would send Elizabeth a simple mail to say that he was alive, well and trying but had not been able to make any headway to find her brother but had found the family of co-prisoner Azad. She would have to get word to Azad about his wife and son. How, he did not know but then she had confided that she had discovered the name of the prison camp from his medical documents at the Karachi military hospital. She had not shared it with him. He will convince her that it was important for him to know the location. Could fate be so cruel that Azad and the others become untraceable.

   Now that he had found Ruhaina and Basheer? Should he call Smita in Ahmadabad and tell her that he had found a way of sending messages to Azad. Ruhaina would be overjoyed by it. Brother wanted to share the possibility of it with Azad's dear ones but then if it failed he knew something like this could only end in bitter disappointment. He would wait. So much had happened on the very day that he had returned. He did not have time to attend to the music classes that had become a regular feature. Mr. Johnson his music assistant seemed to be doing an excellent job. Brother felt happy for Johnson. He was a retired school music teacher and Brother had asked him to help with his classes and it looked like Johnson had taken on both their shares of work. *'Maybe I need to hire a lady too, so that the girls and little children feel more comfortable learning.'* Suddenly, his life was brimming. It was good to be home to your own bed and today had been a long day. He yawned and turned over into the old brass four-poster. Thoughts floated towards Sheila till sleep took over liberating him to dream on.

   Sitting over a steaming cup of tea Brother looked at the telephone and the number that would connect him to Victor. The verandah doorway curtains swayed gently, twirling like ballet dancers to the early morning sea breeze that brought with it the flavors of Chapel Road. Someone was frying bacon and someone else was trying to keep the pressure cooker whistle from blowing too often. It was just eight in the morning but the best time to catch those who leave early for work. Brother dialed the number and braced up to introduce himself. Victor would have been told about him. Elizabeth was taking a big chance by even offering to get word to the Indian prisoners and Brother knew the consequences of being intercepted. He was going to keep conversations on the phone discreet. It was as though he was being tapped. This was free India but the psyche of a man who was used to talking in hushed tones and had flown out of a cage by sheer providence, was to continue ducking. It took more than it usually did for Brother to respond on the phone today. Nobody would have guessed that he had drifted off into his thoughts while the person at the other end had picked up the receiver and was trying to get a response from him "the caller".

   Brother got up from his chair rapidly and apologized for being inattentive. ' Please wait, let me turn the radio a bit low.'

'Sorry, but I am Brother James and are you Mr. Victor.'

'Yes, and you must have received the letter I posted a week ago?'

'Yes, and I am very happy to know that Elizabeth remembers me. I had no way of communicating with her and it is great that you are here in Bombay. From your letter I guess you live in Byculla.'

'That is correct. I have a small apartment and work in the docks as a crane operator.' He laughed at himself giving time and space for Brother to understand that he was talking to a simple and hard workingman who was probably just making ends meet. Brother picked up the cue correctly and added.

'Oh! I was an officer and fighter pilot in the air force but today I am teaching music to children and am very happy with whatever I get. In Bombay survival is not easy but not very difficult either.'

'Yeah you're right Mr. James, I wasn't very good in academics and wanted to become a pilot or an engine driver but I finally wound up doing what my father did. I get enough but sometimes it is difficult. I did not marry because I couldn't have supported a family.' He laughed again. 'You must tell me about flying and the war sometime. I love listening to war stories and never miss a war movie man. Did you see "633 Squadron" or "Tora Tora Tora"? I have seen them three times each.'

Brother was amused at the quick informality generated by this man. The conversation was everything other than what Brother had wanted it to be. His aim was to get in touch with Elizabeth through Victor and all he wanted to know was, is Victor Gomes real, or am I getting tracked by some powers that do not want me to rake up this issue of prisoners of war still in Pakistan. Reasonably satisfied that Victor could be a confidant and a conduit to Elizabeth, Brother suggested, 'let us meet sometime.'

'I would love to Mr. James. Elizabeth has told me a lot so I would like to meet you too.' Brother's hopes arose. *'Maybe Elizabeth has told him the location of the camp. This is God sent. Things will become so much simpler if I can tell the authorities about the location of the camp. They will definitely want to know as to how did I suddenly remember the name. To hell! I will tell them that it was my memory loss that had prevented me from remembering but it has all come back in a flash. After all it is they who had declared me unsound of mind, so I can always fall back on that. I cannot give away the presence of Victor or the role of Elizabeth. It could be dangerous for them and even fatal for the remaining prisoners. Nothing should happen to them or to Elizabeth.'*

'Can we meet today?' 'Oh sure! My lunch break is at one pm and you can come to the Princess dock gate. I will be there. I wear jeans and check shirts.' There was another apologetic laugh and he added ' You will easily recognize me. I am a body builder. You need muscles to operate these huge cranes. Lifting weights at the gym gives me the strength and guts to lift those huge containers. Never had an accident in twenty years man, touch wood.' Laughter again and Brother couldn't help but join in. The man had an infectious presence. It could be an interesting afternoon.

'I will be there at 1pm Mr. Gomes, also in a pair of jeans and a check shirt. I like the combination too.'

The receivers squawked with laughter.

Brother waited outside Princess Dock. He had reached well in time, ahead as usual. The security guards looked at him suspiciously and Brother sensed a game. *'Keep them guessing. Maybe they think I am a terrorist or suicide bomber. These days clothes don't maketh a man. Crooks and saints come in all sizes shapes and even colors.'* Suddenly there was a flurry at the gate and the guards were waving at him to clear off. He just stood there spreading his arms in helplessness.

One of the guards came across and told him, 'don't stand at the gate— there are VIPs coming this way.' It wasn't yet time to disclose his identity.

Brother sniggered, 'who is this VIP and isn't this a public road where anyone can wait?'

The guard hadn't expected the response and it took him by surprise that quickly graduated to annoyance and he threatened, 'do you want to be locked up?'

In the mean while Brother espied a white car with a flag. It was a Vice admirals' flag and there was a cavalcade of three cars behind it. He also saw a short stout man in jeans and check shirt approaching the gate from within. That must be Victor. Brother poured out boiling arrogance.

'Why should I be locked up?'

'No one is allowed near the gate when there are VIPs, now move or…'

'Or what?' was Brother's staid reply. The gate barriers flew up and the cars went through; the guard turned around and clumsily threw up his rifle in a salute. Brother noticed that the VIPs seated within had not even noticed him or the guard at the gates. They were busy in their own conversation. He had been a part of the armed forces and felt a little cheated at being treated as some trash.

'I am a retired air force officer,' he mentioned to the fuming guard. It only managed to increase the scorn.

'We don't care for that; there are many like you; so what.'

'So, the least you can do is ask me who I am or check my identity and not just yell as if we are cattle. I am not obstructing your entrance so what is all the sycophancy for?'

'You come with me to the guard room, we will tell you what is the problem.' And he blew a whistle for help.

Brother stood his ground and soon there was a small gathering of people that rapidly grew. In all the faces he saw a kind of curiosity and helpless viewer ship. And then he heard a loud authoritative voice. It was Victor in his check shirt. Brother and he recognized each other simultaneously. Victor confronted the guard on the goings on.

Brother heard Victor saying, 'he is my friend and you don't know him, he is a fighter pilot, war hero and fought the war with Pakistan and was prisoner, how dare you treat him like that?' Pushing through a circle of watchers, Victor reached Brother and shook hands. 'I am sorry they behaved like that. Don't worry, they know me, it is all right now, let us go somewhere and sit down peacefully. Everyone here thinks he is a VIP and even these guards want to show that they have some great authority. They know me; so all you should have told them is that you have come to meet me.'

Much to his disgust it reaffirmed Brother's suspicion that in India you had to know someone and everything would fall into place.

*'If you knew someone important or powerful, they would believe your story and possibly move things to get the other prisoners freed. If the judge or his daughter Smita had to tell the government that Ruhaina's husband and others were languishing in prison for no reason; they may believe it. But if I had to say the same thing they will declare me mentally unsound. No wonder Dad had to request a VIP; the local member of the legislative assembly that I was missing feared dead and that they had yet to receive my death benefits in spite of the air force declaring me missing for more than six months. Sheila also had to wait for a long time to receive Kailash's benefits and insurance payments.'* Brother bit his lip in revulsion.

'Oh! I didn't know that if I had mentioned your name, they wouldn't bother with me.' He laughed aloud. 'Then you must be a VIP Mr. Gomes?' It had broken the ice and laughing arm in arm they moved on away from the gate.

'Let us eat something,' said Brother.

'Sure, joined in Victor, there are some reasonable places here.'

'Let us go to City Kitchen,' said Brother.

'Oh! Their vindaloo is excellent,' slurped Victor; 'have you ever tasted it?' Brother recalled a meal there long ago with some friends.

'Yes I have been there years ago when the restaurant must have just started Victor.'

Brother's juices churned. *'So this is the secular and democratic India a mix of 'isms' where secularism is purely a word for rhetoric. Only the powerful, the rich, the VIPs and the connected have the right of way and privileges. They are above board exempt from being asked questions and to be seen or associated with them can make all the difference in getting your rights or be heard. Isn't secularism something to do with all pervasive equality and democracy and something definitely applicable the least to basic rights? That guard's behavior was reminiscent of feudalism.'*

Most of the tables were full with people from nearby offices and some college students. A Goanese Olympian hockey player started the City Kitchen restaurant meant specially for sportsmen to have a good and affordable meal. Unlike today sportsmen in those days as a rule never had fat purses. Quite likely he was from Chapel road or nearby, thought Brother. So, the menu was simple and rates even easier. Brother gave Victor the pleasure of ordering lunch. Studying his face while Victor poured over the dog-eared daily menu card, Brother waited patiently to begin his questions. Victor was sure hungry. He ordered one full plate of pork Vindaloo and another full plate of fried Pomfret and then asked Brother, 'What will you have?'

Brother settled for half a plate of rice and chicken curry.

'Is that all you will have?'

'I am a small and slow eater and will give you company. Don't worry about me. You go ahead. Maybe I will take a bite of the Pomfret fish from you.'

'Most certainly. Elizabeth told me that you were quite unlike a lot of military men in your habits. I believe you don't drink or smoke and you never use slang or curse words that is a bossy style in military men's conversations.'

Brother passed it off and asked, 'didn't she tell you that I was going to die?'

'She had said that you were very sick but your will power to live was very strong. She gave me the note to post here in Bombay on the belief that you would have surely survived.'

Brother suppressed a surge of mixed emotions. It was so good to be alive after the hopeless existence as a PoW. Would he ever be able to unshackle himself from those memories, or was captivity in his fate. Maybe, it was better this way. *'At least it keeps me motivated to find the survivors of my friends back in that hellhole. I have to get them their freedom.'* Sitting physically in the restaurant he was actually faraway.

'What else did she say Victor.'

'She wonders about her brother who was taken PoW in Longewala. You know the famous tank battle place?'

'Yes I do. I had flown some missions against the enemy Armour there.'

'Tell me about that battle please. I have read about it. I wish I had been there. I can do anything for my country. And… in hushed tones, do you think Elizabeth's brother is alive and still a PoW. Do we also keep PoWs as hostages for exchange at convenience? Can we find Elizabeth's brother? His name is Edward Fernandez. I think he was a Captain. Elizabeth said, that you were the one person she trusted, could find him.'

Listening in silence, the sounds of City Kitchen in the background, Brother studied the man's face as he raved about Longewala. It was as though he had missed a party. There was awe and patriotism too in Victor's gestures and voice. So far Brother had only talked to Sheila about the war and it was more about his angst about the whole experience than the missions and glory. Here was someone who wanted to get first hand information to be able to feel the heat of the battle. Victor was thirsty for the romance and glamour portrayed in the war films he watched.

'I will tell you some other time Victor but tell me what did Elizabeth tell you about me and to be honest, I have no clue about Pakistani prisoners being held by India. I do not know anything that could lead to her brother Edward. It will not be easy to find out and anyone asking about such issues is bound to attract undue attention. I had promised her and have tried but so far have no information. I have to get in touch with some very close air force friends who may possibly tell me the realities in pure confidence or they may not even want to talk about it. And none of them is in Bombay.'

Victor looked disinterested, 'yes Brother I do understand and it is so many years ago so who would have kept track of prisoners. I have tried to convince Elizabeth that she should forget waiting for her brother but she believes that he is alive. Some prisoners were released by India just after the war and one of them told her that Edward was still a prisoner. The Pakistani government thereafter approached our authorities with his name but were told that there was no Edward Fernandez as prisoner.'

'Did Elizabeth tell you anything else about my prisoner days or the place?'

'Yes she had mentioned that there were some more prisoners being held by Pakistan according to you and that she believed you and also that she had found your documents in the Karachi Military hospital saying that you were arrested for being a Christian priest in Pakistan. I found that very amusing. Did the authorities of your prison camp make those false papers? You were a prisoner after all eh?'

'You may believe what you choose to was Brother's terse reply.'

'Of course I believe you, I hope I didn't offend you?' Brother wanted to ask him if he knew anything about the location of the prison camp and his mind was racing.

'Should I ask him or shall I wait. Elizabeth may not have told him and I will look silly asking him that question. I need to tell Elizabeth that I have located the family of Azad Khan and that she should try and get word to Azad that his family knows about him. Can I include Victor in the knowledge that I have found Ruhaina and Basheer? Why are there so many questions in my mind whenever it has something to do with the prisoners? Everything I am doing after being released is still connected with my past captivity. Either I am searching for relatives of prisoners in India or for a Pakistani prisoner in India. I'll be glad when I finish finding all that I am searching for. Looks like the rest of my life will be searching for clues and people. Will I ever get the time I wish to spend with Sheila? And thanks to her it was she who found the first clue in a newspaper that set the ball rolling. I wonder where and when will all this end.'

Brother's thoughts had taken his eyes away from Victor and this was taken as his reaction to the sick humor. 'Look Brother I am terribly sorry for insinuating that you were not a PoW. Please forgive me. I should have known better because Elizabeth had told me the truth about your prison camp past.'

There was a sudden glimmer of hope in Victor's apology that Elizabeth may have told him more, so Brother put the question discreetly. 'I don't mind the humor Victor but was wondering if Karachi is very far from the prison camp because she said in her note that she could take messages across to the prisoners. Tell me, you have been to Karachi. How far is it from the camp?' Brother threw the dice.

'I am sorry Brother but I never asked Elizabeth about the prison camp or its distance but she said that she would have to take leave to go there. I visit her once in every two years and am like a son to her mother after Edward went missing. Aunty Jenna is a great cook and I love her recipes. She looks forward to my visits. I could take all your messages if you want. I will do anything you want Brother. After all you have done such a lot for the country. For me you are a real hero. You have fought a war that we won and we taught the Pakistani's a few lessons. I wish my aunt and Elizabeth migrate to India but they have always lived there, even before the partition. My aunt was also a nurse in a hospital. They do not want to come and live in India. I wonder why.'

The dice had rolled off the table. Brother's disappointment and urgency was like a neon sign. Victor was a great talker but Brother was waiting for specific information and now it was evident that he would have to ask Elizabeth and she may never tell. It was dangerous and she knew it. Elizabeth had not been careless in telling Victor. Women with secrets no matter how educated, affluent or not always knew what they should do or speak. He was in a way happy that she had been discreet. She was capable of reaching his messages to Azad and the others. She would be careful. She had to be kept going.

Lunch was served and Victor had seen Brother's embarrassed smile. He was however quick to serve and offer Brother some of what he had ordered. There was no show of any acquired politeness or table manners. Victor was bluntly honest to the point of being crude. They chatted on in between morsels. At times Victor's mouth twisted to accommodate the food and conversation. Brother noticeably maintained his modified British manners but Victor wasn't fazed by it or he didn't show it the least.

'It is good that we have met. I will e-mail Elizabeth from a cyber café today to give her the good news. She will be overjoyed because she knows you will trace out her brother. If there is anything I can do towards that, let me know. Oh! She asked me to give you her e-mail address. Please write it down. It is friendlyliz@hotmail.com.' Brother hurriedly took out his pen and diary to write but was at a loss how to write it. He had never needed anyone's e-mail address and in fact did not know how to even write an e-mail address.

'Can you write it for me here Victor?'

'Sure, but it is so simple, should I spell it out.'

'I have never noted any e-mail address so I will be grateful if you show me by writing it once.' Victor almost choked with laughter that bordered on sniggering.

'You mean you don't know about e-mail and how to write these addresses. Those Pakis sure did a good job on you man, eh?' Brother could only look him in the eye helplessly but with growing resolve on his lips.

'Show me your diary, I will write it down and you must get yourself a computer and ask someone to show you how to get onto the internet. I do it almost everyday and it can be interesting. Once you learn, you will be hooked man.'

Brother continued to smile as Victor wrote down the address. He had a good handwriting for a man who was almost gross.

'Thank you Victor, just meeting you and knowing that you are willing to help is great for me. Are you permitted to visit Pakistan in less than two years.'

Victor lowered his garrulous volume, 'I know of people who go there quite often but why do you ask?'

'Good, I may want to send some message that cannot be sent on the Internet. After all the Internet I believe is not totally secure.'

'Yes, that is true. Traveling is expensive but I can do it for you Brother. What message do you want to send?'

It was in hushed tones and in a broken sentence Brother replied, 'Nothing… as yet… but… I will let you know… and… if required… make arrangements to pay…. for your fare.'

'Hah! Victor can afford anything for a war hero.' It was said out loud and Brother winced. 'Just let me know and I have accumulated leave that I can take anytime, so I am at your disposal anytime sir.' Victor looked around and smiled at those who had heard him. The waiters knew his ways and smiled in a knowing way. He wasn't going to miss the opportunity of being close to a hero and not let the world know about it.

It brought a smile to Brother's face. The sheer honest though crude energy of the man could change the ambience of a place. Azad used to have the same effect on him and Brother felt annoyed with himself for not yet opening up fully to him about Azad, Ruhaina and Basheer. He began but Victor cut him off in a hiss.

'I once took a Muslim girl from here to Pakistan because she was not permitted on her own. There was some suspicion about her family being linked to smugglers or terrorists I don't know but she was the sister of a friend, so I did it for him. She was to be seen by some relatives in Pakistan for her marriage. The girl is now married and lives in Pakistan. I have two sets of passports. Went as a married man with this girl and came back as myself.' His laughter that followed was almost lewd but Brother followed suit in a controlled appreciative way, ending it by wiping his lips with a napkin and coughing into it gently. Their presence drew the attention from all the other tables. Brother felt exposed. Victor extended his laughter as if to give cover to Brother and everyone went back to their food. Bombay recognizes laughter at a bawdy joke quickly and is even quicker at overlooking it.

Here he was about to tell Victor about Ruhaina and Azad and surprisingly the man had almost read his thoughts and confessed to an illegality that Brother's mind was rapidly considering. *'Ruhaina had said that she would go to Pakistan to find her husband if that was the last thing she did. Here was the man who had gone into Pakistan once and would surely do anything for me his "war hero".'*

'That must have been very risky Victor.'

'Not as risky as flying your war planes in a war Brother. These migration, customs and police officials on both sides look after people from their own community. Let me know if you want me to go across to Karachi with messages or escorting someone and I will be there without fail.'

Brother suppressed the urge to take him into confidence. *'I need more time to think about any such course of action and also about Victor. He is bold but I do not want problems. It feels dangerous. '* He shook hands across the table genuinely grateful at Victor's offer. 'I will let you know Victor, if ever I wish to send something across. I will need your help I think. Thank you very much for the offer.'

'Be my guest anytime but you must tell me about your attacks on tanks at Longewala.'

'That's a deal.'

Their plates were empty and Victor reluctantly ceased chewing on the fish bones. They seemed juicy but Victor's chewing them in a restaurant was something Brother wasn't expecting but had to overlook this afternoon. Yet he had found renewed strength to go forward in his mission. The crane operator sure knew how to raise spirits. Brother had one more supporter to push his plans into action.

Returning home Brother narrated parts of his encounter to Sheila on the telephone. She was amused with his experiences and asked him if he had learnt how to send e-mails. The sweet memory of his failed lesson had resulted in laughter at both ends and he was gently reminded to go to the nearest cyber café to get an e-mail ID and also learn how to send mail. Brother was more than eager to do this now. His apprehensions of the computer seemed to have vanished. This was one more small challenge at hand.

'I have to learn a little about computers mother, he said to Martha.' Brother sat with his mother after a restful night over a retired cup of tea. It was 8 am and he liked to plan his day.

'Why would you want to do that now?'

'Sheila says it's the easiest way to stay in touch with anyone and covers the whole world. You could send a message to your sister in Australia in seconds.'

'I don't believe that James and who do you have to keep in touch with that you are going to learn it now? You can always phone Sheila and any of your other friends. And by the way our phone bills are really shooting.'

'I know you are telling me about my long calls to Sheila.'

'Oh! I didn't mean to hurt you, its just that it was hardly anything earlier and Sheila is a nice person to talk to.'

'Then why don't you call her up sometimes mother.'

'Tom and I hardly made any calls other than to the doctor or the parish priest. These days the tones in the phones have changed and sometimes I can't even make out if it is the dial tone or something else. Phones without a dialer, I don't even know if the number has got dialed or is in the process and before you know the tones change even before I have finished with the keys. And sometimes there is a strange voice that talks to you in Marathi or Hindi. I guess I don't understand the language and these things anymore. It is good that you are here.'

'Oh mother! You make me laugh. Anyway, I am off in an hour to that cyber café on Hill Road to learn something worthwhile. Or very soon I will also become ancient like you.'

'I am not ancient. I can follow whatever is said on the television and these days the starlets dress up in things that we would never dream of wearing. But they look nice, don't they?'

Brother ignored Martha's last comment. 'Do you need anything from the stores or chemists.'

'Get me some peppermint and come back soon. You have been away for all these days at Ahmadabad and are becoming so busy now. What's going on.'

'I will sit with you sometime mother.'

Martha had wanted to ask Brother about Sheila but did not know how to. Her senses had appreciated their vibes and she was a mother who wanted to know more.

Brother stood on the pavement opposite from the cyber café studying the clientele and waiting for the traffic and some courage to cross over and enter the net realm.

*'What should I tell that lady who runs the cyber cafe. Will she laugh that at my age I don't know how to even switch on the machine. And then I have to explain to her that I also want to send e-mails and Sheila said that*

she would understand and do the needful. Why is it so complex? My aircraft had so many switches and lights so why does this computer make me so apprehensive. I think I am just a bit scared or is it that I am ashamed of my ignorance. Maybe a bit of both. It's not my fault that I don't know about computers. They never had them in the Air force. I wonder what else have I missed out in these last twenty-nine years. I guess I have to catch up a lot. Let them laugh. I have to do this for my guys. Soon you will know that I have kept my promise to you. Elizabeth will get to you guys.'

An hour later Brother walked out of the cyber café on a cloud. The lady running the café was the owner and a good teacher too. She had taken one look at Brother and diagnosed his fears.

"Keyboard dilemma", she called it. 'Do you want to learn or just send some mail?'

'Do you think I can pick up how to operate a computer and send e mails and other things?'

'I think you can do a lot because at your age you have the courage to make the attempt to come here. Only, you have to continue by telling yourself that it will not bite or explode on you. It only does what you tell it to do and don't worry too much about how it works or the links up through the Internet. But if you are still really interested, there are some beginner's books available. Read them.'

She had shown him the procedure to start and switch off and also the ease with which he could get onto the net. Thereafter she had helped him register his e-mail ID. Brother felt ecstatic that he had a one-line address that would let him be in touch with the rest of the world. He was now brotherjames@hotmail.com. He was connected and his note to Elizabeth read.

Dear Liz

Thank you for your note. Sorry but truly I had never expected any news or message from you and am glad you took the pain to write. I met Victor. He was interesting to be with. We had lunch together yesterday. Haven't found out about your brother Edward. Will try harder. My friend Azad you remember? He was my closest friend there. I located his wife Ruhaina and son Basheer. They are fine and are overjoyed to hear about him. Can you reach Azad? I am fine and so is my mother. More after hearing from you. I have learnt how to operate a computer after taking some lessons at a computer café or cyber café as it is called. I hope you get this letter.

Regards
Brother

*'Liz is like my angel in the sky. She can reach Azad and convey my message. Azad will be happy to hear that he has a son. This e-mail facility lets me fly freely and takes me close to my friends with renewed hope of freedom for them. How I wish I could fly them all out of that place.'*

This computer is another dimension of freedom, he thought.

*'I must have my own link to this freedom. I need a computer soon. I could even send e mails to Sheila or would she consider that to be too bold?'*

# Chapter XIV

Abdul sat on the hillside with his head leaning against a rock. The warmth from the rock was soothing to his back and shoulders. He had not fully adapted to the awkward loads he was made to carry. It was noon and Salman along with Rasheid and Hamid the two Kashmiri militants slept in the shade of the rock. It was August and Abdul had proven his resolve through the summer to assist the mujahideen in their raids on border villages near the line of control and into India near Baramulla. They could now rest without having to keep a constant watch on him.

This resting hideout and launch base was south-east of Timarkot on one of the seven hills that lay in the fork of the Jhelum flowing southward towards Kot and Mirpur further to the south. A group of huts went by the name of Bagh village. There were several such resting points concealed from the searching binoculars of Indian troops. They were to wait till five in the evening and then begin a trek towards the road running south from Uri to Poonch. Both these were small border towns well protected by Indian army pickets and bunkers on the western slopes of what formed the Pir Panjal range. The range was an obstacle in reaching Tangmarg, Shupian and Srinagar in India from the west but also afforded hidden infiltration routes and ambush points to the mujahideen in their raids on supply convoys between Baramula, Uri, Poonch and Akhnoor.

Forward ammunition and supply posts were lucrative targets for the militants in causing tension and disruption for Indian soldiers patrolling the range or troops simply keeping watch for mujahideens using the mountain passes. Ammunition and food was always on critical demand. Both, the soldiers and mujahideen needed it.

The lower slopes of the Pir Panjal facing Pakistan provided good grazing grounds for sheep sometimes left to graze on their own or with shepherds who ignored the skirmishes between troops and the militants. Indian army troops could even recognize the regular shepherds and sometimes just the behavior of the sheep provided warning to everyone, of strangers in the ravines. They would scramble rapidly up or down hill away from such intrusions by the mujahideen or troops and the whole hillside would seem to be undulating in their slow rolling gallop. Sharpshooters would get ready and scan the hillsides behind with their telescopic sights. Many militants and even greenhorn soldiers of the Indian army had met their bullet on these slopes.

The mission today was to carry ammunition from the hideout at Bagh to a point on the Poonch road running south to Akhnoor on the Indian side. Kashmiri militants would receive the supplies carried by Abdul, Salman and the other two to boost their operations further east in the valley of Kashmir. On such missions there was always a fight on hands. Indian troops invariably found out about these rendezvous points and laid ambushes for the store carriers and the desperate Kashmiris coming for the pick up. Abdul watched the Nanga Parbat wear its midday crown of clouds. The peak used to be northeast from the prison camp but now it appeared almost north to him. That brought him closer east to India and he needed the right opportunity to break free.

Abdul looked at his boots. They were a hard leather brown pair with laces up to the ankles. Good in their softened midlife, now they were frayed and worn out at the heels and soles. His toes often felt the harsh knock of rocks and pebbles on the rugged mountain tracks or when they crossed stony riverbeds. These would not let him cover distances that he would want to in his bid to escape. He must a get a better pair, but how. From his elevated position Abdul could see for miles but not around bends and over the hills. Sections of the road that they were to reach and follow south were visible and otherwise he watched for rising dust behind hillocks from Indian army tyres on the dusty Poonch to Akhnoor road. Traffic was always more at noon and then it would be the odd straggler or a command jeep that would be racing against the sunset. All vehicles were better advised to reach destinations and protected zones at least two hours before sunset.

Rugged hilltops and craggy overhangs met Abdul's scan. He was on watch for any convoy movements that could well be the ambush troops being dropped at intervals to take up positions before dark. The ammunition drop was always very close to sunset so that any engagement with the enemy would be short and escape more feasible under cover of darkness. Eyes narrowed automatically from the harsh reflection of sunlight off bare rocks and from the sheer tension of it all. Abdul watched for signs and contemplated the success of this mission. His own plans to escape filled the gaps of his always-alert mind. If he had to be captured, not many would believe his story of being a prisoner of a war and that there were more PoWs left behind and forgotten. Suspicious Indian soldiers wouldn't show too much mercy unless there was an officer around. Troops had their own method of quick justice in these harsh surroundings. For them it was, the more militants you snuff out the better it was for your own survival. The rocks and peaks with their scarred faces rapidly imprint a new "bare fangs" personality into these soldiers. Far away from their own homes and the comforts of a peace station, soldiers like animals blend with their surroundings. Younger soldiers were quicker in donning the newfound viciousness within. The older and experienced knew how to protect their sanity and humaneness but even they had to survive so they were only a shade slower to rage.

Abdul watched the trees near the bottom of the valleys and the snow line where they ended. His newfound restricted freedom allowed moments of indulgence in appreciating such beauty. The forests were like stoles carelessly thrown across the shoulders of mountains but to the rigidly trained professional men in uniform it was all like a shroud. Within these tranquil forests were the mujahideen waiting to dash your hopes of retiring with grandchildren on the knees.

Abdul had been on a dozen raids in the last three months but he had yet not been given a weapon. He was to arm himself with an Indian soldier's weapon. Those were Ozero's orders. For that, he would have to kill or steal and wasn't sure he could ever do either. Not even for his own freedom. A weapon would give him more courage to escape. In a situation, he could even kill his captors to escape but had strangely begun to like Salman. He felt compassion for Salman and the way he had been forced to become a militant. And Salman was entrusted with the task of ensuring that he didn't escape.

He looked at them lying exhausted in the shade. It wouldn't be very difficult to snatch one of the weapons strapped at all times to their tired sleeping bodies but failure would result in sure death for him. There was temptation and he had seen opportunities but he was still not ready to becoming treacherous with his captors nor a traitor to the Indian army.

He thought. *Maybe today evening I will get my chance. I am to carry some of the load nearer to the valley bottom rivulet while the others will be not very far behind on the hillsides. They will be covering me and each other and come down to hand over their loads only after I make contact. That could be my opportunity. I will need to hide in the rocky hillsides for maybe thirty minutes and then it will be dark.* 'Allah, will you help me today.' The prayer left his lips and it reached Hamid through his fitful sleep.

'What is it Abdul?'

'Oh! I was only trying to finish my prayers before it is time to get into action Hamidbhai.'

'Yes we will need His blessings today because this is the most risky area of operations. There are too many informers in the villages across from here. There were some shepherds on the Indian side that I noticed just before we took shelter and they could very well have sent message to the platoon that is about twenty kilometers from here. I don't like the route at the bottom of the valley. We are exposed to the ridges above and easy prey for an ambush. Has there been any vehicular movement in the last hour.'

'None that I have seen Hamidbhai but there is likely to be the last evening run truck from Akhnoor to Poonch that should be passing by very soon. It is now almost 4pm. We have to start in an hour. I can scout around alone if you want and give you a signal if there is any danger. Should I?'

'No, let us stay together and if required fight our way out. Why don't you get yourself a weapon? We could use extra fire power.'

'I have never been able to get close to the soldiers Hamidbhai. How can I get a weapon from them unless we get close and then, you don't expect me to charge at soldiers who are firing at me with this staff? You are armed but I only have my staff to defend myself, that too only in close combat.'

Hamid smiled at him in a way only someone who knew the impossibility of the situation could.

'Will you be able to reach one of their soldiers, if I manage to injure or kill him and then you could run across and finish him if he is still alive and there, you will have your own automatic.'

Abdul opened his palms to show his helplessness and said, 'I could do that and thank you for considering to help me. I will remember it.'

*'Why does he want to help me or is he just trying to feel me out to see if I have thoughts of escaping. I have to watch out for Hamid or am I being too suspicious. I am sure these guys trust me now and genuinely want me to also have a weapon and add to their strength and capability. I have proven my loyalties so far and I think I should just be watchful and I will survive them and be free soon. Soon but when? It is now more than five months after the Ahmadabad riots and killings. I pray everyday for you Ruhaina. I hope you are safe. We will leave Ahmadabad for some better and more peaceful place.'*

It was time to move. Hamid's conversation had woken up Salman and Rasheid. They had not arisen but were listening. Salman wondered what he would do if he saw Abdul trying to escape. He thought. *'Abdul is an Indian at heart and will definitely want to reach home. Don't I also sometimes long to be back with Ammi and the rest. I will shoot him if he tries to escape. After all my sister too was not spared by these Indian soldiers like him. So what if he was a prisoner and has now changed his loyalties. Ozero will not spare me if he escapes.'*

With an almost painful sigh Salman raised himself and smiled at Abdul. ' Did you see anything across the border?'

'No Salman bhai, but Hamid has some apprehensions so let us be cautious and wait for some more time.'

'Yes even I think we should move only when the hills cast their shadows. Let our friends reach the pick up point and wait for us if required.'

Rasheid turned away from them and raised himself on one arm and thought. *'This Abdul is a tension for us. Why is he in our group? The mercenaries and Ozero never take him with them. He is baggage for us. Let him go for the drop. If we see him making it safely we will quickly follow. We should stay concealed till he makes contact with our Kashmiri brothers. We can then be ready to withdraw if he is ambushed. He can be sacrificed. After all he is an Indian soldier. Let his brothers kill him. We can use him as bait from now onwards. That will give us a better chance.'*

Hamid was the accepted leader of this small band of three Kashmiri dissidents and one Indian soldier turned militant. Watching his team Hamid sensed the dilemma like always. But he also knew that they had a better chance by moving together, providing covering fire from different directions. To send Abdul ahead had silently crossed his mind but he had discarded the thought faster than the contemplation now being loudly deliberated by Rasheid. Salman was the youngest and eager to finish the task.

He blurted, 'Let us wait till just before sunset and then move fast.'

Surprisingly, Hamid had no argument or premonition. So they waited. The shadows grew long and the Poonch to Akhnoor road became less visible. The lengthening shadows even managed to create images of fictitious Indian troops taking up positions on the slopes and a solitary startled deer on the road suddenly trotting off kicking a puff of dust set them off in a whispering argument that it was Indian soldiers on patrol.

'What was that? I think it is a sniper taking up position to take a shot at us. Get down and wait.'

Abdul sniggered, 'it is only an animal.'

Salman challenged him and Abdul pointed out at the animal behind some bushes.

'Look behind those same bushes from where you heard the sound. It is a single deer trying to get out of our way without being seen. Watch its tail quivering in anxiety.'

They all breathed again. His experience and survival instinct did not go unnoticed. There was silent admiration but never the body language of trust.

Shadows from the setting sun swallowed the peaks and ridges in the east. Hamid crouched and took a last look all around. They knew it was time to march. Each man secretly stole a look at the other ones face to see signs of fate. They believed, death shows on a man's face before it arrives. Body language sends its own messages.

The hand signal for silence was given and Hamid started forward. The track was narrow and steep making its way down to the road across the unmarked border. They moved in single file keeping fifty paces between them. Abdul followed right behind Hamid and the rear was brought up by Rasheid with Salman behind him. Salman almost felt over burdened with his added responsibility to ensure that Abdul did not desert or let them down. At fifty paces he could down him with a single shot but the track was becoming more difficult and he was losing sight around bends at times. They reached the road in twenty minutes and took up positions along it spread out over a distance of five hundred meters. And then Hamid darted across. They waited for gunfire. There was none.

Abdul quickly crossed the dusty road with his heavy load leaning on the staff. Rasheid leapt across expecting an ambush and rolled in the dust and took cover rapidly behind some rocks. The harshness of his maneuver could be heard by all of them in the silence of the wilderness and it brought angry frowns at the possibility of being discovered. Fortunately there was no fire from the ridges across. Resting for a moment and listening to the sounds of the wild, Hamid was satisfied that they could move on. He cursed silently at having forgotten to slip of the safety catch of his AK-47 and hoped that the others had been more careful. There was to be no talking so he couldn't check or warn them. He just looked back at them in fear but his face was not visible to the others. It was getting dark. In half crouched and bent over position he began the arduous trip down towards the rivulet at the bottom of the narrow twisting valley. Abdul followed close behind. They moved sideways down the slope and kept looking for signs of an ambush from the high ground. It was more looking without seeing. The pace was gradually increasing and confidence levels rising. They had given the slip to the patrol or the informers had failed. Hamid's mind strayed to the comfortable bed at Nathia Galli and Rafiqbhai's stories but his eyes kept searching.

Abdul used to be the scout on watch and ammunition carrier on all their raids. He would take up position and warn the others of approaching convoys or patrols with hand signals. And when required his voice was loud enough even above the gunfire in the heat of their hit and run battles. His timely warnings had proved invaluable and they had not lost any of their team for sometime. There was a silent gloved reliance on him. And he was quick to sense it. He was straining hard now in the failing light and the winding track was not allowing a clear view. It was taking some of his concentration away. Their steps became slow. A sprained ankle at such moments was suicidal. They were nearing a bend in the rivulet. The drop was to be in the vicinity of this bend. A few rocks slithered down the hillside opposite the bend. The single file froze. Hearing your own breath when you want to hide can be disconcerting. The rockslide had to be by an animal or human beings. Rasheid, bringing up the rear moved stealthily sideways up the hill opposite to the source of the rockslide. Height would give him a better view of the source and also more effective field of fire in case of an ambush. Abdul dropped the load on the track and took cover in a nearby bush but Hamid continued to crawl forward looking for a place to take cover if required. He cursed that the Kashmiris had not yet turned up.

A single shot from a high-powered rifle shattered the calm. Nesting birds at sunset screeched and flew aimless in frenzy. A bundle rolled reluctantly down the slope on their side of the valley.

Abdul made out the body of a man in typical Kashmiri attire, arms flailing, rolling helplessly down the hill on their side. His eyes searched the opposite ridge. The Indians had a sniper. From the brush near their track three more Kashmiris appeared from nowhere and there was rapid dialog between Hamid and them. Abdul dumped his remaining backpack payload off the track and suddenly felt free to fly. The backpack gone he was agile and rushed backwards along the track away from the gunfire and danger. The others also dropped their loads and followed suit. The Kashmiris were quick to pick up the ammunition and disperse for cover into the nearby tree line. Rasheid opened fire at what he thought was the Indian troop location high up on the ridge. Now there was return gunfire directed at them from all sides. Abdul concluded there were probably six automatics in all. Hamid returned the fire from wherever he thought it was coming.

Abdul yelled to Salman, 'follow me,' and left the track to charge through the brush uphill. It was almost towards the direction from where a short burst had come. They had to cut across and get out of the bowl of fire. Dodging between rocks, small trees and thick bushes Abdul struggled uphill not knowing that he was headed towards one of the Indian soldiers.

Something moved on his left in the near distance and Salman opened fire ahead of the area that Abdul was running towards and they continued moving towards the top of the ridge. They had to reach the road and cross back to safety. Salman smaller and quicker was no longer behind Abdul. They were moving more parallel upwards to the road. Coming around a boulder Abdul stumbled shocked at the sight of an Indian soldier trying to crawl on his stomach to cover. He had been hit. One shoulder dragged uselessly as he heaved himself with the other. He glanced around for Salman. This was probably what Salman had fired at. And if he had not, it would have been the end for him or both of them. In a flash here was his opportunity.

Abdul stopped and looked at the soldier who turned and stared back at him. His arm bled like a spout and he was in pain. A semi-automatic 7.62mm self-loading rifle lay a few feet away. Abdul reached for the weapon and his blood raced. Was anyone looking? He was within touching distance of the soldier and could read his nametag. It read Harnam Singh. There was no fear in that injured face, just hate and a look of desperation. Abdul had to decide fast. It was not yet fully dark and the other two militants may soon be withdrawing along this route as he. They would find Harnam Singh alive if he left him in the same place. He looked up and saw Salman scurrying through the brush upwards not looking back at him. Abdul gripped the soldier under his arms and quickly dragged his struggling body into the cover of a bush that enveloped a couple of rocks. The surface was uneven and the wounded soldier moaned in pain. Abdul pointed the rifle at him and whispered to him to be quiet.

'I will not harm you. Just be quiet or they will get you. Your friends will find you but be silent for at least half an hour. By then we will be far. I am an Indian soldier, Azad Khan, para-commando.'

There was a look of utter disbelief from the wounded man. He spoke with his eyes to say a silent thank you. Abdul had to do something much against his conscience. A backhanded fist on the soldiers nose knocked him out. Slinging the automatic across his shoulder Abdul was about to leave when he saw the man's boots. The gunfire seemed to follow him now and a few shots scattered the area around the bushy shelter.

'Sorry brother but I can do with these.' He was quick to unlace the soldier's boots, pull them off, tie the laces together and throw them over his shoulder. Undoing the unconscious soldier's ammunition belt was easy. He would need that. Picking up the Indian soldier's haversack that contained even more ammunition Abdul turned and raced upwards breathing gasps of air but could not see Salman. He was suddenly alone. There were shots being fired but it was now directed away from him. He guessed Hamid and Rasheid were making a fighting withdrawal. There was return fire from the Indians too and Abdul's experience pinpointed their location. He was almost at the road. Turning towards the Indian side Abdul thought. *'I can hide till it is dark and then surrender to the Indians.'* He pointed his automatic at where he thought the Indian soldiers were in their pursuit. Opening fire was like a burst of freedom. But he had deliberately fired above their heads. It even brought a smile to his face. Hamid and Rasheid would appreciate that surprise burst of covering fire. The Indians turned their attention to him and he had to duck away from the bullets singing around him. It gave Hamid and Rasheid the chance to run. Abdul did not wait to engage the Indians any longer. Gathering himself, staying low he leapt across the road in seconds. He had to escape from this area. There was no possibility of his escaping into India or surrendering tonight. They would find him with an Indian weapon and have no mercy.

Something caught his eye as he crossed the dusty road. Taking cover on the edge of the road in a lying position he strained his eyes through the fading light at what appeared to be two people in a scuffle on the road. *'Is it Salman.'* They were hardly fifty meters away. He recognized one as an Indian soldier and the other was a woman forced to the ground. In one motion the soldier now tore away the kameez from her body, as she lay struggling on the road. Abdul recognized bare flesh. The soldier was tearing at her clothes. He now stood up and tried to drag the Kashmiri woman off the road. She resisted and he swung at her and she went motionless. He must have knocked her out, Abdul concluded. The semi automatic aligned itself in Abdul's hand and he looked down the sights and fired a single shot at what he thought would be below the waist of the Indian soldier. He wanted to give the woman a chance to escape. Also, he could not live with the blood of an Indian soldier on his hands. He didn't wait to see the soldier hit the dust as the shot found its mark and bodily lifted him into the air.

Lungs bursting, Abdul slithered downhill away from the road and heard a muffled shout.

'This way Abdulbhai, hurry up.' It was Salman.

He ran in the new direction and was face to face with Salman so quickly that it took a moment to realize it. Abdul wondered if his thoughts of an escape showed on his face. They looked at each other panting and Salman smiled at his success. Abdul looked at the ground.

'So, you got yourself an automatic. I also saw you fire at that rapist. Ozero will believe you now. You are now truly a mujahideen.'

*'Just as well you did see me fire at an Indian soldier,'* thought Abdul.

Darkness had set in and the firing became sporadic and distant. A single shot or burst at uneven intervals kept everyone alert. In the dark you even fire at shadows. It however gives away your position. The Indians were trying to recover their wounded in the dark and firing at random. Hamid's group was split but they were alive. It did not bother Hamid whether the Kashmiris made it or not. One had died but who cared. Such images just made the desire to survive stronger. They had dropped the load and it had been picked up. The mission was successful. The Pakistani bosses will be pleased. That's all that mattered. Abdul put one hand on Salman's shoulder and between gasps for breath managed to convey that he had got one of them.

'Your shooting saved my life Salman and then I finished him off with my staff.' He even showed off the new boots to Salman. The act was convincing.

Retracing steps was always welcome but had to be done with caution. There had been occasions when the Indian army troops had deliberately allowed an escape to track down withdrawing mujahideens to their holding and resting places. In the darkness, mujahideens and villagers would then all become lucrative targets. Salman and Abdul could see the first few lamps framing the windows of the huts on the hillside at Bagh. They looked like blinking orange demonic eyes in the deepening darkness but served as the beacons to which the militants were homing after a lucky escape.

Salman beckoned to Abdul silently. 'Stay here while I skirt around the village to see if all is clear. If you hear shots give me cover from here. There could be Indian soldiers in that village. It is too close to the line of control.'

'Be careful Salman. Why don't you stay here and I can check out the place for those Hindu soldiers. I know how to deal with them better and now I have a weapon too.' It was a desperate attempt to join up with his Indian brothers.

'No, you stay here. Our orders are very clear and you are still to be accepted as one of us. I know we can depend on you to help if required. Stay here, I will signal if all is clear.'

He was being trusted to stay back alone. He could now easily escape under the cover of darkness.

Left alone Abdul took a deep breath and again felt the rush of freedom. Almost instantly his throat went dry and he felt eyes probing at him from the dark. The Colonel's words rose up fearfully from his stomach. *'There will be many opportunities to escape, be patient and do it when they least expect.'* This is another test for me. Hamid and Rasheid maybe lying in wait somewhere on this track towards the border waiting for me to make a break. Or even Salman may vanish in the dark and position himself from where he can watch me. This seems to be too easy an opportunity. He smiled. 'I will stay here Salman. You cannot trap me so easily.' Voices and fortunately not his thoughts carried a long distance at night. There was no other sound when he thought he heard a few short rapid muffled words of Hindi in the distance. In contrast Kashmiri language otherwise rhythmic, spoken by these militants was quite guttural. Recognizing was easy.

The voices came from somewhere behind and from the road that they had left on the Indian side. *'Those sound like Indian soldiers searching for their comrade. I hope they find him or he will surely die of bleeding. That wounded fellow looked surprised that I did not kill him. It was easy. I think he recognized my features that I was an Indian and not a*

Kashmiri. I could have stayed and helped him and hidden there to be found by the other Indians. They would have been grateful. I think I have missed a great opportunity. Oh Ruhaina! Have I blundered? In my eagerness to get a weapon I overlooked the opportunity of escape. What should I do? '

His thoughts went back to the prison camp and how it had affected his reasoning. Captivity had made him suspicious, over cautious to the point that he either became suddenly withdrawn and at other times unpredictably impulsive and irrational. The reasoning process had become purely for survival. An impulsive mind cannot reason or look ahead. He had missed what he regretted, a huge real opportunity.

'I must think clearly and act fast or the next time I may blunder even more and get myself trapped by these mujahideens or shot by the Indians. But now I have a weapon and the next opportunity I get will not be wasted. If Salman and the others try to get me, I can retaliate and fight my way out. I must not hesitate in shooting at them. They are mujahideen and ruthless with anyone and they are continuing to wage a war against my fellow Indian countrymen. It is my duty to wipe them out.' And then he was again overtaken by the fear of his plan being discovered. 'Now that I have a weapon, they will trust me less and watch me more carefully I think. They could easily do away with me and cover up by saying that I tried to kill them or escape. Will they see the hatred and deceit in my eyes? That Rasheid looks at me with a lot of suspicion. Will he guess that I am just waiting for the next opportunity to escape? The slightest suspicion will be enough for them to end my life. How will I conceal my deep desire to escape? Should I run?'

He heard a low whistle from the huts. That was Salman's signal to them all. It was clear. They could enter Bagh without any fear of treachery or ambush. For just one moment Abdul felt the rush of wanting to quietly backtrack into Indian Territory but he still did not know the whereabouts of Hamid and Rasheid. He was torn by doubts and decisions.

'Either I escape now and take a chance or start back at once before they start looking for me.'

Picking himself up Abdul looked over his shoulder almost mournfully towards the Indian side and started towards the huts of Bagh. Approaching the diffused glow from the huts holding the snatched weapon across his arms like a prize Abdul walked into their midst. Hamid, Rasheid and Salman were already reviving their spirits with a cup of tea sitting at the doorstep of one of the huts vacated for them for the night. They had already heard about his encounter. Salman had narrated. Hamid smiled but Rasheid looked enviously at the prize. It was a better automatic than his own. And Salman beamed with enthusiasm. Abdul had been his responsibility. He had more than proven himself. Now they would all be on equal footing. He could have run free but no he was back with them. He was not the betraying kind. He was a true Muslim; wronged by the Hindus. His revenge had begun. Abdul tried a smile, his eyes trying to project the pride at having been able to kill an Indian soldier and get away with his rifle, ammunition and even the boots.

Rasheid just cursed, 'Dead men's boots are unlucky,' but Abdul didn't care and who would ever know the truth.

Salman offered him a cup of tea but the others just stared. It was never easy to accept new members into the fold. They would have to be more watchful.

Rasheid thought, *'Why don't we just get rid of this fellow tonight. An Indian soldier turned traitor and now a mujahideen is certainly a kafir we are not accustomed to. He is armed now and can be dangerous.'*

After a sparing wash, they ate an equally silent head down meal. Water had to be carried up from a nearby stream; so bathing was not a practice. Salman kept first watch while the others stretched quivering and tense limbs within the poorly lit hut. Abdul hugged his new companion close. A rifle was good sleeping company. It had been long and the feel of a cold steel barrel was surprisingly welcome. The others, Abdul imagined were looking in his direction through the dark. He could not see their expressions but felt their probing minds. Tomorrow would be a new day. They would get used to seeing him with the automatic. Maybe give him space and respect too. The image of the Indian soldier molesting a Kashmiri woman floated into his mind. It triggered disgust.

*'Is this what our soldiers are doing in this beautiful valley called Kashmir? Anyway, I hope my shot did not kill him. Did the girl escape or would the other soldiers catch and brutalize her? Women always face the brunt of war during and long after it is all over.'*

They had to get back to Timarkot and wait for instructions. He almost longed for the next mission. It won't be long he concluded and snuggled with his newfound Indian companion. Turning away from the others, he smiled at the cold wall. *'Soon there will be no walls or mujahideen or even Indian soldiers to keep me away from you Ruhaina. He kissed the captured automatic.'* It was his passport.

# Chapter XV

Chapel road was sprucing up for Christmas. Brother sat hunched on the swing in his verandah. If body language could replace vocabulary— Brother on the swing could be the epitome of "contemplation". The aroma of warm, freshly baked cakes mixed with sounds and spicy odors of the street was like a feather that tickled the average Christian senses into an auto-infectious smile generating a permanent glow almost in concert with the blinking lights and decorations all around.

Light bulbs hanging in dilapidated yet snug verandahs wearing their Stars of David swayed to the gentle evening sea breeze dancing in tune with the carols that played from antique stereo systems side by side with LED flashing DVD players belting out jazzed up versions of the Christmas mood. The widely different beats and sounds left a relaxed frenzy on Chapel Road. You could pick it up and do your thing and no one would be wiser or disappointed. Chapel Road was seasoned beyond such mundane gyrations. The singing children had just left after their special evening Christmas carol session and Brother had led the chorus with mixed emotions. The children or was it the songs, he wondered, had vibrations that stirred him. Just a year ago it was during Christmas that he had first reached for his guitar and it had changed a lot in his life and he was still savoring it, slowly but surely. There had been so many dark Christmas eves within the damp walls of the prison camp. And there were so many things that were happening now, that it would be an understatement to say that it just kept him marching on.

*Destiny, perceived by others who know not the efforts is often labeled as fortunate or unfortunate.* Brother was putting in efforts towards a goal that no one could even dream off. His destiny would surely draw interesting adjectives from an audience that knew not the plodding.

Sheila was now much more than a friend. It was a spacious bonding. Through challenges they had held each other closer. Their intimacies making living apart in the same city a kind of self-imposed exile. Together they seemed to retain their own space effortlessly. He had talked about marriage and she had not said no.

In a giggle she said, 'it makes me feel young again but do you know what you are saying Richard?' It was not always that she addressed him by his first name. It was intimacy.

'I am saying that we have a good chance of becoming a part of each others lives in many more ways than now.'

'It is possible but it needs so many adjustments Brother.' She had held him close. Brother also wondered if he could make the changes after all the years of regimented captivity.

'I understand and like you once said not to expect too much out of you; I can only add to that and say that I too may bring some disappointments but I think Sheila, you could be the guide on this journey.'

'Richard, I sometimes wonder if you will ever be free of the commitment to your friends out there in captivity.'

'Yes I would like to complete that part of my life and then we could consider my proposition.'

'That sounds reasonable Brother. I cannot go through another loss like Kailash.'

'I understand that and appreciate your concern. Do you feel that something will happen to me suddenly?'

'It is not that Brother. I think it is just a very possessive feeling when you are not prepared to part with something.'

'You don't have to Sheila. I think I want to be with you always.'

Looking into the future she had expressed that she just didn't want to experience another loss. The loss of Kailash was in no way fresh but his presence in her life had a flavor that she could never imagine being without. Brother tried to understand but couldn't quite fathom this still water. He just put it behind as one of those feminine emotions that was beyond the comprehension of a man. *'Does she mean wait or is it a no. How do I know what women say and mean?'* Martha had been his only feminine experience and he had gone into training after which he hadn't been close to a woman for the best part of his life. Yet Sheila the woman, became his catalyst in all that was happening and they both knew it and accepted it silently. His willing acceptance of her superior role in his judgment system drew them even closer. It was a bond that was strengthening. In spite of their age there was always a halo of youthful exuberance in their intimacy or association with the world and it willingly enveloped those that cared to share it with them. They could be a jolly good pair.

Fourteenth of December was spent together. Sheila set up a prayer altar at home. Rani and Ravi unabashedly held hands during the prayer. Brother had gradually been included into the small family inner circle. He had squat Indian style next to Sheila. Ravi had gradually become deeply respectful of Brother. They prayed for Kailash's soul. It was the day that he had been shot down in the war of 1971. It was also the day that Brother had been taken prisoner. The prayers were peace for the departed soul and thanksgiving for what they all had and hopes for the future.

Christmas was a few days away and Brother had received a greeting card and letter from Smita. The letter had news. Smita's judge father's friend, a retired General lived in Calcutta and had found out that there had been three army officers in the western sector with the surname of Ganguly in 1971. One had retired and died much after the war in a hospital, the other had recently retired. The third was missing feared dead and his wife lived in Calcutta. Her name was Radhika Ganguly. Brother could not remember if Major Ganguly had ever mentioned the name. Why would he and to whom would he talk what, about his wife within the darkness of a prison camp. The major had buried himself with sketching and painting but he never painted any figures of human beings. His works were always about nature and sceneries. The news of the Ganguly woman had been shared with Sheila and they had decided that Brother could make the trip to Calcutta and meet this Radhika Ganguly. His tickets were booked on the Geetanjali express for 28th December. Brother had been to Calcutta as a young air force officer and knew that Christmas and New Years was a happy experience in the "City of Joy." He would have to shelve plans for New Years Eve in Bombay with Sheila. It did not pain them to be apart. After all, they had found something that every moment together had become a celebration.

Every day spent away from each other became the tacit reason for even more fondness. Separations were not dreaded.

Legs dangling from the swing Brother's mind drifted to the cold mountainous memories of Pakistan, trying to figure out the likely events at the prison camp. His mind walked between the prison billets and dark alleys. He saw too many things and wasn't prepared to accept any. Elizabeth had not been very prompt after his first few e-mails but of late there had been a series of them, each one exchanged left him a bit more anxious. He had found Azad's family under very unique circumstances and now he had come upon information about a Radhika Ganguly, who could well be the wife of the major in captivity but also as it seemed from Liz's email; one of the prisoners was missing. There was little Liz could confirm as to who it was. Was Major Ganguly still alive or had met his end at the hands of some whimsical Pakistani prison guard. Anything was possible in prison camps and Brother had been witness to even cold-blooded murder at Daud Khel. The incomplete information gave flight to imagination and horrible visions seemed to close in on him. Christmas was not a nice time to feel this way. It was a time for celebration and he was soon going to set out on a new mission to Calcutta. The discovery of Radhika Ganguly could be another happy experience. Or was it going to be the wrong number? Brother recalled the events of his meeting and dialogue with Ruhaina and her expressions as she had absorbed and begun to appreciate that her husband Azad Khan was still alive. He wanted to relive such moments. The heart was greedy for rejoicing. However, he re-read the e-mail that gnawed at his soul:

Dear Brother

After your mail about finding one of the families, I took leave and went to meet your friends but couldn't see them. It was too difficult. My being an Army nurse did not help in letting me enter the prison camp as a simple visitor. Do you remember Fatima? I came across her. She somehow conveyed to me and I think; now there are only three of them. One was taken away, according to her. She could not explain which one and I showed her a snap of you that I have, to win her confidence. She recognized you and was happy and understood that you are well and have found the family of one your friends. I could not get across more, we had little time and she just could not relate with the names you gave me but she said she would try to inform the senior most of them about your being alive. Maybe you can describe the features of the person that you are referring to. Poor girl, if only she could hear or speak. I just could not figure out about who has been taken away from that place. It is all such confusion in my mind. What else can I do? Let me know.

Best wishes
Elizabeth

All he needed was the name or nearby location of the prison camp. The Indian authorities could then consider his story and possibly begin an inquiry. Is that what he wanted? No, he really wanted them to be freed like him and the imponderables were eating him up.

*'For fear of being discovered she is not going to write the name of the prison camp location, even on e mail. She must have found a photograph of me from the hospital papers. There were several of them with my medical documents. Fatima, the poor girl may eventually find a way of telling the Colonel about me. She, with her challenges will convey some news about a family that I have traced out all right but the poor guys; each one will think that it is their family that I have found. It will create tensions amongst them. What if Fatima is caught and tortured. She may lead them to Elizabeth or even convey that I am alive in India. It would be a tragedy and then they would take immediate precautions to erase all traces of the prisoners. The Pakistanis may free them from life. One of them must have been taken away to be done in or has he been released like me due to sickness? They were all healthy when I left. Which one of them could have fallen so hopelessly sick to be released and with what kind of false papers? Am I pursuing this mission only to find that my efforts precipitated the death of my friends? In that case I must stop it now. Or should I ask her the name of the place in some way that even if the mail is intercepted, there is no danger to her. In the worst case, Elizabeth may just stay silent or reveal it to me in a discreet manner. It is dangerous but I will have to try. There is little time.'*

Brother jumped off the swing and went into his bedroom. The second hand computer on his study table with its web of cables was becoming his best hope. Come what may, he had to ask Elizabeth the name of the place at the risk of getting caught. Who would monitor the mail of a hospital nurse? The Pakistanis were far from being as smart as the Americans and the CIA. Bin Laden took even the CIA for a ride. Brother watched silently as the computer logged in after being switched on. Sitting at it was a bit like being in the cockpit. There were so many things and the whole Windows thing just amazed him. He typed out his simple message.

Dear Liz

You give me a lot of hope. Thank you for going to meet my friends. Unfortunately they were all not there and also you couldn't meet anyone of them. I understand that one of them has shifted permanently. Since you have not mentioned his name can you find out and let me know his whereabouts. Also can you give me the postal address of the others so I can write to them? Unfortunately, before leaving that place I never noted anything and did not know what to write or whom to ask for the address. I will be grateful for the address. You cannot imagine my joy if I get their address. Hope to hear from you soon. I am leaving for Calcutta to meet another family. Will keep in touch from Calcutta with you. Happy Christmas and New Year to you and your mother.

Regards Brother.

This was Brother's third Christmas after being released from Pakistan. The first had been just after he was shipped home on a stretcher coughing in spasms suffering from Tuberculosis. The recovery had been marvelous. Martha had a lot of faith in mother Mary. She had taken Brother to Mount Mary at Bandra's lands end to pray. He had looked frail sitting in the wheelchair as they went through the service. Through the prayers Brother had resolved that if he survived, he would locate the families of his prison mates to let them know that their loved one was still alive in Pakistan and should be freed. Prayers, Martha's unfailing attention and gallons of hot broth prepared with almost a desperate urgency had pulled him through. She had clung on for his life even as she bent over frail with age. The sleepless nights staying by his side fuelled the flickering hope and desire to live and Brother came through. Martha had simply prayed. *"Oh Lord, you have given me back my son. His whole life went by behind some prison walls for no real fault of his. What was the real purpose of that? Why did you give him this freedom after that, only to die of a sickness that was never to be his? Maybe it is our weight to carry. I have always believed in you and that everything you do is for a good cause. Save him, so he gets all the opportunities to laugh and fly like a free bird. Heal him from the nightmares of agonies that he must have faced. Let me be a good mother and nurture him the way I could when he was a child. You have brought him back to me. Grant me the energies that I need at my age. I thank you for giving me this opportunity again. Whatever it is, thy will be done".*

Lying in his bed Brother had seen his mother doing her best to make him healthy and well. Today sitting on the swing in the verandah he looked at Martha and remembered all the testing moments they had gone through together. Those struggles to just survive urged him on to overcome apprehensions of his ongoing search. Aware that his co-prisoners may have given him up for dead had its own negative strokes. They would never know his fears, challenges, frustrations or the silent tidal wave of joy that consumed him in that moment when Ruhaina had begun to believe that her lost husband Azad was still alive. He had seen the years of trials and tribulations and all the hopeless situations overflowing through frail crystal eyes and then it had all vanished, replaced by a fierce resolution to rescue and reunite with her husband. Brother had to make that happen if only to relive such joy to make up for the starvation of joyous moments in his captive life. His true emotional partner was Sheila and they shared a strong desire to reunite the captives with their loved ones who also remained captive to their uncertainties. He had to go on. It was a mission launched by his own choice.

Christmas was here. Sheila had baked a cake and it was Brother's maiden attempt at turkey roast. They were going to have Christmas dinner together. Rani and her fiancé had also agreed that they should celebrate at Brother's cottage on Chapel road. In a few days Brother would be going to Calcutta to locate Radhika Ganguly. It could be another success for Brother. Sheila and her little family understood it well and wanted a confidence and courage building evening for Brother. Meeting unknown people and trying to change their mindset about a missing person could be frustrating. Brother had oft felt helpless when people found it difficult to believe that he himself had been locked away for so many years. It seemed unreal to everyone. Sheila had understood Brother's vulnerability and feared that this would one day overtake him and terminate his search. It would mean failure and Brother she feared was not yet ready to handle a failure. There would be no one or nothing to blame for this failure and that could be disastrous for Brother. He would end up blaming himself. It was not what she wanted for him. Moreover, she had seen him gradually coming out of his cell. He was certainly rejuvenated after the trip and success in Ahmadabad. He was riding a swell now. It had also taken her to love him as a man and make him believe the powerful primacy of his passions as a mortal. His presence in her life had revived her own resilience. Women are no doubt born with it; unfortunately not all men acknowledge it. Those who willingly accept it can draw from it. Maybe, the ability to draw such strength is what is termed as "always a great woman behind every great man". She had often smiled secretly as Brother revived her soft emotions as a woman becoming a different person and very rapidly too. Her own loss of a husband to a war was like being cheated by faceless gamblers. Brother had been the first man who had brought her face to face with the dice and she had been finally accepted widowhood. Her imagination and visions to keep Kailash alive in her life had been shattered. Through the broken bangles that she wore till then Sheila had accepted her widowhood and with it came the courage to move on. The step was huge and Brother had unknowingly held her hand through it. There had been no one with whom she could emote or connect with about her unfortunate past. It was now her turn to help him through his mission with the hope that it would finally release him from being fettered to his captive past.

Seated on his swing Brother watched the road for Sheila's car. He was accustomed to wait outside their billet in the prison camp. Azad and he used to scan for the birds flying eastward towards their nests in the mountains. They would count the flocks and sometimes even predict the number of birds in a flock. On some days they would correctly forecast the time of arrival of flocks over them as though each flock had an identity. A flock with lesser numbers than predicted would cast a silence between them. Some birds must have been hunted down or had gone the other way; forsaking them. Predictions of numbers that came correct drew a smile and even laughter. For a prisoner, simple hopes was all they could cling to. Hope of being free. Wrong predictions made them sad as though the birds had let them down. But they never lost hope. Here he was. Hopeful of finding Major Ganguly's wife. Here he was, looking forward to Sheila's company and laughter. Yet his thoughts could never unshackle from the damp prison walls and its inmates. Sometimes he almost believed that he had deserted them. They had become a little family. He had not left of his will and wanted to return and free them. Let Christmas celebrations be over. Meanwhile he used to talk to them.

'I will go to Calcutta. There is no time to waste. I am quite sure Radhika is your wife Major. Then I will find your family Colonel sir and Pawri, I remember how you cared for me on so many nights when I was sick. I will find your parents too. It is time I walk into Army HQ and tell them about you guys. The Air force did not believe me. Maybe my Army friends, if they are still there, will listen. In Ahmadabad the Army helped me find your wife, Azad. The other day I saw an article in the newspaper. It was about some fishermen who had been kept in prison for over ten years in India. They had *strayed into Indian waters. Maybe the authorities will start believing that Pakistan could also still have PoWs held in captivity for over twenty years! I will return to free you guys and you will be happy to know that I have a special friend, Sheila. I am sure you will all like her.'*

Sheila's car appeared at the turn a few houses away and Brother recognized it and stood up in a graceful reflex. He couldn't wait for anything now. His mind had developed the capability to fly fast and his thoughts could travel and simultaneously focus accurately, briefly and surprisingly on completely unrelated issues. In the prison camp there were only survival issues but now there were so many and quite a few involved him and his new dependency, Sheila.

Martha had not celebrated Christmas like this before. They never had any Hindu friends who would want to visit and have Christmas dinner with them. Hindus, Muslims or others would visit, wish or pass by with a joyous wave. There was no real reason for get togethers with people from different communities. To non-Christians it was just that Christmas was associated with joy and merry making. "Merry Christmas" itself signified the effervescent happiness of the Christian community and some others just joined in. Non- Christians met their social commitment by wishing every Christian they knew and not many Christians organized parties to entertain. These were hard times. Chapel road was lively and you could invite yourself to any house on Christmas and quite a few people did that but Christmas dinner was still very much a family affair. Earlier, Tom and she would go to church like good Christians and have a nice meal at supper, sit in their porch till late night and watch television and sometimes recall the times they had before Brother had left home for training. Celebrations on Chapel road now had many forms. From jazzed up carols on the street to private parties where the wine overflowed and dance music and sounds of laughter burst unashamedly from overloaded cars, to another smaller private party of the sixty plus sitting on old cane chairs and talking of bygone Christmas celebrations. Everybody was free to celebrate in their own ways and choose their own company but everyone wished everyone and smiles were in abundance.

At Martha's there was a freshly decorated Christmas tree in the hall that was old. Tom had bought it for them but the Christmas of 71 had been shattered because Brother had been shot down and they were only told with regret that he was missing in action. What else could the Air force do? No enemy tells you that one of your pilots is their PoW and not always is his body found and neither do your own authorities want to give you information without proof. "Missing" was the easiest way to describe the dead or captured. The Christmas tree had only come home that year and now it had been taken out because Brother had wanted to decorate the house. Martha through her tears had told him about the tree in the storeroom because Tom and she had never decorated or truly celebrated Christmas with its joy ever since he had gone. Brother had given the finishing touches to the verandah with a delicately arranged crib with hay, the wise men, Joseph, the holy virgin mother and her child.

Greetings exchanged, the evening resounded with their laughter and gifts were opened and appreciated. Martha searched for the right words to say their prayers at supper. Sheila was a Hindu, so how would the prayers be said. It would be fine she mumbled to herself because Sheila liked Richard and it brought warmth in her cottage that had been missing for long. The time came quite soon and it was as though suddenly they were all standing with joined hands at the dining table. The table had been laid with care and Sheila's cake, Brother's turkey and all the other little side dishes with sauces and salads had been arranged with a touch of elegance that made the rest of the room glow with the mood. Brightly lit candles all around danced in unison. Martha looked at Brother for support that she thought she needed. He just nodded and smiled and she was sure that they would all be with her on this day in her prayers to the Lord. Brother's one hand in Martha's; the other found Sheila's. Following the cue from Martha their eyes closed prayer just followed her simple words.

'Oh Lord, we thank you for all your kindness and blessings that have been bestowed on us in our lives. You have brought happiness to this house of Tom and we remember him with fondness and hope he is rested knowing that our son Richard has returned and I am not alone. We are happy to have Sheila and her family with us to share our joys and are thankful to you for bringing them into our lives. Whatever you have given us this day we are thankful and more than happy to share.'

Brother's hand tightened in Martha's and like some current he felt strength from the gentle clutch of Sheila's fingers. The prayer over, they smiled as if on a cue and Brother broke the somber silence.

'Mother, there is some wine I have chilled, it is your favorite and I am sure you haven't had that for sometime.' With that he brought it out of the refrigerator and Martha's eyes blurred with the memories.

'Sure Richard, just very little for me. First pour some for Sheila,

Rani and Ravi. I don't know if wine is good for me but I will share some with you all today. Sheila, my dear, nobody drinks in this house but we do taste some wine at Christmas. I hope you don't mind.'

'Of course not Aunty, I am so happy for you that after a long time you are celebrating Christmas the way you always used to. I will have just a little because it will be the first time for me.' She laughed in an apologetic yet warm way and 'it is also the first time for Rani so it is nice that she will taste it in her father's best friends house.'

Supper was a sit down easy informal exchange of pleasantries. Martha did most of the questioning because she had always stayed in the background where Richard and Sheila were concerned. Today was an opportunity to be closer to Sheila and her daughter and the male friend whose name she just couldn't remember.

There had been a moment when Sheila had not known what to say to Martha's simple enquiry.

'Why is Richard going to Calcutta? He was in Ahmadabad for a few days and I missed him. I don't know what he went for but he has become quite busy after that trip. Is it some job that he has got or is he just meeting friends. That is what he tells me but I am sure you know better eh?'

'Yes aunty, he went to see the family of one of his mates who is still in the prison camp.'

'That is really cruel. Why can't they free them? The war was over so long ago. I don't even want to think about all those years of suffering for my Richard.' She quickly wiped away an imaginary tear.

'Richard wants to bring some joy into their lives. They will now know about the existence of their loved ones as prisoners. Most of them would have given up but Richard hopes to free them from their uncertainties by bringing them the good news that they are still alive.'

'Wouldn't it make them feel more pain and helpless?'

'It may but then they will have reason to push the authorities to get them back.'

'I can't understand why have they not done that already. Richard must have told them. Anyway, I don't want to know or hear about these things today. I will pray to Jesus for mercy and he has always helped.'

Sheila wondered if she had said the right things.

As Sheila drove home, the evening gently replayed through her mind. Brother had sung some carols and they had joined in. He had actually carried them along.

'*He sings well. His presence and easy conversation lightens the* atmosphere. Looking at everyone in turn he in fact illuminates the place. He must have been a popular person with all his colleagues in the air force. That was a good place for him. All that company and laughter must have been oxygen for him. Kailash was full of fun too. Brother is more approachable. Are fighter pilots all like this? Martha is a caring mother who still worries about Brother but keeps her distance. On the contrary Brother never seems to worry about Martha in spite of her ageing and infirmities. He appears to be so effervescent, almost childish. But he has a deeper side that hates violence and detests regimentation of the mind that the air force tried to instill in him. I have felt his pulse and breath. For a bird like him, the prison must have been living death but he has come out unscathed at least on the surface. His deeper wounds are healing. He will overcome and complete his mission, I think.'*

She was not upset that Brother did not share all with Martha. Yet it did bring forward some feelings bordering on regret. Rani shared so much with her. Martha was missing out. Even Brother was missing the warmth of sharing with her. Maybe Brother could share more without getting her alarmed that he was on a search that could trigger a movement and lead to complications for him. If he could make her understand the importance of his search; all would be well and maybe she could motivate him even more. *'Martha feels that I know the truth about his activities and that Brother does not share with her as much as with me. Is this the time for Brother to improve mother and son relationships?'* Sheila would wait and tell him. He was leaving for Calcutta in two days. She sighed wondering how and when would it be the right time for Brother to share more with his mother and then was it really so important. Brother adored his mother and maybe it was just pure concern that he left her out of his mission. Sheila had no doubts about that. Maybe sons behave differently from daughters in their bonding with mothers. *'How do I know? I have only a daughter and thank God we are close. Brother is a good man and a loving son. Time may bridge the gaps that I imagine. Maybe they are close and I cannot see it. Was Martha trying to understand how close Brother is to me? I bet she understands and is just looking for a confirmation. Or am I being defensive? In any case Brother needs to share more with Martha. Being secretive is probably the conditioning he received in prison. He did not have time to think about his relationships. His is a relentless mission to find a few souls and set them free. This Christmas evening has been good for us all. I am happy to be here.'*

Brother felt Sheila and her family coming closer into his mother's cottage. He slept with a secretive smile on his face.

*Women rarely miss the vibes. They are naturally equipped with sensors to catch what is flying in the air. Evolution needed one of the sexes to sense accurately to build and sustain strong bridges across the ever-changing expanse of humanity. Man was designed to be assisted by their sensors. Women with active sensors know how and when to wait. They may suffer loneliness but come to terms with what men perceive as a kind of captivity when lonely. For women waiting is a willing submission more like an offering to some cause. Waiting is not diluted by feelings of captivity. How many men would wait for their wives "gone missing in action" and bring up the children or run the business with the hope that she was still alive and may return one day? Men would be condoned for not waiting. I wonder if our world would endorse such a judgment if a woman did not wait. The world has seen too many wars and separations. Men always justify wars, or the taking of prisoners and even holding them without reason. Freeing captives therefore becomes secondary or unimportant to man. In this regard his cause or fears becomes more important than the issue that they should be freed after the war or there is someone waiting for such unjust captivity to end. Brother without knowing was trying to free these women and others from what he perceived as their captivity to uncertainty. Waiting was like being captive in Brother's comprehension. Freeing them was however secondary to letting them know that their own dear one was alive. He was more eager to take away the pains of their imaginary loss. He could not understand why at times they disbelieved his story or even their damp expressions after being given the good news of their loved one being alive. Even news like Kailash's end was relief for Sheila. Brother continued to believe he had freed her of some bondage. Women search truths and their moral fibre carefully yet almost spontaneously accepts what they sense clearly and being thankful that "He" is alive is more succour than gaining freedom from their own captivity to uncertainties. Some men are more fortunate than others by conscious or auto acceptance of such emotionally different polarities. Brother would never understand for he was not conditioned to do so. He would remain captive to his mission in spite of reaching the families. In his search to experience the joy he brought to them; he could never be free. It however gave him the fuel to overcome fears and disappointments to plough on towards finding them. His willing emotional reliance on Sheila and the growing joy of their relationship and the final reunion of families is what he wanted to gift his captive colleagues.*

## Chapter XVI

    **A**hmadabad has its Christian population but unlike Bombay with its Chapel Roads, Byculla, Colaba, Bandra, Borivili and other larger congregations of the community; Christmas is given visibility by the presence of discount sale banners displayed at almost every store. Here many storekeepers forget to take these banners off or leave them swinging in the breeze intentionally because it attracts shoppers and it is not that the discount sales were still on. You can tell the real from the make believe discounts by the banner condition. The faded tattered ones were the forgotten advertising memories of festivals that helped make up for the poor sales in the year that had gone by. Some of these are even left overs of the festival of Diwali. Diwali in Ahmadabad is like Christmas in Calcutta or Bombay. Celebrated with fervor. The spirit of celebration is all that there is in common between the two. Christmas comes ever year on a fixed date. Not so Diwali and most of the other Indian festivals. These religious occasions have become buying sprees for everyone. It is not by any chance the benchmark of levels of happiness nor has it very much to do with any deep religious beliefs. It would be unfair not to mention that there is definitely an atmosphere of celebration in which everyone, the rich and not so well to do, all make an attempt to inject a dose of joy that enthuses them on. Bonuses are announced and new ventures launched. It all begins in August. Christmas in December is by default the closing curtain of festivities because New Years Eve is really a western thing! Not that it is not celebrated but is probably rung in with differing revelry than in the western world. The Hindu calendar has its own New Years day and it is surely celebrated and not wined in.

Most of those at the bar in the Ahmadabad High court were members of the Club. It organizes a New Years party more as a routine and reason to have an event where everyone can come together. The heads of government departments, the police chief, armed forces seniors and some select bosses from the industries would be on the invitee list. Judge Sudhin and his family made their presence every year as it gave them an opportunity to informally meet even those they would never be seen with. A judge had to appear unbiased and secular. The judge's daughter had wanted to wear a new outfit for the occasion and who could tailor it better then Basheer.

Smita got out of her car and walked towards the steps of Kasim Khan Outfitters. She was to collect her embroidered ensemble for the new years' party. Recognizing the lady customer already inside the shop at the counter the spring in her steps died. Basheer Khan was at the counter handing over clothes tailored at his training institute to another customer; a middle aged lady from the Army cantonment. She was someone, you could tell from her presence and she had a young soldier standing obediently at a discreet distance outside the entrance. He was the driver of the staff car in which she had come to collect her clothes. She was the Area Commanders wife known in many circles as the social worker who did days of selfless voluntary service in rehabilitating victims of the Godhra riots and later for victims of the floods that had washed away the blood stains from remote corners and walls but could not drown the screams of those who were systematically butchered and the wails of those who were even made to watch the violations. That tidal wave had left behind silt that had the potential to harden into rocks that could fly at random and once again erupt into a revengeful fire more dangerous than volcanic lava. The Army could do a lot. It could not voice opinion or take sides but it had the wherewithal to snap into action and control breakouts like that at Godhra and what was doing the rounds is that the committee set up for the post riot enquiry was questioning the delay in calling out the Army to control the riots. There was a history of the Army at Ahmadabad being called out in such situations in the past and they had often been credited in saving the day. There was no absence of precedence in calling upon them. The decision to call out the Army is taken at the highest levels of the local civil administration and of course with the nod from the Central Government in New Delhi.

Smita entered the shop. Basheer had seen her much before she came in but he never displayed emotions other than his permanent soft smile that always stayed in his eyes. The lady was talking to him.

'Basheer bhai you are most welcome to come to our health care center and use the physiotherapy facility. Let me see your fingers. They seem to have healed well. We are all proud of you in the cantonment that you have opened an institute for women to learn embroidery. I may also send some of our jawans' (soldiers) wives to learn the art.'

'Sure madam and we do not charge any fee for their learning period. They afford their own material for learning and sometimes we help them in little ways. Some of them stay on to be employed and get paid a commission on their work. Some just learn the art and leave. We do not believe in holding anyone against his or her wishes. It makes us happy to know that our ancestral expertise is appreciated and we are not disturbed by any competition.'

He smiled and continued, 'thank you for patronizing my grandfather's shop. We have been here in this cantonment from my childhood and it is the business we get from your army ladies that has seen us through many of our commitments. Please keep on coming.'

'Surely Basheer, I may start giving you material for embroidery and then put it in our welfare shop for sale. Some of the money earned in this manner goes towards welfare activities of the women and children of our soldiers.'

'It will be our pleasure to contribute to your cause madam.'

'Thank you Basheer bhai and do remember my offer for physiotherapy. By the way, is that a picture of your father who I have heard was a gallant soldier of the Parachute regiment?'

Basheer just smiled. There was no exuberant response announcing that his father Azad was believed to be alive and still a PoW. News of Brother's visit to the Ahmadabad cantonment had not yet spread for the senior most lady to know about the discovery of PoWs and the missing Naik Azad. Ruhaina and Basheer had decided to keep it a secret for good reasons.

Smita stood behind the lady who was in conversation and unintentionally heard the entire exchange. She took in and liked the colors inside the shop. Basheer had good taste. The wall cupboards were of dark mahogany with simple flush fit brass cups to slide them open. There was a black leather covered couch settee for waiting customers that had a comfort inducing sloping cushioned back and it could double as a place to sleep for one person however with not much space to change sides. The seating was so designed that the sliding glass cupboards began a distance above your head and there was a mirror on the opposite wall that would give one a full view of all that was on hangars or shelves in the cupboard. It also gave depth to the not so big shop. The glass shelves now were premium thick glass probably selected as hindsight to the shattering experience of the riots. The tailor master's counter was no longer made of glass shelves inside a wooden framework. It was more like a well cushioned bar counter with the wooden edges well polished. The entrance instead of an all the time fully open front now had a glass swing door with wood paneled cupboards on either side. You could see and enter through the door that could be electronically locked from the counter in an emergency. Secure from inside it had been sensibly renovated after the riots.

As the senior lady turned to leave, their gaze met and there was recognition. 'Oh hello, you are Sudhin's daughter, aren't you. What a lovely embroidered kameez you are wearing.'

'Oh this! It was tailored here at Kasim Khan's rather, Basheer is the one who designed and tailored it,' Smita almost blushed in reply and glanced towards Basheer. The lady smiled politely and left.

He had turned his head away to conceal his full bloom smile. It was not that he turned away from the compliments. Basheer did not want anyone to see the emotions that glowed in his eyes whenever Smita was around. This was a change from the times before the riots. Hooligans that had attacked him had even accused him of intimately associating with her as they tried to beat him to death. It had been a shock for him and he was sure that through the pandemonium he had heard correctly. He would be cautious even with his emotions and body language whenever Smita visited their shop. He wanted no hurt for the only source of inspiration he had.

'Salaam Smita,' Basheer greeted her with a restricted smile more like the ones he gave to all his customers.

'How are you Basheer. I am happy that the local cantonment army people are aware of your incident during the riots and are appreciative of your work and contribution. Your father will be proud if you get involved in teaching embroidery to the jawan's wives.'

'It is more my mother who runs the institute and teaches helpless Muslim and other women. I am more into cutting and tailoring.'

'But haven't you made my party clothes yourself and also the one I am wearing now?' With that she pirouetted watching herself in the tilted wall mirror behind Basheer while his eyes couldn't resist taking in her womanly charm that ended quickly as he glanced at the doorway. He thought,

*I hope no one was watching her. I have to somehow tell her to be more discreet without offending or hurting.*

'Yes I did but my mother's hands are far better,' he smiled apologetically.

'I have only learnt a little bit from her and Baba will be proud of her. I would have been happier if I could have joined the army into Baba's regiment but that is history now. Let me show you your New Years ensemble.'

He turned to reach for it as it was displayed in a special glass case in a corner. Smita whispered with concern, 'I hope it did not put strain on your fingers.'

'I cannot be here and do nothing Smita. Your work has in fact rekindled my confidence that my fingers are still functional for intricate work.'

With that he brought forward the combination that Smita would wear. Her eyes brightened into shining diamonds and almost immediately withdrew in a blur within a film of moisture. Basheer was quick to notice because he always watched his customer's eyes and listened for their breath when they accepted his tailoring. He knew it was the true assessment of their work. Words could never replace their body language. He could deal with appreciation or criticism but he was not adept at handling a customer whose beauty filled his mind enough to make his eyes and fingers move with needle and thread like a musician, specially when her eyes could get wet with concern for him. Basheer desperately tried to find words to distract them both. Time recorded a silent emotionally flooded gap as it ticked away. Smita raised the dress so that it formed a curtain between her and Basheer. She did not want him to see her tears. These were tears of joy for the man who had been her companion through her youth. Their association had unintentionally contoured her impressionistic emotional sensitivities gently and ever patiently through her frivolous exuberance of youth. Her self-analysis had often revealed that many of her successes in the court was due to the soft yet rock like confidence and patience she had experienced with

Basheer in their friendship. All her achievements became irrelevant in comparison to this nobility born in a humble family that had climbed out of the debris so often always with a smile.

'It is just gorgeous Basheer. I could have never dreamed of these little flowers with matching shaded pearls embedded in the center. Finding and matching these pearls with the color of threads would have taken you so much time and also they are so small that I cannot imagine that just a few months back your fingers could not even move and now look at the intricate embroidery you have done.'

'How do you like the small bees and butterflies, Smita. There are just a few.'

'Where are they Basheer? See, I always miss the wood for the trees. I like the idea and yes I see them now. You should have been a poet. Your imagination and creativity is so unpredictably stunning.'

'Smita how could I be a poet when my grandfather was just a tailor and my father a soldier and I was never good with language like you were in college.'

'You know, your biggest problem is that you just haven't learnt to accept compliments Basheer.'

'That you come to our shop for all your clothes Smita is our biggest compliment and we can only accept such a compliment by living up to your expectations.'

'Beyond expectations is more like it Basheer. Please charge me correctly for this piece of art.'

Basheer gave her one of his oldest spontaneous smiles. She was familiar with that one.

'No, I will not accept it for free Basheer. You have gone through so much effort and pain I am sure that this deserves to be paid for or I will feel guilty wearing it.'

Basheer took a deep breath and said, ' Did you not tell me once that the best things in life are free?'

Defenses broken, the lawyer just crumbled against such an honest appeal.

'Basheer then I will gift you with a sherwani. Will you wear it for your occasions?'

'You have already gifted me back my life Smita. I will always be indebted to you. I would have never come out of that trauma if it had not been for your constant attention. That must have also occupied your mind for endless hours and pain for my difficult behavior. The time and effort spent by me on this dress for you is nothing compared to all those days you suffered on my account. So please accept this as a small token of our appreciation of all that you did. Had it not been for you maybe that retired air force officer who was a prisoner with my father would have never located us. Can we ever be grateful for that.'

'These are very kind words Basheer but I will feel more comfortable if I can present you with a sherwani and you promise to wear it.'

For those few minutes that they exchanged their own reasoning, Basheer felt his cup filling up and Smita found herself drifting back to their college days that was littered with such endless debate. Sometimes genuine yet sometimes those youthful conversations were spontaneous exchanges mutually seeded to bring out emotions or provide an excuse to spend more time with each other. Time was like a huge container and it always seemed empty those days. They spent a lot of time together to try and float to the top of that container and experience fulfillment but somehow they always felt that time had run out for them. Today also time was hanging and the vibes had rewound to their early years. Between them this magic never took any time. They could go back instantly. Theirs was a bonding beyond religion, status or any of the artificial abstract roadblocks created by scheming tunnel vision minds. Smita had spent just a few minutes with Basheer and had enough time today. Basheer could not contain his urgency to terminate their back scrubbing. He was subject to fears that he had been made conscious of.

*There are many in India and the world that have similar bonds that leap across barriers created by history, country, politics, religion, tradition, color of skin, society and even parental disapproval. Theirs is a conscious struggle to sustain the joy they have discovered from within. Some graduate to levels of consciousness that it no longer is a struggle. Others travel a distance and succumb to the fatigue and some even fall prey to the vicious repercussions that can get triggered. Such bonding is not the majority and could be termed as the exception and a lot of us secretly hope that we progress towards a conscious freedom that is promised by just being ourselves and democracy and secularism. Yet many remain captive to obsessions that we have never bothered to analyze. Time for analysis has been engineered away from us by too many factors that are so entwined that the only way is to shed fears and come out but then fear is also one of the baser emotions that can take credit for man to evolve from the stonage and fabricate weapons and implements for pure survival that have evolved and also created the weapons of mass destruction. The desire to reach sunlight is what makes a plant bend, twist, lean and climb into the open. Man can generate equally strong forces.*

*Secularism is a sunlight that can be reached. There will be a price for a release from Captivity to Inheritance. It will be not be without resistance and pains.*

Basheer felt the pain rising. He had to tell her his fears about their association. It would be difficult for her to accept. He knew her rebellious foundation. All the same he never concealed from her and the earlier he shared this concern would be better for them. He could not breathe freely while there was a section of society that had leveled a charge that had colors to stain her chastity and his character.

'For me to wear a sherwani there will have to be an occasion and I cannot see something like that Smita.' He began to shuffle behind the counter as though he was looking for something. Smita noticed this unease and wondered why he had suddenly begun to hop around like a rabbit seeking cover from a stalking hunter.

'Well, what is bothering you suddenly Basheer. Am I holding up your work?'

The comment stopped Basheer from fidgeting around and their eyes met. 'Nothing is so important that cannot wait but there is something I have to talk to you about and am unable to do so here.'

'You can tell me whatever it is Basheer. If something is bothering you, it is best that you share it and maybe we could find a way.'

There was no way out of this dark corridor for Basheer and as suddenly as he had said, he now felt an uncontrollable urge not to tell her as it would most certainly leave Smita disturbed and feel responsible for the attack on him by the Hindus.

'Is it about the riots Basheer? Have you found out any information about those miscreants? Or is it something about your father? Is Ammi all right? Basheer you must tell me because you have triggered my curiosity.'

The quick staccato of her guesses left him even more confused as none of them related to what he had wanted to say to her. His eyes refused to meet hers and kept traveling from shelf to floor and back to the ceiling. Smita withdrew into a tight-lipped hum, letting him think and humming just to keep his attention held to her presence. She wanted to know his mind and had a strong suspicion that it was unpleasant and was discouraging him from telling her. He could go into a cave very fast. She had to keep him connected to her presence and coax him silently to climb through his apprehensions and share those thoughts with her.

Basheer took a deep breath and started, 'Will you understand if I tell you that you should not visit this shop as often as you do now.'

There was silence as the words ended and they looked expressionless at each other. Smita trapped an immediate question to his words and allowed herself to rapidly consider the reasons for Basheer's almost death sentence like statement.

She thought, *'my visits to this place began more than fifteen years ago. What has happened now that makes him say such a thing. Should I ask him or will it be something unpleasant and is best left alone for the moment. Why should I stop coming here unless it is something that will be harmful for me or for both of us? There is no such place that I visit that can be detrimental to me so why should my coming here become so? Perhaps he has some apprehensions. Or he is scared that I may convince him to lodge a case against the rioters. I will not contest his statement now and maybe I will understand more about it in time. This family has been close to me for so many years. This is not going to be easy. I hate this kind of imposition and need an explanation but it should not hurt him in anyway. I can ask him. He will be patient and explain, I am certain and if it has to be the way he wants it then I will accept his rationale.* Pacing along the counter she broke the silence entreatingly, 'Basheer, I am sure there is very good reason for what you say. I am not hurt by what you have said. I am just confused at this very unexpected request made by you. It is something I cannot understand.' It had the desired effect on Basheer.

Leaning on the counter head between his hands Basheer shied from his reflection on the glass top to reluctantly begin. 'Smita, there are people who watch you coming and going. There is nothing wrong about your coming here. I also know you enough to understand that you will do what you feel irrespective of my explanations. Also, whatever happened to me during the riots is something that was circumstantial. It has nothing to do with anyone. We have seen so many of these communal incidents. The mob was in hysteria and Ahmadabad has seen such behavior in the past. It is happening all over the country.'

He looked up groping for more words and to feel for her pulse. Smita was a picture of calm and it gave him the courage to confess his innate fear.

'Those people who attacked me said something not nice about my association with you. We have been friends for so many years and I have never heard something so shallow. I respect your feelings regarding religion, family and friendship. In fact it is because of you that I believe that those that hate us for being Muslims are few. There are many more who respect and appreciate us for what we are. That itself is reason enough to disregard verbal abuse such as what happened during the riots. It is just something that worries me. I want no harm to you. You are a married Hindu woman. I am an unmarried Muslim. Those who watch us conversing, laughing or your coming here even just to see Ammi will never understand. These are people who play with public emotions through lies and fear. I pray that something so unclean is never even dreamed about you.'

Basheer was forced to stop his monologue because Smita began to giggle building to a choking laugh. He grew nervous and his eyes kept darting towards the doorway and street beyond. Above all he wasn't sure if what he said was shameful or acceptable as a conversation between man and woman. He was not exactly an upwardly mobile man of the 21st century. His words were more forced from an aged value system, which however would not be very much out of place in the modern world. Men and women share much more verbal intimacy today but Basheer had not been exposed to it. Such a situation had never occurred in his dreams surrounding her. And he had dreamt for many years. Secretly loving, then admiring and finally just respecting and being thankful for her as an experience Allah had privileged him with. She remained his central pedestal of emotions and as the years went by he made a few adjustments to continue with his own battles. He thought his words must have hurt or embarrassed her.

'Have you finished Basheer?'

Basheer tried to elaborate. 'I am sorry if this has hurt you but it has been in my mind for a long time.'

Smita heard him through her exhausted laughter now dying into an almost rhythmic snigger. Her eyes though conveyed much stronger emotions. She was not one to succumb to any kind of threat or ridicule. Hers was not any kind of brazen attitude. Rather it was courage that was born from clear thinking and self-reliance. There had been many situations in her youth that had her mother adopting a firm attitude and even pleading with her in vain to be more conventional and surprisingly it was her father who never intervened and his silence for her non-conformist attitude had charged her on to being a woman who could stand her own in a male dominated profession and society. She was not about to back off from her commitment to her beliefs. Society and their words were purely incidental and any comments from such sources was like water on her duck's back.

'There is something I came here for Basheer. It was not just to collect my clothes. Will you understand if I tell you that I need your assistance to identify one of the criminals who has been arrested for looting and arson during the Godhra riots? One of the girls working for you during that period has already identified him as one of those who attacked your shop, injured you and also kidnapped the women in a stolen van. If you identify him independently, the law can take its action on all the other evidence that is available.'

With that she sat down on the couch meant for visitors. She usually went behind into their home if she had the time to sit for a while. To keep her in his vision, Basheer had to look down at her. It was as though she was going down on her knees, requesting him. It uplifted Basheer against his wishes. He would come down and he did. Coming round from his side of the counter he stood in front of Smita never losing eye contact. Smita now looked down at the floor waiting for him to agree to her request. It would not be easy, as he had refused to even give a statement to the police after his injury and removal to the municipal hospital. Smita had tried but he had not seen any purpose because he wanted to forget the incident whilst a statement to the police would keep taking him back to the hell.

'I am not sure I will be able to recognize this person Smita. I do not want to implicate the wrong person. Allah has been kind to us and even if we lost something during those riots, we also got something much bigger than life. It was during that period that we came to know that Abba is still alive. He may be a prisoner even now but he is alive and there is hope that we will recover him. Nothing can be a greater gift and justice from Allah than that for us. For Ammi it was getting back years of her life. She smiles now like I have never seen before. There is hope in her voice and in everything that she does there is a trace of getting ready to receive Abba. We can forgive these people who looted and damaged our shop. See, even my injuries have healed completely and this dress that I have completed is the first one after those days. It is a milestone for me. In all sincerity I do not wish to identify this person. I would rather forget all their faces. Allah, be merciful to them. They will get their judgments from Him. I am sorry to disappoint you this way Smita but I trust you will understand. Also if my request not to visit often has hurt you— please forgive me for telling you the truth as it has lain in my heart. You are free to do as you please.'

Smita had expected a negative response from Basheer to identify one of the criminals. Hers was a life and commitment to uphold what the constitution and the law of the country assures. Basheer's tragedy had brought the failures of the whole system to her doorstep. She had promised herself to move heaven and earth to bring relief and justice to those who were violated. Smita offered her services without any fee to Muslims families that had been attacked during the riots. Her father had not contested this decision at all. He had experienced her desperation to save Basheer's family and he had taken his own firm decision to follow the procedures of law in every case that came to him for judgment. Smita's services did not involve any search or coordination with the police or the Government team carrying out an enquiry ordered after the massacre. She had only gone forward to provide legal help to all those who approached her with their complaints. Strangely, even the worst cases were not forthcoming. Their reluctance to respond to her offer was not initially understood by Smita. It however did not take long for her to gather that they feared a backlash from local gangs that had support from quarters that could manipulate evidence. The refugees had no confidence in the system to protect them if they complained or even gave evidence. The law was shamed by its incapability to protect the minority community for over two weeks while the mob went about wreaking havoc. Smita had visited some of the relief camps that had been set up to provide shelter and protection to Muslims who had been driven from their homes to avoid getting trapped by marauding gangs. Her reassurance to women who had been raped and those whose men and children had been slain before their eyes fell on deaf ears. Most of them retaliated not willing to believe that she would help them if they complained. Others just suspected her intent and kept silent. Smita had never seen so much fear in human beings. It only made her more determined to get them to register their complaints. It also devastated her to be part of the system that was supposed to generate confidence among the weaker sections of society. They were the ones who really needed the protection and they had lost faith. Truly, the rot had set in deep. They could remain captive to the pain, hate, suspicion cycle for maybe generations. What a trail.

Basheer's reluctance was expected but his rationale was on a different plane than what Smita had encountered in the relief camps. He wanted to forgive, free himself and leave the memory behind.

Smita found herself mentally fatigued and she said, 'Basheer, you know that there are very few who are coming forward with their complaints and evidence. It shatters me to see their plight and the fear in their eyes. Witnesses are a must if the courts have to dispense justice. I respect your personal reasons for not agreeing to my suggestion but have you lost your strength to uphold the truth. By assisting the law you will be upholding it. Can you not set aside your personal feelings and consider that your cooperation will be giving support to those who are really helpless and weak.' She grew tired.

Basheer had listened to her carefully and he said, 'to be frank with you Smita I have a lot of faith in the justice system. I also believe in all the things you have just said. Witnesses and evidence is the basis of deciding the dispensing of justice. The law can help with the help of citizens as you have yourself said. Doesn't that imply that the law needs support to do its job? The law is helpless without us. For us to help strengthen the hands of justice, we have to be alive and to be alive we need to protect ourselves to some extent. It is the fear of ones life that prevents a lot of Muslims from taking your assistance. For me to identify this person is not the issue. What is more important is that I am not sure that you will have enough protection from those who may seek revenge for your involvement. Even asking you not to visit us too often is to protect you. Your position in society demands an above board character and you must give no opportunity to them to tarnish it.'

Basheer had lit her fuse. 'I don't care too much about what people say about my character. I have to able to live with my conscience and for the time being it dictates that I don't change either my coming here nor will I stop pursuing these criminals and get justice for those whose lives have been permanently damaged. And Basheer I am thankful for your protective thoughts. Only don't let it change things too much.'

Basheer could only smile and secretly he was proud of her sword out attitude. His love and admiration was on the right horse. Their different rationale was one of the strongest factors in their marriage of minds. Their minds were always in search of each other.

Smita smiled and said, 'Basheer, you have a way with convincing. I am not happy that you will not come for this identification and I am also not convinced that I need to be careful about coming here. Let us agree to disagree. Like the old times?'

They were smiling now and it was as though the stage was set for Ruhaina to come in from the rear entrance of the shop. She stopped for just a moment watching them both without knowing about any of the discussion they had just terminated.

'Smita it is so good to see you, how are your parents?'

'They are fine Ammi and how are you.'

'I must tell you something Smita and I may need some help from you.'

'Tell me Ammi, I will do whatever I can.'

Basheer withdrew behind his counter as though making space for his mother.

' Smita do you have the address and telephone number of that gentleman, Mr. James who was a prisoner with my husband.'

'Yes, I have it.'

'I need to write to him and ask him a few things because I am planning to go to Pakistan to some relatives we have in Karachi. I think I will be able to somehow find out the whereabouts of my husband. We can then officially try to rescue him. What do you think about it?'

Basheer had no inkling of his mother's plan but it excited him and his immediate gut feeling was that she would be successful. Ammi had a way of unraveling most mysteries. A father whom he hadn't seen was truly a mystery for him and he wanted that to change. Smita was taken aback and her first concern was about Ammi's capability.

*'Would she be able to travel alone and then convince relatives she hardly knew about her missing husband. Would she be able to withstand opposition or would she get the support she expected. What if she failed? There was just a chance that she may succeed but Brother James would know better. He has to be contacted.'*

'I hope you are able to get clues to your husband's whereabouts. For that if you plan to go to Pakistan, I think it is a positive step and I will help you with whatever needs to be done Ammi.'

Ruhaina beamed courage and confidence as Basheer saw off Smita with his most courteous smile. She left the shop not quite successful but hugging the dress that Basheer had created for her gave her enough to feel good about.

# Chapter XVII

'Dada (elder brother), I haven't eaten for three days. Give me a rupee for a cup of tea. God will bless you.'

Brother took out a five-rupee coin and placed it in the leathery palm of the beggar woman with a child tied around her waist. 'Buy her some milk,' he said instinctively not knowing but just presuming that the child was a girl.

'Thank you "Dada". God will bless you always.' The woman touched his feet but without any trace of change in expression in her eyes. Beggars were captive to their sinking state and expressions were long ago blanked out of their wiring.

Brother had just stepped off the train in Howrah Station, Kolkatta to this strange greeting that he was long gone familiar with but deprived from experiencing in the years of his captivity. In Kolkatta everyone was everyone's elder brother. Brother James did not feel out of place.

An arrival in Kolkatta through the portals of Howrah station can only be described as a controlled stampede. Indian railway stations are a reasonably good portrayal of the city or even village. It offers the real people, sounds, smells and the voices with its local language that can bring you home or put you out like a "Robinson Crusoe". Victoria

Terminus of Bombay in comparison is an ocean of people all flowing in one direction. No stampede here; direction of flow varying very much like the tides of the Arabian Sea that it is surrounded by. Howrah station built by the British was like a maze to Brother as he looked for retired General Nagchoudhuri's driver who was to receive him. Situated on the river Hooghly that flows into the Bay of Bengal, Howrah evokes history and intrigue in a visitors mind. It is not just the stonewalls, cobbled stone streets or the cacophony of the crowds. The people have an intriguingly ageing look like the city that is truly old in Indian and World history. The imposing structure of the Howrah Bridge speaks dominatingly saying, "Try me for size and strength" and it is truly amazing at the way traffic disappears across the ancient bridge into Kolkatta. Nowhere in the world will you find a traffic sign that says, "Infiltration Left" allowed. Kolkatta, the city where the British laid the foundation of their trading and business is till date a trader's make or break. It is also a city where women are visibly treated with almost divine respect. Chivalry in this world still has a cushioned bar stool, in Kolkatta. Brother had come in search of Radhika Ganguly the wife of his co-prisoner, Major Ganguly.

The retired general's driver Gautam had been described to Brother on the telephone and also that he would have a placard with Flight Lieutenant James written on it. Brother looked around and walked past some of the cars that were angularly parked adjacent to the platform; something only Howrah station boasts of. Parking next to the platform so you can get off the train and hop straight into your car. Very "Propah!" and comfortably British. Gautam was found leaning on his bonnet with the placard held in one hand. It almost looked like a notice held up reluctantly for the car to be sold. Brother imagined that Gautam would have come looking for him but here he was waiting to be spotted.

Brother introduced himself and the driver saluted. It reminded Brother of his Air force days. Throwing him back a rakish touch to his temple, he got into the rear seat with his baggage— one suitcase.

The driver ordered; "The guest was to have lunch with the general". It was indeed around noon.

'Can we go to Fort William so that I can drop of my suitcase, wash and change?'

Gautam was silent for a moment and then he was firm, 'the general has said to bring you straight to him.'

Brother was not new to Kolkatta roads and tried to sound convincing. 'The general lives on Chowringhee lane and the Fort is pretty much on the way, isn't it? I need a few moments.'

'Every place can be on the way sir, I have my instructions from the general and I have been with him now for ten years. He does not appreciate any changes without his approval.'

'Right then take me to him,' Brother acceded and reclined back to think about his meeting and watch the streets of Howrah as they meandered through lanes that defied any memorizing of the route.

The general was judge Sudhin's friend. He had fought the 1971 war and knew a lot of top brass in the army. It was all Brother had gathered from Smita's letter and phone call as far as bio-data was concerned.

They reached Chowringhee before Brother could get a fix on his whereabouts. Gautam navigated through crowded streets with trucks and bullock carts, across some wide roads with smart policemen, a few narrow lanes with houses on the street almost touching the cars and buses driving past and then suddenly into an open avenue with beautiful trees suddenly ending with a turn into a non-descript arched drive in with a dilapidated gate to stop in front of the Edwards Court porch. It was old, British and under renovation. Gautam got out like lightening and was at the rear door before Brother had glanced around and mentally prepared himself to get out. The door was held wide open and Gautam reached for his suitcase.

'I don't need this now', was Brother's halfhearted protest.

'My orders are to bring you up with your baggage sir.' There was a smile on Gautam's face and it surprised Brother that he could.

*Maybe this was also a part of the General's standing orders. These retired generals like to command. I wonder how many troops he has now. Poor Gautam, he must be the only soldier left. All the same he is a dedicated fellow. I must tip him.'* Brother searched for an appropriate rupee denomination to give Gautam. Taking out a hundred rupees he held it out to Gautam. Another big smile greeted him this time with all stained brown teeth exposed, Gautam accepted saluted and wheezed,

'Sir I have yet to drop you today at Fort William. And I will be with you everyday during your stay in our city.'

Brother found his entry into Kolkatta most intimidating. Was this a harbinger of the days ahead? He was certainly not hoping for too much opposition. In Ahmadabad it had not been very difficult to get across to Major Dilip and then Smita. There had been a few doubtful moments but he had been convincing and with their help he felt quite a team by the time they reached Ruhaina and then Basheer.

'Lead the way then Gautam, the general probably has been

waiting. You don't want him to get angry? Lead the way.'

'Oh yes sir, he briefed me three times in the last three days. Is it a fact that you were a prisoner in Pakistan for twenty years.' It was the first sign of striking a personal note and Brother felt his calm return.

'A little more than twenty but how did you know?'

'The general, he knows everything sir, you will be amazed, follow me.' They climbed old and bleached wooden stairs.

The introductions over Brother sipped a snifter of gin at the orders of his host while the general gripped his glass of beer.

'It is a great privilege for me to have you here with us Brother and I want you to understand that I will give you whatever help you need while in Kolkatta. I wonder how many people you meet will believe your story but Sudhin told me that you were a man with a mission to find one of your co-prisoner's families here in Kolkatta. It is a great service you are doing. Not all prisoners released by the Pakistanis or any country would spend the time and energy to go and look up relatives leave alone finding them without any definite clues. I wonder why you haven't gone to the government. They must help get our boys back. This is preposterous that these officers and men are being held so long after the war has been over.'

Brother recounted his deportation followed by the Indian Air force experience; finding Kailash's wife and the general believed him when he admitted to total ignorance of the PoW camp location.

'We also held Pakistani PoWs from the liberation of Bangla Desh and there were strict instructions that no one was to reveal the location. It however amazes me that the air force did not take up this issue with the government but I am not totally surprised at this response. You know how the bureaucracy is and there is always a tussle between them and the armed forces. They will not believe you and take the risk of an international misunderstanding, that too with Pakistan. Just recently, India released quite a number of Pakistani fishermen who had been caught fishing in Indian territorial waters. They had been held for over ten years. Amazing.'

Brother was tempted to tell the general about Elizabeth's e-mails and of her cousin Edward who was still believed to be held by the Indian Army, also as a PoW. *'It will be too many inputs for the general. I think I will keep it for a later date.'*

The general leaned back in his rocking chair, looked at Brother with far off eyes and said, 'tell me seriously, more about this place in Pakistan. What did the countryside look like from your prison camp? I was a Brigade Commander in Poonch and have a fairly good memory about the terrain across the border. We were ready to launch an offensive right up to Islamabad and I wish the war had not been stopped so abruptly. We could have ended this two nation business and rolled back history.'

Brother described his capture, the different places he remembered being at, the cruelties, their days in prison, the executions, the nasty events and all about the other PoWs with him not forgetting the beautiful mountains and Nanga Parbat that loomed near yet was so far for them during their imprisonment.

The general heard Brother's story with singular concentration and after a light lunch led him into his study. There was an old map framed and hung on the wall. It had a big caption. "NAGCHOU WAS HERE". A closer look showed the area of Poonch.

'This is one of the maps I have preserved for a long time. My lead assault battalion, from the Madras regiment over ran the enemy's Company HQ and brought back this Pakistani map. It does not have any information other than the local deployment of their forces during that operation. It has all the other natural features in great detail. Maybe we can both look at it and from your description of the view that you got at the camp, be able to narrow down our guess as to the likely location of your PoW camp.'

Brother's eyes lit up because he had flown missions in the same area around the same time. The map had a strange effect of camaraderie on them both. Their smiles had now become less formal, friendlier and even mischievous. The frequency match of old soldiers happens on the strangest platforms. Two veterans can start a riot and no one would have been wiser today to guess from the appearance or conversation of these two— were they old or new friends?

After an hour of discussions with the general, providing detailed descriptions of sunrise and sunset, the shape of mountains and the color changes with seasons, they were no wiser about the PoW camp location. The general finding the smallest places and marking them with a color pencil, they finally sat down.

His final declaration was, 'I think your PoW camp was somewhere north of Nowshera. I am concluding from the description of your specific view of the Nanga Parbat peak and the barren areas opposite your camp in Pakistan.'

Finding a willing listener the General during his trek on the map had taken the subject away to the night of their assault, the battle and how the air force had helped and also failed them in the hour of need. They now looked at each other making their own assessments of each other as professional soldiers. Brother tactically diverted him to the point that he wanted to know where to find Major Ganguly's wife.

'Oh, I must put you onto my morning walk friend. He is retired Wing Commander Siddharth. You may be knowing him.' The name seemed familiar but wasn't from among Brother's close colleagues.

'Is he Siddharth Bose?'

'Yes, I think so. I have his telephone number. Let me call him up. He does some work for the ex-servicemen's association here in Kolkatta and it was he who found out the address of this lady you are searching for. Her husband, a tank man was deployed at Sialkot before he was declared missing. Siddharth Bose has gone into the army records available and has all the details.'

The general reached for his telephone diary and wet thumbed to the page he was looking for. Finding the number he called up the friend. They spoke briefly and then the general handed Brother the phone. 'Here, he wants to speak with you.'

Bose happened to be in Halwara with Kailash around the time that he was shot down. Brother and he chatted for a while and the general looked pleased. To him it seemed that Bose knew about him but Brother was not very sure about Bose since he was from the bomber fleet. Brother was flying the Gnat fighter from Pathankot and Bose was from Canberra bombers.

'You fellows are a strange breed. A fighter pilot does not know a bomber pilot?'

Bose had found out the address of Radhika Ganguly who was presumably— the missing Major's wife. She lived in Jodhpur Park, an upper middle class suburb and Brother took down the address and decided that he would meet Bose at the Fort William Officers' mess the following evening. Before that he would try to find Radhika's house in the morning and meet her if possible. The general looked tired. It was past three in the afternoon.

'I think I will rest now Brother. My driver will reach you to your quarters and he is at your disposal whenever you want. Just let me know a day in advance. If you need any help in your dealings with this lady, what is her name...'

'Mrs. Radhika Ganguly', Brother helped.

'Yes, you can tell her to speak to me if she has any doubts about you or your story. I am with you son. We must get the boys back, right?'

'Yes sir', was Brothers affirmative. The two shook hands. There was recognition for each other's contribution to the country. They had fought the same war. One became a general with his performance and another was not so fortunate. The general looked proudly at Brother as his son.

'You are doing a fine job, young man. You have my best wishes and support always.' *'These generals think everyone is a young man. Their presence makes you feel young?'* Brother smiled.

Gautam appeared from nowhere and Brother followed him out. His suitcase was already in the car. He just chuckled at Gautam's efficiency and generally at the very gregarious afternoon. Tomorrow would be an important day. Today he had met two interesting people. Gautam and his "General". They had become his partners in the Kolkatta mission. Getting off at the Officers' mess in Fort William, Brother was quick to slip another cash tip into Gautam's shirt pocket. It earned him a cracking salute.

'Thank you sir, what time do you need the car tomorrow morning.' Brother was no longer surprised. He understood the general and his management to know that Gautam had been briefed to take him around whilst in Kolkatta.

'Please tell the general that I will be very grateful if you can pick me up at nine in the morning.'

'The general has given clear orders that I will be your local guide and take you wherever you want to go. He does not go anywhere because he is suffering from cancer of the lungs. They have given him six months.' Brother was taken aback. There had been no trace of the general being sick or suffering.

'*What a soldier.*' Brother could only mumble watching an equally amazing Gautam who spoke with his arms and head moving in unison.

*'These air force guys don't even salute when you see them off.'* Gautam wondered if he wanted to continue helping Brother.

Brother felt at home in his room at the Officers' mess. After a quiet evening in the library he slept peacefully. He had a long day on the morrow and this time he was setting out by himself. He would have to deal with the Major's wife just by himself. His thoughts floated back to his association with the Major. He would have to be convincing for the woman to accept his story.

Gautam was there in the morning at the dot of nine. Brother wore his favorite jeans, a check shirt and had his leather jacket thrown over one shoulder. Kolkatta gets cold in December. As they drove past Park Street Brother warmed at the Christmas decorations. In Kolkatta these decorations continue till the New Years Eve. He had spent one

Christmas here in 1970. He was based near Kharagpur; just three hours drive from the then Calcutta. He wondered why it was now spelt Kolkatta. *'Must be like Bombay which is Mumbai now eh?'* They were in their early twenties and six of them on three bikes had spent three fun filled days in "Calcutta" during Christmas. It had been a weekend. He remembered Swapan challenging him at the Trincas in Park Hotel to ask Pam Crain the crooner to let him sing a song. Brother never backed out of a challenge. And he had crooned with her, "Oh Darling" by the Beatles. Ms Crain had accompanied him and the evening was one of the highlights of his singing career. He was in the war the very next year and now he was back in Kolkatta but not on a spree.

They reached Jodhpur Park. Gautam kept up a steady guided tour monotone, explaining the route and sights. Kolkatta was modernizing with flyovers, wider freeways and high rises. It was all so different from 1970 when he last visited. The city almost felt alien. Brother was happy with his own thoughts but he pumped in some comments every few minutes so that his self deputed guide was not disappointed. They did not have to search for 171 Jodhpur Park. It was at the junction of two roads with a lake in the background. Gautam was good at driving and looking for house numbers. It was as though he knew where Brother was headed.

Brother opened the gate and walked in slowly, expecting that someone would hear him opening it. He thought about Major Ganguly briefly. This was his home and he had been long gone. There was excitement in his stomach. They will be overjoyed. The ground floor house had a grilled balcony facing the road. There was a faded nameplate that said, Dr. Pulak Ganguly MBBS on it. He rang the bell and heard it chime somewhere far inside the house. After a few moments a maidservant opened one of the doors leading to the balcony and asked him in Bengali,

'Whom do you want and what is your name.'

Brother guessed what she meant and replied in Hindi, 'I am Flight Lieutenant Richard James, a friend of Major Ganguly. I want to meet Radhika Ganguly.'

The maid frowned on the alien Hindi language words. Without a word she retreated into the house. She was back after a few moments and opened the groaning grilled door to let him in. Leading the way into a poorly lit room the maid announced Brother to a frail woman seated on a wooden stool by a window. She was looking outside as he came in. The light was switched on and he saw an old man also seated on a couch, wrapped in a woolen shawl. They both looked at him expressionless. There was no response to Brother's smile. He was not even asked to sit down.

'I am Richard James and was in the air force. You must be Major Ganguly's parents?'

The old man rasped, 'what is it that you want? Prodeep died in the war. They did not even find his body. Who cares? They took so long to give us his money. Now we don't even get that. Have you come from the government? We are not interested in any of their charity schemes for war casualty survivors.'

The old woman shrugged and went back to looking out of the window. Brother sensed their anguish and loss. He looked for a place to sit.

'Don't waste your time. We have no time for you people from the armed forces. Not one of Prodeep's friends ever feels that they should visit us. They only came to meet his pretty wife for a while and then we were forgotten. Even she does not care for us.'

Brother decided to burst abruptly into this vicious backlash of neglected parents. 'I was a prisoner of war in Pakistan and your son is alive. He was with me.'

There was disbelief on the father's face. The old lady Brother presumed was the mother now looked fixedly at him and said, 'my son died for his country. What have you come here for? Are you also one of those who are interested in his wife? Let me tell you, she is the most loose-character woman. She may be having a lot of his money because she got all Prodeep's benefits but she is no good. We had to tell her to leave us alone because she even started drinking and smoking and having her friends over here for parties.'

Brother was lost for words. All he could offer was, 'I am sorry for you both, but I have come to tell you that Prodeep is alive and I must meet and tell his wife about it.'

The parents did not believe a word of what he said. There was no sign of joy or surprise. This was a home that had got destroyed by one single event. The death of an only son.

'Please go now. We do not like to be disturbed. Prodeep is dead and so is his wife as far as we are concerned. We do not want to talk about this anymore.'

There was hate spewing in every breath here. The maid was summoned. Brother regretted his failure to hold their interest about their son. It was no use at the moment. He would have to find Radhika and tell her. He got up to leave.

'I only want to say this that your son is alive, still a PoW and he paints and sketches very well.'

They did not respond. Brother turned and left, wondering how could parents become so miserable. There was much more than the eye could see, he thought. Radhika was obviously hated here. He had to find her. Gautam waited for him at the kerb.

*That there was a possibility of disbelief about Major Ganguly's existence did not deter Brother from coming to Kolkatta. He did not have much by way of evidence than himself and whatever he had learnt about his co-prisoners from living together. The hearing he got from Major Dilip in Ahmadabad and then from the General in Kolkatta was in fact proof of their belief about his story. They had nothing to gain or lose from it. Surprisingly they were more than willing to help. In contrast those that had experienced the loss were reluctant to accept that they could recover something after all. The near impossibility created an invisible barrier in their acceptance. Losses like this could cause permanent damage and dislocate the reasoning system. Brother had set out to carry the message of their son being alive. He was not starting a movement to free them nor was he in a position to assure their return. For a man who came back from the dead and forgotten, Brother couldn't do more than carry the message he had. Remaining captive to a loss can deny reception of so many positive changes that those so afflicted can sink into the ocean of self pity and reach the bottom where there is only hate, mistrust and depression going beyond the reach of any help. You can only rise up to the surface yourself. That was what Ruhaina was trying to do. For her Brother was just a bit of sunlight through the dark waters. He too was trying his best to shake off the past by carrying his message of hope. He would never realize that he could not free them of their captivity. He could only hand them a bunch of keys. They would have to open the doors themselves.*

'What happened sir? You are back so soon. Were they happy about the news?'

Brother did not expect Gautam to know his mission. He realized that Gautam knew all and it started a wave of strength that surged through him. Gautam was like a teammate in grief and crisis. His mind with its back to the wall, Brother said, 'Gautam, I presume, the general has told you all. I am back so fast because I failed to touch the minds and heart of these people. They are the old parents of a co-prisoner. They think he is dead and I cannot blame them for that. They also seem to have had a difference of opinion with their daughter-in-law and she does not live with them anymore. They behave like they have lost everything in their life. Everything inside there is like a waste including their existence. I have been through a similar experience. It was my duty to tell them. I think there is a lot I expect in terms of their response. I expected everyone would be happy when I returned from my exile. There were a few who were happy, most of them were shocked but there were also a few who suspected so many things. People respond according to their conditioning and priorities. Why should I wait for their response? Mine is to only carry the message. I guess I have to be just a postman. It is not important that I wait for their responses or a tip. I should go on. We have to find their daughter-in-law and then I can move on after telling her. There are others I have to find. I think I will finally go back to Bombay and start working on carrying the Lord's real messages to those who think they have lost everything. I am now ready for my future. Let us go.'

Gautam was speechless at Brother's declaration. 'You are a wise man and speak so much sense. I thought you were a pilot; where did you learn all this? Are you a priest?'

Brother could not contain his nervous laughter. It was a good release after his deadpan interaction with the Gangulys. 'They call me Brother but I am in no respect a priest or maybe we all are a bit of a priest; even you Gautam. Where do we start our search for their daughter-in law? You have any ideas?'

Gautam looked around helplessly, a bit out of his class. 'In Kolkatta the Pan shop (Cigarette & Betel seller) guy knows everything that happens in their locality and their families. They are the best news carriers. It may be a bit difficult but if you give them a tip, it may work.'

Brother did not like the idea of a tip but he could compromise on his principles because he had to locate Radhika. They drove around the block and found a Pan shop with an old man squatting like only Pan vendors can. One leg impossibly folded under his seat and the other dangling out of the shop. The shop itself was like container where the owner could effortlessly reach all the wall shelves storing cigarettes, chewing tobacco and other tidbits of addiction, without having to get up or stretch too much. Gautam stopped the car across the road. Brother got out and walked towards the "Information center".

He tried to draw the shopkeeper into a conversation, 'do you know or have heard of the Ganguly family's only son Prodeep. He was in the army.'

'Who are you, mishter?' Was the terse reply without even looking up at him. The man continued to apply some reddish brown paste to the betel leaf also known as pan in India. Brother watched the artistry taken aback at the man's reply in English.

'My name is Richard James. I used to be in the air force.'

'Then why hab you come to me? Go to your authorities to phind out about thees army phellow, Prodeep Ganguly.' This was not going to be easy. Brother searched for better lines.

'Well actually I have found out from the authorities that his parents and wife live here and I just wanted to know if there is a problem in the family because the parents did not let me meet the wife.'

'Why do you want to meet the wife?' The man's eyebrow shot up.

It was not rude here to discuss someone's family or your personal life, its intrigues or even your intentions. Pan shops in Kolkatta or anywhere in India are like miniature gossip clubs. The grapevine roots very often are in the Pan shop. However any questions about women were not considered in good taste because women in Kolkatta enjoyed special status. Dare you ever tread on their character? It could precipitate an instant brawl. Brother was aware of this social aspect about Kolkatta and he smartly maneuvered the conversation.

'Actually I know her husband and have some news for her.'

'Didn't he die some twenty-phive years ago. Poor phellow, I remember him from his school and college days. A real brave boy. He saved the life of one of these urchins from drowning in this lake behind us. Everybody stood watching while Prodeep dived in and rescued that boy. That boy remembers him even now and prays for Prodeep's soul every year on the day that he was rescued. He libes just two blocks away. Do you want to meet him? I can send for him.'

Brother knew he had pointed the man in the right direction. He would have to coax carefully and this guy would lead him to Radhika and more stories. He waited for the man's spittle coated ramble to run out of breath.

'Prodeep was such a phine lad and he married a real gem of a lady. Poor girl became a widow at such a young age. She should have re-married but I think she still believes that Prodeep is alive. Out of phrustration she has started smoking. She buys her cigarettes from me and no one else. I believe she even drinks now because of her problem with the in laws. Don't quote me; I have only heard this from her maidservant. If she re-marries I think she will be fine but now she is old, who will marry her.' Brother listened closely, making his own conclusions.

After a pause the man continued. 'She has many friends and they are all very modern and have parties every weekend. Dance parties, you know? Where men and women touch each other and dance and God knows what else. Kolkatta girls were nebher like this. All this TeeVee and films has ruined the youth. Don't all of you drink a lot in the armed forces? I have heard a lot about it. Don't you get an unlimited supply of liquor and at cheaper rhates than the market? I don't drink but sometimes I have a little brandy when it is cold. Do you drink?'

'Sometimes, and I also drink only when it is cold.' Brother had to lie, for moral synchronization. 'Do you like brandy?'

'I love it. My brother-in-law, he is in the naebhee. He gets me imported Napoleon whenever he comes home ashore on leave. You armed phorces guys really have it lucky.'

'Do you want some brandy? I am coming this way tomorrow and can get you a bottle of good brandy. It may not be as good as Napoleon but it will be the best Indian one.'

The old man smiled. All his stained teeth showing the tobacco chewing habit. 'This is what I like about you "phaujis" (military men); all of you have a big heart. My sishter was lackee to marry thees naebhee boy. If you want to meet thees lady, you will have to go to 201 Jodhpur Park. It is on the other shide of thee lake.'

'Hey you!' He motioned to Gautam. 'Take him from that road which has a water tower and turn rhight at the corner. 201 is at the end of thee road.'

Brother thanked him profusely and reaffirmed the bottle of brandy.

'Oh, it is all right, I can do anything for a phauji and for Prodeep's wife. She is like my daughter. I hope you have good news for her.'

Brother almost told him the real story but something cautioned him from narrating it. He did not want the whole locality buzzing with this information. The man yelled across the street as Brother got into the car.

'She may not be at home now. She warks for a beeg modern company. I think she will be bhack by noon. Today is a Saturday. They have a halph day today and party in the evening.'

'He sure knows a lot', Brother enjoyed the incident with Gautam and the peculiar English pronunciation, himself.

'I told you sir. These Pan shop guys know everything. Soon they will be talking about your visit here.' They both laughed, each for their own reasons.

It was past 11am and noon was not too far. Brother sat back while

Gautam slowly cruised to the end of the road as directed. 'This is too easy Gautam. I never thought locating people is so easy like it is here in Kolkatta.'

'Yes sir we Bengalis are a big family. We know where everyone stays, always help each other and share each other's problems.'

Brother thought, *'this was very much like Chapel Road, but the rest of Bombay was not so close knit. You sometimes didn't know your own neighbors and often there was pure hate and even hostility between them. I guess the big city and multi-culture phenomena coupled with material selfishness, jealousies, mistrust and greed has got the better of people in the consumer society.'* They found a lock on the door of 201 Jodhpur Park. Brother decided to wait. He did not miss the nameplate. It still read Mrs. Radhika Ganguly. She had retained her surname by marriage. It was encouraging.

Passers by gave the car and its inmates a suspicious look. Strangers were not really too welcome here. It made Brother uneasy to see the obviously hostile looks. The worst images of bus burning, football stadium riots and Marxist political strikes floated in his vision. In Kolkatta, crowd mentality and frenzy was never too far away with its volatile people.

'Should we go somewhere else like a restaurant and wait?' he asked Gautam.

Gautam was surprised. 'Why, is there a problem. Are you uncomfortable in the car? You can stand outside if you wish to or go for a walk. Why waste money at a restaurant? I can wait here.'

Brother took his suggestion and stepped out for a walk. It was easier to look people in the eye walking around than sitting in a car outside someone's, especially a lady's house and being stared at.

*'Maybe what the Pan shop owner said about Radhika and her ways with smoking, drinking and parties is known by everyone who lives in this locality. A strange man in a car waiting outside her gate is therefore not very socially acceptable. In Bombay a single woman with friends, partying at home or even smoking and drinking will not attract comments from the local moral brigade. Here it is a hot gossip topic. And a drink to beat the cold was perfectly in order and not otherwise.'*

Brother continued with his observations about the two cities. *'It is amazing that all these cities, towns, villages and even localities with so many people who speak so many languages and have different social customs and values, live quite harmoniously. You may not approve of a custom or lifestyle but that was not reason to insult, maul and violate each other. Why is there no communal riot between the Christians and Hindus? In some pockets there* exist the suspicion of conversions of Hindus to Christianity but there were no outbreaks of riots. Why then was this hatred between the Hindus and Muslims. It could not be only the cow or temple/mosque factor. Christians eat beef but there is no communal disharmony on that account. Maybe Indians allowed their Christian British masters who took care of them.'

Brother walked around the lake, his mind dueling with the Ahmadabad riots, Pakistan and their hate for Indians and then to the present. Radhika lives on her own and supports herself. She has her own circle of friends and obviously her in-laws disliked her lifestyle. He wondered if she was in contact with them at all. Also, with so many friends, she would surely have some male friends. What if she was intimate with someone?

'I have become intimate with Sheila. It just happened and there is no right or wrong in it. I am single and she is a widow. We are mature individuals with a right to define. Here, Radhika is not a widow. She has however accepted widowhood since she does not know that Prodeep is alive. It is over two years since I was deported. No one truly knows if Prodeep is still alive at this moment. Even I have become a captive to this uncertainty now. Radhika's relationship with a man cannot be weighed in a morality balance. Morality is a personal issue collectively evolved around many factors. You can go along or break away but the consequences are always yours.'

Gautam came half running and walking from behind, disturbing his chain of thoughts. He was left undecided on some morality and real life issues.

'Sir I think the lady has arrived. She is with a man. I think they had a case of beer with them. They looked very close and happy.'

It was one in the afternoon. Brother was in a jam. His immediate preceding thought process put him into a conflict. Should he present himself now or only when Radhika was alone. He thought systematically.

'She is a mature woman of this world living with her emotions, borne her losses and faced her challenges. News about her husband is a truth for me. Truth does not require specific audiences or settings. She has a right to accept or reject the message for its trueness. It has nothing to do with her current relationship or lifestyle. I will not be intruding or exerting any kind of pressure on her. Why am I concerned about the effect of my message? My message about her husband may result in some guilt feelings or it may not have any such effect on her considering the time that has elapsed. Does she not have the right to continue with her life and build relationships that emancipate her? I came bringing good news that can free her from the captivity to uncertainties. Who decides whether it is good or bad news? Will *this truth in the presence of her male companion have an adverse effect on their relationship? Why do I presume a relationship? I do not wish to break or spoil things for her. I expect to see her happy after receiving news about her missing husband. Every woman hopes for health and a long life for their partners. It is nobody's specific responsibility that events in her life have been as they are. There is no right or wrong that she is in male company today. Maybe I should just wait for her to be by herself. That way she is getting a better chance to appreciate my message and deal with future developments.'*

Brother's pure concern for Radhika and the Ganguly family's response to him made the decision. He spun out a plan that only quick thinking fighter pilots could.

'Gautam, will you do me a favor?'

'What can this simple driver do for a great man like you sir?'

'It is very simple. You have to wait here till the gentleman who is with the lady leaves and then follow him to find out where he lives. I think I need to know more about him before I meet her.'

'What if they both leave the house?' Brother smiled in appreciation of his intelligent question.

'Gautam, I like your quick mind. Just follow them and if it is getting later than 6pm, you may leave them and see me tomorrow morning at 9am. It is a Sunday and I will be able to visit her without any problems.'

With that Brother got out of the car and walked to the main road and hailed a cab to go back to his quarters at Fort William. A sense of relief overcame him as he leaned back in the Kolkatta cab no longer debating his decision to wait at Radhika's but consciously assuring himself that he was giving everyone a chance without playing God.

That evening he was at the Institute bar in Fort William. It was a Saturday and there was a sprinkling of visitors. Weekends are occasions to gather and the Institute generally has some event and special eats on these days. A few senior couples that looked like retired service officers talked in hushed tones. Some younger couples that were probably serving officers with their wives or girlfriends were present and there also seemed to be a few civilian guests. Brother did not feel totally at home. He had always felt like that when he was at any mess or service institute outside his home base. Knowing the barman's name was like being in comfort zone "A" and here he did not know anyone. Not knowing the layout of the place with its counters and doors leading to the dining hall or washrooms contributed to a mild sense of being at sea. In such a situation some become fidgety and others flamboyant. You can be picked out very easily. The body language of a newcomer is visible to all. Brother always tried to counter this with a confident stride and a growing smile. It worked at times and more than anything it provided a psychological screen that shielded him from penetrating eyes.

Wing Commander Bose was first to spot Brother with his cup of coffee at a table near the bar. He was late by a few minutes and apologized profusely cursing the slow moving traffic in the same breath.

'I remember you very clearly now Brother. Your face hasn't changed much. You were based at Pathankot and were part of a formation that was from different bases. In fact I was in the Canberra photo recce flight that did the photo run on the Gujranwala bridges two days before your strike.'

Brother felt at home immediately and said, 'isn't it such a coincidence that we never met then but were destined to meet here under such strange circumstances?'

'Yes and the General is a close friend of mine and we meet almost everyday in spite of his ailment. He is one of the few retired officers I know that has contributed a lot for the welfare of war widows. He has narrated your story to me and I am truly amazed with you. You are in very good shape and look fresh. There is no adverse sign of your long exile.'

'Do you doubt my PoW days?' They laughed simultaneously.

'It is not that. I have met quite a few officers and men who were captured in the 1971 and previous war. Frankly, they look quite bitter. You don't.'

'Thank you for the compliment sir.'

'Call me Siddhartha. How was your meeting with this Major Ganguly's wife?'

His guard going up Brother said, ' I found their house and met the parents but she was at work so I couldn't meet. I will visit her tomorrow and hopefully meet, as it is a Sunday.'

He did not share his emotions and mental debates with Bose. Brother was protective about the Gangulys' apparent plight, emotional desert and Radhika's association with a man.

'Tell me, how was your experience in Ahmadabad. The general has told me the unique circumstances under which you traced out the family of an army soldier who is still a PoW.'

Brother was not good at selling himself and anything that even had the trace of his own achievement was automatically played down. Not all fighter pilots were the back slapping, loud talking type.

'In Ahmadabad I was fortunate to have the assistance of a junior army officer who took me around to locate the house of this victim of the riots and then there was a lady advocate who knew the family and she helped a lot in convincing the wife of this PoW, that I was genuine and that her husband was in all probability alive the way I had narrated. I couldn't have convinced them without the help of these people. They don't give you a certificate to say you were a PoW, so that everybody believes you.'

Brother continued after looking for signs of boredom or disbelief. 'I don't even know the name of the place I was kept. These are my handicaps. The people I am trying to locate and meet have probably tried their best with the authorities before reluctantly accepting the missing feared dead fate of their husbands or sons. After so many years their mental reluctance to believe my contradiction of the authorities is inevitable. My arriving into their present with news that is more like some fairy tale is not easy for them to accept. I was fortunate in Ahmadabad. During my interrogation after being deported, I had given all the names of my co-prisoners. There was not much else I could offer to justify my long imprisonment and I guess that was reason enough for them not to even consider informing these relatives that there was a chance that their loved ones had survived. It is unfortunate but true. I am only trying to reach the message of their existence and not trying to start some movement to free them. I am in no position to do that. I owe it to my co-prisoners that I tell their near ones that they still breathe.'

Bose was visibly moved. 'What you say is the hard truth Brother and I think all of us who have worn the uniform know that becoming a PoW is something none of us imagined. To be honest, becoming a PoW is still considered an act of disgrace. We never spoke about it so our families never consciously went to that zone. The response you are getting from these relatives is something very few have had to face. Your courage is admirable. I feel personally thankful for your persisting efforts. If there is anything I can do to make things easier for you, please feel free to ask.'

Brother thought for a moment and asked, 'Can you find out the home address of one Colonel Sunderam of the Madras Regiment. He was a PoW with me and was truly our father and guide during those trying days. I must reach his family. They may be in Banglore. I owe it to him to make it through my sickness and sufferings in that camp.'

Bose was helpful. 'Consider this done. Is there any other help you need?'

Brother's hopes rose. 'Also there was a Lieutenant Pawri, a medical officer who was also a PoW with me. He provided a lot of care for all of us. I need the location of his parents. They are either from Pune or Nasik I am not sure.'

After a pause Bose said, 'I am an active member of the ex-servicemen's association here in Kolkatta. It will not be a problem to find these addresses. I will have it before you go back or I will mail it to you as soon as I find out.'

'Bose sir, there is just one more request I have. This is a personal favor and you may refuse. There is a Pakistani officer Edward Fernandez. He is the brother of the nurse who cared for me when they had given up hope for me in the Karachi hospital. Her brother went missing in the same war of 71. Is there a chance that we have detained some PoWs like they did? Can you find out if he was taken prisoner and is alive or dead.'

Siddhartha Bose's face lost its color. Brother guessed that he had made a mistake in his eagerness and judgment or both. Suddenly the flavor of their conversation and camaraderie seemed to evaporate.

Laughing unexpectedly Bose looking him in the eye loudly proclaimed, 'let me show you around this army institute. I am sure the air force does not have anything like it.'

Brother understood the cue that Bose wanted privacy. They got up and Bose waved to some friends seated at nearby tables as they walked towards the exit. They waved back with greetings. Brother just smiled. They were soon outside in the driveway.

Bose turned to Brother and looking around to see that there was no one present, he said, ' your return from the Pakistani camp has its own controversial and incriminating story that you had defected during the war and stayed there as a priest. Everyone does not know the story but I have a friend in Air HQ and some people are aware about it. I am not saying that I believe in that story. In fact I find it impossible to believe. You have my assurance that I will help you in every way but if you go around trying to find out about some Pakistani PoWs and their location and other information; you are asking for trouble Brother. Why are you getting into deep waters? The easiest thing for anyone to believe will be that you have been sent back to dig up information. Can't you see? If you can just find the relatives of your co-prisoners and put their doubts at rest— consider it as your mission complete. Then go home and live in retirement.'

The earth moved under Brother. He had never thought about such a complexity. The cold fear of the PoW camp returned. He was not going to let them arrest him on some false charge of espionage and lock him up in a jail in his own country. They stared at each other and their thoughts raced. Both could see the rapid thoughts speeding in all directions and Brother felt he was going to be betrayed. He thought of Martha and imagined Sheila fading in the distance. This could take him away from them both. They would be very sorry if he got involved in some new problem that kept him away from them. Another separation would kill them. Something screamed from within.

'*No one believes and cares whether you are genuinely trying to help and rehabilitate others. Only you know what it is to be behind cold damp walls unsure of seeing the sunrise. They don't. They only judge you by their suspicions, fears and priorities. They only understand what they want to hear. You have no evidence to back up any of your claims. For them your version is just words without its emotions, sufferings and realities. You can be sacrificed. They do not want an International mess. You gave a promise to Elizabeth to find information about her brother. Has Elizabeth told you about the location of the PoW camp in spite of going there to meet your co-prisoners? That is all you really need; the location. Without evidence your own people will not hesitate to suspect you and they will believe the Pakistani story about your wartime defection even more now. You maybe honest and Elizabeth risked her everything to find out your friends and get word to them that you made it and have met one of their relatives. You can and must find out about Edward for her sake.*'

Bose put his hand on Brother's shoulder but could not detect the flinch of revulsion. 'I am your well wisher and am willing to forget that we had this conversation. Please forget that you asked me about Pakistani PoWs. There has been another war in Kargil before your return. There were a lot of casualties. We did not find all the bodies and still do not know with certainty whether they have withheld PoWs again. Do not quote me but whatever I am sharing with you is only because I trust you. How do you expect me to ask my still serving friends in the army or air force about this PoW brother of some Pakistani nurse who may have helped you? What do I say and will they not wonder as to what is my interest in something so old, gory as that. All of us know that keeping PoWs after a war is unlawful. It is suicidal Brother, to even mention such a thing to anybody.'

They were walking slowly and reached the swimming pool. Without looking at him Brother said, 'have I made a mistake?'

'You sure have Brother but you can trust me that I will not talk about this. You don't have to look over your shoulder.'

Brother had not given up because he had never succumbed to any threat. That was one of his characteristics that brought him through many life and death situations as a prisoner. He had to decide on whether he was willing to pay the price and face dire consequences in the pursuit of the information he needed. He turned and faced Bose.

'Will you believe me if I forget that I ever met you. But I will still find out about Edward. You will never fathom the grief of being kept in the dark about your loved one. You don't have to help me with anything. I will never put you into trouble if you also forget about this request but I will pursue it in my own way.'

Bose laughed aloud. 'Brother you misunderstand me. I deal with ex-servicemen everyday at the association. Many of them look for employment and some of them have disputes with the service or other civil organizations in getting their rightful dues. They all demand justice. I am familiar with the feelings of desperation, disappointment and disillusionment that many ex-servicemen suffer. I advise them to address the correct forums, follow the correct procedures, have patience and decide what is more economic and beneficial to them. Satisfying the ego is a fruitless expenditure that many indulge in. The price is what you need to evaluate. Often time is the price and sometimes effort. I understand that you have been wronged and maybe this nurse and many like her have got a raw deal. What will you gain by finding out about Edward? Would it satisfy you if I made you a false promise that I will find out and a few days later tell you that yes there was this Edward Fernandez PoW but he died in captivity during the war?'

Brother could only look down at his feet. He did not want to hear Bose's justifications any more. They stood there with Bose getting the silent message to stop but he continued all the same.

'On the contrary I am advising you to avoid this pursuit. How will you deal subsequently with the possibility of this nurse going to her government and claiming that her brother was being held in India without reason? The whole issue will blow up in the Parliament and the world. Do you think the Pakistanis will not find out the source from where she got the input? They will trace you out. You are playing with fire. It can destroy you Brother. Just leave these stones wherever they are. You lift one of them and it will explode like a mine. You have been in uniform and know that some issues are always left alone. It is not economic to pursue them. The end result maybe some good but there can be a lot of damages too.'

Brother hated the business like attitude Bose was selling. Though he knew that all that Bose said had some truth. Satisfied that Bose was sincerely concerned with his safety, Brother withdrew and said, 'I will be careful but if you do get any input, let me know.'

'I will not make any extra effort Brother; I think you understand that you can trust me and the general to do whatever we can under the circumstances. You understand our limitations, hopefully?'

Edward remained important because Brother owed his life to Elizabeth and she was still his only connection with the co-prisoners whom he wanted to free. The issue of Edward Fernandez and Bose's intervention in his journey could not stop him from his personal commitment. He had opened a new chapter in his mission. Not just the relatives of his co-prisoners. Information about Edward Fernandez could become the force that could convince Elizabeth to give him the name of the PoW camp location. This was his personal war and mission.

The evening over after a snacky meal at the bar, Brother retraced his steps to his room.

*He hated the way Bose and many like him who react to situations where truth was being pursued. Truth gets a price tag because of consequences. If there is nothing to lose, the abstracts of an attached price becomes clear and converts into a synergy that could move mountains. Truth was that Pakistan had kept some prisoners. Truth without real evidence placed in front of those who have already succumbed to hopelessness like the elder Gangulys and Boses was akin to a flickering lamp in the wind to recreate intangibles that we had once believed in but shamefully deserted and re-acceptance now that "there were some PoWs left behind" was now more like rebuke. Ruhaina had come through because she wanted to believe and had not lost hope. Tomorrow he would meet Radhika and it would be another tryst with beliefs. These were all minds that were captive and he would have to work on them to set them free in spite of the truth he offered. Brother looked up at the sky. There was a full moon.*

*'We all believe in the moon because we see it. If it did not appear for a considerable period would we believe that it was the same moon or some other planet? The secular moon is worshipped by Hindus, Muslims and others albeit the shape and phase. Then why has a truth like secularism or "left behind PoWs" been forgotten? Reluctance to accept could be a reason.'*

Brother lay down with thoughts about Radhika's likely response to his arrival in her life. In spite of his fears a courage born in solitude was gaining momentum.

## Chapter XVIII

'Good morning sir, what is the task today? The General has sent his regards. I waited yesterday till six but no one came out of the house at Jodhpur Park. I told you the couple had a whole case of beer, so that takes time to enjoy.' Gautam smiled ludicrously standing at Brother's door. He had come to take him around for the day.

'You don't think they finished all the beer yesterday? What will they offer me when I visit them today, Gautam.' Brother knew how to humor simple and direct people. Vehicle drivers in the air force had been quite similar to Gautam. Brother was nice to them. They drove but he flew. The challenges were not quite incongruous yet not parallel.

Gautam arrived like a disciplined trooper in the morning. Brother was ready for him. Their two-day association had developed into infectious smiles, appreciation and a joint commitment to his mission. Of course it had the generals sponsorship. He got his debrief everyday from Gautam and Brother's mission had suddenly begun to occupy his full attention too. The specialists at the military hospital had given General Anil Nagchoudhuri only another six months. He was not going to accept their verdict and fight to the end, proving them wrong. He thought of ways to make Brother's mission a success. He did not have much time. Brother's uncompromising attitude appealed to him. 'I don't believe that the air force can produce dedicated soldiers who can charge into certain death,' he had once said in a forum after a joint services briefing during the war. It was shared with one of his bacthmates in the air force and they had elbowed each other on it. He had become unpopular for adding, 'they are good at turning out show boys and opportunists who zoom into battle when it was convenient and the enemy was not in the air.' Sitting in his study with Gautam dispatched for the day he was willing to take back those words after meeting ex-PoW Flight Lieutenant Richard James. The mission was like a breath of fresh air in his chair borne existence.

'You know where to go Gautam?' Brother asked getting into the back seat.

'Yes sir, 201 Jodhpur Park.'

'Lets go because I have only today. Tonight I go back to Bombay.'

The streets looked friendlier today. It was the last day of the year. Brother did not have any plans for the evening. He would have liked to be with Sheila in Bombay. He couldn't anyway as his train would be leaving Howrah around midnight. It takes atleast thirty-six hours to Bombay by train.

They arrived at Jodhpur Park and Gautam parked the car at a convenient shaded spot. 'How long will you be sir?'

'I have no clue after yesterdays performance. If I am good in my act, it may take the whole day or I may get thrown out within minutes.'

'Sir, I am going to take a nap here so if you need me I am here in the car.' Gautam started unbuttoning his well starched and ironed driver's tunic before Brother had even crossed the street.

He rang the bell and stood with no real opening words. It had been his predicament. He never prepared his opening sentences. It worked for him sometimes but he was sure he could do better with some good lines. Now he thought feverishly before someone responded to the bell. *'Was she alone or? How does it matter? I have to deliver my message and remember not to be moved by the response. I am now used to glum faces. People have truly forgotten how to respond to good news or maybe they just don't want to share their joy. What do I say?'*

He heard heeled footsteps from within. The door opened and he was looking at a woman who had deep lines under her eyes. She was in an elegant dressing gown and her hair was combed loose. She is quite attractive, Brother thought.

'Yes, what is it please', the lady enquired. Brother liked the sound of her voice. It quivered just a little bit and was soft yet with its tone of authority. Not musical but it had richness to lend to a melody. Brother could recognize voices that he could accompany with the guitar.

'I am retired Flight Lieutenant Richard James.' She judged him with a quick head to toe sweep.

'Oh! Do come in? Can I get you a cup of tea? I was just having mine. Please be seated I will be here in a minute.' Brother was talked into the sitting room and his eyes took time to adjust to the dim lighting. The curtains were drawn and did not allow light in too easily.

*She sure has a cozy nest and prefers her quiet than the bustle that the beginning of a day can bring. This is comfortable. What I am going to tell her needs her to focus.* 'Thank you, I would like a cup of tea.' Brother sank into one of the single sofas and immediately leaned forward to keep up a business like posture.

In a few moments the tray she set in front of Brother had tea in a silver teapot, with bone china cups, a sugar pot and milk in a tasteful see through glass jar. 'Will you help yourself please? What did you say your full name is?'

'Call me Brother. It is easier but my name is Richard James. I live in Bombay.'

'Oh! I love Bombay with its Marine Drive and fast food. People in Bombay never bother about what you do or wear, you know Kolkatta is so conscious of your lifestyle and everybody makes it their own business to comment. I think Bombay is a lovely place to live in.' She smiled appreciatively about Brother's living in Bombay. Her smile gave him the gap to contribute and make it a conversation.

'Yes it is but people here in Kolkatta are probably closer to each other like one big family. Everyone is so helpful. In Bombay unless you have friends, it can be lonely.' Radhika's eyes narrowed just a little and Brother was quick to notice.

She asked, 'does your family like the life in Bombay?' Brother detected the leading question.

'I live with only my mother. I never married.'

'Oh! That is why you think it can be lonely in Bombay. I suppose we all need friends. Friends have become my biggest support. Sometimes just one or two friends are enough. Life is so hectic. How come you are in Kolkatta and how did you find my place.'

Brother started at her in-laws and back pedaled his entire story to the PoW camp and Major Ganguly. Radhika listened with intent asking a few questions softly, to fill her into the gaps that were there in the sequence of narration. Brother had never felt so comfortable, at ease in his mission. She was a good listener and asked relevant questions. Her neutral reaction to news about her husband created doubts in Brother's mind.

'I don't think she has understood or I am not convincing. She is just being a polite listener.'

Her response allowed him into her thoughts.

'Why haven't you gone to the government, the air force, the army, the ministry of defense to expose the Pakistanis and get these prisoners freed. Maybe there are more prisoners now especially after the war of Kargil. I don't know what to say and believe but it is such a long time ago that Prodeep went away to the war.'

'Mrs. Ganguly what can I tell you about the authorities when you have probably personally experienced their tunnel vision. I am glad that I could trace you and give you the news about your husband.'

'I am a totally different person from the wife I used to be. He may not even recognize me. I had to reinvent myself to survive and I have no regrets. The army did not give us any news about him for a long time. I had become frantic and tried to contact some of his colleagues who were still here in Kolkatta but they had no information. Then one day we got a telegram and then a letter and finally someone from the local unit here came to tell us that he was missing feared dead.'

'That is sad but even my parents got the same information about my being missing. There is nothing much the government can do at that time.'

'His parents were devastated. It took me two years to restart life and I went back to college, did my graduation, took up an advertising course and then got a job. We waited for some news about him and then had to approach the army authorities repeatedly for the financial benefits. It was so humiliating at times. Unfortunately, the departments that we had to deal with were full of civilians who think Officers are a spoilt and privileged community and war widows are people who just want to grab the financial benefits to splurge. Empathy does not exist in those dark official corridors. There were a few who helped though.'

'I have tried telling the authorities about the yet not released PoWs but they do not want to believe it. There is a trace of belief on their faces but they always want concrete proof and that is what I don't have other than my word. My word is obviously not good enough for them. I can imagine the torment you have had to undergo specially with the civilian authorities. They are shallow.'

'We needed every penny to survive. There were expenditures for the treatment of my in-laws and I had not received all the money but they wouldn't believe me. It was such an unbelievable change I saw in them after the tragedy of their son. They even accused me of bringing ill luck into his life and that my bad luck had killed Prodeep and was the cause of their plight. In fact they approached the army so that Prodeep's death benefits could be given to them instead. Fortunately some of his colleagues used to visit and they gave me the sense and courage to stay firm and take the benefits in my name. And now you are here telling me that he is alive. I am so happy for him and am sure we can do things now to get him released. You are new hope that I hope does not end like a mirage.'

Brother was moved by her struggles. He had been witness to a similar tussle between the parents and wife of a colleague who died in a fatal crash during peacetime. Survivor benefits are supposed to rightfully go to the immediate closest survivor and nominee but it is sometimes viciously contested.

'I am sorry for you Radhika. All I can say is that I am trying to reach the relatives of those who were with me in that prison. I only want to reassure them that they are not dead. There were other prisoners with me but many of them were shifted to other camps and I have no inkling about their whereabouts. Some must have been released after the war. Unfortunately our authorities did not believe that I was locked up for so many years and sent back only because they expected me to die of tuberculosis. I survived and am doing what I can now.'

Radhika thought of his situation and suggested, 'I am grateful to you for the news about my husband but why don't all of you who were prisoners, meet sometimes at some occasion and exchange notes. You may get to know the name of your camp if you interact with each other. Isn't there a PoW day like Victory or Liberation Day.'

Brother couldn't suppress a smile. 'Becoming a prisoner is still considered an offence and a PoW is not a hero or even thought of on the same honorable terms as others who also fought the war alongside and were fortunate to come through safely. There are no PoW day celebrations Radhika. There is a victory day celebration where all are expected to mingle and rejoice. As an Ex PoW I prefer to stay at home.'

Conveying the message to Radhika had been easy and her measured response strengthened Brother's resolve. Thoughts of retracing his steps back into the military and bureaucratic castles with a desperate assault on their conscience without fear of any consequences hovered in his mind. Radhika had a catalytic presence. She had withstood pain from her own in-laws to pick up her life and move on. He could also stake whatever he had for the sake of a cause. Brother was ready to go to battle with the deprivation of these women as his energy source. Would they join him and how could he surmount the stigma attached to his own deportation. He had not felt it necessary to disclose the lies attached to his return. It didn't bother him but he knew it would come up in an open war with the authorities. He would deal with it in time.

'I am glad that you are happy about Prodeep and have gone ahead with your life in a profession and have friends. We will try to get him freed. I cannot promise because you just heard the circumstances. It is sad that your relationship with his parents has soured.'

Radhika fired back instantly, 'it is not sour, they hate me for everything,' her glaring eyes holding him captive. 'They cannot tolerate my having a good job, having friends and my own lifestyle. My smoking and drinking became a public laundering issue and that is when I decided to leave them alone and find my own place. I still deposit money into their account for their needs, or else they have nothing but the house that my husband also contributed for.'

Brother was frozen by her magnanimity. Ill treated daughters-in law was not a new happening but Radhika's continued care for them was a window to her character. There was silence for a few seconds and then Radhika slipped into a silent sob. Hiding her face in her hands she leaned over and sobbed in desolation more than just grief. Brother remained still in the cutting cold of the blizzard of emotions that flowed. Joy and grief both had their own place in Radhika's emotional upheaval.

She left the room to regain composure. It was not often that she let her big eyes go wet. A woman whose husband had died on some battlefield that not many had heard of; a woman forsaken by her in laws the only remaining link with her dead husband grows to hate the taste of tears. Her life had brought many situations to master the art of controlling tears. Today was different. Tears were only a visible expression. Radhika had graduated to controlling her invisible expressions. She had swallowed a lot.

The mood in that living room had changed so dynamically from words to emotions that it left Brother a little numb. He however became a shade more aware of the slow torture that these women survivors of a war had undergone. The prison camp days looked easy. He had to shift his attention from the overwhelming moments to the wall clock that could now be heard ticking or it would be very easy for him to also slip into remorse. Pacing around the sitting room he looked without really seeing the display of all the little curios, memorabilia and photographs. There were a few photo frames. His attention recovered. Recognizing a family shot his eyes moved further to a frame that had a young man in uniform. It was Major Gangulys' portrait in a silver frame. Prodeep Ganguly had a very appealing smile. Brother had never seen one of those smiles at the camp. The Major was a controlled one.

Brother was unaware of Radhika when she came back into the living room. He was startled to hear her, 'will you do me a favor Brother James. I want you to meet someone. His name is Prasanjit Roy. He is heir to the owner of the company I work in. Without his guidance and help I would not have survived. He has been a source of inspiration and helped me along in almost everything I do. Can you explain to him about my husband? It is important. I cannot bear to tell him. He is a special friend. You will be doing me a personal favor if you meet him.'

Brother couldn't understand the importance but he was ready to do what Radhika wanted. After all he had to just meet the gentleman and tell him that Major Ganguly was alive and a PoW.

Taking the address from Radhika, Brother woke up Gautam from his deep slumber in the front seat and they were off to 23 Golpark near the lakes. It was not far and they were soon along the lake and past Anderson Club. It was a swimming club on the lake. Gautam was not familiar with the area and had to back track a couple of times before he found the narrow shaded lane at the end of which was the place they looked for. Brother had dressed up more than his usual self. He was in his favorite blue blazer with an open collar light blue shirt and gray flannel trousers. Very military in a corporate leaders house.

The watchman at the gate took his name and used the intercom to speak to someone. Brother was then handed the intercom. It was a clear, slow voice on the line. 'Mr. Richard James, where have you come from?'

'I have come from Bombay but I have just met Radhika Ganguly and need to talk to Mr. Prasanjit Roy about something important.'

There was a moments hesitation before the voice said, 'I will be down in a minute. Can you give the phone to the watchman please.'

Brother waited while some instructions were given. He was quickly ushered into the premises and made comfortable in the porch adjacent to a lawn with a putting green. There was a hole with a small flag. Someone was using it to lower his handicap and get ahead. He had heard that the "short game" mattered a lot. Golf had been a mystery for Brother. He had watched golf being played and seen the phobia of golfers over even one extra stroke or a chipped drive that went asunder. Crew room or bar; golf talk fitted in anywhere. As he waited for the host Brother was glad he had dressed. The golf green, house and the ambience complimented his formal attire.

Prasanjit was in his tracksuit and sneakers as he came forward smiling and shook hands with Brother. The grip was good. He was Radhika's special friend and had helped her to get back into the mainstream of life. Brother had served with one commanding officer that had the same firm grip. Alas! The forthright blunt attitude had not taken him too far in rank but those who served with him were all strong, like Brother.

'What will you have, some tea, coffee or a cocktail?'

'Thank you sir, I don't drink in the day but would love a black coffee with sugar.' It was ordered into a phone.

'Tell me what brings you to me from Radhika's house?' There was a trace of urgency without any accompanying display of anxiety on the face. In its place there was in fact a smile that made Brother comfortable as only men feel with men before getting down to business.

'I am a retired air force pilot and was a PoW from 1971 to 2000. I was with Radhika's husband Major Ganguly in a PoW camp. He is still alive, I presume because we are now at the end of 2002.'

Prasanjit was looking at Brother without any expression. Only his hands came together in a grip that tightened. Realizing his own stiffening Prasanjit got up and shook Brother's hand again. Holding his hand he said, 'you are the next best thing that has happened to Radhika. The best is that Prodeep Ganguly is alive. When is he coming back?'

After Brother had narrated a shortened and need to know version of his mission and past Prasanjit leaned back in his chair. They had walked around the putting green and come back to their chairs and Brother now sipped his coffee. It was welcome warmth soothing his lately over worked voice chords.

'Did Radhika tell you about us Brother?'

'No, all she said was to tell you what I have, about her husband

and that you have been instrumental in her rehabilitation. Is there a problem I don't understand?'

Prasanjit just lowered his head and let a vocal smile escape from his well-groomed emotions. 'There is no problem. We had a deal, Radhika and me. I was supposed to find out about her husband's whereabouts. He has been missing since 1971, like you just said. I have tried many sources. You have done for me what I could never have done by myself. The wait is now over for both of us. Our deal was that Radhika was agreeable to marry me if I found out about Prodeep's fate. We had almost accepted that he was a casualty. I know Radhika. She will keep her deal but we must reconsider the issue, now that the search is over and if what you say is true. I don't think she had catered for a situation like this. I don't want her to do something that will leave stains on her conscience. She is a survivor. We will both wait for his return. What is the plan? Can I help in this in anyway?'

Brother sat watching Prasanjit's eyes and found just a flicker of pain but there was a lot of genuine joy there too. Strange how varying emotional colors blend without the necessity of mixing. Within visible moments Prasanjit's face now took on a determined look that gave Brother even more confidence that he would be able to garner support to start a movement for the freedom of his colleagues.

'My plan is to find the relatives of two more co-prisoners. One is a Colonel and the other is unfortunately a very junior officer whose career as a doctor came to an untimely end. Once I find their families my job will be done. There is not much else I can do under the present circumstances. Radhika will explain to you why my hands are still tied. There is a lot I have to still do to set myself free of some shackles.' Brother got up to leave and they parted with the assurance of keeping in touch. Addresses and telephone numbers and also e-mail addresses were exchanged. Gautam waited with a smile. He watched the two men walk down the drive and then Prasanjit held the door for Brother to get in.

Gautam beamed watching Brother in the rear view mirror, ' you look happy today sir. I think you have been more successful than yesterday. Who is the man you just met? He looks like the one with that lady yesterday afternoon with the beer. I waited till six in the evening as you had said but he was still there so I left. He looks like a very rich man.'

Brother only heard him in the background. His mind was speeding on its way. *'Have I spoilt things for Radhika and Prasanjit? He is a powerful man and can help in mobilizing efforts in the right places and he is also so fair. I have learnt something today. Justice is another form of love. I must wish goodbye to the general and thank him for his support.'*

'Gautam can we go to the general? I have to catch the night train to Bombay. Before that I want to say goodbye.'

Gautam was left with his own imagination about the rich man and single woman. Brother had never said anything about the lives of Prasanjit and Radhika. He felt left out and resigned himself to his duty. To drive.

Golpark to Chowringhee took them twenty minutes. It was a weekend and the last day of the year. Kolkatta was gearing up to dance away the night. Brother would be on the train heading back to Bombay. Radhika and Prasanjit would probably be together as the clock struck 2003. They reached the general's house and Brother did not waste time. Before the car had stopped fully, he was out and knew the way to the apartment. He did not wait for Gautam to lead or inform the general of his arrival. Brother however threw him back a smile and Gautam smiled back realizing that he was in a hurry. He would get the scoop from the general anyway. They were companions of a sort.

The general was visibly surprised to see Brother. 'I wasn't expecting you Brother. I hope all is well and Gautam is behaving. Sometimes he talks a lot. How was your visit to the Major's wife today? I heard that you could not meet yesterday.'

Brother smiled; Gautam was reporting all activities. 'I notice your intelligence system is very prompt and efficient. Gautam never misses a thing.'

The general's face grew serious. 'We could have saved many lives if the air force gave us better photo-intelligence in the wars. Intelligence and good administration facilities are almost a prerequisite to winning any war. Field Marshal Montgomery was a firm believer of having good intelligence and adequate administrative support and that's how he beat the great Rommel who ran out of gas.'

'No doubts and I got the point sir, my mission here in Kolkatta has been possible because of your good administrative support; I mean you, Gautam and the car. Thank you sir. I came to say goodbye as I think I have finished what I came for.'

The general accepted the compliments and gratefulness with a smiling nod. ' I am glad I could help you. Was your meeting with this Mrs. Ganguly fruitful and is she the person you came looking for?'

'Yes sir, she is the wife of prisoner of war Major Prodeep Ganguly and she was very happy to hear the news about her husband. I have given her your telephone number, just in case she needs any assistance in the future.'

'Good and if you ever need any further help, let me know. Wars only end for the politicians and civilians who forget the soldier once it is done. We in the uniform continue our campaign in many different ways. Look at you. You are still gathering scattered broken pieces of a war and puzzle long forgotten. Your task is a difficult one and if you are able to reach these families and free them from their uncertainties; you have done your bit as a good soldier.'

'Do you hate the Pakistanis, James?'

Brother had never thought someone would ever ask him this question. 'I hated being a prisoner but that was the hand of fate. No I don't think I hate them. It was a war. Either you get them or they get you. And the enemy never has a face. That is the game but I never liked the rules. Keeping us beyond the end of the war for whatever reason was not justified. Worse, our own system not believing me about the other prisoners is something regrettable and I guess the price to recover the boys is not something they are willing to pay as yet. A lot of others are suffering due to those wars. People who were in no way connected other than being a relative, friend or colleague. The war still lies at their doorstep and visits them at random leaving behind ruins every time. It has become my personal campaign now to bring the truth to them. I am certain, Pakistani families and individuals could also be facing similar agony. No I do not hate them. I hope I have answered your question.'

'Well spoken my boy but you cannot train a fighting force on that logic. We have to be aware but set aside this rationale and focus on the professional aspects of being a good fighting machine and become part of a complete system that prepares for war and win them because that is the only time we can prove our worth. There are no runners up in a war. The pains will always be there. You are courageous to take on the task of healing some of the wounds of long forgotten victims. I wish you the best of luck.'

They shook hands and Brother started to leave.

'James, there is an envelop on the table. It is for you.'

Brother picked up the envelope and looked at the general. The general turned away in his swivel chair and spoke. 'It has something you are looking for and my gift to you. Go ahead open it.'

Brother opened it and found a piece of paper with well spaced neat typing.

It said:

Captain Edward Fernandez, 12 Baluch Regiment, captured Longewala, shot trying to escape from PoW train. Buried Ambala military cemetery. January 1972.

Colonel Chokkiah Sunderam, Commanding officer 7 Madras Regt. Missing feared dead. Survived by Wife and Daughter presently Capt. Tapashi Sunderam posted as Army Intelligence officer with 7 Madras Regt. in Baramulla, Kashmir. Home address: 18 Fraser Town, Banglore.

Lieutenant Pawri medical officer, 5 Kumaon Regt. Missing feared dead. Unmarried. Parents address: "Shamrock", 10 Dairy Farm Road, Deolali, Nasik.

The information sent shock and relief through Brother. Bose had told the general about their confrontation. They had both used their contacts to find out this information for him. Edward was dead and he was holding the addresses of the survivors of his co-prisoners. A feeling of gratefulness swept over him. Walking towards the seated general, clicking his heels Brother held out his hand in a gesture. The general shook it and said, 'we trust you will be discreet, even forget that you ever came here.'

Brother had no words to offer. This was probably the last time they would meet. He hoped the general would live more than the six months he had. He would want to share the joy of freeing the prisoners with this man. The information in his hands was invaluable and he could have never got access to it unless the authorities believed and trusted him. They didn't but these two here in Kolkatta were helping him to open the doors for so many. He would carry the key safely. They smiled at each other, shook hands firmly. The general winked. Brother stepped back and saluted, 'thank you sir, I will remember this,' turned on his heel and walked away.

Gautam was ready for him. The general would want him to be with Brother till departure but he wasn't sure of his next destination. Brother was overtaken by a sense of gratefulness that usually portrayed a saddened face for an onlooker. Having the addresses of the Colonel and Pawri he would waste no time in these visits. It had already been a long wait. Any further delay to retrieve them could endanger their lives. His simple mission to find and release the families from their captivity was surging into an uncontrolled urge to rescue and bring their men home. He was no longer searching in a haystack. Travel to Nasik or Kashmir, he would set off immediately.

Gautam stood with the rear door open and mumbled, 'Sir you look worried. Are you all right? Is the general unhappy about something? He is quite a fussy man. Don't worry he will be fine soon. That is the best part of him. He forgets fast and can never truly be angry with anyone.'

Brother wasn't attentive to Gautam but had heard and registered relevant information like pilots do while their minds focus on multiple tasks. He hesitated, sighed and replied 'the general is fine and he is a great man. You are lucky to serve him. I wish I had a master like him. Will you take me to Fort William? I need to sleep for a few hours so that I am fresh to travel tonight.'

'Most certainly sir and the general has given instructions to see you off at Howrah Station,' he conveniently presumed, 'so I will be with you.'

Brother laughed, 'You want to make sure I leave eh?' They both laughed on various issues on the drive to Fort William as Gautam extracted some of the information of the day's proceedings from Brother.

Brother could not share all with Gautam and would have to decide what to convey to Elizabeth about the circumstances of her brother Edward Fernandez's death. It would shatter her hopes but then it would free her from the darkness of waiting and uncertainty. Getting off at his destination Brother took a hundred rupees and put it into Gautam's shirt pocket. 'Buy yourself something Gautam. You have been great company.'

'Thank you sir, I will buy something for my wife. It is going to be a Happy New Year tonight.'

Reaching his room Brother washed to get ready for lunch at the mess. In the mirror he found a face different from his earlier one that had deep furrows on the forehead. The permanent lines were there but suddenly looked less prominent. For a moment he looked away wondering at the change. *'I think I haven't looked at my face closely for long. Those lines seem less prominent. Maybe I am imagining.'* He took a closer look and even his eyes looked less distant. Sitting dressed up in front of a mirror was not his style. It occurred to him that he was wasting time now. He could be on a flight to Bombay and surprise everyone for New Year's Eve. The pressure of his search had suddenly diffused, allowing him to look at himself and letting his brain consider sensible options like the one he was. *'I have the addresses* of Sunderam and Pawri now. The trip to Nasik can be later this week and next week I can be in Srinagar and reach Baramulla the same day. Poor Edward. I don't have to search anymore. My job seems to be over. There is nothing more to search. If only I had the name of that camp. Well, I wouldn't be here and the boys would have been freed by now. Or they would kill them if our government brought up the issue with this information. What do I do with my life now? Once all the families are informed I am free. How will I get the boys freed? All these relatives should get together and go to the government. Do they need me? They will and if the government is involved, I will be roped in soon. I will have no such luck of being free. Well, I need to talk to Sheila. I feel light. A few days ago I was in the dark about Radhika and today I have all the information I was searching for. The general and Bose have opened a huge door.'

He picked up the phone and dialed the number. It rang a few times and then the voice message came on saying, 'Bose's are out for lunch. Please leave your message after the beep. Wish you a Happy new year, we will get back.'

Brother left a message. ' Siddhartha, I never expected it but got all that I needed from the general. I owe you one. All the best Brother.'

Looking out of his window he could see the generals car in the car park. Gautam must be sleeping inside. He could sleep standing the way Brother could during his academy training days. You just needed a wall, a balustrade or even a cooperative colleague standing next to you would do. Brother whooped a shout. A cheerful release that he was famous for, during his crew room days. *I am going to catch a plane. That will be fun. I haven't flown since my last trip on the Gnat at Gujranwalla. Hah!'* As if on cue, Gautam's arm appeared in the front seat as he shifted position in deep slumber. It brought a mischievous thought into Brother's mind. He would steal the keys, have lunch and then ask Gautam to take him to the airport. Let Gautam sweat for a while. *'I haven't had fun in a long time. The first part of my mission is over. Till I get into the ring with government authorities, let me have some fun. And then it will be more fun. I will hopefully have a few angry tigresses on my side.'*

Taking out the keys from its ignition slot was easy. Gautam slept while Brother went into the mess for a quick lunch.

He was standing outside the car sunning himself in the winter noon when Brother came out of the dining hall. 'Gautam I think I will catch the earliest possible flight to Bombay. Can you help getting my train ticket cancelled and then drop me at the airport.'

Chuckling, Gautam said, 'that's the best thing to do. The general never travels by train. You are an ex fighter pilot. You should also only fly.'

'I will be down with my suitcase in a minute. Are you ready to move?'

'Yes sir, whenever you say.'

'Should I call up the general and tell him?'

'No, he sleeps in the afternoon. You can call him after reaching Bombay. I will tell him. He will be happy that you will be home for New Years Eve.'

Brother took the stairs leading to the first floor two at a time. The knowledge that he had been more than successful in Kolkatta was like a second in. Physically in Kolkatta, Brother was racing mentally towards Bombay, Nasik, Srinagar, Baramulla and beyond. *'Colonel Sunderam sir, can you hear me? Soon, you'll be back home in Banglore and you should be proud that Tapashi your daughter is an Intelligence branch officer in the same regiment that you commanded. Major Gangs, your wife is there for you. I don't know if all will be well with the two of you but I think your wife will know best. I am sure you will reunite and your parents will come back to sanity. Pawri, your parents are close to Bombay. I'll meet them this week. They will be happy. Now I must catch that plane to Bombay. Will call Sheila from the airport. No time now.'*

He was down at the car park with his suitcase. There was no sign of Gautam. Looking around Brother waited giving finishing touches to his plan of getting Gautam into a corner for the car keys. Instinctively his hand reached inside his trouser pocket. The keys were there. *'I want to see your face Gautam. The general will have you out on punishment parade for misplacing the keys.'* Gautam emerged from a washroom for drivers in the car park and ambled over in his usual waddle. 'Lets go', Brother said. 'I will get late. We also have to cancel my train ticket. Man don't delay me now.'

Gautam winked at him and said, 'I think you are keen to drive. Go ahead, you already have the keys. I will relax in the back seat and watch the fighter pilot drive.'

They laughed and Brother moved forward to hug him. They held each other for a few moments. Brother sheepishly handing Gautam his car keys.

It wasn't difficult for Gautam to get the ticket cancelled at the Railway office in Chowringhee. He just barged into the queue barking in fluent Bengali, 'this man is a war hero, his ticket has to be cancelled first otherwise he will miss the plane. Please move, didn't you hear me he is a war hero?'

Jostling his way through. 'You can wait two minutes for a war hero.'

The man behind the ticket counter was quick to realize Gautam's imposing manner. He took the ticket and returned the money, deducting some for the last minute cancellation. Gautam almost yelled accusingly, 'why are you deducting money, this is an emergency, my boss has to travel fast to be in Bombay. You cannot penalize a war hero?'

Brother was standing some distance away and almost intervened but Gautam gave him a laser-cutting look that froze him in his tracks. Brother just fumbled around apologetically. Gautam drove on proud of his achievement and Brother almost wished he had stuck to traveling by train and avoided the embarrassment.

At the airport Brother tried to hand him another well-deserved tip. Brushing his hand away gently, Gautam reached for a package lying on the front seat. Opened it. There was a beautiful bunch of yellow roses. Handing it to Brother he said, 'I have never met a fighter pilot and you must have surely taught those Pakistanis a lesson. You have already tipped me. Please accept these flowers from me for New Years.'

With that he saluted the way only a general can teach a driver and he was gone.

Brother was not impressed by the flight to Bombay. This plane was nowhere near his little fighter. The Gnat.

He stepped out at Santa Cruz airport clutching the bunch of roses. Flowers would have never been held so close by anyone. It was 10.30 pm. He had been given a seat in the 8 pm flight. Gautam was not there to help the war hero get a ticket for the earliest flight and Brother did not complain. Waiting at the airport had given him time to call Sheila and his mother. It would be late to go out for New Year's Eve with Sheila but she promised to visit and spend the next day with him. Brother had not spoken a word about his achievements. Telephones were to be used with caution. He would wait till they were together. Martha was glad he was going to be back for New Years Eve. Mother and son just watched the celebrations on television and wished each other at midnight.

# THE YEAR 2003

# Chapter I

'We gave up hope after a few years. They told us you were missing feared dead. We waited eagerly for you when Pakistan and India exchanged prisoners and were broken hearted that you were not there with those that returned.'

Brother could feel the pain as he watched Martha recounting the days during the war of 1971.

'Tom wouldn't speak for days. He would only talk to Father Nerris and spent long hours in the church. The air force authorities in Bombay sent us invitations to come for the Air force day celebrations for about two years. Their Commanding Officer used to call Tom and also send an invitation card. Tom was never keen to go for that party and celebrations because it was a happy occasion for them and we would feel out of place. It was nice of them but after sometime even the invitations and calls stopped.'

Getting up early Brother spent time with his mother in the morning over cups of tea and they talked about his visit to Kolkatta. He asked Martha about their feelings after he had disappeared. Her recapitulation of those days pained him and he explained to her about the families that he was now trying to locate. She had tears of joy and was proud of his efforts. He was however guarded about what he told her. There was no reason to get her involved with the demons in his dreams. They liked sitting in their balcony facing Chapel Road. Brother preferred to keep his air force past buried away from Chapel Road. The road had taken him sometimes reluctantly to school— to his exciting days at the training academy and then to war. He did not want to ever spoil its ambience with his fears. Chapel road with its morning habits was like an anchor to life; young people returning from a morning workout by the sea; elderly couples making their way back from the morning prayer and mass; the indomitable bread and milkmen on their overloaded cycles and children dressed in freshly ironed school uniforms. Martha had watched this road for a long time. Now she had company again.

'It is nice that Richard is telling me about what he is doing. He was secretive like this even in school. I had to keep guessing if he was included in the football team and were his teachers happy with him or not.'

She couldn't stop one tear from rolling down. Brother wiped it off with his long shirtsleeve. She let him.

'Will it be possible to get the other PoWs back Richard? It will be such a happy moment for all of them.'

'I am trying my best. There are some difficult issues that the governments have to resolve in getting their release. I am hopeful but it is going to be very difficult mom.'

'I only got to know about your return from Pakistan when you called from Delhi and it was unbelievable. It took me a couple of days to believe that it was you who called. There was no one who could tell me anything about your release and for a few days I even thought I was dreaming or someone was just making crank calls. Your second call, saying you will be home in two days started me to get your room ready.'

Brother compared his recent experience with the Gangulys with what his mother had felt. 'What would you have done if someone had to come and tell you that he was with me in the prison camp and that I was still alive.'

Martha took a deep breath that quivered from the emotional storm set off by his question. 'It wouldn't be easy for me to believe but I would have gone to church and thanked the Lord for sparing your life and pray for your return. Yes, I would pray a lot for your return. I would have told all my friends and tried to get in touch with the air force authorities to find out more about you. You are back now and I never want to think of those days and now I will pray that your friends are also brought back safely.'

'Mama, I am going out for the day. Sheila is picking me up and we will go into down town. I shall be back by the evening. We will have supper together.'

'You go son. I'll be fine. Sheila called me yesterday after you called from Kolkatta and told me about your arrival. She called everyday while you were away. It makes me feel good. I am glad you have a good friend.'

Brother had turned away so Martha couldn't see his smile. He had a long day ahead. *'Sheila will be so happy about Kolkatta and we will make a plan.'*

She was punctual. Dressed in a white churidar and kameez with the borders delicately hand embroidered in white thread; Sheila blew freshness ahead of her. In the car Brother talked about his entire trip. They were sorry about Gangulys parents but understood that they would probably reconcile if the Major comes back. Radhika's struggle and her relationship with Prasanjit led to an interesting discussion. Sheila was glad that she had moved on in life and become independent but worried about the adjustments if the Major had to be freed. They decided to make a visit to Nasik on the coming weekend. Sheila would drive him. In January, Kashmir is cold but Brother was keen to go to Srinagar and meet the Colonel's daughter.

Success in Kolkatta encouraged Brother to suggest, 'why don't you to come with me Sheila? It will be a change for you.'

Sheila laughed placing her fingers on his knee, 'you are going for a serious purpose and also how will I explain it to Rani? I can come to Nasik for the day since we will be back home the same day. You go on; it is better that you go to Srinagar without me. Maybe someday we could.'

Their conversation filtered through silent smiles and sometimes, loud careless laughter as the day progressed. Silent moments were very few. There was such a lot to catch up on. Hands found each other instinctively during their conversation in the car, at the shopping mall and they even found a nice corner at Café Mondegar where they could just look carelessly at the younger world seated around. Sheila dropped him home a little after 6 pm. It was New Year's Day and she did some shopping at the discount sales. Brother was happy carrying her packages. The trip together to Nasik was finalized. It was just two days away.

Martha handed him a letter that came in the noon post and Brother went into his room to switch on the computer and catch up on his mail. She watched him a little worried as he opened the envelope. He recognized Smita's writing. Brother was grateful for his breakthrough in Kolkatta and owed a lot to her. He would reply at once. It was she who had pestered the "Judge" to find out a contact in the armed forces and General Nagchoudhuri was his bridge partner from college days. Smita had been his gateway. He would e-mail her.

Skimming through the letter Brother slowly turned pale. Resigned he lay back on the bed.

*'Ruhaina is planning a visit to Pakistan. She has some relatives in Karachi. One of them was in the police force. They will help her locate Naik Azad Khan through their contacts. This is dangerous. How can I stop her? Azad is her husband and she is determined. I saw it in her eyes. The general thinks our camp was north of Nowshera. I can give her that information or should I? What if it all blows up? They will kill the poor guys in the prison and wipe out all traces. I haven't even met Pawri's parents and Sunderam's family. This is happening too fast. If Ruhaina waits a bit the survivors could all go to the government together. Sunderam's daughter is in the army intelligence corps. She can certainly mobilize and raise a storm with the government. How do I convince these people to act fast?'*

He shuddered at the risk to his comrades.

Sending a thank you e-mail to Bose helped distract him. He wrote another one to Smita and confirmed receipt of her letter with Ruhaina's plan. All he could write was that he had found Major Ganguly's family in Kolkatta and now had the addresses of the others with the help of the general. He couldn't resist asking about the dates when Ruhaina was planning her visit and added it in the end. That night he couldn't sleep. Suddenly his efforts and plan were being overtaken and this latest development could lead to a drastic end for the guys out there. Pacing in his room, sitting in the porch or just lying in the bed staring at the ceiling for conclusions and solutions worsened his apprehensions. He had lain on a hard bed in prison just staring at oblivion for so many years that the very act of looking at a ceiling now had become unbearable. It dragged him back into a hole, than offering a bouncing board for his thoughts. After a fitful night and restraint in calling up Sheila he sat contemplating on the swing in the morning. He tried tuning the guitar. It had been sometime since he played music or gave his time to the students who religiously came every evening. He tried strumming Lara's theme from Dr. Zhivago. It was one of his favorites. He had often caught himself humming it in his head. Such humming moments were purely to keep going and not for any specific reason. He was going to continue with his plan towards Nasik and then Kashmir. Stopping Ruhaina could not be justified. He was not in any position to assure anyone about the safety or return of the boys. Fate was going to play some more rounds of dice. Who was he to play God? Let everyone try.

In the evening Sheila called to reconfirm their plan about going to Nasik and Brother was excited. They would leave early morning in the cool when the traffic was least.

'Do you have the address Brother?'

'I think so, otherwise we can ask around and am sure we will find it, ha hah.'

'Brother I don't have time to waste.'

'But you promised that the whole day was going to be ours. We will have breakfast on the way.'

'All right, I'll pick you up at 6 am.'

'I'll be ready Sheila.'

Brother slept early but was up at midnight. He dug out and was looking hard at an air force map that he had saved during his days in the squadron. It was in his personal baggage that the air force had sent home to his parents. The Indian border was clearly printed and his eyes searched for Nowshera. He found Nanga Parbat, the peak that had become a flag of freedom in their dreams and a beacon for their escape plans into India. Locating Gujranwala was easy. That was the town that had the bridges that he had fired on just before being shot down. Nowshera was northwest of Gujranwala town. Just north of Nowshera were the foothills of mountains that became craggy with steep slopes forming ravines through which flowed the river Indus. The area was labeled the Northwest Frontier. There was a road leading from Islamabad to Peshawar. Nowshera came before Peshawar and to the north of Nowshera were a group of small towns and villages.

*'According to the general our camp was in all likelihood situated north of Nowshera.'*

Closing his eyes he visualized the whole picture and tried to recall the view that had got embedded into his memory.

*'In front was Nanga Parbat and to the left were the mountains. The area immediately around us was a pleasant plain. The birds used to fly into this plain for food. Azad and I would watch them fly back east every evening.'*

Brother looked hard for a railway line because they used to hear the whistle of a steam engine once a week. He found a narrow black line on the map that led from Wah to Nowshera onto Mardan and then went further to a place called Malakand. Beyond Malakand to the north were the hilly regions and the railway line died just short of it. The camp had to be either at Malakand, Tangi, Katlang or some other village or township that was not marked on his old map. Ruhaina could begin her search around Nowshera. If one of her relatives were indeed a policeman, it would be relatively easy for him to locate the whereabouts of a military camp. Not many would otherwise get to know about PoWs inside the camp and any enquiry could become very sticky.

*'I guess Ruhaina will have the good sense to deal with that situation.'*

Brother's mental tussle about Ruhaina's visit rested in a resigned state. He now wondered at the debates that would take place in Smita and Ruhaina's minds after he told them about the likely location. Breathing deeply he muttered loud enough to hear himself and drifted into a slumber.

*'I am as lost as you all are. Only, I have a little advantage because I was there for all these years. I can even recall the smell of the grass after the rains. North of Nowshera, is my gut feeling— backed up by experience, reason and maps. The general is clever. You people will have to trust me about the place and the way in which I have arrived at it. There was no reason for me to conceal anything. I just wasn't sure before meeting the general. Best of luck Ruhaina.'*

Switching on his computer early morning Brother wrote a detailed letter to Smita about telling Ruhaina about Nowshera. There was a short paragraph of the need to exercise extreme caution. The life of three close friends was at stake. Death in captivity was a catastrophic possibility. Pakistani authorities, if discovered, were not exempt from the fear of being accused as war criminals. Criminals become desperate in a corner. Holding military PoWs was a serious crime in the eyes of the world. *'How many eyes would ever be permitted to reach some vague place north of Nowshera to catch the Pakistanis red handed or ever imagine what we went through as forgotten PoWs.'*

It was close to 6 am. Brother waited in the porch sipping his ginger tea. He was carrying a flask full of coffee. Sheila preferred coffee. He also packed some potato wafers bought from A-1 bakery. They were the best and Tom had often taken him there for a treat. Especially when he did well in class tests and always after a football match. Sheila's arrival caught him with a half full cup of tea. Leaving it in the kitchen he tip toed past Martha's bedroom. She surprised him.

'Richard, what time are you going, there is some cake I baked yesterday for Sheila and you. It is in the fridge.'

Brother was startled at her voice. He was sure she was sleeping. *She always worried about his comforts. Life had taken away so many opportunities from her to fuss like only mothers prefer to. Motherly instincts and sensitivities also deserve fulfillment. She was going to make up for it in full measure.*

' I saw that mom but didn't know it was for us. I am leaving now and will take some of the cake. You have some too. I will be back in the evening.'

Brother almost leapt out of the porch with his bag of goodies and jumped into the front seat. Chapel road had not woken up. He leaned over and kissed her cheek forgetting that walls sometimes have eyes too along with ears. Sheila tried to resist and then relented to his almost boyish affection and excitement as they slowly wound their way out of Chapel road at dawn. Brother couldn't wait to tell her about Ruhaina's plan and his e-mails to Smita.

'You don't have to worry Brother; Ruhaina knows discretion better than anyone. Let her go on her own mission. She will find a way and I think she just wants to find the place and confirm that Azad is there. You watch she will come back and be at the government's throat. You then have to just be with her as a support because the whole process of freeing them will probably need tons of diplomatic influence, confidence and assurances at the highest level.'

Brother leaned back in his seat, watched her drive and said, 'you make it sound as if my job will be simplified and others will take care of the issue.'

Sheila turned towards him in a possessive smile, 'haven't you done enough and isn't it time you thought about yourself and moved on. Or will it make you feel jobless if someone else takes the lead?'

'Oh no I will be more comfortable if Ruhaina or anyone else begins talking to the government. I prefer the backbench than getting into cross fires.' Brother leaned back thinking of a situation where he was in the background.

Sheila continued. 'See Radhika; she moved on when she thought she couldn't do much living with her in-laws. Learn from others Brother. Think of what you want to do because you will reach a day when you will be free from the past. You came along in my life and suddenly I was free. You will also soon be without your worries of the past.'

Their fingers searched, found and held on while Sheila drove letting some moments pass silently.

The drive to Nasik was through beautiful countryside. Sheila stopped at the hilly section of Igatpuri. They shared some sandwiches made by Sheila. The wafers tasted crisp between soft sandwiches.

Martha's cake kept them attached to warmth generated from a mother's love and Brother's coffee fired them on. It was just past ten in the morning when they drove into Deolali.

Deolali is a small military town offset from the industrial hub of Nasik. Its place in India's history under the British is permanent. Tales about British troops, skirmishes with thugs and Maratha chieftains, the impeccably dressed officers, fair skinned golden haired young ladies, croquet, club nights and romantic intrigues and affairs abounded. It was more like folklore. Some old cottages lay unused till date because of the ghost stories linked to them. These cottages bore a very British look and funnily fit into the landscape that was also quite Scottish. The locals sometimes spotted British ghosts. The whole cantonment is on undulating comfortable hills. The British must have found a home away from home here. Their departure did not cease to affect the future of the subcontinent much after they could imagine. Today the Artillery of the Indian army makes its own history through their gunnery and golfing at Deolali.

Sheila absorbed the outdoor quiet. The ambience was ethereal. They both looked around for Shamrock, 10 Dairy farm Road as she crawled along. They enquired at the Military Dairy farm and the watchman said, 'this Dairy farm road ends at a crossing of four roads. The house you look for has to be between here and the end. There are no by roads, just straight.'

What he meant was, the straight road had sharp curves, gentle climbs and dead ends if you were not careful but all on this very small stretch till the crossing. Their search looked easy. Lieutenant Pawri sure grew up in a military yet gentle on the mind surroundings.

Brother contemplated loudly, 'Pawri was just twenty when he was captured, so the parents after thirty years should be in their seventies.'

Sheila listened and her expression conveyed that she wasn't sure they would find both parents alive.

'At least one of them will be alive,' he mumbled, responding to her thoughts. 'He had a younger sister in school at that time. She could be around too.' Brother looked at each gate for the house number and name.

Some cottages had a nameplate and others just a number. They drove past a nice open field with cattle grazing. Sheila stopped to admire the scene.

'Isn't it a beautiful place to have a home? It is so untouched and the cows look at peace. The mountains in the distance give it a protected look. The world will sure take some time to reach here. Walking here on the roads or just across these meadow like spaces could be so heady.' Brother had not noticed this side of her. Sheila just leaned on the steering wheel and stared out on her side. In her silence there were so many messages that there was no language that could translate all of them into words and feelings. Silence, unlike the prison camp quiet he was beginning to realize, could also be like a well-harmonized state of existence.

'Let us walk,' she said. 'It will be easier to find the place and also enjoy the sights.' Brother liked the idea. It was getting stuffy in the car after the four-hour drive.

They locked the car and started walking. The road went slightly uphill. Brother's hand found hers and helped her along. She didn't need the assistance but the presence along with his touch provided the words to the music playing in her heart. The end of the climb came quickly and they could see the junction of four roads. Between them and the junction there were no more cottages. A motorcyclist came into view as he turned onto the road towards them. Brother put out his free hand in a request to stop. The rider, it turned out was an officer from the cantonment. He stopped and said, 'can I help you sir.'

Brother acknowledged the respectful greeting and help, 'we are looking for this address.'

There was no sign of recognition of the address that Brother mentioned. Sheila asked, ' actually the address is of a family with the name Pawri.'

'Oh! Their house, it collapsed a few years ago around the time that I had come here for a short course. It was in 1998; I think. There was no one living there at that time. I think it was there.' He pointed in the direction of the cows and the open space that they had just left behind. The cows continued to graze undisturbed in the open space.

'Are you sure,' Brother asked in an anxious tone.

'Did you know the family sir?' The officer tried to understand Brother's anxiety.

'Yes, I knew someone there,' Brother sighed. 'He was a doctor in the army.' The officer took off his helmet and parked his motorcycle before saying more.

'It is very sad. The Army doctor's parents both died within a week of each other. I think they died in 1990. Their son died in the 1971 war I believe. I was still in school then, so I have only heard from my colleagues here. Everyone here in Deolali knows the family. Dr. Pawri was a very kind and charitable man. I think all Parsees are like that.

He gave free treatment to the poor and even those whom he charged was purely at their will and taken as a donation. Mrs. Pawri died of heart attack and he died a few days later in his sleep. All the officers in the cantonment knew them as they sometimes attended a memorial function for the martyrs who died in the various wars. The son's name is on the tablet for martyrs. They had a daughter. Their neighbour, an old Parsee lady still lives in that cottage opposite to that open space. She may be able to help you with more information.'

Brother and Sheila were left looking at each other while the officer saluted and left. Without a word they walked towards the open space. Reaching it they found the remains of what must have been one of the pillars of the gate. Brother bent down and rolled it over. 10 Shamrock was still etched into the concrete pillar. Touching it with his fingers Brother folded slowly to steady himself on his knees and haunches. This was the first dead end he had reached in his search. The pain rose in his chest.

*'Lieutenant Pawri had stayed with the casualties and it resulted in his capture. In the camp he had taken care of even the enemy. He had saved Fatima from violation. When he comes back there will only be these ruins in front of him. It is not fair.'*

They had to find his sister. Over his shoulder across the road was another dilapidated small cottage more like a shelter with portions of the roof without its protective tiles. The once garden had grown into an uncontrolled heath and a narrow path led to what must have been a door. Brother crossed the road and led the way. Sheila's own loss to the war and what she saw here made her move physically closer to Brother. Not ready to lose anymore, she held on to his arm as they found their way up that narrow path. Knocking on the door seemed rude, so Brother called out.

'Is anybody there?'

He had to repeat it a few times. Sheila also called out to help him. They heard a fragile coughing from within the shelter. Brother moved to a window that was still in tact. In fact it had beautifully painted panes like many Parsee homes have. Only these had become dull and caked with dust and dew. Peering inside he saw an old woman sitting on her bed. It looked like she had just arisen but was too weak to get up. Brother tapped on the window to attract her attention. The woman looked up and said, 'Mohan have you brought the bread?'

Brother could barely hear and concluded that Mohan must be someone who visited her and brought her a few daily requirements. She stared at Brother, a new face. 'Come inside', she said hesitatingly.

Brother and Sheila pushed open the door. It was not latched. The woman tried hard to look at them. It was not very bright inside.

She said, 'who is it; I cannot see you too well. Can you come closer?'

Moving towards her Brother said, 'we have come from Bombay and are friends of Lieutenant Pawri.'

'Oh! Dr Pawri, he died many years back. He died of grief after losing his wife. They used to look after me. Now there is no one. It is time for me to go. Did you see Mohan anywhere? He is a good fellow. He was to bring me some bread and butter for my lunch.'

Sheila said, 'we have just arrived and didn't see anyone,' and after a pause, 'do you like sandwiches? Cucumber sandwiches?'

'I love them but it is too much for me to make them and Mohan doesn't know how. I haven't had that treat in sometime now.'

Brother asked Sheila to stay and happily went back to the car. There were a few sandwiches and cake left over. Sheila had struck up a conversation with Meher and by the time Brother returned she had told him that Brother had known Dr Pawri's son in the army. Old as she was; she was fidgety and conscious of her clothes and condition and didn't register much of what Sheila said. They pulled an old table close to Meher. Brother opened a newspaper to cover the dusty tabletop. Looking around he found a cracked gold-bordered china plate with very fine flowers painted in blue. The center of the plate had a dream cottage that appeared to emerge from it. These were the remnants of a glorious past that had slowly ebbed in the absence of human breath and touch. The solitude of the lady in her house energized them both. Sheila and Brother reached out with all their attention. Meher soon had a plate with sandwiches and Martha's cake placed in front of her. Smiling for the first time she looked at them for long. She must have been beautiful in her youth. Her smile had the elegance of a not so distant past. The damp walls had some oval frames with black and white portraits of very handsome men in traditional Parsee headgear and beautiful women in flowing gowns. Brother was guessing.

*'Which one of them is Meher and look at the ageing that neglect and loneliness has hastened? My mother must have been lonely after father passed away. Is this what would have become of her. Thank you God for bringing me back. Dr Pawri, you are blessed not to have had to cope with the darkness without your partner. In the prison at least we had each other. For that matter, I had so many friends in the air force. Where have they all gone? I wonder how they are. If we all lose touch, age will take its opportunity to*

catch up. *Once all this is over I must find and visit my old friends. Circumstances just pull everyone apart. It is so much joy when someone visits you. Look at Meher. She is smiling.'* Brother was now staring between Meher and the walls with photographs.

Meher chewed slowly on the sandwiches with her gums. Brother and Sheila became her hosts and it transpired that Dr. Pawri's daughter was mentally challenged from birth and was shifted to a home that Meher wasn't aware of. Brother thought, *'Lieutenant Pawri used to take care of Fatima with such dedication in the camp but we always suspected that he had fallen in love with her. He had found another sister, I guess.'*

Meher spoke slowly between her chewing. It fatigued her. She had to speak, wait and then again start chewing ever so slowly. Sheila had moved closer to her and was holding her frail bony hand. The fingers had twisted with age but it couldn't take away the shapely taper with her well-proportioned nails. Meher was looking far away when Brother asked her, 'What happened to Dr. Pawri's house?'

'There were some builders who wanted to rebuild their cottage into a hotel. They offered to provide him an apartment in Nasik. Pawri wouldn't sell it for anything. That house belonged to Pawri's mother. There used to be a statue of her near a fountain in the center of their driveway. We would all sit there and play cards, sing and the children came from all over to play hide and seek. It was so long ago but I cannot forget. Their son died in the war and Bacchi didn't ever believe it. He will come back to this house someday, she would say.'

Breathing hard from the talking Meher looked at them and smiled weakly. Then continued.

'I lost my husband in 1982 and they never let me feel alone. After Bacchi died of a heart failure— poor Pawri, he never spoke to anyone after that. He died in his bed and was found by their gardener. He was very attached to her. I heard those builders tried to demolish the house a few years after Pawri died. The local people stopped them. They loved him.'

Brother and Sheila could not respond more than being still. They could hear an old clock tick harshly on one of the walls. Meher tried to complete the picture with a few more strokes of her failing voice.

'This house and property has become such a mess. My husband Sohrab, was a judge in the Supreme Court. We had many servants to look after this place. Sohrab chose to retire in Deolali because he wanted to get away from people who kept bothering him to fight their cases even after his retirement. The servants all left slowly since I couldn't afford them anymore. Mohan is the son of our erstwhile gardener. He takes care of me. Sometimes I give him some money whenever the banker visits me to give the interest from our savings. We moved here in 1965 from Delhi. I have no children. Sohrab willed this place to an orphanage in Bombay. I hope they get it soon. It is time for me to join Sohrab, Bacchi and Pawri. It is nice of you to come and visit Dr. Pawri but bad luck for you— it was a little late. I will tell them.'

She smiled and they both smiled at her uncanny sense of humor. Meher was visibly tired from the effort of speaking. She left a piece of half eaten cake and flopped back on her pillow. 'I will surely tell them when we meet upstairs. What did you say was your name?'

Sheila answered the question.

'God bless you. I haven't seen such happy and peaceful faces like you two for a long time. Do you have children? Children are the real diamonds in all your jewelry. I never had any but there are some children I took care of and they come to see me sometimes. Everyone is busy, I understand. Take care of your children. It is a long distance to Bombay. You better go.'

She tried to hasten them on their way by waving goodbye with only her fingers. To lift an arm would be too much effort. Brother had so much to say but in parting managed to only express, 'aunty, we will visit you again, soon. Pawri's son is alive. I was with him as a prisoner in Pakistan. We are trying to get him back and free.'

'Poor fellow, he was very attached to Bacchi. He will miss her. Remind me, Meher "chocolate aunty", to him when you meet him.' She didn't ask any questions about anything that Brother mentioned about being a prisoner.

*'I guess she doesn't care about the prisoner bit. She was just glad that young Pawri was alive and felt sorry for him about his mother. Martha had said the same thing. She would be just happy to know that I was alive. So many of us don't realize the truth about just being alive.'* Brother held Sheila's hand as they got up to leave.

The drive back to Bombay began with silence. It was like a plateau after the mountains of the day were left behind at Deolali. The plateau was dotted with snippets of conversation they had with Meher. As the distance from Nasik increased, their focus shifted to Brother's plan of visiting Srinagar and finding the Colonel's daughter. Entering the busy suburbs of Bombay the crowds seemed to collapse onto them. It was the down slope from their peaceful plateau. The visit was a good change reminding them that they had each other with so much more and the realization needed no words. A touch and eye to eye conveyed what volumes cannot.

Sheila convinced Brother to catch a flight to Srinagar instead of the long train journey. Brother was keener to take the train. It would take longer but he would be traveling down memory lane. He had only caught trains during his air force days. Made many friends during his journeys to air bases or homewards for vacations. The railway tracks of north India knew him. He had flown over them and they always amazed him. The way it ran all by itself. Here and there you could come across a train that looked like a toy and that used to be fun for fighter pilots. Towns resembled a spider's web with tracks emerging in different directions.

He booked his ticket by Indian airlines for the 15th of January. A week was what he would get in Bombay. Sheila offered to share the cost of his flight because his mission was now hers too. Brother tried his best to refuse. Sheila bought him a new leather jacket instead.

'That will keep you warm. It is my contribution to our mission.'

He had company now. Sheila had been just a support. Now she had become a partner along with the Smita, Ruhaina and Radhika, not forgetting Bose and the general who was like a stoic manager in absence of a little team he knew not existed. In that week Brother tried to meet the Army bosses in Bombay with just a hope that they would help in contacting Captain Tapashi Sunderam and inform her about his arrival. He had to tell them parts of his story but they just smiled. His mission of carrying the message of some prisoners still being alive and in captivity rang too many warning bells for the army brass to even remember him as he left their offices; their halfhearted promises, hung like hollow bells filled with air behind him. Brother knew within, they wouldn't do much. He would not stop knocking. Someone would open the door and help him. He wasn't concerned about any repercussions anymore. No one could envisage the team he had built and the force it could generate. Women deprived of their rights could be like a tidal wave. Brother just smiled at such uniformed audiences and their shining peacetime medals.

'Watch out soon you will regret. Don't say I didn't come to you. You had the chance to help.' Brother grit his teeth every time and moved on.

He trusted the information Bose and the General had given him about the Colonel's daughter but wanted to be surer about her identity and location. He would have called her if he knew her numbers. That would be too much information to expect from the army officers that he managed to meet in Bombay.

The air force Commander was more helpful. Brother's arrival as a guest in Srinagar's Badami Bagh air force mess where he would get a good centrally heated room was assured and the request was sent ahead by a signal message. He was even given a copy of the message. That was as far as the air force helped. The air force boss had been apologetic.

'Your story about prisoners still being in Pakistan is information only you have. There is no proof of it Brother. I understand your predicament but our hands are tied. We are a small unit here in Bombay. Your information and any action on it can only be taken by Air HQ. It is so long ago and without any tangible evidence; I doubt if anyone will entertain you at the headquarters. Try them, but don't quote me.'

That was the air force Commander's advise. Brother was grateful that they were keeping a room for him to stay in the air force mess. Maybe some of the old waiters or orderlies there may recognize him. He had visited the same mess and stayed there for short durations before the war.

*'This could be an opportunity to locate some of my colleagues. They would be very senior and some retired. Hopefully none of them has passed away.'*

Sheila accompanied Brother to the airport. It was 15 January 2003. The flight was via Delhi to Srinagar. They reached the airport well before departure time and decided to have some coffee at the airport restaurant. There was no anxiety about the oncoming separation. Sitting close to each other was more of an emotional than physical need. Both knew that this was the end of a phase in his search. From here onwards a lot would depend on how the forgotten prisoners' families moved. They would have to open the chapter with the government. Brother could not be blamed for informing them unless he was proven wrong. That was the only danger but it would be impossible to prove him wrong. That was the irony. Even so it could be taken care of. Sheila had spoken to a lawyer who would protect Brother's rights.

Through the steam of her coffee, Sheila looked at him and thought, *'One day this will all get over. It will be a personal victory for you Brother if it is proven that Pakistan still holds some Indian soldiers as prisoners. Those poor guys; they must be reunited with their loved ones. It could become an international matter. Maybe the United Nations, like you once said, will take it up. You may get involved in a lot of controversy. You will overcome with your truths. God will protect you. No country should be* spared for such an inhuman act. If we are holding their soldiers, they should also be released. I hate this Hindu and Muslim thing that keeps surfacing in our country. It has only resulted in destruction of lives. You think, one day Pakistan and India will become one. Why not? The Germanies became one after so many years. You have courage that cannot be stopped. I cannot imagine any harm coming to you. What should I do? You have truly given me my second chance at life. I never want to lose you. A marriage looks more possible now. But to have and then lose you will kill me. I cannot leave Rani alone to marry and live with you Brother. And it will be cruel to take you away from Martha. Maybe we will find a way. I think we can talk after this mission is over.'

'You seem to be lost somewhere Sheila.' Brother moved his arm to hold her fingers lightly across the table. He liked his coffee a little cold. She had finished hers with the speed of her thoughts. Their fingers gently grappled; she to get a better hold. He allowed her. 'I will be back soon. Nothing will happen to me. I am carrying the leather jacket. It will keep me warm. Thank you for it.'

'There are so many who should be thankful to you Brother. You are giving them another chance in life.'

'I got mine Sheila, don't you think we all deserve it? Someone or something always comes along and helps out. I am doing my bit, I hope everyone gets their opportunity to pick up life again.' The announcement for passengers to check in interrupted their musings.

'I think that is your flight Brother. Better go and check in. I also have to rush to work. There have been too many days that I have taken an off, or am found going in late.'

Laughing at the changes in their lives, Brother gathered his suitcase, jacket and Sheila picked up her leather bag. They walked down to the departures gate. Brother asked her to go. He would rather see her going than she wait till he disappears into the crowds and security check. She waved goodbye and walked away briskly not looking back. They had both learnt not to.

## Chapter II

The flight to Delhi took Brother climbing into his criss-cross webs and conflicts of conscience and reasoning. He had not sent any information to Elizabeth. She too was waiting and it was her e-mail that set him guessing about the one prisoner that had been taken away from the camp. He did not know which one but it had put the urgency into his search. He had to reach the families before it got too late. She had not and understandably could not disclose the location of the camp. He accepted. Bose and the General had given him information on condition of extreme discretion. They also needed cover like Elizabeth. The information of the tragic end of Edward Fernandez weighed heavily on his conscience. Concealing this information gnawed at him. It was not just the fact that he was no more. He had seen co-prisoners shot for lesser reasons than trying to escape. It was more the guilt at not informing Elizabeth for the fear of losing her. She may just go underground. He needed the link. If anything he felt that Elizabeth was someone out there who knew about his whereabouts and the twenty-nine years. She knew the place and he needed to hold on to her hand more now than ever. Edward Fernandez had died in almost anonymity other than some records in a dusty old file. Edward's role in Brother's search for a release for so many had become a window that could close everything forever. Brother expected that Liz would tell him the location at some point.

Persist and appeal and she will tell. He had to maintain contact. She may finally be the angel that leads everyone to the others and also exonerate him. Freedom never looked so close.

Captain Tapashi Sunderam's location came to him in a most unexpected way. He had tried in Bombay but failed to establish the authenticity of the information given by the general in Kolkatta. The army in Bombay was far away from PoWs still held in captivity and the presence of an ex-prisoner almost threatened to dynamite them out of their offices. They got rid of him with promises. Not a pin would be moved out of the plush cushions on their well polished glass topped tables with a battery of telephones that could easily confirm if there really was a Captain Tapashi Sunderam in Baramulla and also get word to her that one of her father's friends was going to visit her. He did not doubt her existence but would have been more comfortable knowing that she was real and going to be there at the end of his journey. He wanted to meet the daughter of the man who played a father, mother and brother role on his road to survival. The trip to Ahmadabad and even Kolkatta for his search had kicked off with similar unconfirmed information but now nearing the end of his search, he needed to be surer. It was almost like the last check he did on his Gnat fighter before getting into the cockpit. The ejection seat safety pin had to be in place before being strapped into it and then removed so that he could use it to escape if the need arose. Tapashi Sunderam was important. She was an army officer whose father lived. He was given up for dead by the army but his daughter would be told the truth in a few hours. Brother's anxiety about Tapashi's existence at Baramulla surged. The General's information could be old.

Ruhaina was leaving for Karachi any day. He had received an e-mail reply from Smita telling him that they had helped her get a passport and the visa through her father's contacts. Ruhaina had been briefed about Nowshera. The tigress would be in that area soon. Everything could blow or end well. Too many "ifs" and "buts" defied his imagination.

The transit time for Brother at Indira Gandhi (New Delhi) airport was only two hours before he would board the plane to Srinagar. Pacing in the lounge Brother could have made holes in the marble floor. He would travel to Baramulla after checking into the Srinagar air force mess at Badami Bagh. The image of the air force mess he was familiar with provided momentary consolation. He was not totally at sea.

The way he peered through his window on the flight to Srinagar, looking at the countryside below would give one the impression that here was a truly keen "Tommy tourist". Only he did not have the tell tale camera, haversack, pamphlets and road maps. On the contrary he was scanning for the minutest clue that could reveal to him some information relating to the location or cross-country routes to the prison camp. At height you can look miles into Pakistan. Unfortunately the wintry weather allowed only small gaps in the clouds and mist that left Brother stuck with his nose to the window.

Airport security personnel at Srinagar looked happy that they had something to do. There were only two flights a day. Dressed in khaki they were watching the arrivals and scrutinizing passengers carrying their hand baggage. Brother walked through the swing doors into the lounge and then out onto the road in front of the terminal. Taking a cab he gave directions to take him to the air force mess at Badami Bagh. There was an air force transit mess just outside the airport. Brother saw the roadside board with an arrow pointing towards the location. He decided to get into the city air force mess without wasting time. The drive from the airport to the town would be within the hour, he recalled. Brother and the other pilots used to drive down this road in a jeep singing songs and buying almonds or apples on the way. He looked for familiar signs on the route. There were none. Times had violently changed the people and places. The women who sold apples were not there and very few shops that sold tea, almonds, walnuts and snacks were open. Everything looked abandoned. The driver was not very co-operative either and Brother failed to strike up any conversation. He just gave his name as Quadir. Questions from Brother got no replies. He could well have been deaf. The beautiful landscape felt ugly within the silent cab. Reclining back Brother made his plan. He was on the move based on inputs from Kolkatta and his own recent successes that relied totally on self-belief. Approaching the city he saw a milestone pointing towards Baramulla. He looked in the direction. There were mountains ahead. Some had snowy peaks. The driver knew his way in the city and Brother was soon outside the air force mess. He was expected by his name and shown into a comfortable room. It was past three at noon and the senior mess caretaker discouraged him from a trip to Baramulla as vehicles needed special military clearance to be on that road after dark. Sunset was not far away. It grew dark by five. Brother had carried his favorite author. Leon Uris and Exodus were with him on almost every journey now. He never tired of reading how they reached freedom and the Promised Land.

There were a few fighter pilots at the mess bar in the evening. Brother ordered some Brandy and sat near the welcome fireplace. His salt and pepper blended with the character of the polished pine wood furniture all around. The young pilots in their leather jackets and boots were a jovial lot. They were picking on a colleague who had obviously messed up something during their flying. It was normal to do that. Others in the bar just smiled, enjoying the joke but not daring to add any fuel. That was a right reserved only for squadron mates. There was one grim faced army officer who was conspicuous in his mess dress uniform. He wore a black trouser; white shirt with his medal ribbons, name tab and his trim waist was enclosed in a black and red striped cummerband.

Brother introduced himself to this army officer. He could be a good conversationist in such familiar surroundings. Small talk in the bar with visitors usually centers on personal biodata and purpose of visit. You don't look much at each other. You just nurse your drink and glance at the mirror reflections in a wall mirror behind the barman that could tell stories if it could talk. A retired officer who had fought a war was always held in awe. Some gravitated to them and others just let them be part of the furniture. Some thought;

*'These old timers had a ball of a time and love to add spice to what it really was in "those days". Who is interested?'*

He decided not to talk about war or the past at all. This was not the time and place for facts or bravado. He was a casual visitor to meet someone and gathered that the army face was attached to an air force squadron as liaison officer for joint operations. Brother knew their role and purpose. He took him aside and came to the point. It was almost like a hold up. The officer did not flinch.

Brother asked him, ' where can I contact someone from the Army intelligence branch here in Srinagar. There is some information I have for them.' It just brought a sarcastic smile to the grim face.

Nursing his drink, grim face thought, *' Oh! Here is another one of those counter-intelligence types in civilian clothes that probe around and gather information that really is so mundane but they think they have solved some huge mystery.'* It was written on his face.

Brother guessed and added, 'I am not what you are thinking. It is just that I am looking for a friend's daughter. She is a Captain in the Intelligence branch. I just need to get word to her that I am here.' Tapashi Sunderam's name was scribbled on a bar chit and handed over to him.

The officer was overtly helpful. 'Sure, where is she located sir.'

'Baramulla I think and she is in 7 Madras Regiment. Brother watched him at the bar telephone, as he dialed some number from memory and spoke in a language that Brother recognized as Tamil. Grim face, he guessed correctly, was a south Indian. Colonel Sunderam was also from south India but he was not mentioned here today. Brother was following a plan. He heard his name being spoken into the mouthpiece. There was emphasis on the "retired officer" part.

Captain Bala walked back to Brother and said, 'Sir your message will be passed. You may get a call if this Captain Tapashi is there in Baramulla. Is there anything else I can do for you sir.'

Brother was grateful, standing up and almost hugging him said, 'I will remember your name. What you did was a big favor.'

Grim face just shrugged. 'That was no favor sir.' He just withdrew, *'these retired types are strange. Looks like a bit of senility has set in.'* Clicking his heels Bala turned and left for the dining hall.

Brother requested supper to be served in the room and left more than a message with the barman, 'any call for me, please transfer it to my room and here, this is for you. He signed for two pegs of rum for the barman. That had been his habit and now he was in familiar surroundings for it to be revived. It had taken a long time for him to feel the necessity to be back in air force surroundings. His last days in the air force had not been quite very pleasant.

Watching television in his room Brother waited for his supper. An old waiter brought it. This was Inthekab. He liked to talk. Soon Brother was telling him about the 1971 war. Inthekab added his own because that was the second year of his service in the air force mess. He remembered the squadrons and some of the names of pilots who had operated from Srinagar. The airfield had been bombed and one of our young boys gave a fitting reply but he was shot down as he was alone in the air. He got one of them.

'Did you shoot down any enemy aircraft', he asked Brother.

It was Brother's quick wit that took over. ' I couldn't because they shot me down but I survived.'

It led to a look of disdain from Inthekab. 'They shot you down? What were you doing sir? Didn't you see them coming?'

It was so easy for a waiter to cross-examine an ex fighter pilot. Brother had begun sipping his soup and sandwich supper. Between bites he was running a conversation. Inthekab's questioning was not a new experience for Brother. On many air bases there were old employees, especially those who worked in the officers' mess. These men had seen many officers' come and go. They sometimes knew them even by first name if they had stayed long enough. Brother could not recall Inthekab but it was possible that he was in service around the time that Brother had passed through Srinagar. After a break he finally replied to the question.

'I was shot down by ground fire in Pakistan and not by an enemy fighter.'

Inthekab forgave him because being shot by ground fire was not a crime in his judgment. The Lord help you if instead it had been enemy fighter action that brought you down. He could even call you a traitor and get away with it. Waiter Inthekab's long service was the last word with officers.

Brother changed the direction of conversation from himself to the frequent militant action in Kashmir. Inthekab relished talking about it and in hushed tones began.

'The Indian army is partly responsible. They have ill-treated many innocent villagers taking advantage of their poverty. They harmed the women. Most of the attacks against the army are for revenge.'

He asked Inthekab about his loyalty.

'I am an Indian first and then Kashmiri. Kashmir is slowly going towards Pakistan. The Hindu Brahmin's have taken advantage of Kashmir and become rich. This valley was so peaceful and there were so many tourists that came here for their honeymoon and just to see the heavenly places but the Hindus were not happy that this was a prosperous state. It has led many young men to turn towards militancy and terrorism. It pays well. There are few jobs and so many to feed. Join the training camps in Pakistan and you earn enough. Some men have of course been forced into it. This valley is a dangerous place. Why have you come here sir?'

Brother was not surprised but the discussion was not exactly going the way he wanted. 'I have come to meet someone in the Army.' Inthekab's blunt submission on the reasons for militancy did nothing to help him take his mind away from the vigil. He was waiting for the phone to ring.

It did but much later at night. Supper was over by seven and Brother had tucked into his blankets by eight. It was late, as his day had started early morning in Bombay. Brother reached for the phone and asked the operator to hold while he switched on the light. The clock showed nine.

'There is a call for retired Flight Lieutenant James from Captain Sunderam sir.' It was the operator; a military operator, Brother could guess from his words and speech that appeared to come from a long distance. The line was faint but clear enough to follow. He was ready.

'I am James. Please put the call through.' There were a few clicks before there was another operator who asked Brother to be on the line.

'Connecting sir', came the distant voice.

'I am holding,' was Brother's controlled impatience.

A woman's voice from far away said, 'Is it Flight Lieutenant Richard James.' Brother was galvanized into life. It surprised him that his fingers were quivering in nervous response.

Checking himself and standing up erect he said, 'Yes it is me, James from Srinagar. Are you Colonel Chokkiah Sunderam's daughter?'

There was a moment's hesitation and then, 'Who are you, yes that is my father's name.'

This was more difficult than he had imagined. How do you tell a girl who probably could not even remember her father's face that he may be alive? She was only two years old when he disappeared.

'I have come from Bombay and was with your father during the war.' There was no response from the phone. Brother glanced at the handset as though it had gone dead and then anxiously said, 'are you there, I know your father and have to give you some information about him.'

'I am here tell me what is it. He died during the 1971 war.'

Brother did not want his information to travel on phone lines. It was too inanimate for the sensitivity of his message. And he wasn't sure if she would stay on line if he said what he wanted to.

He simply said, 'I cannot tell you anything on the phone. Can I come and meet you.'

After hearing her breathe for what seemed like ages the female voice replied, 'I believe you are in Srinagar. Where exactly are you. I can come and see you tomorrow morning by ten. My mother is in Srinagar. I will bring her along. Are you in the Badami Bagh mess for air force officers.'

'Yes, I will be waiting for you in the lounge of the mess.'

'How do I identify you?'

'You won't have to, I will, if you look like your father. I have my identity card so you will have no problem confirming my identity.'

'I did not mean identity the way you have understood it sir. I meant to ask you for some description of yourself. Just one question please. How did you find out about me?'

Brother wasn't prepared to answer an Intelligence officer's

questions and this one took him off guard. The ex-fighter pilot managed to say, 'let us meet, tomorrow I will tell you whatever you wish to know.'

The night had set in and the mist made Brother's windows opaque. Opening the door he stood outside testing the cold air. This was the same chill he had borne for all those years in that dormitory prison. It had affected and almost killed him. He was now back to fight it regardless of consequences.

'Didn't she sound like Colonel Sunderam. Her speech was very much like his. Controlled and sure. What is her mother doing in Srinagar? May have come to visit her. What do I tell them about Ruhaina and Radhika? She is an army officer. Tomorrow she could well be fighting the army to get her father back. That is if she believes me.' Brother felt the chill surround him. Going inside he looked at himself in the mirror. 'Do I look like someone making up a story. Ruhaina and Radhika believed me. It may take time and I have enough time. This is the end of the road for me. Hereafter a lot will depend on the others.'

Brother almost overslept. The night had been without any more mental conflicts. Waking up his first thoughts were about Tapashi.

'I will be meeting Tapashi and it is she who can help the most in getting back my guys.'

He then thought about the distance he had traveled from Bombay. From Ruhaina to Radhika, to the Colonel his thoughts finally settled on Sheila. 'You would have loved this weather Sheila,' he smiled. It was Inthekab who shook him out of the daydreaming with a hot cup of bed tea. From under his covers Brother watched television as he sipped the officers' mess tea. They always over brewed it. It was not to his taste but surely helped in driving home the fact that he was really back home now. As a bachelor in the air force he had lived in messes and its rooms had become his nest and fort. He had grown from boy to man and the tea had probably played its own role.

Dressed in his blazer and flannels Brother threw the leather jacket over his shoulders as he read the newspaper waiting for Tapashi's arrival. It was a cold misty morning and the snow peaks were not very visible. Anxiety pushed him frequently out of the lounge onto the deck that overlooked a garden that now had a desolate look with the plants in various stages of decay because of the intense cold. From his perch Brother could see the entrance gate of the mess. He did not have to wait for long. A jeep with a light machine gun cradle mounted on top drew up at the gate. Militants were targeting army vehicles so they never moved without weapons. The watchman was doing his job. Entry and departure timings were recorded. It was waved in and the driver knew his way to reach the main porch. Brother watched as the driver got out and opened the rear door of the jeep. A young woman in crisp battle camouflage shirt and trouser jumped out from the front seat and Brother assessed her agility. A relatively old lady came out with some difficulty from the rear end. She must be Capt. Tapashi's mother he presumed. Brother had never felt so moved. It took time for the lady to walk to the main entrance steps and then she took every step deliberately, looking up frequently. Her every step after the Colonel was declared missing must have been an effort that only she could measure. Although they were visible to each other now and just a few moments away from Brother; he felt cold and under scrutiny. The Captain had the same bearing as her father. Lean and erect she wore her navy beret smartly tilted at the correct angle.

Stilled by the sight of the jeep and the women Brother waited for a few seconds praying. He did not do that often. This could be the winning stroke for so many. He moved forward with a purpose now. Apprehensions had to be left behind. He had to narrate what he had undergone and it was the simple truth that they would have to bear.

Recognition was instant. The Captain and he saw each other at the lounge entrance door simultaneously. She displayed just the trace of a courteous smile and Brother extended his hand to introduce himself.

'You must be Captain Sunderam, I am James.' Brother had got the mess staff to arrange a card table with four chairs near a window overlooking the front garden. Guiding them to sit he stood and asked politely.

Brother was being the good host. 'Will you prefer tea or coffee and can I get you something to eat?'

The daughter replied, 'Coffee will be fine but without sugar for my mother.'

Brother did not have to do much. Inthekab had been briefed to be in attendance and he was more than willing to earn an extra tip. He had heard about Brother's generosity with the barman. Captain Tapashi had a folder under her arm that she placed gently on the table. It was like a signal for their meting to begin.

Brother had gained some practice now and he was getting better at making opening addresses. Looking at the green felt tabletop and stroking its smoothness Brother began, 'I am Flight Lieutenant James and was a prisoner of war for twenty-nine years. You can call me

Brother. That's what they called me in the air force.'

The two women scrutinized him as though this information was irrelevant. 'Colonel Sunderam and some other officers and men were PoWs with me. Some were released and some held back. I was released and sent back in the year 2000 and the Colonel must be still a PoW but the air force, army and government do not believe me about this reality.'

Mother looked at the daughter and Captain Tapashi just looked around unbelieving. *'This is a mad man,'* she thought. Looking around to focus on something, her piercing eyes bored into Brother. Reaching for her beret she took it off carefully not disturbing her long hair tied into a tight knot. Placing the beret on the table she gave him a "get lost creep" tight-lipped smile. The conditioned military features showed no other emotion. There was no dialog for a few moments and Brother curtailed his urge to continue with his experiences at Ahmadabad and Kolkatta.

*'Let them think and ask questions rather than my flooding them with too many facts.'*

Mrs. Sunderam leaned over to Tapashi and whispered in her own language. She was clearly agitated in contrast with her daughter's calm. Brother wasn't interested in catching their confidentially whispered reactions. He would wait for the Captain to fire her first shot. It would dictate the course of the discussion and events hereafter.

'How do you expect us to believe what you say?'

It was expected. This was not a poor wife who had struggled to bring up her son. Neither was this a wife ill treated by her in laws, now with her own Bohemian lifestyle getting ahead in the world, living only for tomorrow. Brother raised the sluice gates just enough to pour out his experiences with the Colonel and then his visits to Ahmadabad and Kolkatta. It was too early to tell her about Ruhaina's Karachi trip and mention of Nowshera seemed as far as Nanga Parbat used to be for the prisoners as they strained their eyes towards the homeland.

'Where is he then', was the aggressive challenge.

Brother had acquired grace under pressure. Looking her straight in the eye he said, 'if I knew I wouldn't wait for this day and you. Your father would have been home or dead.' Truth has a sharper edge than the best brands in stainless steel. The Captain froze.

'I need proof to believe you sir.'

The woman's eyes in a Captain's uniform had its own fiery

language. She was displeased with Brother's parry. The mention of death made her eyes just a little moist. They had not forgotten softness but there were too many shields protecting that zone. In growing up she had only sensed the pain her mother had suffered in all those years. The difference in their responses was visible. Mrs. Sunderam just looked away at the mountains, the crumpled garden, her own feet still holding the fort. Mother was holding daughter's hand. The fingers were clasping and unclasping like a fish breathing desperately out of water. One hand covered her mouth with a handkerchief. She whispered to Tapashi again. Some of the emotional tide was lapping at Brother. He got up and poured the coffee trying to detach from their expressions.

This was his last stop and Captain Tapashi could get into the driver's seat from here onwards. She had a valid argument though about needing proof. Judges and the jury are not new to situations where there are only clues that point at the truth because truth stands on its own. Evidence is a very mortal requirement. Eyewitnesses are not always available. Truth is as true as a belief. And belief is subject to personal appreciation and very often needs. You can be left to believe or remain in doubt forever.

Mrs. Sunderam spoke for the first time. 'Is Chokkiah alright?' Brother was reminded of his mother.

'He was fine when I was deported Mrs. Sunderam. We have to get going to get them all back. Please believe me. I was there and that is the biggest proof I can provide. I am sorry that there is nothing else I can do or say to make you believe.'

Hands on the table palms facing up Brother made his final plea. 'I thought it was my happiest day to find out that Colonel Sunderam's daughter has joined the army as an officer. She can do what none of the other surviving families can. I have been waiting for this day to meet you.'

The meeting became silent but the turbulence was evident. Inthekab stayed on the perimeter and Brother looked away in the distance. Captain Tapashi Sunderam faced a challenge that she wouldn't back out on.

'Give me time. I need to do some checking out and then I will be in a position to believe or not.'

Brother was happy. He was dealing with a challenge that had definite parameters. He had survived the first round. The next one would be easier as he had deflected the first few blows.

In a very polite and collected tone Tapashi asked, 'How long are you here in Srinagar sir. I'm sure you can stay a few days.'

Brother made his honest declaration, 'I have conveyed whatever I wanted to and have to get on with my life. I want to go back to my quiet life. I have an old mother who worries whenever I leave home. She suffered for many years in my absence especially after my father passed away also during my absence.'

His mind was made up. He would not wait. Brother knew that before noon the bells in the Army and Air force HQ would be ringing and by evening Tapashi would have her confirmations. He could well be home in Bombay late tonight. There was a flight out of Srinagar just after noon. He had three hours to go.

Being in Bombay was some protection. At least he would be safe from the immediate tentacles of the system. Delhi and Srinagar for the Army are on the hotline. Bombay was out of quick reach, more for peacetime soldiering. He could build his defenses before they reached him there. Sheila and Martha would also be with him.

'Can you not stay till I confirm a few facts from my HQ. It may take a day.'

Here was just the right mix of a personal request and impersonal bluntness. Brother decided to be unequivocally honest. This woman would leave no stone unturned in finding out about him. It was better he tell her what to expect. 'I can stay Captain but it will be of no use. You will be disappointed when you check back with your HQ. They will tell you that I am not to be trusted. That I am a deserter who stayed back in Pakistan as a missionary and also that I am mentally unsound. You will be no wiser and probably believe nothing that I have told you today.'

Brother was not willing to recount the hell that he faced on his return from Pakistan. Tapashi could not fully understand his version of the feedback that she was likely to get from her sources in the service headquarters.

'It is up to me to accept or overlook whatever they tell me.'

Brother was direct. 'Are you asking me to stay?'

Tapashi was aggressive. 'You can do whatever you think is best sir.'

Mrs. Sunderam sensed the battle that was on. She interjected, 'if you were with my husband then you have a commitment towards us and that is why you came here. Please respect your own commitment and stay for a day.'

Brother had tied himself up. The elder woman touched his shoulder emphatically and poured oil over stormy waters, 'it is not that we don't believe you son but this is a matter that should be taken up with her HQ and they should clarify and give us the true picture. We are free to trust you in spite of what they say. Don't go back today. We will not hold you longer than maybe a day.'

For Brother there seemed no other way out and he smiled at the elder lady and holding her hand in response to her touch said, 'I can wait because I have waited for a long time and only want the best for everyone. In this process I have faced many difficulties. My commitment to my brothers in prison is that I will not fail them. I will stay as you say.'

Mrs. Sunderam was thankful and Tapashi came of her horse to say, 'you are a gentleman and we respect your commitment and word sir.'

It did not take long for this first meeting. In less than an hour Brother was left to start preparing for the next round. *'I must tell Sheila that the armed forces and government will soon be at my doorstep in Chapel Road. I will need legal advice on my fundamental rights of speech and information. The easiest thing for them is to arrest and lock me up here. This time I know they cannot do it for long. There is only one person who can help in giving evidence that I was a prisoner and also that there are others too. Will Elizabeth do this for me? How can she come here? I should have told her about her cousin Edward and also the situation I am in. But that would have alarmed her and she could go underground. This is not the solution. Stay calm. Why don't I inform Smita? Her father is a judge and who can be better than her to protect me. Will General Nagchoudhuri help?'*

His gallop was reined in by, 'There is a call for you on the phone sir.' It was one of the mess waiters and Brother thanked him and went down the hall to the phone. He looked at his watch. It was an hour after their meeting at twelve noon.

Captain Sunderam sounded relaxed and friendlier on the phone. 'I am speaking from my mother's quarters. She stays here in the separated family quarters that the army has given me.'

Brother listened. 'My mother and I never imagined a day like this would come. She of course never lost hope over the years. It is difficult to accept that someone from your family is dead when you haven't seen the body. It is equally difficult to accept what you have told us today. Over the years we have adjusted to his not being found. As an officer I know that normally prisoners of war are not held back after a war is over.'

Brother silently clenched his teeth and stayed online.

'It is unbelievable that my father is still alive in a PoW camp as you say. My mother has asked me to thank you for your concern to find us and come here. We understand why no one believes you especially after your return and the facts of your case as you have told us. Their disbelief is consequential to lack of evidence. Do you know someone else who can say with conviction that what you say is correct? My mother does not want troubles for you and is willing to forget that you told us anything. She is grateful that my father is alive. I am unsure of whether I should speak to my HQ or not especially because it may cause serious problems for you. Personally, I am interested to go to any extent for the truth.'

Brother was in turmoil. How could he advise her? To say yes was knowingly locking horns with the system and to say no would be denying her the opportunity to go further into the issue. It was becoming a test of loyalty and Brother was not about to fail.

'I think you should try to find out about me because there will be none who will be able to tell you anything about PoWs or your father. My credibility is not acceptable to the system. Neither can I prove my statements nor can they simply declare that I am lying. It is a sensitive issue that can have far reaching consequences. For the system, it is easiest to bury it. They tried to do that by declaring me unsound. The military and government play games to have an edge. They don't always talk or think like teammates. You will be digging many military issues that the government lacks courage to deal with and it can cause trouble for me but for you the truth or ignorance about your father, either way can become a permanent sore that you will have to nurse for the rest of your life. The army will not appreciate your digging up this issue. If you go ahead, I can only assure you of my word. I have no backing or evidence at the moment other than; I have been through that hell myself. I am guilty of not doing anything for two years till I came upon the Godhra clipping in the newspapers on the atrocities in Ahmadabad. I was unarmed to do anything with the armed forces or government. It is fortunate that I could trace you like the other two families. Please do not insist on the sources of my information. I cannot divulge that ever. You will appreciate that I had to work silently because I owe it to my brothers still in that camp. I am hopeful they are alive.'

Brother sensed that the debate between Tapashi and Mrs. Sunderam had become increasingly difficult. They were the ones who bore the loss of a husband and father and here was their chance to recover something. Their minds would be racing back and forth into the grief of the past and the challenge of the present offering a miraculous revival of hopes for their tomorrows. He was their brief mirage in the desert.

A service officer is trained to withstand pressure and uphold the truth fearlessly. Brother and Tapashi had this in common. What was truth for Brother was presently fiction for Tapashi. Fiction that offers the possibility of relief from doubts and opens the doors for joy becomes extremely desirable. Tapashi was in no way going to let this God sent opportunity pass.

'I will try to find out without creating any problems for you sir. That is all I can promise.'

Brother wasn't sure if what she said was possible but he had taken the plunge and he was sure of surfacing. He had faced the authorities once and this time he was stronger. They will come for him, he knew.

'You are a brave officer Captain. To join the army after having lost your father is being brave. You are both brave— your mother and you. Go ahead with whatever your conscience tells you. I will be there.'

# Chapter III

Traveling at the back of a beaten American Land rover always gave a sense of freedom and bravado to the band of militants under their raid commander Ozero. The journey from Tangi to Abbottabad by rail and road had become a routine and Abdul had done it with them by day and at night. They knew the bends and even fallen trees on that road. Abdul always hugged his stolen Indian made 7.62 mm self-loading semi-automatic close to the body. It had been captured almost a year ago and been on many raids and recruitment visits for aspiring militants near the Indian border. Abdul was always positioned on the Pakistani side of the border. He was to give them covering fire if required. On one occasion he had sprinted across the line just in time to lift the injured hateful Rasheid and bring him to safety from the fire of approaching Indian troops. A bullet had grazed Rasheid's thigh and knocked him down. Abdul had prayed not to be hit by the Indians and it was as if they had heard him. He had escaped carrying Rasheid to safety. The man had more respect for him thereafter. Abdul had gradually won their admiration and trust beyond doubts. After that day he had noticed that they did not bother to keep a close watch on his movements. His baptizing though, was not yet complete. He still had to kill Indian soldiers in full view of them.

They would rest at Nathia Galli for the night and rise early and in the cover of darkness cross the border near Uri to set up an ambush on the road to Baramulla. This was a bold operation. It was winter but the roads had been kept open by the Indian Border Roads organization. The snow was not very deep but enough to slow progress on foot. January was not a month for raids and the Indians would have their guard down. It was a Friday and information had it that it was the day of the week when a supply convoy regularly dropped ammunition and food for a border platoon of soldiers. Everyone needs stores in the freezing winters and you could kill for a can of kerosene fuel to keep you warm or cook. The Indian Platoon was conveniently situated on the fringes of a non-descript group of huts usually occupied by shepherds while grazing their sheep on the slopes. There were two families that had settled here staying through the winters and the Indian soldiers watched them carefully but also shared their stores with them. Shepherds new the way and were the best guides and informers. Loyalties could never be above board with this floating nomadic population. They could disappear without warning. The Platoon commander had however made them a part of his force with stores and bottles of rum.

Ozero and his men were to ambush this convoy of two trucks and an armed light machine gun jeep before it reached the hutments. Abdul was to be included across the border for this raid. They needed every man to fight and then carry as much loot to make the raid worthwhile.

Abdul always paired up with Salman. At Nathia Galli they sat around Fazalbhai's fire after a meal making their final plan. The cold had made them weary and slow. Hamid had suggested they wait for another day and attack the Platoon instead of the convoy, in the late evening, escaping under cover of darkness. The Indian soldiers would be playing cards, listening to music and having their rationed rum. The stores would be in one place in a hut and they could sneak in and overcome the two guards silently and then make off with their requirements. A confrontation with the armed convoy was taking too much of a risk. Ozero however had his eyes on the jeep mounted light machine gun that he thought would be easy meat if they ambushed a convoy. An LMG would increase his capability and following.

Abdul had observed these men in combat. Their resolve evaporated under fire. Unlike trained and motivated soldiers they were more like thieves and ran for cover whenever there was retaliation. They were good at ambushes to rattle regular soldiers but to overcome armed men and then take away their stores called for guts and needed a larger force with someone giving covering fire. They were only seven with six of them armed. Fazalbhai their host at Nathia Galli was cleaning his AK-47 as he was accompanying them this time but Rafiq the driver of the Land rover was just an unarmed carrier. He would get some share of the captured stores. Such was the poverty and need that they became foolhardy to even go on a raid unarmed.

The alternate plan became an argument and Rasheid with Ozero on one side were trying to cow down Hamid. Abdul never contributed unless asked and Salman was too young and inexperienced to have the courage. The two of them preferred to listen.

Hamid said, 'Ozero, you are a mercenary and don't care about your life. You are greedy for the money. It gives you enough to waste with the women and booze in Islamabad. I know all your activities.'

It was not a time to fight but Ozero barked. 'If you are so scared, why don't you go back to your village in Kashmir and live like a worm under the Indians. Your wife must have borne many children by now. It is two years since you saw her. Indian soldiers must be paying her good money for her services. Go and be with her. You will not have to work or risk your life. You have no place as a mujahideen.'

Rasheid also ganged up to taunt him, ' why don't you join the Indian soldiers as their guide. Show them all our hideouts. They will reward you.'

Hamid was not to be down trodden. The man had guts. Uncovering his AK-47 and leveling it at them both he shouted back, 'one more word about my family and I will send you to your graves, you rotten scoundrel who doesn't even know who his father is and you Rasheid, you are just a puppet. You forget that it was me who saved you from being butchered by those Indian soldiers. I should not have risked my life to rescue you from their camp. It would have been better if I had left you tied up there or put a bullet through you to keep our secrets. Let this raid get over. I will join Muzzaffar's gang. They do not behave like murderers and thieves that you are. What have we got under this mercenary Ozero? He collects his payments and Majidbhai gets richer.'

They had not expected Hamid to draw his weapon and now they stared in disbelief as he raged at them finger on the trigger.

'Neither are we recruiting those frustrated boys from the valley nor hitting the temples and the Kashmiri Brahmins who have looted us dry. You think Kashmir will get freedom from India by these stupid raids. The Indian army will never leave the valley unless we create an uprising demanding freedom for Kashmir.'

Hamid looked at Abdul for approval for his logic about the Indian army. Abdul just stared back and Hamid continued his tirade.

'Pakistan depends on us to create this uprising. The only way is to hit deep in the towns and create panic. What do those rich merchants in Srinagar know about hardship and poverty? They are corrupt and have the politicians in their hands with their money and comforts. Even the police support them. Innocent people are arrested and tortured and it is publicized as the capture of some deadly terrorist. We should be supporting our brothers in the valley by terrorizing these rich and the corrupt politicians to strengthen our own party and demand freedom. Have you got the guts to join Muzzaffar's gang? They now have a group of dedicated boys who don't mind blowing themselves up with dynamite strapped to themselves. Let me see you tomorrow leading the charge at the convoy. What do you know of Jihad, Ozero?'

Fazalbhai was the eldest and he was not a core militant. They needed extra hands and he could do with some supplies. Intervening he said, ' what is the use of this argument. I am in support of Hamid's plan but if you want I am with you for the ambush also. What do you think Abdul?

He was dreading something like this but at the back of his mind Abdul knew his time was coming to change garb and become Azad again. He would wait.

'I am with whatever the majority says Fazalbhai.'

Ozero was incapable of dealing with mutiny. He only thought about himself. Remaining silent for a while he said, 'we will march at 3 o'clock; get some sleep. Majidbhai will decide after we get back home if Hamid is to be part of my group anymore. Till then you will do as I say.'

Hamid sensed that any more arguments could lead to a shoot out and that was of no use because the mujahideen did not spare mutineers or deserters. He would escape after the raid and join Muzzaffar's gang. It would mean three days march through the snow but he would do it. He wanted to free Kashmir and not remain a thief under Ozero. Shifting gangs was acceptable amongst militants.

The night had been cold and the pre-dawn march in the cold darkness through snow was tougher than Abdul had imagined. He thought, *'These militants really know their way through these ravines and hills in the dark.'* It was early morning and they were climbing up a hillock and Ozero went on all fours to crawl the last few yards. Reaching the top they looked down on a bend in the road from Baramulla to Uri. They could see about a kilometer down the road towards Baramulla. The supply convoy would be climbing up this road. Behind them after a fifty-meter clear patch there was a thick wooded slope of tall Chinar trees and bushes. It was good cover for an escape. They were almost ten kilometers inside Indian Territory. It was quite a distance but escape would not be difficult. The Indian army would not chase them through the snow covered ravines and hills. The final plan was to steal as much as possible and hide it in one of the many caves enroute and collect the stores after a few days. The distance was too much to carry away heavy loads and withdraw safely. The Indian Platoon may send out a patrol to intercept them but they would hide their stores and cut across into safety.

Ozero deployed his force keeping Rasheid with him. From a small mound Hamid was to open fire from the front as the convoy climbed round the bend. Fazalbhai and Rafiq were with him. Ozero would fire at the convoy from behind. Abdul and Salman were to rush the convoy from the opposite side of the road at the bend. Everyone would close in after the light machine gunner was silenced. They would cut down the few soldiers as they came out of the trucks. It was just past sunrise. Abdul and Salman went down a steep saddle in the hillock that led to the road. On signal they crossed and took up position just inside the Chinar trees across and close to the edge of the road. The convoy would be abreast of them when Hamid opened fire. That was everyone's signal to attack. Abdul and Salman would have to take a few steps before reaching the edge of the forest to get a clear field of fire.

Salman whispered to Abdul. 'This is your first engagement with Indian soldiers. In all the other raids you only had to provide fire in a withdrawal. In this one we have to attack, remember. Have you got enough ammunition? Everyone will be watching you.'

A para commando was being given last minute instructions by his eighteen-year-old keeper. Abdul put his hand on Salman's shoulder and pulled him close. 'Don't worry son, you will see what a real attack is like today. I will charge and you stay back to give me cover.' Looking around in all directions he said, 'keep an eye on our rear and on the other side of the road. Never underestimate the enemy. They could easily have a dawn patrol that could be approaching from our rear. You will have to take care of that.'

Salman nodded and smiled at being given the responsibility. His face showed appreciation for Abdul's attention to this unseen possibility. He had hidden admiration for Abdul's professionalism. The thought that he was responsible for Abdul's loyalty and the action to take if he contemplated an escape never crossed his mind today. Abdul had proven his loyalty. He was one of them and it felt secure to be with him. He was a good fighter.

Abdul positioned Salman into cover. 'You stay here while I get into a better attack position.' He crawled to a position about a hundred yards away closer to the bend nearer to the edge of the tree cover. Salman and he could see each other clearly. Abdul ensured that he could clearly see Hamid and Ozero's positions. This could be his chance.

They all heard the sound of a vehicle. It came from the wrong side. Someone was driving towards their position from Uri. Automatics were loaded and safety catches slipped off. An open jeep with a mounted machine gun came into view at the bend. It was from the Platoon at Uri. Abdul was quick to understand. It was going to meet the convoy and escort it through the last twenty kilometers. Most of the ambushes took place near the border enabling the militants to disappear rapidly into Pakistan. The Indians rarely ventured across in a chase. The armed jeep was to discourage an ambush. He wondered if the others understood. There was no way of communicating. He would be careful, as the Indian firepower was more now.

Within an hour after the jeep had crossed, the sound of vehicles lumbering up the hillock broke the silent tension. Their moment had come. Abdul looked back at Salman. He was ready face covered with a dark cloth. Abdul could see a little distance down the road from his position and he saw a jeep in the lead, followed by two trucks and then there was another open jeep at the rear. A soldier in each jeep manned the machine guns and were sweeping the hill slopes heads on a swivel.

Hamid's first burst was accurate. The driver of the lead jeep was hit and the vehicle swerved overturning off the road. The gunner was thrown off. The trucks pulled up immediately and about ten armed men were quick to jump out and take up positions on either side of the road. They were returning the fire that came from Hamid and Ozero at height. Salman had not opened up because he could not see the soldiers who had taken up position very close to him between trees. They were guarding the convoy flank facing Abdul and Salman.

Abdul looked back at him and warned him by pointing at the soldiers taking up position. Salman saw them, stood up and fired a burst and hit two of them. His fire attracted the trailing jeep with the machine gun. The gunner swiveled the weapon and in seconds the Chinar forest was being torn by machine gun fire. Pieces of bark and twigs flew as though a sword was at work. Salman was shuddering on the forest floor. Abdul waved him to join him and started moving away from the immediate scene.

He was going to attract the fire towards himself so that Ozero and Hamid could close in. Abdul charged firing towards the overturned jeep and the trucks, running parallel to the tree line. Salman was running hundred yards behind, firing at the rear towards the soldiers trying to enter the woods. Abdul was careful to fire at the truck tires avoiding hitting any of the soldiers that he saw. This was going to be his test but he knew it was well nigh impossible for any of the gang to see his bullets. The bend in the road had become a rain of fire from the militants at height. The soldiers took cover and returned the fire. Abdul and Salman were cut off from their comrades. Leaving the area would be suicidal because they would consider him traitor. Abdul continued parallel to the road, firing sporadically. His fire was returned by the men on the other side of the road. He saw three of them crawling up the gap in the hill towards Ozero's position but did not fire at them. He had used the same track to come down. Praying that Salman had not seen them he jumped onto the road near the overturned jeep. The driver looked dead blood still trickling from his chest and face. Salman was nowhere to be seen but the intensity of fire near his position had increased. Abdul knew theirs was a losing battle. They were outnumbered and the Indians looked like they had expected an attack. It was time to withdraw but the firing from Hamid and Ozero kept the soldiers dug in.

They could see him from their higher positions as he reached the jeep. The gunner was trapped in the crash and couldn't move. He saw Abdul coming and tried to reach an automatic that lay close by. Abdul kicked it away. The air around the jeep was dense with bullets whizzing past. The Indian soldiers had seen him. He ducked and was flat on the ground next to the trapped gunner. Using all his strength the wrestler Azad managed to move the jeep's upper frame to free the gunner's legs. Pushing him away from the firing he said, 'go take cover I am Naik Azad Khan, 9 Para Commandos.'

There was another burst of fire behind him. Salman came racing out of the woods towards him. Abdul saw three soldiers behind him at the tree line. They were giving chase. He fired at them, keeping his fire slightly above their heads. It stopped them enough for him to grab Salman. He was breathing hard in fear and exertion.

'You run Salman, I will cover you, go now!

Salman looked at him face ashened. Abdul pushed him on, 'don't worry about me; you have a whole life ahead of you. I will keep these soldiers occupied. You climb up that hillock and give me cover; I will join up with you, now go.'

Pulling out a bag from the jeep he dumped it on Salman. Here take this bag of ammunition. I will need it later. It is for my Indian automatic, go.'

Salman scurried in a bent position and was soon climbing the hillock between rocks and trees. Abdul covered him. Firing from Ozero and Hamid's position had ceased. What could have happened? Abdul recalled the three Indian soldiers climbing up the gap between the hillocks. It would have taken them under cover to point blank range behind Ozero. Ozero wouldn't have a chance. Suddenly Abdul realized that the firing had reduced. Whatever was being fired was at him around the jeep. He saw a few soldiers trying to creep towards one of the trucks to get nearer to him and the overturned jeep. Abdul threw his automatic for them to see and rose slowly hands high up from behind the jeep. The soldiers stopped advancing. There was no firing. The bend in the road was full of smoke. One of the trucks was burning.

Abdul was panting from nervous exhaustion. He shouted, 'I am Naik Azad Khan from the 9 Para Commandos. I was a prisoner of war in Pakistan. They had kept me captive.'

He walked forward into the open from behind the shattered jeep his arms still raised. His own declaration echoed through his head through the smoke and chaos. All firing stopped for a moment. Azad glanced back up at the hill. He couldn't see Salman through the smoke. He must have reached the top and escaped. 'Allah is kind, he was good lad to me', he murmured. 'I will soon be free.'

The momentary silence was shattered by a few shots from the hill behind Azad. Dust was kicked up near him and the jeep. The soldiers took cover and fired back at the hill. The battle was announced closed with those shots. Azad heard a voice screaming from the hillside. Was it Salman calling to him? He couldn't make out. He lay on the frosty wet road. It felt cool. Some soldiers had taken off up the hill from where the shots had come. The others were on him. The smell of Indian battle fatigues and their voices sounded familiar. He saw the insignia of the 7 Madras Regiment on their shoulder flaps. It reminded him of prisoner Colonel Sunderam. Wasn't he from 7 Madras? He had fallen into good hands. *'Ruhaina, now I am in safe and good hands. These boys will understand my true identity. They saw, that I did not shoot to kill. I could have. Now they will believe me and also that there are the others. I will be with you soon.'* He turned to one of the soldiers and said, 'don't shoot the boy, he is a Kashmiri....not a terrorist and has looked after me.'

# Chapter IV

At the Brigade HQs in Srinagar, Captain Tapashi Sunderam was on the hot line to Army HQ Delhi. After calling Brother she called one of her lady officer batch mates in the HQ Intelligence group in Delhi on the long distance exclusive army line. She did not mention anything about PoWs still being held in Pakistan. All she wanted to know was about Brother.

'Sheema can you hear me; this is urgent and very important. There is a retired Flight Lieutenant Richard James here in Srinagar. He was taken prisoner during the 1971 war and released in 2000 December. Came to meet me. Can you check with Air HQ about him? I need the information immediately. Please be discreet. He had some problem with the air force and I don't want any more problems for him. Just check if he was a prisoner and any other information if possible. Be discreet. I will be available on this telephone for the next two hours. Thank you.'

Sheema didn't get much chance to clarify but she got the message. Find out and be discreet. Hotlines were for short messages. *'Tapashi sure had her enquiry figured out to the last dot.'* Sheema scribbled the name Richard James with his rank and the year he was released. It looked like a mistake. Twenty-nine years in a PoW camp! *'Tapashi was meticulous in training school, maybe her dates and calculations are not correct.'*

Captain Sunderam called Brother. 'Can you give me a statement in writing simply saying that you were with my father and that he is still a PoW?'

Brother smiled. He wasn't going to fall for this one. 'Do you have internet facility here in Srinagar?'

Tapashi was surprised by his strange question. 'I could arrange for it or we could find a cyber café, but that may take time. I am expecting a call and have to be here.'

Brother had a plan. 'Take me to a computer with Internet whenever you get free. I can show you something that may help you. I will wait in my room for your call.'

*'What can he show me on the Internet?'* Tapashi waited at the Brigade HQ and decided to pick up some of her official and personal mail. She asked a dispatch rider to collect all personal mail for Officers and troops of her regiment. She would carry it back and never forgot to do this on every trip she made to Srinagar. Soldiers serving on the front always waited to hear from home. *'This Brother James is a peculiar fellow. Sounds convincing but has no proof. Why the Internet?'*

She didn't have to wait too long. The telephone rang. It was for her. The operator held the line till she went into the confidential call booth in the office. Sheema would be using the scrambler. She had. The descramble phone booth was accessible to few. "Top security cleared personnel only" was the WARNING stuck on the door of the booth. It needed a swipe card. Tapashi had hers.

'Tell me Sheema. Could you find out anything interesting?'

'Yes, your man was a fighter pilot shot on a mission to Gujranwala. Accused of desertion, he absconded for twenty-nine years in Pakistan before being apprehended by their police. Was there disguised as a Christian priest. Is a bachelor and has only his parents living in Bombay. Insisted he was a PoW but could not provide details and names of the places that he was held. Was declared mentally unsound and suffering from terminal TB. He gave the names of a few other prisoners but I was not given the names, as those were not available in the same file. To get that information you will need special permissions and clearances. I suggest you don't because the air force officer I asked wanted to know our reasons for this enquiry. I just told him that you are in touch with this James in Srinagar. He wanted to know more about James' purpose in Srinagar. Keep a watch on him Taps. The air force officer seemed to know this fellow James. Said he was bad weather and a mental case. I don't really know what he meant by that, so you better watch out.'

Tapashi thanked her colleague. It was quick, within the hour she had whatever file information could be shared between security cleared Intelligence branch officers of the two services.

'There is no difference in what they have on him and what he said. I will need to work on him. I suspect he knows the place in Pakistan but has not disclosed it because of some reason. It must have been a harrowing experience if he really was a PoW. The court martial must have also grilled him. He is hiding something but has come all the way here because he thinks I may help. His effort definitely has some benefits for himself. Let me give him an ultimatum. Threat works sometimes. I will have to make this official; otherwise this kind of investigation could go against me.'

She dialed the Srinagar air force Base Security and Counter Intelligence officer's number. The officer agreed to meet her at the air force mess in an hour. She could work on Brother till then. 'Let me win his confidence before I get tough.'

Brother picked up the receiver in his room. 'Is that you Brother?'

It was the first time she addressed him so. It did not go unnoticed. 'Yes and is that Captain Sunderam. I recognize your voice now.'

She waited for the ripple of familiarity to pass. 'If you are free can I come and meet you.'

Brother extended himself for a lady whenever opportunity arose. He was reading Exodus and planning to take a nap before lunch but said, 'sure I am free how long will you be?'

'I can be there in fifteen minutes and won't take too much of your time. There are a few things to show you and then we can go to a friend's place for the Internet.'

'That will be great.' Brother was delighted.

They met at the same table in the lounge. Brother had quickly tripped down to the mess from his room. Her presence without the mother was singular and she came across as a polite and self-assured person. Seated at the table she opened a folder that had papers, photographs and news paper clippings.

She handed it over to Brother saying, 'these are a few memories we have. I thought of sharing them with you.'

Brother was excited, 'that is very kind of you. Can I see them.'

She handed the folder over and watched him closely. Brother opened the folder and was leisurely about it, asking questions at almost every bit of the assembled memory.

Colonel Sunderam was a first class first in college with

mathematics. *'Why then did he join the army?'* In his training days he was an exceptional rider, marksman and had also won the Inter-Squadron debating competition. *'No wonder he spoke with such confidence and logic.'* He topped the young officers courses with record-breaking marks. His Company was the best repeatedly in the Battalion assessments. His father was in the Maharaja of Mysore's polo team and the Colonel himself played for the army team and had won the National Cup in 1967. An extract from the Battalion history attracted his attention. One Captain George Joseph had penned it in 1972 February. Brother read it a few times and tried to mentally build a picture.

*'Our position had been overrun by Pakistani tanks at Shakargarh. Colonel Sunderam ordered the Platoon and me to withdraw. Staying back with just a section he fought to slow down the enemy tanks so that the Platoon could take up a new position to counter-attack. Out of the ten men who were with him only six bodies were found. The others we presume had been taken prisoner. After a counter attack our troops could not find any of the four missing. Colonel Sunderam was declared missing. The Battalion honors him. He was awarded the Vir Chakra gallantry award posthumously after the war.'*

Closing the folder he looked at Tapashi and handed it back. 'None of us knew about how he was taken prisoner. He never spoke about it. And he doesn't know that he was decorated for gallantry.'

Tapashi had shared with him something that increased his urgency to rescue the war hero who had sometimes nursed him through his delirious fevers. She insisted on him, 'have you tried to recollect the names of the places you had been taken to.'

Brother recalled all the names that he could remember. 'It is important that you try to recall something about the camp.'

Brother thought and said, 'we used to see the Nanga Parbat peak in a north easterly direction but I have no guesses about the distance and there were foothills of a higher range of mountains to the north of us. The place maybe somewhere near Nowshera or to the north of it.'

Captain Tapashi's face lit up. 'Nowshera is not very far from where I am stationed at Baramulla. We have informers who give us information from across the border at Uri. Now I want you to understand that making a false accusation against the army or government that they haven't done enough to get our prisoner's back, can be a serious crime. In your own interest you should tell me anything else you know about the place or other facts in writing. You say that Pakistan still has our men held as prisoners. I will get to the bottom of this and if you are proved to be wrong; it could be bad for you.'

Brother stood up slowly, surprised at the officialdom that hurt but he stayed polite. 'I have not come all this way to be threatened by those who do not believe me. It will be in everyone's interest that you get to the bottom of this issue.' His firm stand had hit the ball right back across the court and she was without a stroke.

An air force officer approached them determinedly. He saw them both and said, 'if you are the Flight Lieutenant James sir, I have to ask you to return to your room and not meet or speak about sensitive issues that you have been telling this Captain. I have orders from my Station Commander to prevent you from leaving the mess till the Interrogation officer from Air HQ arrives. Air HQ is aware of your arrival here. Please cooperate.'

Brother looked at Tapashi. She looked sorry and confused. Brother just smiled and said, 'it is not your fault. This is my cross and I can carry it. I hope you will be as brave as your father to stay and fight. Oh! Thank you for trying to get me to the Internet. Bad luck you missed something. Maybe later.'

Turning towards the air force officer Brother was stern, 'I will be in my room but will leave by the afternoon plane tomorrow for Bombay. You can get back to your Air HQ and tell them that I will not answer any questions of your interrogation officer. Tell them not to waste their time. I have been through my questioning after the Pakistanis released me. Now my lawyer will answer whatever questions are there. Thank you lady and gentleman.'

Turning on his heel Brother left for his room leaving a wake of indecision. His walk suddenly became a swagger only some fighter pilots have. Like at many buffets attended by the brass, two junior officers were left to chew on the leftovers.

The Security officer said, 'Captain Tapashi, it is wise that you told me about this James. I have orders from my boss here and Air HQ has cautioned him that this gentleman is capable of creating rumors and problems for us all and if required we are to arrest and hand him over to the civil police. What is it that you have with him?'

Tapashi mentally summed up the situation and turned away a little annoyed with the interruption. 'It is personal and will not be of interest to you. He was a prisoner of war and has interesting stories. He knew my father.'

There was a dispatch rider waiting outside Mrs. Sunderam's quarters. An agitated mother waited at the window looking anxiously down the road for Tapashi's jeep. The rider waited to deliver an emergency message for her.

Driving back to her quarters Captain Tapashi was undeterred. She had found out about Brother from Sheema. She had also made the mistake of telling the local air force security officer; 'I have to ask this retired Flight Lieutenant James some questions about his days as a PoW.'

'*The air force Intelligence system does not want Brother to speak to anyone anymore. Someone is hiding something.*' I will find out. It may become an inter-service battle now. Her mind kept going back to his last words about the Internet.

Seeing the rider waiting at her mother's place she jumped out of the jeep as it came to a halt. The rider saluted and handed over an envelope. It was a message from the Brigade HQ Intelligence branch in Srinagar. She was there making her calls only an hour ago. What urgency could have developed in one hour? Tearing the flap she read:

REPORT TO UNIT IMMEDIATELY STOP URI CONVOY AMBUSHED 0700 HRS BY MILITANTS STOP THREE MILITANTS DEAD CMA ONE SERIOUSLY INJURED CAPTURED STOP IMMEDIATE INTERROGATION CMA EXAMINING OF EVIDENCE IMPERATIVE STOP.

She had too much on her hands now. Deciding quickly she explained to her mother and used the phone. 'Brother I have to apologize for what is happening. It is your Air force HQ that is taking this unpleasant action. I have to rush to my unit. There is an emergency. Please wait for me; I will be back tomorrow. I can't explain. I have no time now. Be patient and wait till I get back.'

Brother was unmoved. Her emergency was incidental. He was ready for battle. The NDA march past tune was already humming constantly in his head. It was the same tune that had seen him humming through unimaginable solitary confinement and punishments as a disobedient arrogant prisoner. Brother loved the rhythm that made them march together. The big bass drum was like a brave pounding heart for him. He never felt alone and fear was always left far away as they marched forward onto the parade ground. He now also had a strong team of deprived women marching with him.

'Tapashi, I can take care of myself. You will need a lot to handle this situation. I have faith in your courage. All the best. I am with you and trust you are too.'

His sarcasm made her smile. Brother added, 'I don't mind being the guest of the air force for some more time. I will wait for you dear.'

'Thank you sir,' was the crisp reply and she was gone.

Brother looked at his watch. It was past noon. He called for lunch in his room. The earliest any air force officer from Delhi would arrive is tomorrow. He would not be able to catch his plane at midday. Also there was no assurance of Tapashi's return. He would go back to his favorite book but not before he made a call to Bombay.

Brother decided to go in search of a long distance phone. There were a couple of booths he had observed on the way to the mess. He had not stepped out of the gates at all. It was his second day. He decided to go out. The watchman at the gate asked him to enter his name and Brother glanced at the other names as he wrote. The air force security officer must be Sqn. Ldr. Himmat Singh. There was no exit time against his name. He must still be somewhere in the mess. Whistling his favorite tune Brother did not have to walk far. There was a convenience general store that had a long distance phone facility within a ten-minute stroll. It was three in the afternoon. He decided to call Sheila.

'How are you Sheila?' She was at work surprised and caught unawares by his call.

'I am fine, how about you and how is the cold.'

'Not too bad, the jacket is good. I have found the Colonel's daughter and wife and there is a bit of talking we all have to do. It may take another two days.'

'Is there any problem?'

'No major issue. It is the same story about having more proof.'

'Oh! Your mom called sometime back. She said, the air force boss here in Bombay called her to find out your whereabouts and she told them that you had gone to Srinagar.'

'That is not surprising Sheila because now even the Air HQ knows that I am here and they are sending a special guy to talk to me.'

'Brother, are you sure all is well.'

'Nothing is wrong but I may need that lawyer you told me about Sheila.'

'Hey! You said everything was fine but I think it isn't, anyway do you want the lawyer's number. I have it; take it down.'

Brother borrowed a pencil and piece of paper to make a note of it. 'Thank you Sheila, I will call mom and give you a call when I am leaving here. We have to catch up on a lot.'

'Stay calm,' she giggled and it kept Brother connected with his reliance on her support and beliefs. He dialed the Chapel road number.

Martha was happy hearing his voice. 'Have you found that lady officer, I mean the daughter?'

'Yes mom her mother is also here and they are happy. I will be home probably in two days.' He never spoke too much with her but felt good at her involvement with his mission.

*'Lets go back and see what they have for us.'* Brother hummed his favorite tune and marched back.

Tapashi reached Baramulla at four in the evening. The Brigade Commander had been looking for her. Handing over all the mail from Srinagar to a beaming subordinate she got him on the phone.

'I am back sir and will be in the HQ with the captured militant in ten minutes.'

Brigadier Gambhir Saxena was a seasoned soldier and had seen action in Kargil. A couple of militants engaged or captured was not something that excited him too much. 'Yes Captain I am glad you made it back before sunset. These days the ambushes have increased in spite of the winter. Let me know if there is any interesting information you get from the prisoner who is still alive I am told. He is badly wounded and may not make it. The brigade medical officer is attending to him. We lost two soldiers. Remember it is important to find out the locations of their training camps and launch points across the border.'

She was anxious to get going with her job. Any militant prisoner now held much more meaning for her. 'Yes sir I will call you back after the interrogation.'

'Call only if you think it is worthwhile otherwise give me a report tomorrow morning. I have a bridge foursome waiting for me.'

At the 7 Madras regiment HQ cell there was one militant lying on a bunk. His clothes lay in a bloody heap on the floor. A sheet and blanket kept him covered and warm. There were another three bodies covered with sheets on the floor on one side of the room in front of the cells. Each dead militant's captured personal belongings was laid out for her inspection. These were placed in small cloth bundles in which they had been wrapped and placed near the lifeless heads. Their weapons, contents from emptied pockets, pouches and haversack was quite a collection. No one was allowed to scrutinize them before the Intelligence officer had done so. It was Tapashi's job to closely examine all the seized belongings to draw conclusions about their identity and purpose. The medical officer present assured her that one prisoner was alive under pethadine and would come around in sometime. She decided to quickly check the dead bodies first.

Tapashi lifted the cover off the first body. She kept talking and another young officer entered relevant information on a prescribed army form. 'A young man in his thirties. Medium height and built. Seems to be of Chinese or Russian origin with slant eyes. Armed with an AK-47. Death from bullet injuries in the back. Carrying excessive ammunition for a single person in his haversack and wrapped in a warm cloth. I want them to be counted after I finish. His diary has some names and telephone numbers. I will need these photocopied and kept in the safe for my study.'

Leafing rapidly through the pages of the dirty pocket notebook Tapashi did not find anything that attracted her immediate attention. 'Continue writing, some names in the diary are Russian. A hotel bill indicates a meal for two and room charges written in Urdu. The name of the hotel has been torn off. Has a hunting knife and small multi purpose screw driver that looks like a tester and has extra heads stored in the handle. Headgear is made of sheepskin leather with a strap. Did you get it all?'

'Yes madam.'

She checked the cap for any concealed pockets. There was a lump stitched into the side. Opening it she took out the contents smelt it and looked up. 'Carrying about ten grams of opium. Did you get all the information?' 'Yes madam,' was the reply again. The team was well versed with her methods.

She moved to the next body. 'Very muscularly built middle-aged man with gray hair and peppered beard. Looks like a Muslim. Medical officer to submit separate report after inspecting organs for circumcision and other external injuries or marks. His weapon is an Indian made 7.62 self loading rifle.'

She was taken aback by the Indian made weapon found on a militant. *'He must have killed some Indian soldier to get hold of it.'* Reaching inside her shirt pocket Tapashi brought out a miniature but powerful magnifying glass. Holding the weapon by its stock she looked from tip of the barrel to butt end and went back to where the barrel emerged from the wooden stock.

'Note down, weapon has numbers very much like the ones we have. It is 8L 763298. Inform the Brigade Major to check if this weapon is from our brigade and if not which unit holds it on their inventory and who was the last person who drew it from the armoury with names, dates and location please. I want this fast. Keep noting.'

'Yes madam, I've got it, you can keep saying and I will jot it down.'

'Good.' Captain Tapashi gave a quick glance of approval and also looked in the direction of the medical officer.

'He is wearing Indian Army boots size eight. Death from a single bullet in the back. Has a pocket Koran.'

She leafed rapidly through the holy book. Her eyes settled on a page that had something written in pencil. Going back into her office under a bright light, she opened the tight bound Koran fully. The scribbling was not easily visible. It was printed in Nowshera. She stood up and shifted under the powerful table light. Written in pencil there were some names. Her voice dropped to almost a whisper. *'These look like Indian names.'* It read: Vadhera, Gupta, Ganguly, Brother James, Sunderam, Ramesh and Pawri. There were crosses on the names but Ganguly, Sunderam and Pawri's names were without the cross mark. Also scribbled on the next page were Malakand, Tangi, Nowshera, Wah, Abbottabad, Haripur and Nathia Galli. Holding the book with stiffening fingers that would soon ache Tapashi tried to conceal a growing tremble.

Coming out of her office she calmly dictated, 'make a note that I am keeping this Koran for the interrogation of the prisoner and Lieutenant; you can make the inventory for the last body. I need to interrogate immediately.'

She leafed rapidly through the Koran a couple of times to spot any other writings. There was none. She tried to control her excitement. Her pulse was racing she realized. Captain Tapashi knew the weight of this Koran and she was going to carry it and protect it like a tigress. The feline resolve on her face showed. Those around her however wouldn't ever guess the reason. She was known to be a tough officer. Such looks and determination went with her.

Thinking about the list of names repeatedly she realized that it had Brother James's name and also there was a Sunderam scribbled on it. Brother's name had a cross but Sunderam's was without it. It had to be her father. She breezed into the cell where the medical officer was.

'Is he awake. I need to get whatever information he can give.'

The medical officer looked defeated. 'He is only a boy and hemorrhaging and may not be able to speak.'

She leaned over the dying militant. Questioning him in Hindi she asked repeatedly, 'what is your name?'

After a few moments he replied, 'Salman.' His eyes flutterred.

The medical officer quickly made a note on the nearest piece of paper. Blood was trickling from the corner of Salman's mouth.

'What are the names of your colleagues?'

His eyes now steady looked far away and he turned towards the dead bodies and a tear rolled out. Motioning with his eyes he said, 'Azad, Abdul Khan, Prisoner of war, there are others at Tangi.'

As if struck by lightening she sat up and then leaned forward to assist him to sit so that the blood from his mouth would not choke. Pointing at the bodies she said, 'which is Abdul Azad? He could again only point with his eyes. She pointed at the first body. 'Is he Abdul?' He shook his head and she understood. At the second body she asked, 'Azad or Abdul?'

He managed to say Azadbhai and went into coma. Her manner changed. Laying the boy militant gently down she gave instructions to the medical officer and the senior non-commissioned officer. 'The second body is to be preserved. I want to question the convoy in charge immediately. Bring him to me here.'

The senior most junior commissioned officer (JCO) leading the convoy arrived within minutes. His arm was bandaged and in a sling. Tapashi acknowledged his salute.

'I hope you are not injured badly. Can you give me a quick report of the ambush.' She listened carefully making notes as the incident unfolded.

The end of it all interested her and there was a reason for it. The JCO pointing at the body between two dead bodies said, 'he may not be a militant because he said he was a prisoner and his name he gave as Naik Azad Khan. The gunner of the lead jeep says Azad could have killed him but he helped him to disentangle from the fallen jeep and dragged him to cover or he would be dead. Azad had said that he was from 9 Para Commandos. We don't know but he may be a deserter. We saw him send off the boy up the hill to escape and he stayed back firing at us. He fired above us in the air. We saw him surrender but before we reached him the boy on the hill must have fired at him or us. That fire hit him. We returned fire at the boy and he was hit and captured. I think three of them escaped. The others are here. That is all madam.'

Tapashi was mesmerized for a second trying to visualize the whole scene. 'Thank you and will you please make an official written statement along with your report. Mention the details about this Azad and what he was heard saying. It is important.'

The JCO saluted. 'Yes madam the report in an hour.'

'Thank you.' Tapashi went to her office and looked at the wall map. *'Tangi is north of Nowshera. Brother maybe right.'* Opening the page with the names of places she traced the names like a route from Tangi to Nathia Galli near the border and to Uri. It made sense.

Making sure that Azad's body was removed from the company of dead militants, Tapashi called up the Brigade Commander and asked him, 'Sir there is some very important information I have. Can I meet you for ten minutes.'

'Sure Captain, as it is I am losing the game here. No good cards today. I will be in the mess lounge to meet you.'

Tapashi related the entire episode of the ambush and then her visit to Srinagar and encounter with retired Flight Lieutenant Brother James. The Brigade Commander was amazed at the events and information. He said, 'this is a very tricky situation Captain and will surely raise a stink in a lot of rooms at Army HQs and the ministry of defense and foreign affairs. The information is very sensitive and can become an International imbroglio and it is very risky for those prisoners if they are still alive. Can you imagine the embarrassment of the Pakistanis? They could do anything to cover tracks. What do you want to do now, especially since your father's name appears in this list?'

'Sir, I want you to speak to the Air force Station Commander to let Brother James come here to identify the body of this Naik Azad Khan tomorrow. That will be his test. Then we will submit our report. If you permit me, I will take the report and go to Delhi, Army HQ Intelligence Branch myself. It is my father I must get back. Surely, the government can negotiate with the Pakistani authorities. Can I leave early morning and pick up Brother from his mess and bring him here.'

The Brigade Commander smiled. 'Okay Captain you can and I was a very junior officer commissioned during the 1971 war but have read the accounts and know the records of your father. We must get him back. I will do my best. That is a promise.'

She saluted and they shook hands. The Brigadier added with a wink, 'why don't we just send in a commando team and rescue these guys eh?' He laughed and said, 'don't quote me but don't rule out that possibility. Lets see what the Army HQ plans to do. Best of luck Captain, you will need it and I hope you get your father back. We are proud of him. I will speak to the Air force boss in Srinagar for your man Brother James.'

Her office clerk was waiting. 'There is a message from the Brigade Major's office madam. You have to call him up.' Tapashi entered her office. It was seven in the evening. *'Should I call Brother?'* She dialed the brigade major's office first. The voice at the other end snapped authoritatively, 'this is Major Kulwant.'

'Good evening sir I am Captain Sunderam.' Her sense of duty shelved the call to Brother. She also needed to decide what to say to him.

'Your request for information on a weapon is with me Captain. The semi-automatic was snatched from a Sepoy Harnam Singh of the Kumaon regiment about a year ago. The Sepoy has now given a statement to his Commanding officer that an Indian soldier, a Naik was with the militants and took away his rifle and boots but never harmed him. He cannot recall the name of the Naik but says he had a Muslim name. The Sepoy had earlier lied that he had been injured during a patrol and the weapon had fallen into a ravine but when we told him that his weapon has been found with some militants, he came out with this weird explanation.'

Tapashi listened and thanked him for the information. She was one of the three lady officers posted near the border. Every male officer was out to please them. It was natural and she didn't care much about it. *'Guys are like that'*, she would laugh with her mother often.

'Major sir, I think your Sepoy's weird story is true because the weapon was found with a militant who may have been in the Indian army long ago. His body is waiting to be identified. Can you get a written statement from the Sepoy? We will need it as evidence.'

'I will get it and send it over to you personally Captain. Is there anything else I can do?'

'Thank you sir. That is all.'

Tapashi dialed Brother's number. He was quick to pick it up. 'Is that you Brother?'

'Yes Captain, how was your drive and the day. I hope all is well at your unit.'

'Please listen carefully to what I am saying. Some militants were killed while they ambushed our supply convoy to Uri. The one prisoner we took identified one of the militants. Unfortunately he is dead from his injuries but gave a statement that was recorded by our medical officer. His name is Salman and he said there are PoWs at Tangi. Tangi is north of Nowshera.'

Brother sat silently on his bed to absorb what he had just heard.

'Wait a minute. Did you say he said there were PoWs at Tangi? How many?'

'Yes, that is what he said. The body of one of the militants had a Koran with some Indian names and names of places. Your name and my father's name are on that list of names. Tangi is also mentioned along with the names of other places. He did not say how many prisoners were there at Tangi. The Koran with this scribbling is with me. My Brigade Commander will get permission for you to come here to identify a body. Can you please come for some identification?'

Brother was thinking fast. *'PoWs were there at Tangi and one of the militants has given a statement about it. My name and Colonel Sunderam's names are there in some list. I have to identify a dead body? Why?'*

'How will I know a militant Tapashi?' For a moment Brother felt he was being implicated in some controversy. 'I will come but I wonder if I can identify some dead militant.'

'I cannot tell you more now but will drive out early morning and be at your mess to pick you up by nine in the morning. You will know everything after you identify the body. I am relieved that what you said about PoWs may after all be true. My father's name is on that list. Aren't you happy.'

Brother was speechless. 'I am a little amazed at this development. Like you said, I will know more after the identification. I don't know what to say.'

Tapashi realized his apprehensions. 'Whatever I am telling you is true. Don't worry, I think I have enough evidence to prove what you say is true. I have the support of my Brigade Commander. Not many people will have any reasons to doubt all that you have always said about being a PoW. I am happy for you. Don't worry about the air force Intelligence officer's attitude.'

Brother felt her reaching out. 'I will be ready in the morning Captain. Goodnight.'

Tapashi wanted to share all with her mother. *'I need just a little more positive confirmation before I give her hopes. If it is not true, it will just destroy her. Brother, I hope your version is true.'* It won't be long mother. Depriving her the information pained but she had been conditioned. The absence and uncertainties of growing up without a father had its own life's hard lessons.

## Chapter V

Captain Tapashi drove the jeep. Usually she let the driver but today Brother was with her. He couldn't be made to sit behind and neither could she. Brother watched the countryside. There was fresh snow on the peaks and some frost on the roadsides. The Chinar trees dressed in layers of white threw a glow of purity to the otherwise rugged terrain that had hidden hostility embedded for decades. His attention strayed frequently to the road and over the edge into the steep valley. He could relax when Sheila was driving but the Captain had a very different aggressive style. The jeep sped and swerved like an animal in flight.

She guessed his discomfort and said, 'in the valley you drive fast and weave a bit. Difficult target for the enemy.'

'Yes, I understand, we used to fly low and fly fast. We all have our own ways. Don't worry I am comfortable.' She suppressed a smile. It always gave the ones in green a thrill to tease the men in blue, especially if it was a fighter pilot. A case of pure professional pride.

He had flown a lot in the Kashmir valley but never had the occasion to travel by road. Today he was with mixed feelings. It was not any fear or apprehension but there were questions streaming through his brain. He was still not sure of the turn of events and his role. It was not that he had any suspicion about what Tapashi was doing. He just didn't know what was in store and the preventive stance of the air force in contradiction of the army now wanting him to identify a body. It wasn't pointing at things becoming simpler.

He had not insisted on information from Captain Tapashi and she had only asked him, 'are you ready, you may need to spend a night there.'

Brother had quickly packed a change into a bag that Tapashi handed him. He had laughed, 'you sure come prepared and ready for any contingency. You army guys are always prepared.'

She had jokingly replied, 'when we have a meal we put one in the stomach and one in the haversack always.'

'I guess you need to. Pilots normally get back home. Oh! How did you guys convince the air force Station Commander about taking me with you? The air force would I thought be very possessive about their deserter.'

She proudly declared, 'they resisted but everything is official now and we think you are key witness and are also now a civilian. You no longer come under authority like us.'

Brother turned and smiled at her, 'you mean I could have refused to come here with you, right?'

She did not answer. Brother added. 'I hope you remember that I am coming on your request and can leave when I want to eh?'

*'Only yesterday this lady sounded threatening and she had called in the air force and today— what a change. Am I being set up? By sunset I wonder what newer conclusions will I reach. Keep an open mind. You owe it to the guys out there. Keep going.'*

There was enough laughter and casual conversation for the army soldier driver seated in the back seat to conclude their friendly association. His presence was also reason to keep the conversation impersonal and nothing about their purpose was mentioned. Both minds were however considering many eventualities and options.

Reaching the Brigade area Tapashi had to get Brother to enter his personal particulars into the Military Police register for them to issue him a temporary security clearance. The Brigade occupied a large spread. She pointed out various important places as they drove and it was like a small town distributed over a couple of hills and valleys.

'Your unit is located in a very beautiful area with lovely mountains all around. Do you ever trek or go fishing during the summers.'

Tapashi shrugged, 'for us this is a work place. Sometimes we do indulge in the kind of activity that you are suggesting but no place is safe here in the valley. All this beauty and peace is marred by the militancy. Can you imagine I am fighting the same enemy that my father and you fought against? Only now it has evolved into a proxy war.'

On a straight stretch Tapashi brought the jeep to a halt. It was the Quarter guard and two fully armed soldiers stood just inside the fence next to a brass bell on a tripod stand that rang out the hour for everyone to be synchronized. Tapashi's arrival electrified them into an armed drill triggered by a trained military voice that sang out orders to salute. The valley echoed, the orders also announcing their arrival. It had the effect of jarring back to reality. He was entering a process of discipline and formal procedures. The Army regimentation synchronized to perfection was nice to watch. Brother was more tuned to a fighter pilot's codes of order and discipline. The Army had quite a different predictable behavior. A fighter pilot liked springing surprises.

Tapashi's office wore a look of neatness to the point of looking unused. Brother followed her in, as she got activated without even sitting down after the drive. All at once she was calling the Brigade Commander, the medical officer, the Platoon commander, her own Commanding officer and others to gather at the unit mortuary. Brother knew his job. He was being taken to the mortuary to identify a body. He had never done this in all his years. He was still without any leads in his thought process for the purpose of identification.

She glanced at him, 'you look a little worried. I have called for some coffee. We will go down to the mortuary after that. It is within walking distance.'

Brother couldn't help saying, 'you make it sound like we are going to a tea party.'

Tapashi stifled a laugh and managed to say, 'if you are able to identify this person, the party will really get going.'

They walked down after some coffee and biscuits. The others had already gathered, except the Brigade Commander. He was busy and had sent the brigade major instead.

Brother was ushered into the poorly lit make shift morgue. The smell of chemicals in the cold air was harsh on the lungs. Brother almost reached for his handkerchief but saw the others watching him disdainfully, hoping he would not need it. His hand stayed in the pocket and slowly withdrew without making it obvious. The body was on a stretcher placed on ice blocks. Two soldiers held it on either side and lifted it onto a table. A sheet wrapped around the body covered it all. The white sheet added mystery to hushed voices.

Brother was ushered forward by Captain Tapashi as she withdrew the shroud. Brother couldn't see in the poor light conditions. 'Can we have a brighter light', he requested.

A soldier stepped forward with a cell lantern. Tapashi held it to throw light on the face. It had lost its color and the lips were just parted. There was one tooth capped with gold. The light bounced sharply of it and for a moment Brother gasped and regained control.

'Are you all right sir? It was the brigade major.

'Yes I am fine,' Brother was bending close to the face. He had to be sure. It was familiar. Death had tightened the skin and the cheeks had lost their jowls and lines under the eyes. The beard was out of place and he tried to imagine a face without it.

He had seen this face through dim and bright light. It was the face that sometimes wore a smile even while asleep and the gold tooth was often the point of focus for Brother as he spent sleepless nights during his sickness. The beard could not prevent recognition. It only delayed realization probably out of some kind of premeditated concern for him to absorb the shock it could otherwise give him. Brother put one hand on the cold temple stepped back and looked around at his audience. Without saying a word he walked slowly out into the light. The irony and failure of his personal mission clouded his mind. In the cold air his eyes burned and needed relief. Captain Tapashi followed by the brigade major were by his side while the others waited inside as if for some cue.

Brother turned towards her and said', 'I have failed to save my friend. I am shocked and this man I know very well. He was one of us. He has a wife and she bore him a son that he did not even know about. They will be shattered about the circumstances of his end. It is very disappointing for me to even hear that he has been shot as a militant. He is a Muslim soldier, Naik Azad Khan of the 9 Para Commandos captured in the desert near Suratgarh. It maybe better if he is buried here or will the army send him to his family in Ahmadabad? I met them only a few months ago. They will be devastated at the circumstances of his death.'

'Are you certain about his identity.'

Brother had collected his wits and accepted the present but he wanted to know more. 'I have no doubts about him. He was closest to me in the prison camp and gave the Pakistanis a trying time. He has faced mock firing squads many times. It is a big loss for me personally and I cannot believe that he turned into a militant.'

Captain Tapashi remained expressionless. 'I have to take your written statement. Can we go to my office.'

Brother shrugged, 'for Azadbhai I can do more than giving a statement. Can you tell me more? You promised that to me last night.'

She dismissed the others and nodded for Brother to follow. Seated in her office after a few calls Tapashi looked up at Brother. The unknown was unbearable and Brother had never controlled his patience like this for what seemed ages. Drawing in a long breath he made a simple but very firm request.

'Is my job over? If you want anything from me in writing, let me first tell you that if you are trying my patience and politeness, don't.' Lowering his voice to a hiss he leaned over the table and said, ' young lady you will not be able to deal with me if I lose my control. That body is my best friend and you keep me waiting like it meant nothing to you. You are only happy to find your father's name in some book. You could have told me everything when you came to Srinagar. Stop treating me like one of your troops. I can turn around and walk away now and you will be the one waiting. I want everything now here before I say or write anything.'

Captain Tapashi never lost control of the situation. Taking out a folder she read.

'The supply convoy to Uri on 17 January 2005 was ambushed by militants five kilometers from the border Platoon Hq. north of Uri. The engagement lasted fifteen minutes. Two soldiers of 7 Madras were fatally wounded and three injured by small arms fire. During the ambush one of the militants saved the life of the lead jeep machine gunner who was trapped under the jeep by extricating him and also dragging him to cover. The gunner's statement is attached. The militant then dropped his weapon and surrendered. He was shot in the back presumably by his colleagues before our troops could reach him. Before succumbing to his injury from a single bullet the militant had shouted, *'I am Naik Azad Khan from the 9 Para Commandos. I was a prisoner of war. They had kept me prisoner.'*

'The statement of the Sepoy who was closest to Naik Azad and heard him say his name is attached to this report. The militant who shot him was injured and taken prisoner. In his dying declaration he gave his own name as Salman and also identified Naik Azad as Azad and also Abdul Khan.'

She waited for a moment to look at Brother. 'Please read on', he said. She did.

'Salman also said, I quote, '*Azad, Abdul Khan, Prisoner of war, there are others at Tangi.'* The medical officer recorded Salman's dying declaration and his separate report is attached to this narrative. The Intelligence officer examined Naik Azad Khan's possessions. His weapon was an Indian Ordnance 7.62 mm self-loading rifle. It has been established that it was snatched from a Sepoy of Kumaon Regiment about a year ago. The Sepoy's statement saying he was injured in a skirmish and his weapon taken away by a militant with a Muslim name who said that he was a Naik of the Indian army is attached to this report. The Sepoy was not harmed by the Naik turned militant. The Sepoy's boots were also taken away by this Naik Azad Khan and has been identified by him. A pocket Koran was found on the person of this Naik Azad Khan. Names of places and Indian soldiers and Officers were written in pencil between the lines on two pages. The photocopy of the relevant pages from the Koran is attached to this report. In conclusion from all the evidence it can be concluded that the dead militant was indeed an Indian Soldier who may have been taken prisoner of war. The Naik's actions on two occasions of not harming our troops suggests that he may have been forced into militancy and shot attempting to return back by surrendering to our troops during the ambush. It also seems that there are more Indian PoWs. Their names are in the photocopied Koran pages attached. Further, the body of Naik Azad Khan was identified by one retired ex PoW Flight Lieutenant Richard James who came to Srinagar in search of the family of Colonel Sunderam of 7 Madras. The rehabilitated PoW Flt Lt James has stated that he has given names of his co-prisoners during his court martial. These can be ascertained from Air HQs and matched with the names listed in the recovered Koran. He does not know the location of the PoW camp but evidence now suggests that they could be held at Tangi, a small place north of Nowshera. Flt Lt James's brief statement of his visit to Srinagar and the unit at Baramulla for identification of the Naik's body is also attached. Further action on this evidence through diplomatic channels is strongly recommended.'

After reading the typed report Captain Tapashi stood up and saluted Brother and said, 'Sir I have taken the liberty of adding that you have given a written statement without your consent but if you decline, I can change it. I have finished. If you have any questions, I will try to answer them sir.'

Brother had nothing to ask. Providence and circumstances had suddenly laid the whole truth in front of him. His concern for the dead Azad and Ruhaina was, 'Captain, is it possible to reach the body to his family at Ahmadabad. It will release them from so many doubts. Only, I don't know how and what truth will be conveyed to them. The family runs a simple tailoring shop in the cantonment. His son was attacked by a mob during the Godhra communal riots. The Naik was a loyal Muslim soldier. He should be honored.' Tapashi interrupted his further pleas.

'My Brigade Commander has spoken to Army HQ and there will be an air force plane tomorrow to take his body with a guard of honor troop from 7 Madras Regt. I will accompany the body and meet the family. The report I just read out is to be signed by the Brigade Commander. This report will be highly confidential. I guess we can tell his family that he was escaping and shot by militants. There will be no mention of him being a militant. I will try to see to that.'

Brother stayed seated and blank, not hearing Tapashi congratulating him in a modest tone. She had moved to the telephone now and was talking to her mother in her own language. Brother could finally see some emotions. There were uncontrolled tears that suddenly burst streaming down her face as daughter hugged mother from a distance. This family also needed to be released. Officers in uniform were allowed to cry. Brother realized more as truth sank deeper into his Captive mind.

He was suddenly exonerated. In his death Azad, his best friend had freed him from all the suspicions and ghosts associated with his PoW days. Naik Azad Khan remained true to his conviction of escaping. He had broken through the walls that could now reunite and release the others from their captivity. Brother's latent guilt for not locating the families earlier remained dormant.

He did not hesitate this time from pulling out his own handkerchief. An Army Intelligence Officers' office is serious business but tears were not out of place be they from joy or grief. A life locked behind walls had suddenly been released. The created masonry of suspicion and doubt lay shattered in front of him. Brother was ready to fly again. Tapashi was also ready to continue the mission. The flag for the mission had changed hands and this woman fighter Brother thought, was better armed.

## Chapter VI

Brother was surprised to hear the agitated knocking on his door as he packed his belongings to leave by the noon flight to Bombay via Delhi. Opening the door of his room he said, 'you must be Sqn Ldr Himmat Singh. I saw your name in the entrance gate watchman's register.'

'Yes sir, can I help in any way?'

For a moment Brother thought he would take the offer but instead he just sneered. 'News sure travels fast in these parts eh? Yesterday you didn't look too happy about me, but I understand son. It's not anyone's fault, I had to push the system sometime. I guess you were only doing your duty.'

The young officer took the cold shower bravely. It was in good spirit. The air force Security officer was detailed to see off Brother at Srinagar airport. They had arranged for a staff car to pick him up from the Badami Bagh mess. The Security Officer's demeanor embarrassed Brother. He was saluted at sight and his baggage loaded into the car. There was even a bouquet of flowers handed over to him. He would give them to Sheila. She was coming with Martha to receive him at Bombay airport. He left the mess after tipping almost all the waiters and cooks. Inthekab had a forlorn look. 'Take me with you sir. I will work for you till my last days. There is nothing left for me here in Kashmir now.' Helpless, Brother parted with the consolation that he would come back for him soon.

They had driven out from Baramulla at the crack of dawn. It had been a long night with many formalities and reports. Captain Tapashi had reminded Brother about his interest to access the Internet as they reached Srinagar. 'I can take you to my colleagues house and you can use the computer Brother.'

He looked at her and teased, 'more than me wanting to use it, I think you want to see what I was going to show you. It is not really relevant now but all the same I will show you. Let's go.'

They were at Tapashi's colleague's house in Srinagar. Brother opened his mailbox and went to a folder named Elizabeth. One by one he opened his own mail and the replies from Elizabeth. 'This lady nursed me at the Karachi Military Hospital. Her brother went missing during the same 1971 war. I have reliable information that he died. He was shot trying to escape. I have to tell her because I had promised to locate him. And from this last mail, you can now probably guess the name of the prisoner who was taken away from the camp.'

It all amazed Tapashi. She managed to say, 'you are incredible and yes Naik Azad Khan must be the one taken away to become a militant. He must have found it the only way to get out of that hell. Obviously Elizabeth knows the camp location and couldn't tell you.'

Brother got up to leave. 'You are intelligent like your old man.'

Captain Tapashi had said her goodbyes dropping him back to the mess. She was also headed for the airport. Naik Azad Khan was finally going home and she was going with him.

Sitting in the lounge awaiting the announcement for security checks, Brother bought coffee for Sqn Ldr Himmat Singh. Senior officers must take care of juniors he had said when Himmat had wanted to pay. The snoopy was keen to know complete details of his trip to Baramulla. Brother knew the art of need to know.

'Why don't you write a book on your experiences sir', Himmat suggested.

Brother looked for genuineness in that statement. And then, someone from within him said, 'it will not be fair to write a one sided account. I need my friends to be released and then we could jointly consider that suggestion. Even in captivity there is a protocol. I got away but am still part of that team. It is my duty to rescue the others. I wish everyone had understood it that way. Its funny but there is something else I want to know from you. Is there a procedure to declare a person mentally normal after having declaring him insane?'

The PA system came to Himmat's rescue. He smiled and said, 'I will convey your request sir', and saluted. It was time to go.

'Give my regards to your Station Commander. I appreciate the help.'

Picking up his suitcase Brother joined the security check queue. Himmat tapped him on the shoulder and said, ' sir you are with me. Come, you don't need to stand in any queue anymore.'

The airport police sub-inspector saluted Himmat and Brother was escorted into the departure lounge. In a few minutes he would walking on the tarmac towards a new future. He would be back in the air without having to worry about being suspected of crimes he had never committed. The bitterness hadn't left him totally. The court-martial and the constant threat that had delayed him from taking off to officially locate the families of these pour souls in the camp weighed on him. Things would have been so different if they had to believe him. Naik Azad Khan also could have been saved. A staff car drew up on the tarmac and it was flying a flag. It was the Station Commander of Srinagar base.

They saw each other simultaneously. Himmat Singh introduced them. 'I am privileged to meet you sir.'

Brother acknowledged the salute with his classic jaunty movement of the hand and wrist and added, 'It was a comfortable stay and I understand your limitations and actions sir. Thank you for the hospitality. I may visit Kashmir for my honeymoon.'

The Station Commander smiled, 'most certainly; you are still young at heart sir.'

Brother had the last word. 'If you are locked away for the best years, there is a lot to catch up on. Goodbye sir and "Happy Landings." The other passengers were leaving.

As he walked to the plane Brother saw a military aircraft parked not very far away. The Station Commander's car sped towards it. It looked like he was a bit late. The cortege had just begun their slow march from a gun carriage towards the parked air force plane. He saw the coffin held aloft on steady shoulders. Azad was going home with full honors. Tapashi and the Brigade Commander would make sure there were no short cuts. He had been with them at work almost the whole night tying up all formalities. The Brigade Commander had taken the responsibility of the entire proceedings. You had to be convincing if a deceased militant's identity was established as a good soldier. The evidence was beyond doubt. Brother had shared the secret of Ruhaina's mission to Karachi with only Tapashi. She would tackle the issue at Ahmadabad. Smita would assist her to get Ruhaina back. They could preserve the body if required. It was not to be discussed now, she had said. Brother would coordinate from Bombay.

A chill wind blew across the tarmac. Srinagar always was a cold base when they had operated Gnats from it. Brother had fond memories. He watched the uniformed slow march and his heart warmed when he recognized a smart erect lady officer with a wreath following the pallbearers of Azadbhai's coffin. The Brigade Commander waited near the entrance of the plane. Everyone was in their ceremonials with medals. Brother stopped, turned towards them and saluted for a full minute. He could stand forever. He was saluting them all. Without them his irons with the past could have stayed forever. He was now free to go.

*'I'll be back when you guys come home. Now it is Tapashi taking charge Colonel. The ship is in good hands.'*

He boarded the jet that would reach him home by evening. His flight was interesting.

It was obvious that the co-passenger seated next to him had seen him with the uniformed gentlemen in the lounge. Curiosity gets the better most of the time.

He shot, 'are you traveling to Delhi or further. Also you are from the services, right? Are you retired? You must have fought the Kargil war or.... Brother had stopped this barrage with a polite smile that also said, 'please give me a chance.' He had seen this brand of eagerness in his uniformed years. He replied without missing a question.

'Yes I am from the air force and am retired. I am Richard James. No I did not fight the Kargil war, as I was not in uniform then. And I am traveling all the way to Bombay.' Brother smiled and thought there would be no more questions but that was not to be. Some people grab an opportunity to talk to those who have been a part of the armed forces. He tried in vain to catch a glimpse of the proceedings at the military aircraft through his window.

'What do you think of Pakistan training these militants and the increase in terrorism. Kashmir has become one of the most dangerous places. There is no tourism, no income, poverty is all around and they want independence from India.' And as an after thought he put out his hand and said, 'I am Sanjay Hira.'

Abandoning his efforts at the window Brother was patient and for a change did not feel interrupted. 'Do you want my personal opinion?'

'Yes sir.' The man leaned forward looking at Brother.

Folding his newspaper to stow it away, Brother relented to converse. 'Militants are normal people who are tempted, exploited or forced to resort to acts of violence and terrorism. The unethical find militancy a convenient way of progressing their own agendas. Pakistan is a supporter of Kashmiris because of their own agenda. It is not difficult to understand their agenda points. Religious politics is not something new. Militants are one of the tools of religious politics. Whoever trains them whether it is Pakistan or any other nation; it is an act of victimization. The victims are those that get trapped into becoming militants. It is wrong to conclude that Pakistan is training them all. There may be some who get trained there. It is easy to put the blame. The media wants sensationalism. And many like you and me begin and are forced to believe what we read or hear.'

He continued after a pause. 'You are right Mr. Hira. There is no tourism and poverty is all around and that is I think also a part of someone's agenda. After you create disturbed conditions it is easier to recruit hands for militancy in the name of a cause and hopes of better days. It also encourages political parties in Kashmir and the Pakistanis to bid for Kashmir's Independence. Kashmiris want freedom from whom? Who are they captive to? Their mindset has been twisted to believe that they are subservient and will get a better deal as an independent state. Independence is one route to improving conditions. India has improved. It has taken time and a lot of work. It needed good leadership. If Kashmir can provide similar conditions— Independence could be a solution. We need to correct the reasons for its condition as you see it today. It was a beautiful valley not so long ago but religious politics has helped to open the doors that have brought about the conditions that we see today.'

The aircraft had taken off and was on its way. Brother looked down at the valley. On his way in he was looking for some clue about the prison camp. He smiled and it slowly turned into a set jaw. Brother thought he had more than answered his acquaintance's questions. It was not to be. Mr. Sanjay Hira was preparing some more. Brother used the break to think.

*'I think we have most of the clues. It is not going to be easy. Diplomatic channels don't always pursue the interest of the armed forces. Is Captain Tapashi going to get the support? She may become captive to this chase and it could go on endlessly. I wonder now if this will ever end for her. Or for me? At the moment I am the only one who has benefited. They believe me now and Azad is free from his captivity. It doesn't seem fair. I still have to*

*inform Elizabeth about Edward. She will be devastated. I need to take a vacation. Will Sheila accept my proposal? My mission is not yet done.*

'You have a point about this religious politics Mr. James. We have a Hindu political party and the Kashmiris have a Muslim party like Pakistan. I think Kashmir has to go one day. The Muslims are not easy people. It is difficult for us to accept their ways and thinking. I think it is being a traitor when they support Pakistan during the cricket matches we play with them. Also Muslim terrorists are destroying the world.'

It was a territory Brother did not like to talk about. Neither was he a Muslim nor a Hindu. This time he would give a reply that would stem the flow of questions.

'I think differently if you don't mind Mr. Hira. We do not have a Hindu political party. It is a party elected by people to uphold secularism and democracy. Many voted for them because of their promises. Unfortunately that is where it ended. The easiest way for the party to remain popular is to play up to the popular emotions of the masses. Religious politics created Godhra and probably so many similar disasters. Can you blame some Muslims who wave Pakistani flags during a cricket match? They do it because they have probably not been made to feel like an Indian. Someone and the conditions are responsible for it. And why can't you support the team that you like. There are many white supporters of black athletes and vice versa or fans of musicians, film stars and even leaders from different countries. None of these feelings of following are essentially dictated by religion but there are many who are making sure that conditions are created to give importance to religious bias. It is the politicians who have the maximum access to the people and it is easier for them to religiously bias the people. That is how people of different religious following, marginalize others and try to make themselves exclusive. Isolation of both types cannot promote secularism. Marginalization is also one of the reasons for the spate of terrorist attacks all over the world. Terrorists also have their own leaders who understand marginalization and they use it to bias followers for their own agendas. In the name of religion and sacrifice for ones beliefs many are inducted into becoming terrorists. Greed for power and convenient mis-interpretation of religious doctrines made centuries ago has been misused to play with the minds of people. We live in a material world where greed and possession are real. Don't blame the Muslims for terrorism. Blame the leadership that motivates such acts.'

The plane landed at Delhi and Brother was secretly happy that

Mr. Sanjay Hira was traveling no further. He waited while the plane refueled and took fresh passengers. Settling in for a nap he dozed off thinking of Ahmadabad, Kolkatta and home.

It was a rejuvenated Brother that got out of the plane at Bombay. Hurrying through the crowd Brother gathered his suitcase and rushed towards the exit for arriving passengers. He saw Sheila and behind her was Martha. His smiles said it all. It was good to see them together. Freedom was his for as long as he wanted it. He had fought long and survived. He was not ever going to let anyone take it away. He recalled his promise to himself in Kolkatta to serve those who thought that they had lost everything. He would help them to achieve their freedom from what they thought were their losses.

## Captured 1971- Freedom in 2003

Back in Bombay a few days later, Brother sat with Martha on the swing in their porch watching Chapel Road in the morning. In his hands was a letter.

He had spoken to Smita and heard about the respect with which Azad Khan was buried. Azad was a true hero. Basheer was proud of his father. Azad's Koran was with Ruhaina. It would make her more resilient. Azad had freed her from waiting. He had also become free and given Brother the keys to his freedom.

Elizabeth had also replied to his e-mail that had said it all. Radhika couldn't believe his luck on the phone and she was glad that he had been successful. She would wait for Major Ganguly's return.

The General and Bose had got together to celebrate his victory over a couple of beers.

Azad's death pained him a lot. He had lost his dearest friend. He had to visit Ruhaina again. She had tried to reach Azad but Allah was always merciful and his was always done. Azad died a true hero, loyal to his country and the army. She would hold Azad Khan's Koran close to her heart. Brother would also hold this letter close to his heart. He read it again. It was from Air HQ. He would send a copy to the General.

Dear Flight Lieutenant Richard James

We at Air HQ appreciate all that you have done to correct facts that otherwise may have never been known. You have lived up to the finest traditions of being a good officer. It will be an example for generations that follow in the uniform. Your personal contribution in trying to rescue your colleagues and the price paid can never be compensated.

We will leave no effort to recover our brave brothers in arms. Your sacrifices and bravery in the face of unforeseen difficulties has been recognized and we are proposing your name for appropriate appreciation by the government.

We are proud of you and regret any hardships and misunderstandings that were caused by circumstances beyond anyone's control.

We salute you. Many 'Happy Landings'

Yours Sincerely
Air Marshal T K Malik
For the Chief of air Staff.

Holding Martha's hand after reading out the letter to her, Brother thanked her for bringing him out of his sickness to live again.

*A mother was given the opportunity of a lifetime.*

Looking at Chapel Road he wondered where it would take him now. It was narrow like in his childhood. Truly a Trail that opened into the world for all its travelers.

He was going to meet Sheila in the evening. Brother wanted to plan a new trail together.

Brother observed Chapel Road from the swing on their porch. Future now had a clearer space in his thoughts after what had been a long journey that had forced him back and forth on a very narrow trail to emerge into the present. His mind traveled the whole distance. From flying as a fighter pilot to the war, into a hopeless existence in the enemy prison camp and then the trail full of minefields in search of the families of his co-prisoners. The journey had not exactly been easy but it appeared not so difficult in retrospect. Help came from unknown directions. The fears and conflicts about truth and the little world that he had been trapped into had suddenly evaporated without leaving too much sourness in its bubbles. It had taken time and the strong latent desire to free his co-prisoners had kept the embers of courage from going out. There were still those, who now knew that their men were captive and had to be freed. He sat there thinking.

*'Have I unshackled myself to chain them to an impossible trail?'*

Those minds and bodies could now get spun into concentric and intersecting circles full of conflicting interests, denials, fears, frustrations and unknown zones of pain that only faith in the belief that "it is I who can change the present state" can fuel them through.

*Do they have the courage? Did Brother have it or he achieved it?*

*'I have lost so many years. Who is responsible? I am now too old to think of marrying Sheila. Had it not been for that war? Why did I have to get shot on that strike on Gujranwala? Sheila and I would have never come close if Kailash had not died in the war. What was that war all about? The Pakistanis were exterminating their own brothers and sisters; Bengali Muslims in East Pakistan and we decided to "Liberate" them. How were we interested in what they were doing to their own brothers? If I hadn't joined the air force, maybe I would have had a cushy job, a family and all the trappings of the material world that I see around me today. Why was it so difficult for anyone to believe the truth that I kept telling them? Poor Azad. He was an Indian but his family was treated like the enemy because they are Muslims. Why are Muslims treated like this in India? Why are so many nations targeting Muslim countries? What is the war between Muslims and the rest? Surprising but Muslims are also destroying their own brothers. If every Muslim is exterminated, will the world become a safer and better place to live in? How did all this begin? Can all of us not decide to leave behind the past and make a new beginning? We need not forget or forgive but we don't have to let it drag us into revenge and hatred. Entire nations cannot be evil. It is probably just a few who keep these fires of hate burning.'*

*'Religion and political gamesmanship has become the way for the politician and militants. Is it the only way out for such people? Did Azad have any other way to escape? After the prison he was a captive of those militants. He tried but did he succeed. I think he did. He set himself free finally, but what a way. I must leave the past behind. Years that I have lost cannot be made up for but I can try to learn from it and move on. There is a lot to live for now. Have I become free because now everyone believes my story? Or was that freedom really always in my hands? Ruhaina, Radhika and Sheila, each responded in a different way to the truth. They will have to free themselves. I thought I was setting them free but no, they will have to achieve it themselves. They will I know because they all have the courage.*

*They have not lost anything or anyone. You can lose only if you allow someone to take it away. Nobody could have destroyed me because the truth was always mine. Thank God I could shed my fears and get going. Otherwise I would remain guilty of not keeping my word to my friends out there. I will continue working for their freedom. The past is no longer scary or important. I will remember the past but not let it decide the future for me. If it destroys me, I will know that it was for a good cause.'*

Divest means to disassociate. Disassociation with the past is akin to a mutation without uprooting from roots. An amputation with the past would be severing of all links. Without post-mortem a divestment becomes an amputation. Very often keeping alive the memory of an undesirable inheritance assists in the full realization of the benefits of a divestment.

India and Pakistan were born not because of the British rule of India. The British were part of our evolution. In that process the India and Pakistan psyche inherited the dreadful malignancy of a latent hate, suspicion and mistrust between two very prominent ethnic communities of this world. The Hindu and the Muslim. Two nations were born.

Many have tried to wash away the wounds of the past. The amputation of India was harsh. From that pain, recovery will be slow. Forces that push us back into those pains must be dealt with reason. Any more violence to bottle the snake can only increase the venom. It is encouraging that through the smoke and dust is emerging a new desire to put away the past. Hastening the process will be less helpful than taking steps to increase the desire.

Militancy and terrorism around the world or in the context of the sub-continent is not going to suddenly disappear or be smashed by some all-powerful force. It took time for it to surface and has its own rationale. It has to run its course. There are signs of it ebbing. There are also visible eruptions that spread fear, hatred and retaliation. It is our collective captivity to hope that is already working for us to overcome this disease.

It is now time to make the difference. Dismantling forces or erecting walls and laying minefields are not the prescription. Fighting it within with courage and resistance without extravagant violence will stem the growth. Healing can only begin after that. Religion never preached violence and hate. Terrorism and militancy was created by inheritance. It is our burden to divest from such inheritances. The example will not go waste on the negative forces that prevail just outside your doorstep. Divesting undesirable inheritances will be a process. It may look difficult but the inheritance of tomorrow begun today will look quite trivial when it is all over.

Brother escaped from his captivity through courage and perseverance. Chapel Road now appeared to open its arms for him to re-embrace life in his "Free World".

ISBN 141208427-X